A House of Cloaks & Daggers

The Gift War: Book One

Loren Little

LOREN LITTLE BOOKS

A HOUSE OF CLOAKS & DAGGERS

Contents

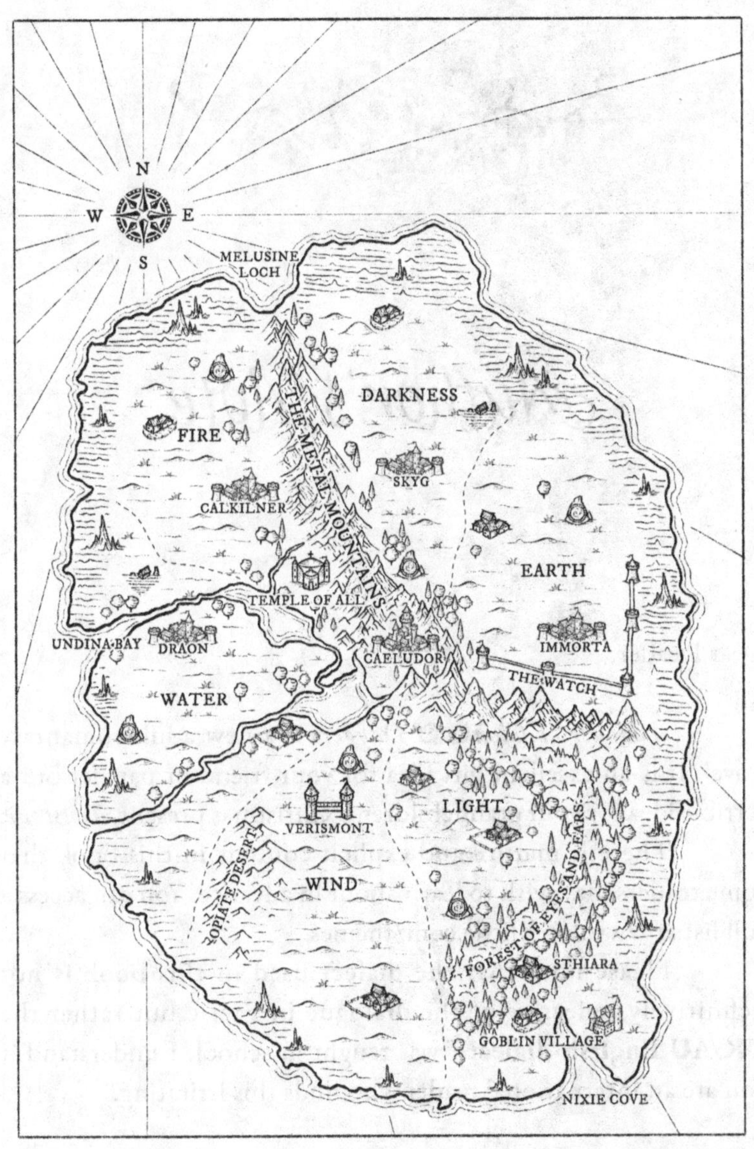

N
W E
S
MELUSINE LOCH
DARKNESS
FIRE
THE METAL MOUNTAINS
SKYG
CALKILNER
EARTH
TEMPLE OF ALL
UNDINA BAY
DRAON
IMMORTA
CAELUDOR
THE WATCH
WATER
LIGHT
VERISMONT
WIND
OPIATE DESERT
FOREST OF EYES AND EARS
STHIARA
GOBLIN VILLAGE
NIXIE COVE

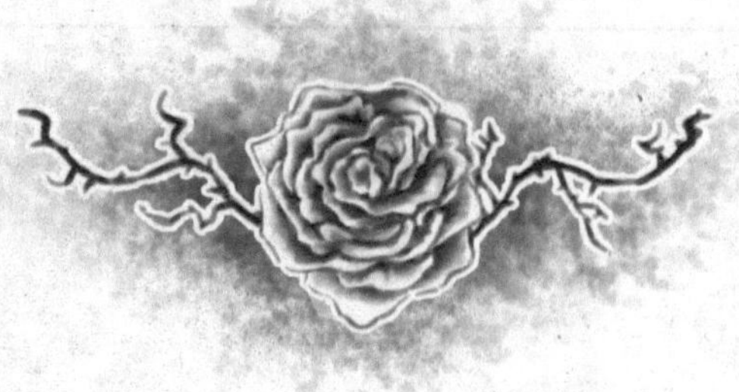

Author's Note

Dear Reader,

    A House of Cloaks & Daggers is a new adult romantasy novel. It is an excellent gift idea for your friend or partner but a terrible idea for your grandchildren's Christmas present. *Trust me*.

    There is mature and explicit content in this book that some readers may wish to learn about in advance. You can access a full list at www.lorenlittle.com/themes.

    Please note that the dialect used in this book is not definitively reflective of the dialogue in Faerie but rather the **UK/AU English dialect** I was taught in school. I understand if you are an international reader who finds this irritating.

If it's any consolation, I always thought that your pronunciation of the letter Z was far superior to ours, and it is, in fact, a hill on which I am prepared to die.

So, since I argued in favour of your Zs against my teachers, <u>I hope you'll forgive me for the Ss and the extra Us.</u>

Love, Loren x

***

P.S: You will find a Glossary in the back of this edition! This includes a list of all the different faerie races, magical and monstrous creatures, place names, and hierarchy of leadership throughout Faerie. I hope you'll have as much fun as I have adding to this in each new book as we unravel the layers of the universe throughout the storyline.

P.P.S: I know I say it a lot, but truly... To all of you. Thank you so much for picking up this book.

Playlist

These are some of the songs I listened to on repeat while writing *A House of Cloaks & Daggers*. Some songs are part of the soundtrack in my head while certain scenes unfold like they do in the movies, and others are part of the personal playlist for a specific character. Enjoy! (Or not. Listening is totally optional and has no impact on your reading experience. If you want my advice on the best time to press play, I might suggest doing so once you've finished the book in order to help with the hangover.)

***

The Apparition – *Sleep Token*

Guilty as Sin? — *Taylor Swift*
I Hate It Here - *Taylor Swift*
I Sent My Therapist To Therapy — *Alec Benjamin*
epiphany — *Taylor Swift*
Family Line — *Conan Gray*
Who are you? — *Bad Omens*
The Bolter — *Taylor Swift*
Bleed — *Connor Kauffman*
Lilith (feat. SUGA of BTS) (Diablo IV Anthem) — *Halsey, SUGA*
Judas — *BANKS*
We Go Down Together (with Khalid) — *Dove Cameron, Khalid*
Control — *Zoe Wees*
i'm yours — *Isabel LaRosa*
Medicate Me — *Rain City Drive, Dayseeker*
Give — *Sleep Token*
us. (feat. Taylor Swift) —*Gracie Abrams*
Blood Sport — *Sleep Token*
TRUSTFALL — *Pink*
Liberated —*Britton*
DARKSIDE — *Neoni*
For the Love of a Daughter — *Demi Lovato*

For the bookstagrammers who hate it here—
This is the key to my secret garden. Now it's yours.

"What did you expect faeries to do?"
"I thought they did nice things, like granting wishes."
"Shows what you know, don't it?"
— Labyrinth (1986)

ONE

Falling Asleep to Sleep Token

The dreams began when the leaves outside my window turned orange and brown with decay, and their branches relinquished custody of them to the smallest breath of wind.

It was nothing at first.

Glimpses of glass, iron, and blood. They were memories that belonged to somebody else. The shards of a shared nightmare piercing through the subcutaneous layer of my subconscious mind. The final piece of a difficult puzzle. The echo of a word—a place or a name—that I once overheard and had since made its eternal home on the very tip of my tongue.

The dreams were bad enough to set off the warning bells in my head, yet not realistic enough to tempt me back to the surface of sleep. It took a couple of weeks for me to realise that each night was getting darker as I tumbled deeper into the bottomless phantasmagoria.

One dream, replaying in my head over and over again.

I saw a wall of glass so pristine that it held my own reflection hostage, offering a mirror to my panicked display of awe. It rose from the meadow like a crystalline tidal wave and disappeared beyond the grey clouds suffocating my sky.

The sense that I was being watched—no, *observed*—sank its teeth into my spine, blurring the lines of reality and gnawing along the very edges of my being as I raised a hand towards the frozen wave—

Darkness. It's late at night. I'm asleep.

Writhing in my bed sheets, I fought to keep hold of the sliver of consciousness that bled through, but the visions held fast.

There was a glitch, and suddenly trees were towering over me. Their trunks were impossibly large and wider than townhouses, their feather-soft branches dangling limply at their sides like unfastened braids spilling over gnarled wooden shoulders. As I traipsed over the muddy ground, there was not a single corner of the forest that openly acknowledged me. I clambered over unearthed roots as tall as cars in complete solitude and stillness. The breeze from the meadow was denied permission to follow me, but despite the heavy silence, I knew I was not alone.

Diamond-white lights sparkled in the underbrush, tiny pairs of inquisitive eyes blinking up at me. Each knife-sharp whisper of breath I gambled was amplified by the hush like I was the only creature left on the entire planet. However, in my peripheral vision, the diamond eyes were tracking my movements, and the trees were trading places with each other at my back. I could not be sure if they were trying to confuse me or conceal me.

I tried to turn away, tried to get out—

A fitted sheet, cool and creased. The knotted tassel of my throw blanket between my fingers.

Another glitch.

Wind tore at my hair, my clothes. It stung my dream-snared eyes into submission, and they squeezed shut as I fell to my knees, groaning when my bones slammed into a slab of rock that sent shockwaves of pain splintering through my skeleton. When the air turned stale and cold, I opened them to a room full of unnatural darkness.

It was the colour of night, only...*more.*

Oozing into the room like an oil spill, it was not the absence of light calling the shadows to life in that place, but rather the *presence* of something wrong and other.

Stone walls, dripping with filthy water, surrounded me. There was a wrought-iron gate bolted into the ground and a small window fixed with the same iron bars high above me. The floor was damp, dirty, and bare save for a large, sturdy wooden bucket, some straw, and a few threadbare rags.

I knew very well that I had found myself somewhere I shouldn't be.

The alarm bells started singing in my head—a rich, angsty melody—and though the song was haunting, it was also hollow. I was not in my own body. My control had been outsourced to the dream maker, and I was left at their mercy as I stood in the corner of the cell, silently begging to be allowed to leave so that I could never, ever return.

And yet, each night, I did.

I returned to that wall of glass, to that forest of eyes and ears, to that cursed prison cell in some forgotten corner of the gloom. My mind spiralled further into unattainable darkness as the shadows bloomed beneath my eyes, and my dreams were plagued by images from someone else's twisted imagination.

By the middle of winter, I had started to scream in my sleep—and I couldn't tell anyone why. I couldn't possibly explain what I'd seen happening to him in my dreams. I didn't even know who he was.

I was never allowed to see his face—only the iron shackles around his wrists, hissing as they scorched his skin, and the chains clanking and scraping against the stone floor as he paced back and forth across a beam of pearlescent moonlight that seemed to drive the sentient darkness into the corners of the room. I'd seen the iron-tipped whip that tore his back open from his shoulder blades to the base of his spine, shredding through flesh and muscle until his blood spilled out like a waterfall. I watched as they crushed his hands beneath enormous stones that sparked as they rolled over his splayed fingers, as they shoved his head into a bucket of water and held him there until he stopped thrashing, and as they beat him with iron bars that left burn marks as well as bruises.

He was so strong.

He fought them every step of the way, muscles rippling and fists and feet flying like a wild horse, but he bit back whatever inner turmoil his pain provoked. He caged it, as they had caged him.

I was never certain if he could hear me—never knew if he resented the sound of my fear, or if he was surviving off it. Either way, I couldn't stop myself. I *screamed*.

For the body of a man, beautiful and mutilated, whose face was forever hidden from me, I screamed at them to stop.

If they heard me, they did not let on. And they didn't stop; they didn't even slow down.

Each night, they began anew. Tearing open the wounds that had almost healed from the night before, changing their tactics, breaking his body in ways I could hardly fathom.

My heart was coming undone, hanging in my chest by a thread as it strained against the agony of watching him suffer. An agony to which I quickly and shamefully became addicted.

I curled up under the covers as soon as the daylight was chased away by the darkness. I was so revoltingly eager to touch that glass wall again, to fight through the intrusive nature of the forest, and to find him still a prisoner in the dungeon.

While the origin of my eagerness was not enjoyment, it was no less disgraceful. I could offer him nothing more than some privacy, and yet I couldn't even bear to give him that.

My punishment was simple and fitting. The more I slept, the more tired I became. And the harder I fought to save him, the louder I screamed, the longer it took for me to wake up again.

In the end, I took the sedatives and then the antipsychotics. I saved the meditation playlists, and I stopped falling asleep to Sleep Token—most of the time. I tried to talk about what I was witnessing, the things that had become so real to me despite being so impossible.

That first night, when my mother came running into my bedroom, the words simply snagged on the petrified lump in my throat. By the time I saw a psychiatrist, they had become permanently lodged there. Even when my little sister asked what was frightening me, I couldn't give her an answer.

Every single time I opened my mouth to tell someone about the nightmares, I felt the sting of a hot silver spoon scalding my tongue. Or I had to run to the bathroom to be violently ill. Or my mind just went...

Blank.

So, I stopped trying to talk about it. But I could never give up my useless attempts at rescuing the man from my dreams. The man who didn't exist, who had sleeves of tattoos with shapes and symbols from a language I didn't recognise inked into his skin, and who had a body of muscle as hard as the stone he slept on after the beatings each night—when the worst part of the dream occurred, once they left him alone in his cell and invisible forces restrained me from going to him.

Coiled up, always facing away from me, he didn't even flinch as I called his name over and over again.

"Lucais."

I'd given my prisoner a name.

And so, he remained within the confines of my wicked subconscious, tortured by my dreams every single night.

Until my twenty-first birthday, that is. When they just...

Stopped.

Two

A Hobgoblin

Dante's Bookstore was supposed to close before dusk.

It was a small establishment on a quiet cobblestone street in the town centre, and most of its customers were regulars. I was familiar with their shopping patterns and reading habits, having spent most of my spare time at Dante's since I was a child, and they rarely came in during the late afternoons.

Sometimes, a college student would wander through when they came home for the weekend, looking for a textbook we didn't stock. Other times, passing tourists would be drawn inside by the dim, romantic glow from the ceiling lights or tempted by the heirlooms displayed beside books in the front window. The bookstore was a haven of tranquillity and old charm, like stepping backwards in time. Even on a street lined by quaint, gracefully ageing shopfronts left mostly untouched since the Victorian era, Dante's allure was unique.

Conventional redbrick walled the upper level, where the living quarters had been turned into a surgery for books in need of repair. The lower level was carved from rosewood and adorned with Belgrave's insignia—the outline of a single flame encircled by straight lines shooting outwards. The insignia dated back to medieval times, long before the modern world. It had belonged to the House of Belgrave, whose Lord had established many townships across the eastern lands as part of an ancient King's Court.

Long gone, long dead, long forgotten. Nobody knew what had driven the nobility away.

There were very few coherent recollections from that era, and most known accounts were infused with so much wartime hysteria that they read more like fantasy novels than history books. Regardless, the insignia was preserved by the council and used to mark certain buildings protected by the Heritage Society. Most of the buildings were skeletal in their remains, so the insignia was either painted on or printed out and hung over their replacements. Dante's, on the other hand, displayed an artful and dignified carving of the insignia in the wood above the entryway that the owner claimed was original.

"Been like that since I was a boy," he'd told me gruffly, on the one and only occasion I had ever dared to ask. "And my father before me. He warned me not to look at it for too long lest ye see the flame start to flicker and ye lose yer wits."

At the time, I was six years old, and the prospect of losing my wits terrified me greatly. The owner himself, John Dante, terrified me greatly too.

He was a miserable, haggard man with an unruly white beard, large hands, and dark, cunning eyes. He lived alone in a rundown cottage outside of the town limits and kept to himself beyond the basic requirements of operating the bookstore. The people of Belgrave called him a Hobgoblin, but John was indifferent. He took no pains to present himself as anything other than the grouchy old bastard that became his natural form.

However, he was the partially estranged grandfather of my best friend, which meant I was permitted to spend my time in the bookstore's reading nook outside of school hours—on the condition that I did not pester him while I was there.

I maintained a wide berth in the bookstore for a decade, during which time I grew up and overcame my fear of both John and the insignia on the rosewood. The marking was merely a lingering trace of history, and the owner an old man who disliked the real world.

The older I got, the more I found that I could relate to those things. So, when I turned sixteen, I began to pester John for a job.

He took great offence to my proposition at first, but thanks to his granddaughter Amelia's persistent lack of interest in reading and business, John eventually conceded that I was his best chance for retirement.

For the first couple of years, I worked to gradually increase my hours while John subsequently reduced his own until I eventually became full-time. He still visited the store, though as his health declined, his visits became fewer and further between. Patricia Farley, the president of the local book club, managed to take two or three shifts on the weeks that John couldn't. I had a sneaking suspicion that Trish stayed out at the broken-down cottage on those weeks, too, but I was never bold enough to ask.

Amelia, who stayed my best friend and remained uninterested in the bookstore, came and went as she pleased. She usually called in during the week to brief me on local gossip, and she always left behind a trail of books she'd neglected to return to their shelves and chocolate wrappers that hadn't made it to the bin in her wake.

I didn't mind the frequent moments of quiet solitude between visits because I liked my own company and the little niche I'd found amongst the avid readers in our town. I also liked the characters in the books that entertained me during the slow times. We had a tight budget, but I managed to balance it between the classics our regulars liked and new trending titles on BookTok and Bookstagram. It was enough for a monthly delivery of new material, which sustained me between my other tasks.

I was seventy-four pages into one of those books—a new adult romance with enough spice to make my cheeks flush—when the little brass bell at the entrance jangled, followed by the sharp *click* of the front door closing.

Glancing up from the page on which the forced proximity trope finally made an appearance, I realised how late it was.

The gentle lights hanging from the exposed rafters were visibly strained against the waning daylight, scarcely able to illuminate the spaces between tall rows of bookshelves. They cast a soft and reflective golden glow on the wood and spines. Craning my neck to peer around the reading lamp in front of me, I saw the empty street outside was already submerged in the lilac gleam of dusk.

"I'm sorry," I called out, in case there was someone still at the front. My voice echoed through the store, sharper than I'd intended. "We're closed."

There was no answer.

They must have seen the front counter is empty and left.

Closing my book, I gathered up the chocolate wrappers Amelia had left behind. She had breezed in and out of the store to invite me to dinner and drinks at The Water Dragon four chapters ago. I'd set myself up in the reading nook to see out the quiet final hour of my shift, and so I told her I'd come out once I'd finished the chapter I was reading.

She'd left with a shrug—but not before agreeing to lock up at the front, which she had clearly forgotten about in the twenty seconds it took her to get from the back of the store, through the rows of bookcases, and out to the front entrance.

Mentally cursing her, I fluffed the pillow I'd been nestled against on the two-seater couch and tucked the book under my arm.

My steps were light on the hardwood floors, creaking slightly in certain places where the wood had warped after the leak a few years prior. I binned the wrappers and shut the door to the office Amelia had left open, flicking the main light switch down on my way past.

Dante's plunged into an earthy gloom with grey, dust-flecked light floating between the shadowed shelves. The day was disappearing fast.

Blinking a few times to let my eyes adjust, I took the shortest route around the outskirts of the bookcases to the front desk. The counter sat to one side of the narrow entryway, which was occupied by a circular oak table showcasing new releases. A few stalls of bestsellers sat on either side of an antique armchair against the opposite wall. Beside it was a solid, gated staircase leading to the book surgery on the second floor—and Amelia had left the gate open.

Picking up my bag and sliding my book into it, I strode over and latched the gate closed.

I have no idea why Amelia would open it in the first place when she has no interest in any of the repairs that are stored upstairs, and she always brings her own food—

The thought stilled me for a moment.

Amelia never opens the gate. She never goes upstairs.

I looked out of the display window into the street, the cobblestone turning indigo in the fast-fading light as greyscale shadows crept up the buildings across the road. Wooden tables and crates had been emptied of their wares, some covered with tarp and others dragged in beneath the awnings. The first of the streetlamps flickered on a few doors up, shining silver onto the pavement below. The person who had walked into Dante's a few minutes ago was gone.

There's no one out there.

I rolled my shoulders back, dispelling the unusual shiver creeping up my spine, and started walking back to the desk.

Halfway across the room, I stilled again.

I was alone, but the feeling of being watched lingered like the brush of a hand along my back.

Somewhere on the upper level, a page flipped over. The sharp scrape of freshly bound and uncoated paper was unmistakable.

My skin prickled.

A sensation like the blow of breath hit the nape of my neck.

Someone is up there.

Tilting my head back, I squinted at the balcony, its railing barely distinguishable above the rafters. I could hardly make out the furniture upstairs through the murky shadows, let alone discern a potential figure sitting at one of the desks, and I had already turned the lights off.

Nobody can read in the dark. Amelia must have come back for something, I thought. I opened my mouth to call her—

No.

The voice in my head sounded strange.

Get out of here.

I took a deep, steadying breath.

Now!

The floorboards creaked—downstairs. Between the rows of bookcases.

That is not your friend.

Soles of my shoes scuffing against the worn boards, I backed towards the door. Two sharp, heavy steps mimicked me. Another creak came from the far corner of the store.

Inky black shadows filled the spaces between the six long aisles. I couldn't see anyone standing there. The distinct, crisp sliding of pages had come from above, but the footsteps sounded from the aisles below, and the floorboards only creaked where there was water damage. The leak had been contained along the wall running behind the front counter, where I'd walked moments ago, where I'd left my keys—

Run!

There was more than one other person in the bookstore.

Three

Jonah

I burst through the front door, bell clanging behind me, and I didn't wait to hear whether it slammed closed again or not.

The voice in my head had been surreal—an inhuman snarl of warning that chilled my blood, so intense and lifelike that it could have belonged to somebody else.

Boots smacking against the cobblestone, I ran down the street in the direction of my townhouse. At the intersection across the base of the sloping road, I ducked around the corner and pressed my back against the wall of a closed shop.

My breathing was ragged, my heart beating hard and fast.

Forcing myself to think pragmatically, I scanned the river that ran along the border of the shopping precinct, separating it from the residential villages on either side of the bridge leading out of town. The voices of fishermen packing up for the night carried across the whispering rush of the water.

Taking shallow breaths, I waited to hear footsteps behind me.

Belgrave was a small town—a small, quiet town. I'd met most of the people who lived there, and nobody ever did anything that somebody else didn't know about. Tourists came through for holidays and weekends. The Water Dragon had rooms available for overnight stays, but the vacancy sign was never turned over. We didn't even have a local police station.

Nothing sinister ever happens in Belgrave out in the open like this...

And yet the bell from Dante's Bookstore jingled again.

My heart lurched, knees threatening to give out as the echo of the door closing swept down the road.

Throwing my head back, I squeezed my eyes shut against the silhouettes of fruit bats shooting across the evening sky like dark stars. I let my mouth fall open, greedy for air, and tried to think through the haze of my fear.

I left the door unlocked with my keys on the front desk.

Frantically, I patted my pockets and the pockets on my bag, searching for my phone.

I must have left that behind, too.

A string of filthy words rang out in my mind, but the truth was that even if I had my phone, I had no one to call. Amelia wouldn't answer when she was out drinking. John lived too far out of town. And my mother was at home with my little sister.

A small whimper caught in my throat as the realisation drove itself into my racing heart like a roughly carved wooden stake.

I'll lead them straight to my family if I go home. If I make it home.

Footsteps resounded on the road.

Slow. Confident. As if they knew exactly where I was and exactly what kind of indecision was keeping me pressed against the wall.

I searched for the voices of the fishermen again, but I could no longer hear them. I could no longer hear anything except the heavy tread of shoes scraping on the road behind me and the bang of my heart, riddled with splinters, slamming against the inside of my chest.

Move!

The voice in my head came back with a vengeance. I could feel the rage in its tone, furious that I hadn't gotten any further away from the bookstore. Realistically, I couldn't blame it.

I tried to move my feet, but they were glued to the ground by the panic shrieking through my veins. My knees locked against the trembles racing down my body, starting from the pinprick of fear that was rooted into the nape of my neck.

Don't look back.

Too late.

My internalised voice of reason came too late.

Two figures were in the middle of the road, drifting between the circles of white light cast by each streetlamp. One was impossibly tall and thin; the other short, wide, and bent in ways that looked entirely unnatural. Both were cloaked in darkness, hoods pulled up to conceal any distinguishing facial features.

I forced my legs to move, and I ran.

Sprinting out into the middle of the road, I made a beeline for the bridge. The sound of rushing water grew louder as I approached, rivalling the whoosh of my blood pulsing in my ears. Stone was replaced by wood, rattling hollowly beneath my shoes, sending vibrations up my legs as I charged across.

The shorter one looked as if their size might hinder their speed. *Perhaps if I can lose them, I can go home.*

Up ahead, the road cut through the two residential villages. To my left, stand-alone cottages and large houses were set along a maze of streets, their interior lights flickering on like a cave of fireflies waking up. That side of town belonged to the upper-class residents of Belgrave. To my right, the lower-class dwellings sat hunched against the cobalt horizon. Rows and rows of small townhouses piled up on top of each other like a small-scale metropolis were flashing with the blue light from television sets by the windows.

I ran for my life towards the housing estate on the right, my bag aggressively smacking against my legs. I did not dare another glance over my shoulder.

The breeze turned icy, blowing the scent of freshly pollinated flowers and chopped grass over me. It swirled and circled, changing direction until the smell of brine and algae from the docks took over and paired with a distinct reek of rotting flesh.

Not fish from the river.

Something else.

Something old and discarded, left to gradually decay in an untouched corner of the world.

Gagging, I covered my mouth and nose with one hand and gripped my bag with the other as I stumbled over a ditch where the road had become unpaved. Drawing closer to the estates, I could make out the furniture in the windows of the grand houses to my left and the washing, strung up with fishing line across the balconies, billowing out over the edge on my right. I was close enough to be heard if I screamed.

But if I scream—

Headlights blinded me when a car pulled out of the wealthier estate.

I skidded to a stop along the side of the road while the vehicle slowed, gravel grating beneath my shoes. The automatic window rolled down with a faint buzz as the car crawled towards me.

"Auralie?" a masculine voice called out. I recognised it as belonging to Jonah Young, the son of The Water Dragon's owner. "Are you okay?"

Silently, I turned and stared down the road, following the harsh beam of headlights shining brightly onto the bridge in a wide yellow glow. The reeds along the riverbed were bent over and rustling in the breeze, and a few dinghies knocked against the docks. Across the water, dotted like stars in the suddenly full night sky, the streetlamps lined the upwards slope into the heart of town on either side of the empty road.

Empty—because nobody was standing there anymore.

And the smell of death was utterly gone.

My body started to warm again.

"Auralie?" Jonah repeated. The engine of his car hummed impatiently.

"I'm okay," I gasped, spinning around to face him. My heart stuttered as heat bloomed across my cheeks, burning logic and sense out of my head. I took a few steps towards the car until I was past the perimeter of its headlights. "I think I left my phone behind at Dante's."

Painted blue in the constellation of lights from his dashboard, Jonah's features smoothed and softened. He looked the same age as me, though he was a senior when I started school. It was the kindness in his eyes.

"Oh," he remarked. "Well, hop in. We'll get your things, and I'll take you home."

"Thanks," I whispered through numb lips.

My skin burned on the surface, emotions heating in the magma chamber hidden far from reach, but the chill in my blood persisted like frostnip. Flexing my fingers, I walked around to the other side of Jonah's car and climbed into the passenger seat, placing my bag at my feet while I clipped my seatbelt into place. It was new and expensive; the interior smelled like freshly cleaned polyester and vinyl.

As I looked up, I noticed my reflection in the side mirror. Shadows clung to my eyes, which were blue and bright with fear. My hair was the colour of an auburn sunset, but it looked darker than it should—more like blood—and flatter, with no trace of my usual bouncing curls. In my haste, my clothes had become ruffled, the strap of my tank top falling off one shoulder beneath my cardigan. And the clasp of my necklace had slipped around the wrong way, pulled taut across my throat like a choker collar.

It was no wonder Jonah had stopped to ask if I was okay.

He took his foot off the brake, easing the car into a crawl. "Katie really wants a burger from Mac's," he began conversationally. His eyes were tired but vivid when he glanced at me, nodding to the baby car seat strapped into the backseat. "Pregnancy cravings, you know?"

I forced a smile onto my face—forced because I *did* know from my mother's second pregnancy and forced because, for some reason, I still had the feeling I should scream. "How much longer?"

"Six weeks." He drummed his fingers against the steering wheel as we crossed the bridge, then slowly brought the car to a stop in front of Dante's.

The sound of the handbrake groaning into place was too loud.

"I'll be out in a moment," I breathed.

He was still tapping his fingers against the wheel. "No rush."

Dante's was completely dark. The front door was closed, though the sign on the door was still turned to *Open.*

I reminded myself that I was tired from months of poor sleep. I had an overactive imagination and a bad habit of forgetting the medication I'd only recently been prescribed. On top of that, I spent most of my time alone in the store, immersing myself in everything from dark contemporary romance to thrillers.

And I lived in Belgrave.

Climbing out of the car with my bag in hand, I let the fresh night air clear my head as I took a step towards the bookstore.

Jonah's car door opened and closed behind me.

The voice in my head went silent.

Approaching the building, I glanced at the window to find Jonah's reflection cast by the streetlamp, circling me like a barrier. He was standing between his headlights at the front of his car with his head cocked to the side, watching me.

My fingers curled around the doorknob as tightly as I could manage with the sweat beading on my palm.

I knew Jonah from school. He was a member of the choir and the maths club. He and Katie had been together since they were juniors. She was the editor of the yearbook the year they graduated. He was the school captain. His father owned The Water Dragon—a business he was set to inherit. And a few weeks ago, when Amelia had dragged me out of the house for a belated birthday celebration, Jonah had driven us home when we were too drunk to stand. I knew him. I'd known him all my life, but the way he was *looking* at me...

Sickness pooled at the bottom of my stomach as I pulled the door open and slipped inside. The bell above me jingled, and I wanted to rip the goddamn thing down for the way that sound twisted my guts.

But Jonah didn't move. He remained in place between the headlights, staring up at me from the road as if he was caught in some sort of trance.

My keys and phone were on the front counter. I moved towards them, planning to call my mother to let her know I was coming home.

But in the unreliable glow from the streetlamp outside, I didn't see the body on the floor until it was too late.

The toe of my shoe connected with something lifeless, something that squelched on impact. I threw myself backwards, recoiling from the deep-rooted shudder that raised the hair on my arms. My bag fell to the floor as I twisted away and slammed my forehead into something as hard as granite.

Not something—*someone*.

I bit back a rising scream as two large hands gripped my shoulders from behind, pulling me away from the pectoral muscles of the person I'd hit with my face.

"Aura," John whispered in my ear. His voice was coarse and low, but my heart pounded a few beats out of order at the sound. "Are ye hurt, lass?"

I shook my head, stunned.

John's grip eased, but I couldn't take my eyes off the stranger looming over me. He was enormous—a tower of muscle, clad in a long black shirt and loose-fitting pants that did nothing to downplay his physique, accessorised by a belt of weapons and eyes that shone like solid gold through the dark. He folded his arms across his chest as he stared down at me, a strand of his tousled hair falling across his forehead.

"You are *joking*," the strange man said. His voice was deep, disbelieving and unnervingly familiar. "I told you to run...and you just come right *back*?"

That voice. I clenched my teeth to keep my mouth from falling open.

He was here *earlier tonight!*

John swore quietly behind me. "Isnae the time," he muttered.

The stranger arched a sculpted brow, but his eyes remained locked with mine as he spoke. "Fine. Get her out of here."

"Nae." Throwing his hands up, John stepped in front of me, pointing at the window behind the tall man. "There's still two out there with the portal wide open—"

"I'll deal with them."

"And if more slip through when ye go back?"

The stranger's golden eyes flashed. "Then I won't go back."

Blinking furiously, I managed to tear my gaze from the molten eyes that hadn't moved from my face and set it upon the old man at my side. He looked frazzled, distracted, and...frail.

John was unwell, and he'd declined rapidly since the last time he visited. I should have realised, judging by the thickness of his accent—it was always stronger when he was stressed, distracted, or in poor health.

"What are you doing here?" I demanded softly.

His dark eyes darted towards me as if he'd somehow forgotten that I was right there. "Alarm went off," he mumbled, gesturing non-specifically to the contents of the bookstore.

"We don't have an alarm system," I reminded him.

"Wasnae that kind of alarm."

I threw a helpless look at the strange man. His full mouth quirked to the side, eyes glinting with wicked amusement.

John began pacing from the display window to the staircase, leaving me within striking distance of his new companion, who was looking at me with near-predatory intensity.

"I should call Trish," I decided, peering around the dark-clad body of rock positioned between us.

"Nae. Keep the lass out of this," the old man replied, shaking his head. He stopped pacing and turned to me. His face was illuminated in the half-light from outside, and there was guilt written all over it in a language universally understood. "Ye must go, Aura. I'm sorry, lassie, but ye must go."

My forehead creased. "Are you...*firing* me?"

John looked as though he didn't understand the question, but before I could clarify, a guttural scream rang out in the street, and I remembered that I'd left Jonah by the car.

All of a sudden, the display window beside the counter behind me exploded in a spray of glass, sending books and ornaments flying as something large and heavy landed on the floor with a dull thud.

I didn't have time to react before the golden-eyed man snatched me with hands that felt like they were made of steel and spun me into the nearest wall, away from the shrapnel. The impact knocked the breath out of my lungs, but one of his hands curled around the back of my head, softening the blow. His other hand was fastened around my waist, putting his nose a hair's breadth away from mine.

Despite the fear that had a chokehold on me since dusk, something warm awakened in my chest and stretched soothing tendrils throughout my body. It caught the scream in my throat and replaced the burning, acrid tang with a flood of honey-sweet relief. Musk and ink and midday sunlight wrapped around me, the scent emanating from my unsuspecting assailant like cologne. And his eyes—I saw the colour moving, shifting like his irises were truly made of smouldering gold.

The moment, the feeling, lasted for no more than a single heartbeat before he jerked away from me so quickly that I couldn't be sure of what I'd seen, scented, or felt.

Heavy breathing filled the silence, followed by the crunch of glass and wood coming from the broken window.

I smelled it first—that putrid, festering decay that had blown towards me across the bridge, carried by the breeze wafting inside through the broken window. Then, out of the corner of my eye, I saw the shadowed, deformed figure from the street beginning to haul their large and lumpy body into the bookstore.

Glass fell from the display, clinking against the hardwood floor. The figure stopped in the beam of light shining in from the street to smile at me.

My stomach churned. Ice-cold sweat trickled down my spine.

It was not a person.

Not a person at all.

As if he had read my thoughts, the strange man pulled out a dagger and said tightly, "No, it's not."

The thing—the *creature*—was not human and not of this world.

It had a head that might have belonged to a mammal if its eye sockets did not look like small mouths filled with blunt teeth and narrow, forked tongues. The creature's actual mouth was empty and cavernous, taking up the entire width of its face, and its thin, chapped lips were pulled back across the dark void of its exceptionally wide throat in a hideous grin. The rest of its body was rat-like; short arms, hind legs and a scaly tail poking out from beneath the tattered black cloak it wore.

It was not human. I was not even sure the strange man with glowing gold eyes was human. But Jonah...

Jonah *was*.

And he was lying on the hardwood floor, his head propped up against the side of the front desk, with his neck twisted in a permanent and unfixable way.

FOUR

Cauldron-Worshipping Death-Wielder

The monstrous creature sniffed the air once through the flat hole in the centre of its face that flared like a single nostril, and then it lunged at Jonah.

My terror never made it out of my throat.

As more debris shifted and clinked onto the ground in the wake of the beast, the strange man and his shining dagger moved with expert skill and preternatural grace. He crossed the room in a heartbeat, meeting the creature with the sharp end of his blade before it could sink its falcon-like claws into Jonah's unmoving body.

A high, keening squeal perforated my eardrums as he drove the dagger into the beast's side. The blade made a wet, bursting sound on impact like the creature's body was a balloon skin of fat and juices stolen from past prey. He pulled the dagger back, spurting liquid I could only assume was blood as the creature stumbled along the ground.

Off-balance, it whirled on him.

Teeth pulled back, mouth closed, and forked tongues wriggling in the air, it let out a seething hiss and settled back on its haunches. Its long, oval-shaped head tilted to the side, nostril flaring wildly, and I realised that it couldn't see him.

Although it had appeared to be smiling directly at me, the teeth in its eyes must have rendered it blind. Instead, its forked tongues seemed to taste the air, and it moved following scent.

The man with the dagger held completely still, letting the creature calculate the distance between them with its other senses—and then he leapt to the side, out of its reach when it sprang forward.

Flying over Jonah's body in a streak of depthless onyx, the creature was still midair when the man appeared behind it, a broadsword suddenly in hand. With breathtaking ease, he plunged the blade through its midriff, all the way down to the sword's leather-bound hilt. He nailed it into the floor, right on top of the body I had stumbled over when I first arrived—which I quickly understood to be the corpse of a similar creature.

Silence blanketed the room.

I stared, biting down on my tongue as I considered whether it was really worth adding to the mess by throwing up the contents of my stomach to ease its sick, tight churning.

Those stunning golden eyes met mine, and the man broke out into a sinfully handsome grin as he braced one foot against the creature's backside and pulled the sword from its rotten carcass. His blade came out dripping with dark blood that smelled of sewerage, which he promptly wiped off using the creature's own cloak.

My stomach roiled, but I decided it was not worth contributing to the horror on the floor.

"What *was* that?" I whispered.

He glanced back at me, cleaning the sword once more for good measure, and sighed. "We call them *caenim*," he answered grimly. He studied the blade, sparkling silver in the light from the rising moon, before sheathing it at his side. "They're the pets of something much worse."

"Malum," John grumbled at my back. I spun around to find him emerging from behind the armchair, brushing dust from his clothes. "Filthy bleedin' things."

John's nonchalance—not to mention his very presence in the store so late at night, and with such peculiar company—diverted my attention from the nightmarish corpses lying in Dante's entryway. Disbelieving, I shook my head at him and turned my attention back to his strange companion with an arsenal of highly illegal and obsolete weapons strapped to his waist.

"Who are you?"

His brows drew together, thinning the circles of gold in his eyes. "You can call me Wren," he told me after a moment. "You?"

"I don't think you're in any position to ask questions." I scowled at the beasts he had slaughtered, slumped over one another at his feet. The reek had miraculously disappeared as if it was coming from their consciousness rather than their bodies.

"No, please," Wren scoffed, all traces of camaraderie lost. "By all means, Auralie, tell me again how thankful you are for me *saving your life*."

I didn't know what it was—that he had asked when he already knew or that he knew my full name without ever having heard it—but something about his tone set my spine straightening, and so I glared at him before turning my eyes towards Jonah's body.

He didn't look good. He didn't look...

I'd seen lifeless bodies before, though never with a fatal spinal injury or any other kind of twisted extremity, and my heart started to sink.

Wren followed my downcast gaze, but I couldn't read his expression in the shadows.

"My life?" I repeated, quietly but not weakly. "What about *him*? What did that thing *do* to him?"

Wren's wide eyes floated back and forth between us a few times before he spoke. "Do I look like a neurosurgeon?" he asked.

Did he—

I groaned, spinning away from him. I had too many things to do that were far more important than coddling a beautiful man's fragile ego.

John was standing by the window, surveying the empty street. Tears pricked at the inner corners of my eyes, but I blinked them away.

Focus. Stay calm. Breathe.

"I need to call an ambulance and someone to take you home," I stated, my throat suddenly hot and thick. I took a careful step towards my boss.

He bristled. "Nae," he snapped. "Dinnae make any calls. There's still one monster out there, and the Oracle knows how many more to come. Ye need to go, Aura. Ye need to go."

Shaking my head at him again, I fought against the urge to turn to Wren for support. I still had no idea how the two of them had ended up in the bookstore together, or how those things even *existed*.

"I told you before that I'd prefer not to have to take her with me, old man." Wren strode past me without so much as a glance. "You get her out of here, and I'll deal with the caenim and the portal."

John retreated from the window, his dark eyes narrowing into slits. "Yer certain then?"

"Yes."

"Aye." A frantic glance towards me. He began wringing his hands and nodded. "Get on with it, then."

Wren pivoted in slow motion, eyes glowing like the core of the sun. He moved towards me, each of his steps silent against the hardwood floor despite his size. It was not just the bodies behind me that stopped me from withdrawing as he approached, but that feeling from earlier, that smell of warmth and comfort.

"Here," he said, in the gentlest tone I'd heard him use yet. He took a small leather pouch from his pocket and pulled open the drawstring to reveal a clump of sparkling silver powder within. He frowned slightly, gazing down at me in earnest. "I've got you."

I blinked back at him, confused by the sudden change in his voice and attitude—right up until he hurled a pinch of powder straight into the middle of my face.

It had a sickeningly sweet odour and tickled my nose like pollen, gathering at the back of my throat as I coughed and spluttered to dispel the amount I'd already inhaled. Swinging my hand out wildly, I knocked it from his grip, sending the pouch careening to the floor in a puff of silver dust.

Wren let it fall.

He stared at me, open-mouthed and wide-eyed.

"What"—I gasped, bracing a hand against the wall—"is *wrong* with you?"

His irises burned down into a subtle copper glow as he gazed at me in wonderment, and then he reached out to brush his fingertips across my upper lip.

I jerked away from him at first, but Wren's touch was magic. The moment his skin came into contact with mine, I felt his warmth all over my body, all the way down to the very centre of my being. It was new and old at the same time, like tasting a brand-new flavour of the only food you'd ever eaten in your whole entire life.

His fingers came away covered in silver powder, but the feeling—the connection—still lingered between us.

After examining the sheen on the pads of his fingers for a moment, he brushed them off on his shirt and replaced his fingers on my mouth. His thumb was so large that it caressed both of my lips and grazed the tip of my nose in one long, slow sweep. And then he repeated the process of clearing away the powder on his shirt before he dusted the last of it from the sides of my nose.

"Odd," he remarked quietly, looking at me as if it was for the very first time. "The fae-lily should have knocked you out cold."

And then, like a stone sinking to the bottom of a lake, it finally clicked.

"You were trying to *drug* me?"

Trance well and truly broken, I put both hands on his chest and shoved him away from me as hard as I could. He staggered backwards, but his pealing laughter made me think the unsteady steps were mostly for show.

"No," he insisted with a chuckle, eyes burning as bright as a solar flare. "Well, okay, yes."

Flabbergasted, I looked to John for backup but found that he was hobbling towards the back of the store—completely unaware, or maybe indifferent. Floorboards creaked beneath his steps, and then the light switch flicked into place as the lanterns hanging from the rafters ignited with a crackle and hum. I'd known it was dark, but my eyes had adjusted to the low luminosity of the streetlamp and fast-rising moon. The electric lights above were blinding, and I winced, angling my head towards the floor...

Where thick, malachite-coloured blood streaked with black was oozing out of the mangled, grey-skinned bodies below me.

Under the light, the caenim were even more atrocious to behold. Their skin was taut over their bones, giving their features horrifyingly sharp edges, and tufts of thinning white hair were visible poking out from beneath their hoods. Forked tongues hung limply from their eye sockets. Their two sets of teeth were indeed ground down into stumps and browned with age and—I gulped—*diet*.

Dante's floor was slick with their blood from the entryway to the centre of the bookcases, where another dead caenim lay amongst a disarray of fallen novels. And above...

I made a horrified noise in the back of my throat and reached for something to steady myself, but my hands came up empty as I turned my gaze skyward. Another monster was slumped across the rafters, dripping the gunk of its lifeblood onto the shell of its companion collapsed between the aisles. One more was heaped behind the railing upstairs, a single clawed hand drooping over the side.

Six.

There were six of those monsters.

Five dead, and one at large.

My face must have twisted in shock because Wren stepped up to my side and bent his head to my ear. I stiffened at his proximity, at the inviting scents falling over me, into me, and around me.

"Like I said," he murmured roughly, his soft breath tickling my nape. "You're welcome."

Angling my head to shoot him a glare, my train of thought stopped dead and derailed as I saw him in the full light for the very first time.

Human—but not.

At his full height, Wren truly towered over me. The top of my head barely reached his breastbone. He had mid-length, wild hair; the blond was as if someone had mixed sand in a pool of molten starlight.

His complexion was glass-like in its perfection, his skin as warm as a sun-drenched desert, tawny beige in colour. His eyes, still glowing like liquefied gold, were almond-shaped and framed with impractically long lashes beneath two thick, angular brows that sat symmetrically on either side of his face.

My eyes followed the slope of his nose, built from the same polished marble as every other one of his features, down to the glittering stubble along his sharp jawline, and then his mouth—curved to one side in a self-indulgent smirk.

I pointedly looked away. And then I looked right back.

Perhaps I should have been afraid, but if I was, it was not provoked by the weapons he carried or the ethereal colour shifting in his eyes. It was his face that frightened me. The look he was giving me.

He was stupidly attractive. He was stupid... He was...

"I have a portal to destroy," he announced at an unnecessarily loud volume, winking at me before spinning on his heels.

My hand shot out to snatch his wrist before I could think twice. I missed, and my fingers gripped onto his unnervingly large thumb. "Wait." I swallowed the lump in my throat as he hesitated, then swung his head around to look at me. "Jonah."

John, I had decided, was a lost cause. Short of swatting him over the head with a hardcover book and dragging him by his ankles through the pool of beast blood out of the store, I couldn't help him. *But maybe Jonah...*

A thick brow rose. "Wren," he corrected with no small amount of condescension.

My pupils flared. "No. *Jonah.*" I let go of his thumb and pointed at my friend, who hadn't moved at all since he was thrown through the window.

Wren tilted his head to the side. "I am *not* a coroner, but he *is* dead."

I knew that. I *knew* that, and yet the word hit me like a blow to the chest, impossibly heavy and painful.

John was clambering around in the office, opening drawers and slamming them shut while he swore in two different languages and continued to mutter nonsense, completely incognisant to who Jonah was or what had happened to him.

Bubbling hysteria began to curdle the blood in my veins. I clenched my fists and shoved it back.

This is on me. Everything is always on me.

Katie was heavily pregnant. Amelia was drunk. Trish couldn't be involved. I didn't have the slightest clue how to explain any of it to the police, and my sister...

Brynn would undoubtedly follow our mother out of the house if I asked her to come to the bookstore against my better judgement.

My heart sank beneath the sudden and dreadful weight.

Wren watched me, eyes flitting between my face and the body of my friend like he was waiting impatiently for the hysteria to kick in so he could try his luck on me with another dose of that silver drug.

"I have no one else to ask," I admitted, shoulders slumping.

Wren took a deep breath, broad chest expanding to twice its size, and nodded once. He stalked around the remains of the caenim and heaved Jonah into his arms. Splinters of glass and wood clinked to the floor as he stepped around the counter, heading towards the back of the store where John was still making a lot of racket.

Arms locked around my waist to hold in any lingering threat of purging myself of my stomach's contents, I followed Wren as he made his way into the reading nook.

Mercifully, that part of Dante's had been left untouched. I had a lot of work to do out the front, between the aisles and upstairs, but my safe haven of peace prevailed. The reading nook—a cosy space at the back of the store, walled by bookshelves, with three desks lined up before three couches that were positioned around an antique coffee table.

Wren went to the couch against the far wall and lay Jonah's body down, his head resting on the cushion I had smoothed over only an hour earlier. He positioned Jonah's arms crossing his chest like they do in the movies and stretched out his legs before he adjusted his head to look like he was sleeping. When I saw the fluidity with which his head moved—as if his spine had been severed at the base of his neck—I flinched away.

The couch became a coffin before my blurry eyes.

But Jonah can't be dead. Katie's pregnant.

"There." Wren flung his hand out towards the body of my friend dramatically. "Now, if you'll excuse me—"

"Help him." I stumbled a step closer, my head drowning in tears that I refused to let fall. It was taking everything I had to hold them back. "Please."

Wren gave me an incredulous look. "Woman," he said roughly, matching my step with one of his own—twice the length of mine. "I am High Fae, not a cauldron-worshipping death-wielder. And that man," he went on, pointing to the couch behind him, "is dead. Gone. Tonight's tragedy, tomorrow's news. And you're lucky that it's not *you* on that couch because—"

I slapped him across the face.

It happened so fast, I barely had time to register the thought before my arm came flying up and my palm connected with the edge of his cheek. His jawline and cheekbones were as hard and strong as appearances claimed—as hard as his chest had felt when I'd walked into him earlier—and took the blow like a caress.

But my hand...!

I yelped a curse, my skin stinging whilst my palm turned a nasty shade of red, and the tears finally overflowed.

Wren smirked down at me. "I am going to destroy that portal now, Auralie, and if you try to interrupt me again, I will toss you into another realm and seal you in there myself."

With that, he stormed off. He left me to scrub the searing tears from my cheeks as I fell to my knees in the middle of the reading nook and handed myself over to a violent assault of spine-warping sobs. I sat there, bent over with my head between my knees until the fabric of reality buckled around me.

Then, silently, I wept and wept.

FIVE

You Read Too Many Books

Truthfully, it wasn't hard for me to believe that Wren, the portal and the caenim were real. I probably would have believed it even if John hadn't set the example of taking the otherworldly chaos in his stride.

As a genre, I liked fantasy more than horror and self-help books, but less than everything else. However, I'd read enough about faeries to face this one prepared. I knew there couldn't possibly be so many veracious accounts of them, disguised as fiction, for the one in front of me to be an apparition or a kook.

Wren fit the bill perfectly.

He was obnoxious, rude, and cocky. He had the most mindlessly handsome face I had ever seen. In the short time that I'd known him, I had witnessed his predisposition to violence and cruelty, and it had quickly become apparent that he had very little understanding of his own supernatural strength.

I had no idea what the destruction of a portal entailed precisely, but I had a feeling that the commotion on the upper level of Dante's was melodramatic at best.

Though he moved with the grace and stealth of any apex predator, the force of Wren's footsteps sent the entire bookstore trembling beneath him as he marched across the second floor and commenced smashing the entire space into smithereens.

Wood groaned as it was pried apart, glass shattered between the deafening *bang* and *crash* of impacts as things were thrown from one side of the room to the other, and Wren roared like some sort of monster as he destroyed irreplaceable books and anything else that had the misfortune of residing up there.

When John slunk out of the office with his fist clenched around the ribbon of an oversized key, I gave him a beseeching look through the tears streaming down my face.

He simply shook his head at me. "Dinnae fash," he muttered. "It must be done."

Another roar from the High Fae bastard upstairs sent the body of the caenim on the rafters falling to the floor with a soft thud, followed by silence. Swaying a little as I climbed to my feet, I swallowed my sadness so I was free to mouth curses at Wren for worsening the destruction of my beloved bookstore.

I do not have time to cry about it. There is never enough time for me to properly cry about anything.

Another minute passed before Wren reappeared downstairs, swaggering out of an aisle like he didn't have a care in the world. He made a point of ignoring me and eyed the key dangling from John's grip instead.

"If you're High Fae," I began, squaring my shoulders as I leaned in to catch his eye, "then why don't you lose the glamour?"

A muscle in Wren's jaw worked as he gave me a sidelong glance. "You read too many books."

I narrowed my eyes at him.

"Is it done?" John cut in, eternally unperturbed. He was answered by a sharp nod. "Good. Good. Here—take this." He unclenched his fingers to display the key on his weary palm.

Wren angled his head to one side and gave him a wry look. "The floor, please."

"Oh! Aye!" With a shake of his head, John braced a hand on one knee as he bent down to place the key on the hardwood floor. He took a step backwards and gestured to it with both hands. "Please."

Blinding light filled the room without warning. It was so bright that, for a moment, I could see nothing but a delicate, glittering sheen of white, silver, and gold. Strangely, it wasn't painful to behold. Images bobbed in front of my eyes, obscured by the light, so faint that I could hardly make out their shapes.

But they were there.

Two people basking in the glow, embracing each other as the light wrapped around them like a swaddle, dancing through time and space—

And then it was gone, swallowed by the hole burned through the floor where the key was only a moment ago.

A small, wimpish groan reverberated from the back of my throat. The hole was tiny as far as holes went, but the list of repairs and maintenance Dante's would require just kept growing.

"Done," Wren declared proudly. He counted with his fingers. "Demolition of portal, check. Obliteration of key, check."

I started to roll my eyes, but he moved into my line of sight.

I froze, stunned. As requested, he'd lost the glamour.

Wren stood even taller than before, and two elongated, pointed ears poked out of either side of his head. He certainly hadn't used the glamour to dull his beauty or stature; however, a silver chain had appeared around his neck alongside silver rings on his fingers, and he had what looked to be crystal piercings through his earlobes. Noticing my gaze, he flashed a grin at me, full of gleaming white teeth, including two large, flesh-shredding canines.

I finished rolling my eyes.

Apex predator, indeed.

I'd read somewhere that vanity was the greatest weakness of the High Fae, so I mentally ticked that off my list of rumours that were true.

"That sixth caenim will be out there, tracking your scent," Wren went on casually, toeing the edge of the burn hole with his boot. "You can stay here—"

"*My* scent?" I interrupted, panic rising in my voice.

"Yes, *your* scent." He surveyed me for a moment, eyes gleaming as he digested my expression. "I take it back. Clearly, you don't read enough books." He sighed. "I told you the caenim are like pets. They're the property of a wicked race of faeries, used as foot soldiers or cannon fodder. They're slow, deaf, and blind but well-trained in their other senses, and the only way to stop them *and* get rid of that nasty stench," he added, crinkling his perfect nose, "is to kill them. Their one redeeming quality is that they're usually a fun fight." He winked at me, irises on fire.

I absently blinked back at him.

"They were hunting you, Auralie," he clarified, as if the truth wasn't already screaming alarm bells in my head and waiting for me to catch up.

They're tracking me by scent.

"Brynn," I whispered. And then I was gone before the High Fae brute could stop me, sliding across the sticky green blood drying on the entryway's floor before I fled out into the dark cobblestone street.

Jonah's car was purring against the curb, keys still in the ignition. Avoiding the baby seat in the back, I climbed in and slammed the door closed just as Wren came stalking out of Dante's Bookstore with a sour expression on his face.

He became a shadow trailing me in the rearview mirror as I tore down the road and over the bridge, nearly sending the car skidding as I made a sharp right turn into my street. I saw our townhouse up ahead, the light from the front porch pouring out in a rectangular beam across the dead lawn. The screen and wooden doors were closed, the second-storey windows still intact. My hands trembled wildly as I half-fell out of the car and stumbled over the gravel, listening for the sound of my mother or little sister screaming.

The house was quiet.

In the distance, a dog barked. Crickets and frogs were singing in the reeds down by the river.

I'm too late, too late...

Nearly colliding with the wood, I fumbled to pull my house key from my bag. It took me two attempts to insert it into the lock. Handle slipping against my clammy palms, I finally wrenched the stupid thing open with a loud bang.

The hallway was dark. Faint light loomed at the end, coming from the kitchen. My mother's bedroom door was partially closed beside me. The television set cast a faint white glow on the walls of the sitting room up ahead. Static filled my ears as I crept towards it, easing my weight onto each foot gently to make my steps as silent as the night. I craned my neck to peer around the door, heart pounding like a racehorse in my chest.

A shadow rose up on the wall in the sitting room, and then—

"Aura?" My mother's voice came from behind me. "You're home late. I was getting worried."

Whirling around, breathless, I found my mother standing in her bedroom doorway, completely unharmed. She was already in her pyjamas—a set of pink satin, with the hem of her long pants tucked into a pair of fuzzy socks.

I glanced behind me. "Ma—"

The shadowed figure emerged from the sitting room, and my heart sank so low that it was no longer a connected part of my being. It was adjacent. Disconnected. Detached.

Because there was my father, a can of beer in hand.

"Auralie." His hoarse voice was like nails on a chalkboard. "You've caused your mother a great deal of stress tonight."

For a moment—for just one awful, fleeting moment—I wished the caenim had followed me there so they could rip that man's head clean off his body.

Gritting my teeth, I turned back to my mother. She was my mirror image in looks—pear-shaped figure and heart-shaped face, a straight nose, and the splotch of a strawberry birthmark in almost the exact same spot as mine, above her left eyebrow—but my opposite in personality. She looked as tired as I felt. Her hair was down, hanging in loose curls over her shoulders, and her face was wan.

"Where's Brynn?" I asked.

"Asleep." My mother tilted her head to the side, a sad smile cracking across her face. "Are you okay?"

"What is *he* doing here?" I mouthed.

She straightened up and swallowed tightly, a silent but familiar warning. "Go check on your sister," she urged.

I didn't need to be asked twice.

Turning on my heels, I swept down the hall without sparing a glance in the bastard's direction as I passed him. The potent, fermented smell of beer filled my nose, and I considered stopping to spit the bile in my mouth out onto his shoes.

But I didn't.

I went straight to the narrow staircase at the end of the hall and clomped up to the second level.

"When you come down, you'll answer to me for what you've done, you little bitch!" the drunkard downstairs called after me.

What I've *done—*

Anger flushed through my veins. My chest filled with hot coals and a cataclysmic pressure.

"Easy," Wren purred from the shadows.

For some reason, I wasn't at all surprised to find him standing in the corridor, leaning against the wall beside my bedroom. I still stopped on the top step and glared at him, but the pressure eased. My anger deflated like hot air from a balloon.

In the dim light coming from my sister's room at the far end of the hall, his beautiful face was painted in a subtle shade of pink. He was a vision of calm and pretty things.

"It's not here," he whispered. "Your sister is sleeping peacefully, dreaming of a handsome High Fae Prince—"

I flicked his arm, careful not to break my nail on his bicep. "Of course you'd think of yourself as a Prince."

Wren's laughter was silent as he extended that large, muscular arm towards her room and nodded. "See for yourself."

Oh, I intend to. I trust a faerie man about as much as I trust a human one.

Our father coming back usually meant that he'd gambled and drunk his livelihood away. It always brought him to Belgrave again to prey on my mother's inability to stand up for herself—and her children—and my little sister's desire to see her father through the child-sized, rose-coloured glasses that I'd handed down to her.

As I padded up to her door, I prayed that she hadn't seen him yet. I prayed that she hadn't felt that bubbling excitement, hopeful for her upcoming birthday to be celebrated as a complete family unit just this once.

He would be gone before then.

He never stayed long—and this time, I would make sure of it. Because with that man in the house, we were in as much danger as we would be if the caenim were in his place.

Brynn was fast asleep, like Wren said. Curled up beneath the blankets, with her stuffed animals arranged around her on the bed, she was breathing deeply and evenly. The curtains were drawn across her open window, overlooking the riverbank and pulling in the scent of brine and damp soil. Some of her washing had spilled out of the basket and onto her fluffy rug, but...

There was no sign of intrusion.

Her night light was sitting on her bedside table, casting the shapes of long-winged fairies and five-pointed stars onto the ceiling and the wall in a soft pink glow.

My cheeks heated as I felt Wren's smug gaze fall on me from behind. He wasn't wrong about her dreams, either. I'd forgotten that Brynn was right into her fairy phase—not the same kind of faerie, but close enough.

Satisfied that she was safe, I pulled her door partially closed and retreated down the hall to where Wren remained beside my bedroom door.

He raised an eyebrow at me as if to say, *"Do you believe me now?"*

I nodded, dragging in a deep and rocky breath.

Wren jerked his chin towards the staircase, the faintest crease forming between his brows. *Who is that man?*

No one. He's no one.

He rolled his eyes at me when I didn't answer and shoved away from the wall, which crackled beneath the force. "I get the feeling you don't like faeries as much as your sister does," he whispered.

"She likes the *nice* ones," I hissed. I knew that I had to go back downstairs, that I was delaying it. "Not the real kind, apparently."

He placed his hand over his heart in mock outrage. "I'm nice."

"Your bedside manner is dreadful."

"I *told* you, I'm not a—"

Wren never finished his sentence. He never got the chance.

It didn't matter that I knew what he was planning to say, or that faeries and monsters were real, or that the two of them had torn Dante's Bookstore apart like it was a battlefield, or even that my father had weaselled his way back into my home.

Every single one of those things ceased to exist when the cry rang out from downstairs. A cry of terror that I'd heard before too many times.

My mother.

Six

Monsters

Wren made it downstairs before I did.

His speed was unnatural. On clumsy human legs, I tried to keep up, but the steep descent tripped me, and the handrail slid out from underneath my grip. I almost went soaring over the last flight, skidding when my feet hit the linoleum in the hallway.

My parents were in the sitting room, where the television had remained static and grey. At the window beside it—

The caenim.

It was the tall one from the street.

In the shadows, its features were hard to discern. It stood outside the window in tattered robes, its hood concealing the ghastly face that would plague my sleep for years to come. A conjuring of darkness and horror made real.

One hand—grotesquely thin and gangly but bearing a nauseating resemblance to that of a human—was pressed against the glass. Slowly, it scraped an iron-tipped nail down the window. The shrill, keening sound was enough to make me cringe.

And enough to shatter the entire window.

My shout of warning was swallowed by the sound of the exploding glass, and my follow-up cry was lost on the breath that Wren knocked from my lungs as he shoved me out of the way.

He prowled into the room, drawing a small blade from his side. I followed at his heels, peering around his wide frame, looking for my mother.

Broken glass littered the carpet and the coffee table, refracting light from the television and the moon. The couch was empty. I took a step further in and found my parents on the floor.

My father was scrambling to his feet. My mother was clutching her left wrist in her other hand.

The caenim stepped over the windowsill, its long legs granting it otherworldly ease. Due to its significant height, it had to bend its neck to fit in the room. As it lowered its head towards the floor, the television light illuminated its face; stumpy teeth bared in its eye sockets, forked tongues tasting the air, shapeless nose flaring widely.

Its attention was locked straight ahead—on the couch, on the people behind it.

The sound of a knife slicing into flesh cut through the room, and I glanced back at Wren to find him holding up his palm, a fast-healing wound dripping blood onto the floor.

My relief that he bled a colour that looked like red was genuine but short-lived. He smeared his blood onto the wall, no doubt in an attempt to distract the monster whose every sense was trained on my parents, and I suddenly remembered that it was deaf.

"Don't move," I cautioned. "Hold your breath."

My mother's eyes flashed to my face. The expression she wore told me she knew that already from years of living with my father. But she also knew that eventually someone would get hurt, and she—

"*No!*"

My shout was too late.

My mother did as she always had, as she always would, and moved to take the blow for her children without trying to find another escape. *Thus, the cycle repeats, and repeats...*

She jumped over the couch, crying out as her injured wrist bent further in the wrong direction, and screamed at me, "Run, Aura! Get Brynn and run!"

The caenim tracked her by scent and opened its mouth into a dark grin.

Wren sent the dagger flying across the room and unsheathed his sword, but the caenim must have felt the shift in the air. It deflected the blade with its iron claws, sending it clattering against the far wall.

"Get her out," he barked at me as he advanced upon the beast.

But even Wren wasn't as fast as my father.

He might have been, had he only known that there were two monsters in the room with us.

My father moved with more determination than he'd ever displayed for anything before in his entire miserable life. He careened around the corner of the couch and grabbed my mother by the back of her neck, shoving her towards the caenim head-first as he ran for the open doorway.

No—not towards it. Right into its outstretched arms.

She screamed as its nails sank into her skin, screamed as a low rumble of hunger filled the room, screamed as the front door opened and closed with a boom, and my father fled into the night.

Wren raised his sword in the air, wielding it as high above his head as it could go, but he hesitated when my mother was pushed between them—like he was trying to decide if it was worth delaying the killing blow to catch her and pull her back. He decided against it, and his sword arced up and then down, where it connected with a gut-churning squelch against the caenim's neck. He halted the sword before the blade kissed my mother, whose slim frame hung limply between its claws, and the beast's head thumped onto the ground, rolling a few steps away.

Blood squirted into the air like the caenim's body was a broken fire hydrant.

I charged forward, straight into the disgusting mist of gunk, and tried to catch my mother as the caenim toppled over, dragging her down with it.

The monster slumped on its side, leaking foul fluid onto the ground. I fell to my knees before it, shards of glass digging into my skin, and found that my mother was unconscious...but alive.

Her breathing was wet and raspy, her pyjamas stained with the caenim's blood.

She's injured. She's injured again.

But I knew what to do. They'd told me what to do, showed me how to treat human wounds inflicted by human hands.

"Turn on the lights," I ordered Wren.

My own hands were shaking as they hovered over the bony, grey-skinned arms wrapped around my mother. My voice was shaking, too.

Wren didn't move, but suddenly the fluorescent light globe in the centre of the room flickered on above me.

A tortured sound escaped my lips.

Under the harsh light, the caenim's skin was translucent, a clear casing over the grey waste beneath. Small, sharp bones protruded from its hands, which were locked around my mother's torso, and blood—red, human blood—was leaking out of her wounds.

It had dug its claws deeply into her flesh.

My every sense told me not to touch the creature, dead or alive, but I ignored them and reached down to grasp its ghoulish fingers and pull them *out* of her abdomen. I kept my other hand close, ready to apply pressure—

"Don't." Wren came up behind me, grinding his boots into the glass as he crouched down. His breath was warm against my neck as he said, "They're plugging extremely deep wounds. She'll bleed out instantly."

Human wounds by human hands.

These weren't quite human enough.

Tears streamed down my face, blurring my vision. "He didn't have to do that," I whispered furiously, flexing my fingers. A dry sob exploded from my chest, and then a feral, raw shriek. *"He didn't have to do that!"* I panted through the violence clouding my thoughts. "He could have gone around the other way. He could have just *left*..."

"He was trying to buy himself time," Wren murmured grimly. "Who is he?"

I swallowed the lump in my throat—nearly choked on it. "My father."

"No..." My mother's eyelids fluttered but remained closed. Her voice was barely a wheeze. "He's not."

More tears raced down my cheeks, and I sucked in a sharp breath through my nose before wiping the sadness leaking out of it onto my sleeve. "No, I know," I agreed, voice breaking. "I know."

Her eyes flew open, bloodshot and swollen. "No," she gasped, chest shuddering beneath the caenim's arms. She pointed her gaze over my shoulder—to Wren. "You *don't* know."

Dazed and confused, I looked at the face of the High Fae man leaning over my back. It was a picture of innocence marred by outrage.

"No," he insisted. "Absolutely not."

I was so distracted by my mother's injuries and accusations that I didn't hear my sister's footfalls on the staircase until it was too late. She appeared in the doorway, blonde hair ruffled with sleep, clutching her favourite stuffed bear to her chest.

Brynn dropped the teddy on the ground when she screamed. *"Mama!"*

Seven

Nothing Fucking Funny About Faeries

I had not realised how confronting the scene in our sitting room was until I saw it through my little sister's eyes.

Dark green, rotten blood soaked the carpet, splattered on the ceiling and the walls—not to mention the disturbing smear of Wren's blood-soaked handprint beside the doorway. Shards of broken glass made a minefield of the floor, and I became painfully aware of Brynn's bare feet as she teetered on the threshold.

"Don't move," I commanded, forgoing gentleness for urgency.

She barely registered my voice, my presence—anything. Her eyes were transfixed on our mother, unconscious in the clutches of a creature that no child should ever have to behold in the flesh. She was steadily bleeding out on the floor, and it seeped into the caenim's filth until our formerly off-white carpet turned a hellish shade of brown.

Desperation began to claw at my chest, a splinter of my soul determined to flee, but I forced myself to turn to Wren and find his eyes through the tsunami of tears stinging mine.

I found them to be mostly empty, the light snuffed out but edged with something like aggravation.

"Fix her," I pleaded. "With magic."

I expected him to object, to make some kind of crack about necromancers or witches or surgeons, and I was prepared to fight him on it. I had seen him use magic when he burned that key, and while I hated to admit it, Jonah had been beyond the point of saving long before I had even asked. But my mother was still alive.

When Wren made no such jibe, my surprise came and went with the twitch of a finger.

He merely clenched his jaw and nodded solemnly. "I make no promises."

"Fine," I stammered. "Fix her—now."

Scooting back to make way for him, I pushed myself to my feet and brushed the glass from my clothes. The sickly green mess from the caenim's decapitation stained my hands, blending into the dark denim on my knees, and my mother's blood was all across the front of my white shirt, soaked into the thick threads of my knitted cardigan. I wiped it off as best I could and went to my sister's side.

"It's okay," I crooned, retrieving her bear from the ground.

Brynn was like a mannequin when I tried to return the toy to her arms. She stared, open-mouthed, at the disaster on our sitting room floor as fat tears silently rolled down her bone-white face.

"She's going to be okay," I promised.

My sister did not reply.

She didn't look as if she was capable of speech anymore.

Heart cleaving in two, I wondered if she would ever find a way to talk, or laugh, or smile again after this.

I wondered if I would, too.

We remained on the threshold together, immobile, because I knew better than to lead her out of the room while Wren worked. Firstly, because I knew the scene before us was burned into the back of Brynn's eyelids regardless of how far we got from the room. And secondly, because I wanted Wren to feel me watching him. I needed him to feel the pressure and sheer importance of healing her with whatever magic he possessed.

Wren didn't look up at me, but I knew he felt my eyes on him. Felt the impact of my sister's tears as they hit the floor.

The light went out.

The television screen turned black.

My hands, stained and smelling of copper, gripped Brynn's shoulders. She was motionless and cold.

Wren lifted his hands, holding them parallel to my mother's chest, and the same pearlescent light I beheld in Dante's Bookstore glowed against his palms.

Gold and silver and white.

The beginning and the middle and the end.

It was ageless and ancient, brighter than any flame and colder than any sun.

He kept it contained to his hands, subtle and well controlled as tendrils of his power flowed into my mother's body. I had no idea what he was doing, but I prayed it would save her.

His eyes shuttered. He fell still.

But his magic continued to work.

Gently, a wisp of his power stretched out from the steady stream of light travelling between his palms and her chest. It curled around the caenim's wrist, holding it up as other, smaller beams of light shot out and wrapped around each of its five long fingers. Slowly, the strings of light removed the claws from my mother's chest, and then her stomach. When they were free, the lacerations were filled from within by a shimmering light.

Wound by gaping wound, Wren's magic stitched, pulled, and knitted my mother's flesh and skin back together. Even the rips in her pyjamas were repaired, the stains burning away without singeing the fabric.

It could have been minutes, hours, or years that I spent standing with my sister in the doorway, watching his powers at work.

It was hypnotic.

He was hypnotic.

As if he heard my thoughts and had something to say about it, a long tendril of his light split from the others and stretched towards me. The beam radiated a corporeal warmth and softness as it stroked over my forehead and my hair. With a featherlight touch, it danced along my shoulders and arms to where my hands rested upon my sister before finally reaching my legs.

The sensation was not like being caressed by a physical or immaterial thing, but rather like the essence of something—or someone.

Wren's essence.

As if in affirmation of my thoughts, I could have sworn I saw him smirk when he indulgently guided the tendril of light down my thighs. I didn't dare move or speak to reprimand him lest I distract him from his continued work healing my mother. And when he pulled the extra thread of his power back, I decided I wouldn't mention it at all—because he had used it to remove all traces of blood and gore from my body, clothes, and Brynn's shoulders, upon which my hands had been resting.

At last, Wren reclaimed every drop of his magic and lowered his hands as the light faded. Gently, he eased my mother into his arms while the pieces of glass from our window rose up from the couch and the carpet, levitating towards the broken frame before piecing themselves back together.

He lay her down on the couch as the caenim's body and surrounding pool of blood burst into flames.

Brynn flinched.

The startling movement relieved me, and I released the breath I was holding hostage in my throat. At that point, any movement from her at all would have had that effect. I stroked a soothing hand down her arm while the fire hissed and whooshed, leisurely eating up all traces of the caenim and the mess it had made in our house.

"She'll be fine," Wren said, striding to the window to draw the curtains closed. It was utterly perfect, somehow in better condition than ever before. "You can go to her now."

My little sister moved like a fairy—or a faerie—and crossed the room in the blink of an eye, throwing herself on the edge of the couch. She sobbed quietly into our mother's chest while I hovered above them to check her breathing.

Slow and steady.

Her eyelids fluttered as if she were dreaming.

"She'll sleep for an hour or a day," Wren murmured. "She'll wake feeling as if the injuries never happened."

"But she'll remember?" I traced calming circles across my sister's back.

"Yes. Did you want me to make her forget?"

I sighed. Of all the memories my mother had from her life, that night would not be the worst, but I still wished that she didn't have to carry it with her for the rest of it. Brynn, too.

"I'm going back to the bookstore," Wren informed me. "Someone has to clean up and get the old man home. I'll check on her again when I'm done."

"Wait." I kept one hand on my sister, who had mercifully stopped shaking, and inched the sleeve of my cardigan down to cover my free hand, wrapping that arm around my waist as I pivoted to face him. "Why did she look at you like that?"

Firelight danced across his face, within his eyes. "It explains why the fae-lily didn't work."

"What does?"

"If that mortal louse is not your father," he elaborated softly, "and one of my kind is."

No. No.

That mortal louse *was* my father. The alternative was unthinkable. I had not endured the abuse of a complete *stranger*—

"But not you?" Internally, I kicked myself for even feeling the need to ask. For acting like I cared when I didn't.

Wren let out a single, harsh laugh and gave a pointed glance towards my hair and then my mother's. "Redheads aren't my type."

I pressed my lips into a thin line and willed the blush to stop spilling over my cheeks. I didn't know what to say. There was no logical reason for me to feel offended by his blunt dismissal.

"Auralie, I promise that I am most certainly *not* your biological father." He tilted his head to capture my gaze, eyebrows raised as if he was waiting for me to have a light bulb moment.

"Oh," I muttered. And then, *"Oh."* Embarrassment coloured my cheeks again. "Of course. Because faeries can't lie."

"No, we can't," he agreed, with no small amount of annoyance. He tousled his hair, brushing his fringe back from his eyes.

"But that doesn't mean you can trust us," he added, striding for the door. "I'll be back soon—or maybe I won't."

I almost laughed as I watched him duck his head to fit beneath the doorframe on his way out, but I didn't.

Because there was nothing fucking funny about faeries.

EIGHT

The Court of Beer and Bets

My mother slept for at least an hour.

When the smokeless fire had finished devouring the corpse of the caenim, I turned the hall light on so we weren't waiting in the dark. I considered trying to move her to her bedroom, but Brynn was asleep, tucked in at her side. So, I sat against the doorframe with the baseball bat we usually stored on the shoe rack and kept one eye on the front door. It was unlikely that my father would return so soon, but I was ready if he did.

"Aura."

At the sound of my mother's voice, I straightened against the wall and whipped my head in her direction. She was in the process of sitting up, bundling Brynn in her arms like an infant, and looked completely and utterly healthy and *alive*.

I was glad that Wren wasn't there because I might have thrown myself at his boots and wept with gratitude.

Knees wobbling, I rose to my feet and stumbled over to them, crossing sections of the room that had been burned clean of the caenim's blood without scorching our worn carpet.

"How are you feeling?" I asked in a rushed whisper.

"I'd love a cuppa." She smiled at me coyly, and I smiled right back. "I'll meet you in the kitchen."

Picking up the bat on my way out—just in case—I padded into the kitchen to put the kettle on.

The soft light over the stove was still glowing, illuminating my father's empty beer bottles strewn across our small dining table in the centre of the floor. I tossed them into the trash and washed my hands before I started on the tea.

Like everything in our townhouse, the kitchen was small. It doubled as a laundry on one side with a fold-out bench next to the washing machine that looked about as old as Wren likely was, and the kitchen counter, sink, and stove on the other. The back door led out into our tiny courtyard, bordering on the strip of council land that sat between the edge of the housing estate and the river.

My mother plodded into the room as the kettle began to squeal, taking a seat at the table with Brynn's head resting on her shoulder. She was still asleep.

I made two cups of chamomile with a drop of honey and brought them over to her, leaving the tea bag in my mother's mug.

She nodded her thanks as she wrestled an arm free from my sister and began to dunk it a few extra times.

"That thing..." she hedged after a few minutes of silence, looking up at me from beneath long lashes. "It's gone?"

"Yes." I pressed the warm ceramic against my mouth and breathed in the heady aroma of the chamomile. "How much do you remember?"

"Everything," she admitted with a grimace. She took her first sip. "I'm so sorry."

I took a sip of my own, frowning at her.

"I should have tried harder to get you to believe in fairytales," she explained, averting her eyes to study the glass cabinet of mugs behind me. "You grew up so fast. Always so practical. I remember the day you came home and told *me* that Santa wasn't real." She smiled wistfully and took another sip of tea.

I placed my mug down on the table and stared at her in astonishment.

First John, and now my mother. Both of them were completely fine with the idea that faeries and monsters were real—that they were the *same thing.* He tried to drug me. Had he already drugged *them*?

"I don't mean to intrude on the reminiscing," Wren said, stalking into the kitchen like he lived there.

I was glad I'd put my mug down, or else I might have spilled the tea everywhere. *He's so quiet when he moves.*

He flashed a wicked grin in my direction as he walked straight to the washing machine and took a seat upon it, causing the steel to groan beneath his weight. He fixed his gaze on my mother, who was watching him with delight. "But now might be the time for you to take back your heinous allegation that you and I..." He cleared his throat delicately. "That we spent time together in the past. A great deal of time, in fact," he added pointedly.

I blushed again, but laughter bubbled up and out of my mother's mouth.

"No! God, no." She gave me a firm but meaningful look. "Aura, no. Your father was High Fae, but not *that* High Fae." She jerked her head towards Wren, who let loose a rough breath. "Thank you, by the way," she said to him. "Aura's father was from the Court of Light, too."

"My father was from the Court of Beer and Bets," I corrected, and then immediately regretted it for the shame that crossed my mother's face. "I'm sorry. I'm sorry, but this is impossible. I've known that man since I was a baby."

Her eyes darkened, lashes fluttering. "It happened while we were together."

"No, it didn't." *That was too quick*. I'd deflected that far too quickly. My brow creased as I bent my head to recapture her gaze. "Mama."

"I am so sorry," she whispered, placing her mug on the table in front of mine. "I knew from the moment I found out about you that you weren't his. I had these vivid dreams of starlight and power, and sometimes, I could have sworn that you were playing with magic in my belly. I had this...this *sensation*. It was like you were dancing as early as six weeks."

"*Mama.*" My voice cracked.

"He didn't suspect it until you were about three years old because you look like me," she went on. "But then he found you playing in the garden at our old house with wood carvings of fantastical creatures that you said your friends had made for you. The Little Folk used to bring you gifts." She smiled ruefully. "I never told him about your heritage, but he grew suspicious about the presents, and one night—"

"I remember."

I would never be able to forget the first time my father hurt her. The night he left her bleeding on the kitchen floor, her lower lip split straight down the middle and a fast-forming bruise colouring her cheekbone. That was the first night he left us, and when he eventually came back, everything had changed.

He'd always been an alcoholic, but he'd never been violent or angry. He returned as both of those things, with the added bonus of a gambling addiction supported by his unemployment benefits.

I'd never questioned what that fight had been about. I'd hidden in my wardrobe and covered my ears until I heard the front door slam and his car speed away, and then I raced into the kitchen to find my mother holding a bloody tea towel to her face.

"He found out you cheated," I finished for her. "But not with...*whom*?" It was better not to refer to faeries as a *what* when one of them was present in the room, I'd decided.

"No, not with whom."

"And were you ever going to tell me this?"

Eyes softening, she angled her head to the side and shook it gently. "You were so human. After we moved, The Little Folk stopped visiting you. You never displayed any sort of powers or even an interest in magic. I thought it was better to let you live a normal life."

A normal life.

I tried not to let my disappointment show—that she thought what I'd had was a normal life. That her denial had caused her to lock us into this existence, taking as many breaths as we could before my father returned and plunged us all into dark waters.

But I couldn't say any of that to her. Not after what she'd been through.

"Three months ago," I began instead. My eyes dropped to my hands, secured around my mug. I swallowed to clear the sudden tension closing around my voice box. "You sent me to a shrink because

I thought my nightmares were real. You convinced me to let them medicate me—"

My mother gasped, prompting me to look at her. "Were the—" She broke off abruptly, glancing at the otherworldly man perched atop our washing machine, preoccupied with picking at his nails. "You didn't tell me what they were about," she hissed.

"I don't *know* what they were about," I hissed back.

It was true. I couldn't remember the details from a single one of the dreams that had woken me, screaming and thrashing in my sheets every single night for three long months. According to my psychiatrist, I'd tried to tell her about them while they were happening but could never bring myself to get the words out. And then, as soon as they stopped, it was like I'd forgotten all about them.

They'd left me with a hollowness, though. And dark circles around my eyes. And two pills to take—one in the morning and one at night—until I stopped thinking about it.

"I'm sorry, Aura. I really am. I thought it was a trauma response, delayed—"

"It wasn't." I refused to look towards Wren, though I could feel him staring at me. "I'm pretty certain now that it wasn't."

The dreams weren't a response to past trauma. I don't have to remember them to know that. Not after tonight.

They were a warning.

NINE

Do You Get a Crown?

"**Y**ou're having dreams?"

"Had," I corrected Wren, refusing to meet his gaze. "Not that it's any of your business."

"Aura," my mother scolded. "Be polite to our guest."

Snorting, I braced my elbows on the table and combed both hands through my hair. I freed a strand to curl around my finger and stared at my murky reflection in the contents of my mug. The blurry image of the girl with pink skin, red hair, and blue eyes tainted by darkness made my heart sink a little.

I was very pretty by human standards, but nothing like the High Fae, and those dark shadows around my eyes served as a cutting reminder of my own mortality. Although, a High Fae inheritance of personality traits would explain my penchant for trying to fight intoxicated men two or three times my size.

But dwelling on the confessions of my mother's infidelity and my questionable paternity was too hard, too confronting. None of it excused the behaviour of the man who had been present on and off throughout my life. However, it did open old wounds—wounds that would flood me with guilt until I drowned or bled out.

I opted to keep my focus on the rest of it instead, though equally as damning.

"It was no accident, was it, that the caenim were following my scent?"

"No." Wren's tone was void of emotion. "I've been hunting them, and they are hunting you."

"Were," I amended quietly, still staring at my own reflection in the tea.

"No. *Are.*" Again—such short, clipped words. "There are more of them."

Finally, I let my eyes slide up to meet his. The gold was duller beneath the kitchen light. He looked bored.

"But you closed the portal," I reminded him, releasing the strand of hair woven through my fingers.

Wren gave me a scornful, lopsided grin. "There are other portals, bookworm."

I squeezed my eyes shut despite the tension headache brewing behind them. "Why would more of them come here now?"

"For you."

"Me?" My tone was flat, but my eyes opened.

"Indeed." His gaze drifted over my hair, my face, my chest. "That dormant magic in your veins must be rather valuable." He squinted at me. "Though I can't see why. We thought you were human."

"What do you mean by *we*?"

Wren clicked his tongue thoughtfully, studying a crack in the ceiling as he leaned back on his hands. "The High King of Faerie was alerted to the fact that the caenim had breached the border in pursuit of a human." He wagged a finger at me. "Naughty. Goes against all the fine print. Breaks a lot of rules." He waved the same hand in the air dismissively and finished with, "He sent me to deal with them."

I sat back in my seat, hands falling into my lap. "What, so now there's a High King of Faerie?"

He flashed his teeth at me arrogantly. "Yes. We all got together and had a meeting and decided that the *High King* of Faerie sounded far better than the *Prime Minister* of Faerie."

"You're so funny," I snapped, smiling venomously despite the hollow ache in my skull.

He bowed his head to me with irreverent modesty. "The Malum have all sorts of diabolical plans, and eradicating potential complications or threats is now at the top of their agenda. Even half-bred, ignorant ones who read a lot of books," he added, inclining his head to me again.

I ground my teeth together at the insult, anger shooting down my arms like the scrape of a hot poker, then glanced to see if my mother was hurt by the jab. I was almost dismayed to find that she was simply watching the exchange with a faint smile on her lips. It was as if she knew the High Fae's violence, ridicule, and cruelty well and adored them anyway.

"In the worst-case scenario," Wren went on heedlessly, "the High King *might* need to summon all of faeriekind to his behest. The

Malum are ugly, bitter creatures, and they all smell *revolting*"—he paused, pinching the bridge of his nose and making an exaggerated gagging face—"whereas the High King is the most handsome, talented, and clever person you've ever met. So, *obviously*, you'd offer your allegiance to him and fall under his protection. The Malum probably want to stop that before it has a chance to happen."

Faerie politics made me want to throw myself into the claws of the caenim, but I kept my expression neutral as I considered the information—specifically, the threat that all of it posed to my family if absolutely any of it was true.

John had sworn, cursed, and muttered something about Malum earlier in the night after Wren mentioned a race of faeries who owned and controlled the caenim. If Wren considered them to be evil, I would spare myself the gory details. *But if they are sending their beasts into the human world, hunting down anyone with faerie blood in their veins...*

"It killed Jonah," I remembered aloud. I squinted at Wren, trying to push my mother's quietly horrified face out of my line of sight. "He wasn't...?"

Wren shook his head. "He was a case of the wrong place, wrong time. Blasted things will eat anything that crosses their path, even on a hunt."

I shuddered at the thought of Jonah being *eaten* and wished the impossibly tall caenim had gone after my father instead.

"That was a little different," Wren murmured thoughtfully. I shot him a startled look, but he was staring at his boots, clicking his heels together. "With your mother, I think it was confused. Her scent is very similar to yours, and they're blind."

The blood rushed to my head. I felt dizzy, sick, and on the verge of tears.

If they come back and get confused again...

"When John told me to go, he didn't mean...home." My shoulders sagged as the blood rushed down, all the way to my feet, leaving me light-headed and empty.

"No. Not this home, at least." Wren raked a hand through his hair haphazardly. "I suppose it will save me a trip now if I'll end up needing to come back for you eventually, seeing as though you can't take care of *yourself*," he admitted, apparently coming to the same conclusion that I was and not caring at all that it was strangling my heart. He hopped down from the machine, as silent and graceful as a cat, and strode over to the back door as if something in the darkness had caught his interest.

I turned back to my mother, lower lip trembling as I opened my mouth to utter words I was struggling to even form in my mind. Brynn stirred in her arms, turning her rosy-cheeked face towards mine, wide blue eyes sparkling with mischief.

"Aura," she whispered, the knowledge of all that had transpired glowing on her face. Out of everything she'd been secretly listening to, she had managed to find the one potentially nice detail and run wild with it in her imagination. "Are you a fairy princess?"

At that, my mother's mental wall crumbled. Tears streamed freely down her cheeks, though she smiled as she stroked my sister's hair and gazed at me with love, sadness, and regret.

"I am," I replied, my voice steady despite the thickness in my throat. I bent my head towards her conspiratorially and grinned. "And you know what? Fairies love even harder than humans do. I loved you before, but I love you even more now. Both of you."

Brynn beamed at me, a little gasp escaping from her lips. "Do you get a crown?"

"I'm not sure," I answered, and I felt the tears welling up in my eyes. I resisted the urge to blink, trying to balance the moisture on my lower lids. "Maybe you can make one for me."

She nodded eagerly. "Yes!"

My mother's hand began to shake as it continued to stroke my sister's head, and I noticed the tears dampening her hair.

The back door flung open, and I jumped, but it was only Wren—who, for some reason, had taken it upon himself to step outside to inspect the washing line.

Not the washing line, I realised with no small amount of horror.

My washing.

"I'll be right back," I whispered to Brynn.

I stood up, chair legs grating against the linoleum floor, and pressed a kiss to the top of my sister's head. Then my mother's.

She didn't say it, though I knew she was thinking it too. I saw it in her eyes as she watched me walk away. And I saved that look, committing it to memory for when I would need it most.

Wren was inspecting a pair of skimpy red lace panties when I stepped outside, closing the back door behind me. He didn't look up at me as I approached, and when I snatched them out of his hands, he simply moved on to the white lace bodysuit hanging next on the line.

"Stop it," I seethed, swatting him away as his fingers moved to unclip the pegs.

He deflected my hands with his elbow, angling his torso away from me as he held the lace up to the moonlight. "Have you made your decision?"

I have.

I saw the look on my mother's face. I felt my heart writhe in my chest in reply.

I had made my decision, and I dreaded it with every single fibre of my being. Wren's obsession with my underwear only lessened the blow slightly, though the heat of my embarrassment and anger had evaporated the tears in my eyes.

"I'll go with you," I whispered. "But you have to make them forget."

He peered at me over one broad, muscular shoulder and elegantly arched an eyebrow. "Excuse me?"

He was still holding my lingerie up to the light, so I took advantage of his distraction and reached around to swipe it out of his grip. He lowered his arms to his sides but didn't turn his body back towards mine.

"I thought you were being snarky earlier, but I've seen what you can do, so I don't want to hear any bullshit about you not being a bloodsucker or anything else. Make them forget the caenim, and the Malum, and everything that's happened tonight." I hesitated, feeling the increasing speed of my heart beating in my chest. "Including me."

Finally, he turned around. "Are you quite sure?"

"Yes." *No, no, no, no. But…beasts with teeth and tongues for eyes and political faerie assassinations and portals and who knows what else.* "It's safer this way, as long as you can remove my scent from the house."

His eyes were glowing like rays of sunlight through the dark, and they studied me with that same predatory intensity from earlier in the night. "You catch on quickly. Perhaps you are part-faerie, after all." He sighed. "If I refuse?"

I rolled my eyes. "Then I guess I'll just have to stay here and pine after you until the day the Malum come to claim me."

He parted his lips, tongue skating over the edge of his top teeth as he stared into the kitchen through the glass door and considered. "I have one condition." With preternatural speed, he snatched the white lace negligee from my hands and held it up to me. "You let me keep this."

"That's my mother's," I lied.

He gave me a crooked smile. "No, it's not. I said that your scents are similar, not that they are the same."

I truly was horrified, even as something heated and clenched in my lower belly and my toes curled in my boots. "You're disgusting."

Looking away from him, I rolled my shoulders back. "Fine. Just...be nice about it."

Wren shrugged, stuffing the lace into his pocket beneath a dagger. "I really can't imagine why you don't seem to think I'm nice. Wait here."

I did as he asked, holding in the word that my mother and I had both heard coming.

Goodbye.

I turned my back on the door as he slipped through it and tried not to quaver at the enormous amount of trust I was bestowing upon such a cruel, apathetic creature.

Wren had saved my life and the life of my mother, but it was only to win my loyalty for his High King. It was dumb luck that he was tracking the caenim while they were stalking me and that he'd been ordered to eliminate them. Any glimpses of kindness he'd shown me in between insulting and degrading me had been the acts of a trickster. After all, he'd had no interest in me—or in shielding me from long-term danger—when he thought I was entirely human.

Maybe he pities me a little bit.

He had such a low opinion of humans and half-humans. Perhaps my father's act of cowardice had stirred some deeply buried semblance of sympathy that I'd been born to him, whether by blood or name.

It didn't matter.

Even as I glanced over my shoulder when Wren finally exited the townhouse to check that my mother and sister were still alive, the voice in my head whispered words of solace and relief. Brynn was yawning in our mother's arms. I turned away before they rose from their seat at the kitchen table, but not before noticing that there were suddenly only two chairs.

The washing line, too, had been magically cleared of all my clothing. I knew that Wren hadn't used his powers to fold it and put it away in my bedroom.

No, it was gone. Like it had never existed.

Like *I* had never existed.

"If it makes you feel any better," Wren purred in my ear, pointing towards the gap in the fence, "there *are* such things as *nice* faeries. We call them sprites."

"I thought sprites were supposed to be wicked and cruel," I mumbled, trudging in the direction he urged me to walk. When I ducked my head beneath the upper beam and slipped through to the other side, I was not at all surprised to find Wren waiting there as if he'd simply walked through the wood.

"Well, they can be, I suppose," he mused. "But I think they'd be quite taken with your sister. They're nice to the people they like."

I huffed a humourless laugh. "And you?"

"I'm nice to everyone."

"Right."

Through the waist-high grass on the slope by the river, we slipped deeper into the night, skirting around the fringe of the housing estate away from the town bridge. Crickets and frogs clicked and croaked along the water's edge, falling silent as we passed them and then picking up their songs as we continued to walk. The moon was low in the sky, a crescent in shades of grey, white, and yellow. Stars shone brighter the further away from Belgrave's township we went, and with Wren walking a few steps ahead of me, there was no trace of that golden light.

He was a being of shadows, darkness, and steel as he led me away from home, his hair gleaming like quicksilver beneath the moon, the weapons along his belt shifting with each long stride. I knew he had adjusted the length of his steps so I could keep up, but I had no intention of quickening my pace for him.

We must have walked for hours before I decided to say something; it was only then I noticed the stars were beginning to wink out and the sky was lightening into teal above us. Belgrave was nothing but a smear of colours and shapes on the horizon. Purple and jade rooftops, yellow brick buildings, and smudges of black, brown, and white. I turned in a circle and tried to name the field in which we were standing, to recall which Belgrave family to whom it belonged. It was so familiar.

"Where are we going?" I asked Wren at last. The first light of dawn cracked over the horizon and bathed the endless long grasses and wheat stalks in the same gold of his eyes.

"To Faerie," he answered simply.

And even though I already knew the answer, had already made my choice, it still sent a wave of dizziness rolling over me to hear that word spoken so confidently out loud.

Wren can't lie.

Although, perhaps he was a kook. Perhaps he had stared at the flame in Belgrave's insignia for too long and lost his wits.

Auralie's father was from the Court of Light, too.

The words rang out in my head as I circled back to Wren and reminded myself that he was real. That *this* was real. And when my eyes fell upon him again, I realised that it didn't matter whether my mother could lie or if Wren was a raving lunatic. Because he was standing a few feet away from me, the tall stalks only passing his knees where they nearly covered my waist, waiting for me to join him.

At a wall of glass.

Ten

The Forest of Eyes and Ears

"**W**elcome to the Court of Light."

"This is an empty field."

Wren's nostrils flared. "No," he tried again, voice straining. "This is the Court of Light."

Fine. I crossed my arms over my chest and stamped my feet into the solid dirt. *The Court of Light is an empty field, then.*

It turned out that the glass wall I'd seen was not actually that at all, but rather a permanent portal into the realm of the faeries that was situated along the border of the Court of Light. According to Wren, there was an identical portal in every Faerie Court leading into some part of the mortal world, and they only existed to those who knew they existed.

When I had questioned him on how exactly I was supposed to believe that my family was safe with a ginormous portal only a few hours away from them, Wren explained that the Malum tended to create their own. Tiny rips in the world, he'd said, instead of the real thing.

He then suggested that I think of the glass wall as more of a gateway and refrain from using the term *portal* unless I was referring to illegal activity.

The real things—the gateways—were controlled by the High King of Faerie, Wren had elaborated when I hadn't moved, and they were protected by runes, spells, and other enchantments far too complicated for my poor half-human brain to comprehend. The High King had to approve all inter-realm travel requests, and he was alerted every time someone ignored the rules and syphoned some of the gateway's power to create a rip elsewhere.

I still hadn't moved any closer to it.

Wren continued, blabbering that the Malum created a portal in Dante's Bookstore through which the caenim had crossed, and John took it all in his stride because he had snuck over into Faerie through a similar rip when he was a boy. And if John could do it, Wren concluded unpleasantly without giving me a moment's pause for breath, then I could stop standing there looking like a *lochgrub* and do it too.

Quite unceremoniously, he then proceeded to snatch my wrist, use it to pull me in front of him and, with both hands on my shoulders, the bastard practically threw me into the wall.

Through the wall.

It was like passing through a body of water with my eyes closed, though it happened so fast that I hadn't had time to shut them, and I came out on the other side in the middle of what was quite literally an empty field. Lilac-coloured wheat stalks with translucent azure spikes extended as far as my eyes could see to the dark and distant horizon ahead, following the much lighter stretch of skyline in every other direction.

The glassy, wall-esque gateway reappeared behind me, rippling like the exhaust of a vehicle. And above...

"What *is* that?"

Wren followed my upturned gaze to the star-filled sky, glittering mutely like someone had dusted crushed diamonds over the spaces normally filled by clouds in the human world. Ether tinted a nebulous shade of rainbow all the way through the spectrum from violet to green to red, the crystalline haze directly above us rippled and shimmered, diffracting in waves like an ocean of colour.

"Should you have your hearing abilities checked alongside your IQ? I told you, we're in the Court of Light." Wren's golden eyes, dimming down to a pale shade of lemon, rolled halfway back into his head as he threw a hand up towards the atmosphere. "What do you *think* it is?"

Light.

The sky was made of light.

Not illuminated by it, and not reflective of it.

Made of it.

I swallowed my pride. "I guess I was expecting more," I lied with a shrug, and took my first step deeper into Faerie.

Wren's eyes flared with an emotion that almost looked akin to hurt or disappointment, but then he blinked, and it was gone. "We're on the boundary line. We have a long journey ahead of us before we're back in any form of civilisation. Normally, I'd evanesce, but—"

"Evanesce?"

He smacked his lips together. "You know," he began, holding his hand up, palm facing outwards. "Make like the breeze and sort of—"

With a swipe of his hand through the air, Wren vanished.

My eyes barely managed to catch his movements from one place to the next. He was standing a few feet away from me at first, completely real and physical, and then he was a fluid blur of dark clothes and sunbeams, finally reappearing in his full physical form before me, his face dangerously close to mine. I could taste the sweetness of his breath as it coasted over my lips.

He grinned, but then had the nerve to look annoyed that it hadn't spooked me.

I held my ground, though part of me wanted to collapse.

Wren had teleported like catching a ride on an invisible wind. As he conceded and took a step back, I noticed that his light hair *was* wind-tousled, and his shirt was pressed against his body, the fabric hugging the curves of his athletic chest like he'd come out of a vacuum seal.

He followed my downward gaze and tugged the fabric loose, smirking.

At a loss for words, I simply nodded to convey my understanding that I could not do what he had done.

Evanesce.

Magic.

And so, we walked.

The pastel grasses parted, laying out an extensive pathway through the field for us. Wren kept his strides shorter to account for my bumbling human legs, but as we walked, the long grass lining the trail on either side tinkling softly like wind-chimes as they swayed, I found that it was easier to keep up.

It was as if gravity held less authority there.

Our silence was tense, and I highly doubted that it was due to the drawn-out physical exertion that my presence demanded of Wren. His legs were long and powerful, and he barely drew breath to spur himself on.

I, on the other hand, was panting by the time the darkness on the horizon finally took shape. My mouth was dry, and my skin was hot beneath its surface, though I could scarcely remember the cure for that as a vast, dense forest grew into the sky before us.

The trees were enormous—tall as skyscrapers, wide as houses. Their trunks were varying shades of black and brown, shale and grey. Some were smooth, others ossified with bark and calluses, and they all drooped with tangles of branchless leaves that looked similar to the fronds of weeping willows.

Close together, the trees left very little space between them. The small gaps glowed with a subdued viridity, more like a cavity than a trail leading into the forest.

The sound of the grasses clinking together faded as we approached, and a thick quiet fell around me like a silent hush of comfort.

"First hurdle," Wren said, his voice tight. "Get through this." He turned to give me a loaded glare. "Don't say too much, don't think too much—which shouldn't be hard for you—and don't let too much show on your face."

My eyebrows raised as high as my forehead would allow them to go. "Excuse me?"

He rubbed his temple. "I call this the Forest of Eyes and Ears. It *knows* things about its travellers, and the last thing I need right now is for us to get separated or sent around in endless circles because it thinks you're trying to find your way home."

"I'm not," I blurted, only half-convinced. I looked at the ground, my black boots coated in a scintillating sheen of gold, and then back to the forest. "It won't."

"Good." Wren stepped over to me and curled his hand around my wrist. His touch was blooming with carnal magic, familiar and soothing, but I eyed him warily. Loosening his grip until his fingers were no longer overlapping, he slid my hand through his and left a solid bracelet of gold around my arm.

I swore at him as my eyes followed the chain attached to the manacle, all the way to his hands, where he was holding a similar circlet of gold and fastening it around his own wrist.

He held his hand up when he was done, jiggling the chain in midair, and gave me a roguish grin. "Humans can lie," he stated with a one-shouldered shrug, as if it was any sort of excuse or explanation.

While delicately crafted, the gold bracelets and chain were unmistakably a replica of handcuffs, and fury simmered in my blood as the High Fae brute sauntered off towards the forest, towing me behind him like some sort of prized cow on a leash.

"This is not necessary," I spat at his back.

Wren's only reply was to shush me harshly.

My mortality—and mundaneness—weighed on me heavily as he tugged me along. It occurred to me that I was likely to die in Faerie, half-blood or not, because I could not match the effortless power he displayed. And if Wren's power trivialised me so completely, what would the power of the High King of Faerie do to me?

Inching through a narrow passageway of wood barely wide enough for the broad-shouldered High Fae bastard to fit, the forest began to feel like a maze. The expanse of trees was so wide. I shuddered as I considered its potential depth, beating away the encroaching claustrophobia. I kept my breathing as even as I could while sucking in quiet gasps of air, too afraid that the wood might shift around us and pulverise me if I dared to speak or show my concern.

Wren vanished around a sharp corner, the shining gold chain grinding against the wood, and I followed him a moment later to find that where the maze ended, the true forest began.

In the midst of the thicket, the gaps between tree trunks left room for me to breathe. Dim sea-green light floated between the shadows of the brushwood and canopy, so thick and vibrant that the air almost appeared to have substance. The pathway straight ahead was clear, though obstructed by small mounds and hills, like solid waves rising from an earthen ocean.

Wren didn't give me much time to survey the foliage before he pressed on, the chain between our wrists going taut. My footsteps were silent on the mossy ground, the sound of my heartbeat quietening as we ventured deeper into the forest. He did not look back or slow his pace, nor did he offer any leniency for the handcuffs linking us, keeping his arm firmly at his side while mine was pulled ahead of the rest of my body.

As we approached the first slope, I felt a mixture of dread and relief wash over me.

Dread because it was not a hill but a massive, unearthed root as tall as Wren and almost as steep as a wall. And relief because I knew there was no way we could climb it while our wrists were still linked.

Wren seemed to realise this too and came to a stop at the base of the gnarled tree root. I waited for him to magic away the handcuffs, trying to conceal my smile. However, when he turned to face me, his eyes were smouldering a mischievous shade of gold, and he put the pointer finger of his free hand to his lips.

And then he snatched me and hauled me over his shoulder.

Pinning my arm to my side with the rigid chain, his elbows locked around my knees as he crouched down and *jumped*.

He was jumping.

Over the root that was at least twice his size.

My stomach somersaulted as the world tipped upside-down. Warm air kissed the nape of my neck, threading through my hair and pulling it across my open mouth, and the firm ground became a depthless shadow beneath us. I pressed my face into the curve of

Wren's shoulder blade to hide my expression and hold in my scream, and I felt the muscles in his back ripple in response.

He landed gracefully on the other side, lowering me to my feet with equal ease. I swayed, and he clamped his fist around the chain, jerking me back into place without so much as a cautionary glance. I might have slapped him again had my dominant hand not been cuffed.

While I contemplated the act of violence in the minute that he allowed for us both to catch our breath, I noticed tiny little lights beginning to flicker within the underbrush and shadows on the tree trunks in sets of two.

The Eyes of the Forest.

They had no visible lids, nor pupils or irises, but somehow, they still displayed emotion—curiosity. They peered at us as if they didn't realise that I could see them, too.

Busybodies.

I read the thought all over Wren's face as he turned.

Abandoning my plans to assault him, I yanked on the chain in silent command and continued to trek towards the next obstacle in our course. Wren fell into step beside me this time, keenly aware that we had company—and probably quite proud that his stunt had attracted so much attention.

Well, I would not have it.

At the next wooden boulder, I came to an abrupt halt and whirled on him with an expression of the most determination and grit that I could muster.

I yanked on the handcuffs. *Take them off.*

He stared back at me impassively. *No.*

Take. Them. Off.

A slow, sensual blink. *I. Said. No.*

Fine!

I shrugged, casting my eyes around the shadowed Forest, and spoke to its watchful presence in my mind. *I no longer wish to travel with him.*

As if Wren had heard my thought too, his eyes flared with ire, and he moved to grab me—but the Forest moved faster.

In the blink of an eye, a tiny sapling rose from the soil between us, the sharp edges of its leaves glinting like steel, and sprouted open like a Venus flytrap. The gold chain links groaned and then broke apart as the sapling chomped down on them and burrowed back into the ground as soon as the chain swung free. The manacle fell to the ground with a soft thump.

My skin grew hot within the bracelet's imprint as if someone was tracing a circle around my forearm with a fire poker. It was intense, yet not enough to cause pain. I didn't even care that it left a tiny, scar-like indentation around my arm that glimmered faintly in the low light.

Smiling broadly, I brushed my hands together and glanced at Wren to see if his handcuff had been destroyed as well. It happened so fast; I almost didn't spot the snakelike vine shooting down at him from the canopy until it was too late.

He sidestepped, swearing viciously as the vine hurled down like an arrow from the sky. Light flared on each of his palms even as he reached for the dagger sheathed at his side, and I could have sworn the entire Forest began to hiss at him in response.

Twirling the blade in his hand, Wren assumed a defensive stance as the vine adjusted its course and speared towards him again. He feinted left, then pirouetted to the right, bringing the blade down in a sharp swing and slicing off a chunk of the vine as it swooped past him.

The vine sagged on the floor as if it was feeling the pain of its wound, but then it was barrelling towards him like a rolling log, aiming to knock his feet out from under him. Wren jumped into the air, tucking his feet and somersaulting right before the vine pulled upwards, and landed with perfect, although entirely melodramatic, form beside me. He tossed the dagger into the air and caught it by the hilt like it was nothing.

"Take it back." His smile was cheerful, but his voice was a low snarl. "Now."

"Promise to forgo the handcuffs," I bartered.

The Forest came after him again, a new vine shooting out from the underbrush and torpedoing between us. It wrapped itself around his legs like a constrictor, though he yelled and slashed it in half before it was done.

"Fine," he agreed, exasperated. He kicked his legs free while a rock came hurtling out of the shadows, barely missing his head as he ducked. Pupils dilating, he raised his brows at me and shook his head. "No handcuffs." He pointed at me with the dagger and looked me square in the eye. "You're no fun."

Another sapling shot up from the ground and knocked the dagger from his grip. He managed to catch it with his other hand, and then proceeded to stamp his boots down on the sapling like he was putting out a fire.

Holding back a snicker, I tried to give the Forest a grateful look. *Thank you, but I'm okay now.*

A vine came slithering up behind me, and Wren brandished his dagger again, halting only when I put my hand up to stop him.

"Wait."

His face creased with annoyance, but he obeyed, holding the blade above his shoulder, poised to plunge into the vine.

It ignored him and his offensive posture, sliding in between us before it rose up in front of me like a snake. There were no visible eyes or ears this time, but I was consumed by the feeling of being studied as its thorny end hovered at eye level in front of my face.

After a moment, it lowered itself back down to the ground and gently nudged my heel.

Somehow, I understood exactly what it was saying.

Wren, however, looked to me for permission to stab it. I shook my head and gestured towards the path onwards. The veins in his neck protruded, and he gave me a beseeching look that almost had me laughing at him out loud.

Instead, I simply started walking again.

And, as I knew it would, the vine followed me. Escorting me in case I changed my mind again.

It did so for the entire journey out of the Forest of Eyes and Ears, much to Wren's discomfort when he finally decided to stop pouting and caught up to my side. He was clearly bothered, which I considered an added bonus of my botanic chaperone.

When we at last made it to the edge, I turned around and stroked the vine in thanks. It leaned into the touch like a dog, and Wren's disgusted expression almost made me laugh again.

I didn't, though.

But I did smile.

Because for a moment—for the blink of two starry eyes—I felt the ever-present tension that had claimed ownership of my soul long ago slacken.

I *forgot*.

And when I remembered...

I was not so afraid.

ELEVEN

A Small Single Bed

There was another empty field on the other side of the Forest of Eyes and Ears.

It was identical to the last, except this one was placed atop a cliff overlooking a restless cobalt and silver ocean. I never strayed too close to the edge, but from what I could see where the land curved inwards before jutting out ahead, it was a very steep drop down to a narrow beach of broken shells and stones.

In the sky above, a rainbow of colours and dusting of crystals still danced and played where the clouds should have been, but it cast a normal, albeit somewhat peach-tinted glow upon the world.

Tawny clay speckled with white made up the exposed earth on the side of the cliff. It could have been any ocean in the world crashing upon the shoreline, based on appearances alone.

"That belongs to the Merfolk," Wren murmured, catching my horizon-bound stare. "You'll draw their attention if you keep looking out there."

I studied his expression, tilting my head. "No," I breathed, a smile curling up on my lips. *Faeries I can believe, although even that is a stretch. But Merfolk?* "Surely not."

Wren cocked an eyebrow and beckoned me to his side. "What do you see down there?" he enquired, pointing to the stony shore.

We were a few feet away from the straight drop down, but it was hard to be sure in the long grass, so I leaned slightly into him as I peered over the edge. He placed his hand on the small of my back like he was about to shove me over it.

Heart lurching, I skipped backwards, out of his reach, and averted my eyes. "Stones and shells. Maybe some sand."

He chuckled darkly. "Bones, bookworm."

A shiver spider-walked down my spine, pricking me with needle-like legs. I didn't dare another glance, but I could hardly accept that it was true—even if I knew he couldn't lie.

"Some human legends refer to them as Sirens, but they're all the same," he went on, staring down at the ocean. The waves began to climb higher and they crashed into one another with a spray of white sea foam. "Vicious, slimy little creatures."

For all of his bravado while he'd cursed them, Wren still promptly grabbed me by the elbow and urged me to quicken my pace as he hauled me further inland.

"So, the Merfolk are faeries?" I clarified, once we'd put enough distance between ourselves and the ocean.

"In a manner of speaking," he answered loosely. "All forms of magic descended from the High Fae, originally."

"Do you call *them* half-breeds, too?"

He faltered a step but didn't glance back at me as he replied, "I'd rather your company than theirs. Let's leave it at that."

"They must be hideous."

"They are."

I rolled my eyes at his back and decided against pressing for more information. He didn't seem inclined towards conversation, and I wasn't sure how many more of his insults and dirty looks I could take on an empty stomach.

Provoked by the thought, my belly began to grumble with hunger.

I couldn't remember how many hours had passed since I'd last eaten or had any water, and I'd skipped at least two doses of my medication. *Though*, I supposed as my eyes bore into the back of the broody High Fae man in front of me, *I probably don't need it anymore*.

Thoughts of home circled my mind for the rest of the day's trek into the Court of Light.

My father would likely be long gone, perhaps never to return after the incident with the caenim, and I could only hope that my decision to leave would keep my mother and Brynn safe. That hope was what I held onto. It was all I had to hold onto.

By the time we made visible progress across the land, almost all of my human needs had caught up to me. I didn't particularly fancy broaching the subject with Wren, considering how little I knew about faeries and their own needs, but I was nearly desperate by the time he finally stopped.

We were at a dirt crossroads, lined with trees of average height sprouting large purple berries. The sky was beginning to fade into violet and silver.

"We'll camp here tonight," he informed me bluntly, his back turned to me. He began to kick at the stones and bark on the ground. "Because I'm sick of walking."

Without uttering a single word about it, I turned on my heels and went to find some privacy.

He *is sick of walking? He isn't even human!*

But I was, and I felt it all over. My calves were cramping, my lower back ached, and as I stormed back the way we'd come and sagged against the last tree on the road, I realised that my feet were numb and swollen in my boots. Very likely blistered, too.

Wren hadn't taken many breaks on the way into Faerie, which meant that I'd been on my feet for most of the day. And with night fast approaching in the Court of Light, it must have been a very, very long day.

Delirious fatigue hit me all at once, and I was barely able to keep my balance as I stumbled back down the road after squatting behind a tree like a dog.

Wren was leaning against a tree trunk on the other side of the dirt road, legs crossed at his ankles, absentmindedly peeling an apple with his poniard as he watched me approach. His eyes remained that soft shade of lemon, and he'd removed the weapon belt from around his waist.

I refused to meet his gaze.

As my eyes pointedly drifted past him, they fell upon a small cottage with a smoking chimney sitting on the other side of the trees. I really must have been delirious because it had not been there before.

Wren jerked his chin towards the building and took a bite of his apple. The delectable *crunch* made my mouth water, and so I followed him—if only to get close enough to steal his food.

"You look like a rabid animal," he remarked as he sauntered down the front path. "Behave a bit like one, too. Did you really storm off to go and piss behind a tree?"

I was suddenly too tired to fight him or feel anything in response to his words. Even as the cottage door swung open to reveal a blazing hearth and small table set with food and silver cutlery, I couldn't muster the strength to ask questions or care if they had logical answers.

The cottage was single-storey and had one room. A bedroom. My eyes locked onto the end of a small bed poking out behind the open doorway, and I made a beeline for it—manners be damned, and Wren be damned, too.

He sidestepped in front of me, eyes narrowing like a panther. "Eat," he ordered, pointing to the table with the hand holding his apple. "And drink something, too. Your lips are as dry as the Opiate Desert."

Ignoring his focus on my mouth, I sank into one of the hard wooden chairs and rested my heavy head in one hand as I peered up at him. I was starving, but something I'd read about faeries and their food nagged at me, and I was too tired to dredge up the specifics of the memory.

"Can I even eat any of this?"

"I don't know," he replied, shrugging as he took another bite of his apple. He licked some of the juice from his lips, and my stomach bubbled and groaned. "Can you?"

I pushed my chair away from the table and made to stand up to leave, but his hand came down hard on my shoulder, holding me in my seat. The fireplace popped and crackled behind me as if it was sharing his annoyance.

"You're not asking the right questions, Auralie."

"I'm tired."

"You were doing just fine."

I sighed. Obviously, the view from his high horse obscured the struggles of mortality. "Is this food safe for humans to eat?"

"No." He removed his hand from my shoulder and walked around to take a seat in the chair across from me, hoisting one mud-crusted boot onto the edge of the table and crossing his other one over his knee. "But you're not human," he said, before I could bolt for the bedroom door and throw myself in a heap on the mattress.

I considered that for a moment, staring down at the spread of food. Most of it looked like the food I was used to in the human world—roasted meats and vegetables, cold salads and platters of fruit, a tray of crackers and cheese and plump berries—but the colours were somehow more vibrant, the smells more potent and inviting.

My stomach growled again.

"Eat, Auralie." He tossed his apple core over my head and into the hissing fireplace before pouring a goblet of water from the jug. He slid it across the table to me. "Part-faerie is still a faerie, at least when it comes to fine dining."

That was all I needed to hear, though I didn't feel like I had even an ounce of faerie blood in my veins, and the way I gobbled down food with Wren's filthy boots sitting directly in my line of sight didn't resemble fine dining at all.

"I'm going to bed," I mumbled, after downing the fourth goblet of water that Wren had poured for me in a few long gulps.

Rising from the table, I felt so full and so exhausted that I almost didn't think I'd make it to the door before I collapsed into sleep.

"I'll be in soon," Wren called after me suggestively.

I froze.

One bedroom.

I peered around the doorway.

One bed.

A small single bed.

I'd read those books before, but there was *no way*—

"I'm kidding." He chuckled darkly. "Oh, don't look at me like that, bookworm. I prefer to sleep outdoors. That bed is for you."

Without looking back, I made a rude gesture at him over my shoulder and strode into the room, slamming the door shut on his howling laughter behind me.

Twelve

Little Pink Pills

Sleep was waiting for me in Faerie.

Like it had known that I was coming.

It welcomed me in an all-consuming embrace as my head hit the pillow, kicking my shoes off at the same time as I yanked the blanket out from under me, and I was unconscious before my boots clattered to the floor.

Lucid dreaming, my psychiatrist had said, would occur when the person became aware they were having a dream. Sometimes, it included an element of control. My dreams had been so vivid that they felt real, despite knowing that I was not within the bounds of my normal reality, and they had continued to plague my thoughts even during the day.

She had given me a sedative to start with—which didn't work—and encouraged me to talk about the dreams.

I explained to her that I couldn't, not that I didn't *want* to, and I told her that they were less like dreams and more like *visions* instead.

She didn't believe me.

Nobody believed me.

Everyone was worried and caring, but nobody believed me. They thought the dreams were so wrong and twisted that I was ashamed to admit to their contents. When I realised, I couldn't cope anymore.

I had a breakdown.

I snapped. I screamed, cried, and shattered a vase the day I told the psychiatrist that I *wanted* to tell her about the dreams, but I was not *allowed* to tell her. Or anyone.

She'd asked me who had said that, and I'd fallen to my knees on her office floor and spit onto her carpet and shrieked as a searing heat burned my tongue.

At the end of the session, she'd handed me a prescription for an antipsychotic medication.

I filled it.

I swallowed the pill every morning.

Four weeks later, on the night before my twenty-first birthday, I had woken screaming at midnight from my very last nightmare.

After that, the dreams just stopped. Like they had never happened.

But I hadn't taken one of those little pink pills in days.

And on my first night in Faerie, I remembered what the dreams had been about.

The glass wall rising up before me, shimmering with my own reflection—the gateway into the Court of Light. The mysterious, sentient woodland with diamond lights—the Forest of Eyes and Ears. And then the dungeon—where my prisoner was tortured every single night as he had been for three long months, left scarred, beaten, and burned.

Burned.

By iron-tipped whips, bars, and blades.

Wren couldn't touch the iron key in Dante's Bookstore. Iron was the choice of every weapon in the dungeon, and wielded with hands clad in black leather gloves.

My dreams were of Faerie.

My prisoner was High Fae.

And I was travelling through it, in real life, towards the cell in which the beautiful, tortured body from my dreams was being held captive.

Wren was leading me right to him.

One by one, the pieces fell into place.

Wren was the invisible force holding me back every night when the torture was completed with that impossibly strong and disarmingly familiar grip. Even his scent had been familiar, though I'd mistakenly relished in the cologne, not realising who he was. Until then.

I was dreaming of Faerie, but this time I was also *in* Faerie.

I've made it this far.

And so I screamed louder than I ever had before, until my eardrums buckled against the decibels and my throat turned dry.

"Lucais!"

And then I woke up.

Two arms, tense with corded muscle, lifted me from the bed. "Aura. Aura, wake up."

I was trembling all over, my head lolling against something warm and hard. My eyelids fluttered against the sleep glue that had stuck them together, straining to burst open. But it was dark in my dreams, the moonlight retreating from the cell as if I'd scared it away, and I was still searching for his face…

His fingers brushed the hair away from my eyes, tangling in my sleep-tossed curls. He lifted my head with that hand while his other arm curled around my waist and my legs, pinning me to his chest.

"It's okay," he murmured. It was like I was underwater, hearing him call out to me from above the surface. "It's just a dream."

Lucais.

Lucais was here. I'd found him. I'd passed through the gateway, made it out of the Forest, and he had escaped from his cell.

I had no idea what was supposed to come next, but I opened my eyes.

It was not Lucais holding me on the bed.

The face staring down at me belonged to his keeper. *My* keeper.

Wren.

Thirteen

Elera

I didn't know if Wren ever truly intended to sleep outdoors because I woke up the next morning to find him lying sprawled across the green rug on the floor beside my bed.

I kicked him awake, and we ate breakfast together in brooding silence.

Shortly afterwards, we left the cottage and continued our walk further into the Court of Light and closer to the dungeon where Wren was almost certainly holding somebody prisoner.

He gave no indication of whether he realised that I knew who he was—that I knew he tortured people, though if it was for his own depraved pleasure or by the order of the High King of Faerie, I wasn't yet sure.

The only thing he said to me was that if I was going to scream like I was being murdered again, I should at least have the decency not to shatter his eardrums a second time when he comes in to shut me up.

Very faintly, I remembered fighting free of his arms and yelling at the top of my lungs for him to let me go. Even less clearly, I had a memory of his face being flattened by complete and utter shock for a brief moment before he obeyed and abruptly dropped me onto the floor with a thud.

The bruise forming on my hip served as confirmation that my recollections were accurate.

Any remnants of trust I felt for Wren from the previous day were long gone, but I made an effort to conceal that truth from him. I didn't know who the man in my dreams really was, but Wren was my best option for finding him—and finding out his identity.

It was the most bizarre notion, but something told me that the prisoner was my friend. *Would* be my friend. More than that, even. Perhaps the only person I could trust in Faerie.

So, I trailed along behind Wren as I had done the day before and as I would continue to do until he brought me before the High King.

When he made his first stop, I noticed that the cottage was no longer visible behind us.

We were travelling along the same dirt road lined with fruitful trees, cutting through a vast expanse of sloping, golden-grassed hills.

Wren looked towards a small thicket to one side of the road and whistled with his fingers.

Moments later, a beautiful dappled mare trotted out from behind one of those trees, whinnying softly as she broke into a canter towards him. I had to do a double-take because she had three pearlescent, twisted horns descending down her snout from the top of her head, gradually shrinking in size.

I couldn't believe it. *Even the fucking horses are faeries.*

She was without a saddle or reins, but she was unmistakably *his* as she nudged her muzzle into his open hand and snorted in greeting.

"Elera," Wren crooned, stroking her mane. "I've brought you some lunch. She's got plenty of meat on her bones, just as you like them."

If I hadn't been in Faerie, I would have thought his words to be ludicrous. Insult aside, the implication should have sounded impossible.

But I *was* in Faerie, so I took a measured step backwards as the creature looked up at me with wide, depthless eyes and arguable weapons growing out of her face. Wren gave her a soft pat on the shoulder, and she lurched for me, swiping her slippery tongue right up the side of my face from my jawline to my temple before I had a chance to duck and roll away.

And then she smiled at me.

The horse—or maybe she preferred the word unicorn—*smiled* at me.

Wren burst out laughing, clutching his stomach. "You should have seen the look on your face!"

Elera seemed to laugh too, letting out a high-pitched whinny as she turned and trotted back to him, long silver tail swishing back and forth with glee.

"Bastard," I muttered, wiping away his beast's slobber with the sleeve of my favourite cardigan. I pointed at Elera, cheeks flaming red, and glared at the golden-eyed fiend beside her. "Do you want me to think that *everything* in this bloody place plans to devour me?"

His broad grin of amusement simmered down into a suggestive smirk, and he trailed his fiery eyes from the top of my head down to my boots with deliberate slowness. "Yes," he answered, meeting my furious stare. He winked. "Better keep your wits about you, bookworm."

And with those parting words, Wren promptly mounted his unicorn-horse, hands knitting in her ashy-grey mane. They broke into a gallop down the lane, leaving me to be swallowed by the cloud of dust they left in their wake.

Fourteen

Get Your Own Horse

I was going to kill him.

If I ever saw Wren's smug, beautiful face again, I was going to kill him in some creative way that would leave him speechless and awestruck before he met his end.

And then I might very well have gone into hiding for the rest of my life out of shame for allowing him to trick me *again*.

As I traipsed down the road with absolutely no idea where I was going or how long it would take me to get there, I went over and over the exchange in my head.

Wren offered to take me into Faerie. He never said anything about escorting me to see the High King. Foolishly, I'd assumed that all on my own. I thought that he would take me to some medieval castle where the High King would ask me to swear allegiance to him in exchange for information about my bloodline and heritage—which I would gladly do in order to render myself and my scent useless to the Malum. And then I would figure out my next move: either find a way to free the prisoner from his dungeon, and free myself forever from the nightmares at the same time, or steal some fancy faerie weapons and go back home.

The latter option required Wren's assistance because I hadn't worked up the courage to ask him *what* he'd made my mother and sister believe about my existence before he'd abandoned me. So, I amended my plans.

If I saw him again, I would bleed him for information first, and then I would kill him.

Because I would go home one day. I wanted to, and one day...I *would*.

Plotting and scheming my way down the unpaved road, I walked until my rage simmered down into smouldering embers, burning the last of my energy along with it.

Without a sun in the sky, I couldn't discern the time of day. I had no sense of time passing or the world orbiting in Faerie, and as far as my mortal eyes could see, there was nothing but more of those infernal empty fields for miles and miles.

Taking a seat against a roadside tree, I smacked the back of my head into the trunk until its bark came off in my hair.

Fool.

I was a fool for following Wren out of Belgrave, for having given it absolutely no thought whatsoever, and for not asking any of the right questions, even though I'd read enough books about faeries to know better.

They are tricksters and thieves.

I should have known better.

I should have stayed at home and mulled over my predicament overnight like any logical and sane person would do.

My mother likely wouldn't have agreed to any plans I made to keep us safe—like moving to a different town—but I was an adult, so I could have found a way to convince her. With some better weapons and a little more research, we could have found safety somewhere far away from any of the gateways into Faerie, and I could have lived out the rest of my life in peace.

But instead, I ran.

I quite literally bolted like a horse out of the gates. I had abandoned Brynn like Wren had abandoned me, and the reason was horrible. It was horrible, and it made me horrible, and everything was horrible.

Folding myself in half against the tree, I bent my forehead to my knees and began to cry. I had time for it now that I was alone, worlds away from any of my responsibilities.

Hours might have passed before my well of tears finally dried up and I lifted my head again, my neck cramping in protest, my eyes blurred by despair. The sky was still bright with colour, the fields of grass still swaying in the breeze, and the road spanned for miles and miles.

But—

There. A dot on the horizon, right in the middle of the road.

I scrambled to get to my feet, shielding my eyes with a hand as I squinted ahead, trying to discern the approaching figure. I took five hasty steps forward before I realised it wasn't Wren and a deathly warning in my head chilled my blood.

Not the caenim.

Something worse.

Better keep your wits about you, bookworm.

Well, I hadn't. I'd stared at the flame for too long when I was six years old and no longer had any wits to keep anywhere. John had tried to warn me.

Running felt futile, but I sprinted away from the creature nonetheless because that's what I did: I fought when I should flee, and I fled when I should have stayed to fight.

I ran until my lungs burned, until my knees buckled, until sweat stung my eyes.

And then I kept going.

Over the sandy, uneven road sprinkled with small stones and rocks that seemed hellbent on tripping me up, I ran until I came to another crossroads, and the berry trees lining the path stopped.

Three possible directions were laid out in front of me because turning back was not an option anymore. I had no idea which way was which, but I'd followed a fairly straight line of direction with Wren. The ocean had to be somewhere to my left, and the coastline straight ahead. In most human lands, the cities were built around the sea and close to large bodies of water. But with cannibalistic Merfolk dwelling below the surface in Faerie, I had a feeling the High Fae might have built their civilisations further inland.

I turned right, and I glanced over my shoulder as I did, only to find that there was nobody on the road anymore.

Skidding to a halt, I circled around to double-check that the Court of Light was not playing tricks on my eyes. I was *certain* I had seen a dark, hooded figure walking down the lane. I had felt their ominous presence, and the warning bells in my head had gone off like a defence siren.

But there was no one there.

Staring back in the direction I'd come, I took a moment to settle my ragged breathing into something more sustainable, and then I turned around to reassess my position.

"The High King."

The creature's breath hit my nose before my eyes registered its presence, barely an inch away from my face; rancid, hot breath, like a draught coming up from a sewer.

My heart skipped a beat, and I felt the blood draining from my cheeks as the air was pushed out of my lungs.

"Where is the High King?"

I couldn't speak. Couldn't find the strength to answer it.

Humanoid in its warped and twisted form, the creature would have stood at my height were it not for the massive hunch in its back. Naked beneath a tattered black robe, it had large breasts, thick thighs and long-nailed hands honed down into claws. Colourless eyes bulged out of its head, without lashes, as it stared up at me like it was seeing into my soul and the secrets hiding out within it were confusing.

"Where is the High King?" it repeated, hissing through a small mouth without any visible teeth.

"I—I don't know," I stammered, fumbling for something—anything—in the pockets of my jeans. They were empty. *Where did I lose my bag?*

I sucked in a breath to scream, though I knew that no one would hear me.

Or care.

"Liar," the creature seethed. "Little human liar. I must see the High King."

At that point, I would have liked to have seen the High King, too.

"Why?" I asked innocently, a pathetic attempt to prolong my inevitable death at the hands of the foul thing. "What's so urgent?"

"None of your concern." It spat curdled raisin-coloured bile at my feet. "Tell me where he is, human, and I might let you live."

"Okay." I held my hands up in submission, though I doubted that the creature normally let its prey live long enough to recognise the gesture. "I'm looking for him too, so maybe we can go and find him together."

The creature's lips curved up into a smile that might have been a show of amusement, or perhaps the practice of stretching its mouth out in order to fit my head inside it. "You don't need to find him," it whispered menacingly. "You need to tell me where he is."

I shook my head, backing up a step. "I can't tell you where he is *until* I find him. And," I added, throwing caution to the wind with my attempt at bargaining for my life, "I'm probably better use to you alive so I have a chance of doing that. Before you eat me. Let's find him first, and then you can eat me. Okay?"

The creature threw back its head and howled at the colourful sky. *Laughter.* A fit of absurdly menacing giggles.

I swallowed the ball of fear in my throat. *Maybe if I can amuse it long enough...*

"The High King must pay, one way or another," it told me, shucking off its robe.

I noticed that its faintly purple skin was translucent in full light right as the creature lunged for my throat.

Panic seized control of my body. My natural-born instinct was to fight, which had never served me well in the past, but that was what forced my fist into the air with enough time to smack into the creature's jaw before it closed around my throat.

Hissing and snarling, it swung back to me with its claws out, a razor-sharp barrier between my fists and any soft part of the creature's body. I backed away, and it matched my movements. Claws extending towards me, the monster advanced, kicking up the dust on the road beneath its predatory steps as I contemplated turning around again and running for my life. It saw my hesitation as the thoughts churned over in my mind and sprang, knife-sharp nails slicing through the forearm I instinctively raised to protect my head.

The pain cut through my thoughts. Through my throat. Through everything.

My balance wavered as blood trickled down to my wrist, leaving me open and exposed for the next attack.

Lunging at me again, the creature tackled me to the ground face-first and landed on my back, blowing its hot and rancid breath right into my ear. Saliva drizzled down my cheek from its open mouth as it held me down against the dirt, claws around my neck, and jerked its head back to let out a triumphant, wolf-like cry before it killed me.

My soul left my body with a wild, final release of my breath.

Shrieking sounded in my ears—a high-pitched, tortured exclamation that shook the very ground beneath me—followed by an equally loud and very final *thud*.

But I felt no impact.

Like I'd left my body behind.

Panting against the road, still somehow feeling the stones digging into my cheek, I lay there in silence for a few moments to gather my thoughts. I strained to view the sky from the corner of my eye, which was still a glittering rainbow. The field around me remained a landscape of gold.

If I'd died, I'd made my way into hell—because I was still in fucking Faerie.

"That was very nicely done, though perhaps next time you could do that *before* the Banshee knocks you to the ground."

Wren's voice came from behind me. I flipped onto my back so fast that my spine twinged, and an oversized rock jammed into my shoulder. Sitting on top of Elera, whose furry lips were pulled back in disgust as she surveyed the body in front of her, Wren was grinning down at me.

I had so many things I wanted to say to him—most of them filthy, prolific curses and threats upon his life—but as I sat upright, wincing at the dirt-crusted cuts on my forearm, I could only vocalise one thing.

"Banshee. Not a Witch?"

He eyed the carcass, the corners of his mouth turning down. "No. Similar, but this one's a Banshee. Witches are much prettier. Less intent on fighting everyone, too. Keep to themselves mostly."

"What does a Banshee want with the High King?"

Wren's gaze whipped to my face so quickly that I almost heard a cracking sound slap the air between us. "What?"

Awkwardly climbing to my feet, I brushed as much of the dust off my clothes as I could using the hand on my uninjured arm and then stepped over to examine the creature again. "It was asking me to tell it where the High King is…" I trailed off as my eyes fell upon the cause of the Banshee's death.

A hole had been blasted right through its abdomen, large and clean-edged as if heat had melded the circumference of its wound back together after blowing out the Banshee's vital organs. I couldn't be certain if the same thing that had created the hole had also created the smoky shadows now licking at the remainder of the body, appearing like mist on a lake.

"What else did it tell you about the High King?" he enquired stiffly.

"Nothing." I raised my eyebrows, sucking in a deep breath through my nose as I nodded in undeniable awe at the killing blow. "Thank you, I suppose," I said, looking up at him.

Wren fought off a smile. "Bookworm, that wasn't me."

"What?" I blinked at him. "Who?"

He shrugged, casting his gaze around the empty fields. "Some annoying little human thing."

Try as I might, I could not fathom the implication. *I did not—*

"I knew you could do it," he went on casually, stroking Elera's mane. "Apparently, you just needed a rather foul-smelling, homicidal push."

Any relief or gratitude I had felt for him moments ago winked out of existence. "This was a *test*? You left me here for some dumb, wicked, godawful faerie *test*?"

Wren rolled his eyes. "First of all, I did not *leave* you. I simply went quite a long way *ahead* of you because, like I told you before, I'm sick of walking. You're slow and clumsy, and Elera and I needed to feel the wind on our faces," he declared matter-of-factly, lifting his chin.

The horse nodded in agreement, and I thought about poking my tongue out at her.

"Second of all, I had no idea that you'd take it upon yourself to pick a fight with a Banshee while I was off frolicking ahead of you." He gestured to the mutilated body on the ground. "Banshees are exiled from the Court of Light—and all of the Faerie Courts under the High King's command—because they don't follow the rules, so one shouldn't have even *been* here."

I was so angry, I couldn't speak. All I could do was shout wordlessly and stomp my foot on the ground like a child having a tantrum under his smug, feline gaze.

"Your wounds have clotted," he noted, tilting his head to better examine my arm. "They'll need to be healed to prevent infection. I dread to think where that Banshee's hands have been."

I held my arm up and looked at the cuts, trying not to feel the sting or the way the sight of my own blood made my stomach churn. I also tried not to ponder the seemingly accelerated healing process I was displaying. With the depth of the wounds, I knew I should still be bleeding out and unable to stand.

"Can you...?" I extended my arm towards him, flinching as the cuts stretched open again.

Wren let out a long-suffering sigh. "Must I do everything for you? I'm really not your father."

My teeth cut into my lower lip to hold back my retort, and the saliva that was pooling in my mouth, ready to aim and fire at him. I held his gaze firmly, a prisoner of my own.

"*Fine.*"

Light encircled my arm, warm and bright, and filled my nose with the scent of musk and ink and—

It was gone. Abruptly, as if Wren had yanked it back at the earliest possible moment. The pain in my arm disappeared, along with the wounds, without leaving so much as a scar.

"Let's go." He clicked his tongue, and Elera began to plod along the road in the same direction I had chosen earlier.

I was right.

The tiniest bloom of pride expanded in my chest at that thought, although fatigue quickly snuffed it out.

"Can I just rest for a minute?" I begged. I was exhausted. Gravity had come back in full swing, intent on squashing me upon the road.

"No."

Scuffing my feet along the dirt, I jogged to catch up with them, shoulders slumping so far forward that I thought I might trip and fall head over heels onto the ground. "Can we at least take turns on the horse?"

"No." Wren didn't look at me.

"Why not?" I complained. I was keenly aware that I was sounding more and more like a whining child caught in a bad mood, but I didn't have the energy to spare on caring.

"She's a unicorn, and she's mine. Get your own horse."

FIFTEEN

Sthiara

Wren wanted me to believe that I had unleashed a kernel of my own magic in self-defence and killed that Banshee myself.

I did not.

It didn't matter that he had come back for me. I still couldn't trust him.

It was far more likely that he'd blasted a hole through the creature himself and was trying to trick me into falling for some elaborate hoax, wherein I would ask him to help me master my power, and he would have me hopping in a circle and chanting nonsense before both he *and* his damn unicorn burst out laughing.

Elera clipped and clopped down the lane in a meandering walk, unsympathetic to the fact that my legs had to move much faster to keep up with her graceful strides. Wren perched upon her back, spine straight and head held high as he scanned the empty fields like he was on patrol. The body of the Banshee was miles and miles behind us when the bones of civilisation began to appear around us.

First, there were fences, smooth wood lining the perimeters of the golden fields. Then, small cottages rose up in the distance, gentle curls of white smoke wafting from their chimneys.

We passed one such cottage that was much closer to the road than the others. It was a cobblestone house with vines of crawling wisteria, a jade-green slate roof and reinforced sash windows. Oozing with old-fashioned charm, it captivated my attention as we strolled past. Brynn would have loved it. Larger and grander than our townhouse, flaunting a blooming front garden lined with spectacularly large and vibrant flowers, it was exactly the sort of home she deserved to have.

"Goblins don't particularly like to be observed," Wren muttered from above me.

I was quickly tiring of his commentary, though there hadn't been as much of it that day, and pretended I hadn't heard him. As he'd done with Elera's introduction, he was likely trying to spook me. Besides, Goblins didn't make many appearances in the stories I'd read. From snippets glimpsed on television shows, they were reportedly greedy enough to covet a dwelling like that, but they would rather strip the house of its riches and drag the hessian sacks of gold and jewels back into their dark caves.

The hedges rustled. Wren swore.

"Oh, *now* you've done it."

There was no time for me to look up at him and discern his meaning.

My eyes caught the flash of mint-green triangles above the hedges in the front yard, and then the ground was ripped out from under me as Wren yanked me up and onto my stomach over Elera's back.

I struggled to right myself, but she broke into a gallop before I had the chance, and it was all I could do to hold onto her flank with my hands and feet as she tore off down the lane.

Auburn curls blowing across my face, I could barely make out the shape of a small, pale green creature as it burst out of the hedges and sprinted after us on all fours. I couldn't be sure I'd seen the flash of silver, razor-sharp teeth or its long, pointed ears either.

Elera had put too much distance between us too quickly. I gagged over her flank as the urge to throw up intensified.

It felt like a long time passed before we slowed to a walk, and Wren hauled me into a sitting position so that I didn't become ill. My back pressed into his chest, trembling shoulder blades against granite-carved pectorals, and his arms encircled me as he reached around to regain his grip on the horse's mane.

"I warned you that they don't like to be watched," he scolded me at last. The vibrations of his voice sent a shudder rippling straight through my body, easing the tightness in my chest from wrestling the sickness in my gut. "Why don't you ever believe me?"

The question was posed so innocently. It was as if he truly didn't understand and genuinely wanted to know the answer.

For a moment, as I sat rigidly in front of him, trying to avoid touching him without falling off his unicorn, I almost didn't recognise his voice. Without the cocky grin across his sultry mouth or the devious glint in his burning eyes, he was less the broody High Fae bastard and more...

Not human. Not in the slightest.

But something closer to it.

"Fine," he snapped, after minutes passed and I had not replied. "Do as you like, Aura, but at the very least, you should stop sitting there like you've been petrified. We're coming into friendlier townships soon, and I'd rather not have people gossiping about us."

I leaned forward, bracing my hands on Elera's neck and clenching my legs around her flank, and relaxed my shoulders. My breath started to come easier. The furious knot in my stomach was mostly untangled. But she snorted in response and shook her large head, the motion rippling throughout the rest of her body in a way that made me realise she could shake me off quite easily if she so desired.

"Not like that," Wren growled, letting go of her mane to grab my hands.

He pulled me upright, straightening my posture with a hand over my shoulder and two fingers digging into the base of my spine, and then reached around to grip my thighs. My breath came in gasps as his palms slid over me, the fabric of my jeans not rough or thick enough to intercept the sensation that came over my skin. It danced out of my reach as I sent a mental net down to capture it before it expanded, the warm flow of awareness lighting up every last one of my nerves.

A pathetic human response. I cursed myself for it.

Wren gently spread my legs wider, and mortification stained my cheeks as they started shaking ever so slightly.

I focussed on my perceived loss of control over my balance. The fear of falling. Anything but his touch.

He slid his hands beneath my thighs, and my breath caught in my throat. I held it there as he pulled my legs up until my feet flattened and heels came down slightly, and then he brought my knees back to the horse's sides with gentle pressure.

I tried—and failed—to release the breath.

Slowly, he began to drag his knuckles up and down my thighs like he was kneading the tension out of my muscles. He leaned down, warm and soft against my hair. "Relax," he purred into my ear.

I swallowed a thick gulp of saliva and exhaled.

Releasing my legs, he brought his hands to my face and combed back my hair until it was no longer windswept across my eyes and mouth. He threaded his fingers through it once—and I could not fight the shiver that ricocheted from the nape of my neck, could not convince myself the sensation was made of anything other than sheer, unbridled pleasure—before flipping it over one shoulder, and then he bent forward to take hold of Elera's mane again.

He'd made no comment, given no inclination that he had felt what I had—that he'd even intended to make me feel that way. He'd only corrected my position on the horse.

But his knuckles turned white.

"Let her movements guide you," he instructed quietly. "Move with her, not against her, and hold your posture. Don't inch away from me, or you'll go too far forward—and, for the love of the Oracle, *relax*. I've done far more exciting things with women than sharing my *horse* with them."

I nodded, chewing on my lower lip. The impact of his words was softened considerably by the heady fog still clouding my mind. With his breath tickling my neck and his body pressed into mine, his intoxicating cologne was weaving into the very fibres of my clothing, inescapable and so resolutely calming.

Too calming.

I had to fight off the tension growing in my muscles, struggling to find a balance between keeping my guard up and yielding total and complete control of my every sense and desire to the man with his elbows brushing against my sides.

"Can I put my arms around you?" he murmured, angling his head towards the side of my face not concealed by my hair.

Blush spilled over my cheeks again, and my voice was shaky when I returned with, "I don't know. *Can* you?"

His low, rumbling laughter sent pinpricks of arousal skittering across my entire nervous system. With a sharp intake of breath, I silently scolded my pathetically human body for its reaction to Wren's pathetically intoxicating presence.

"Hold onto her mane." The tip of his nose brushed my temple as he lifted his head. "She knows where to go, so you don't have to do anything, but it's proper form for the rider in front to hold the reins."

There was no opportunity for me to object.

Wren promptly released Elera's dark silver mane, and I panicked, scrambling to grab hold of it as if we were driving a car and he had let go of the steering wheel. Elera snorted again, rather haughtily for a unicorn-horse.

"I'm going to take a nap," Wren announced, wrapping his arms around my waist.

Once more, I was given no time to object or react before he'd made his next disorientating move. I couldn't keep up.

He rested his cheek on the crook of my shoulder, face turned outwards, and wriggled back far enough so that he could lean his chest against me with a great deal more of his weight than I expected. "Wake me up when we get to Sthiara."

"When we get to *what*?"

He didn't answer.

I knew the bastard couldn't possibly have fallen asleep that quickly, but with his arms locked around my hips, I didn't dare turn to find his face or shake him off because I knew that if he fell, he would certainly drag me down with him.

"I don't know how you can stand him," I muttered to Elera.

Her soft, pointed ears flickered, and she whinnied in reply—a completely neutral sound, as if she was refusing to get involved. I sighed and did as he'd instructed.

Swaying back and forth gently, I let Elera's movements guide me as her powerful legs took up a slightly faster pace, and I was surprised at how much more secure I felt when my hands were holding her mane.

Wren was not asleep.

I was not at all familiar with the High Fae's sleeping habits, but it didn't take an expert to realise that the uneven breaths I could feel him taking against my shoulders were not those of a person resting. Additionally, he would have to have been certifiably insane to have surrendered any of his control to a half-breed after so thoroughly communicating his distaste for them—occasional niceties and disarming touches aside.

And yet, for some reason, I let him pretend to sleep for the rest of the journey to Sthiara.

Sixteen

The House

"**W**hy did you think I left you?"

Wren straightened up as Elera sauntered into the small township of Sthiara, marked by a worn-down sign we'd passed a few moments prior on the side of the road. I felt the loss of his warm cheek upon my shoulder like he had peeled off my clothes, but I steadied myself against a shiver. I didn't want him to touch me, excite me, or comfort me, and so I had taken advantage of the silence while he pretended to doze off, letting myself cool down and work through my feelings.

Eventually, I'd decided to forgive myself for being human and to better prepare myself for my surroundings. Faerie was filled with magic. *Wren* was filled with magic. I could feel it hovering around me, trying to find a way in so that it could consume me.

I had to keep my guard up.

And that's precisely what I was going to do.

The road forked ahead; one side led across a bridge over a crystalline stream that appeared to run straight through the town, and the other veered off behind a row of cobblestone buildings with thatch roofing and smoking chimneys.

Elera chose the bridge.

"I don't know," I replied contemptuously. "Maybe because you told me to keep my wits about me, and then you *left* me?"

I felt him roll his eyes behind me, but his voice lacked all traces of its usual ridicule when he said, "I would say goodbye first, you know."

Something fluttered, heated, and stretched out in my chest, even as I scoffed.

Sthiara was a quaint town that reminded me of Belgrave in the initial years following its establishment. Very few records existed from that time, and even fewer were illustrated, but I had pored over the one book I'd found in Dante's with faded grey paintings and sketches depicting the little township in its early days.

The cobblestone street is almost identical to Belgrave, even down to the curbs and flood drainage system that were installed centuries later, and have rows upon rows of small apartments and shopfronts adorned with wood carvings of—

"That's the Court of Light's insignia," Wren told me, answering my unspoken thoughts. His ability to track and read my every movement, even when he was behind me, was becoming quite unsettling.

"Flame?" My eyebrows drew together.

"Ha!" His exclamation echoed in my ears. "That's an orb of light, not flame. Is that what the humans think it is nowadays? By the Elements, Owain will *never* let me hear the end of it. Whatever you do, don't tell him that."

I blinked, long and slow, at the insignia marking every visible doorway in town. "I don't even know who that is," I mumbled absentmindedly.

Wren loosened his hold on my waist by a fraction. "He's the High Lord of the Court of Fire," he explained. "And he has his own damn insignia, thank you very much."

I shook off the questions brewing in my mind as Elera continued to walk further into town. *How many Courts are there, and is Wren friends with everyone? Why is Belgrave's insignia shared with a Faerie Court? And why isn't anyone moving out of the way of the goddamn unicorn clip-clopping so loudly through the street?!*

The thoroughfare ahead was crowded with beings that may as well have come straight from a drug-induced hallucination.

Horns and tails and claws and wings and hooves.

They were alien-like, and most of them made Wren look exceptionally human.

The pathway was a mirage of different skin types and shades of colour. Some leathery and wrinkled, or scaled and glistening, others smooth and clear, or opaque and matte. Every colour imaginable—and many of them unimaginable—filled the street, a sea of shades and textures to rival the sky.

Some did resemble Wren, standing at daunting heights with beauty to put the world's most striking wonders to shame and clothes of a similar fashion—very simple clothing in plain colours and flattering cuts, neither old nor new in their design. Many of those beings, however, had donned a belt of ancient weapons in contrast to their loose shirts and long dresses. I thought it made for a peculiar sight to behold within such a peaceful and cheery atmosphere.

They were indeed talking and laughing as they strode down the street, stopping every so often to admire the wares displayed on wooden tables and the sills of open shop windows, all of them completely oblivious to the approaching beast with horns sharp enough to skewer them if they got in her way.

High Fae, I thought, *who perhaps consider themselves above moving out of the pathway of a horse—even a magical one.*

But the other faeries, who were lingering at the counters behind shop windows and stalls or conversing on the side of the road, did not look up at us as we passed by either. Not so much as a glance.

Elera jerked to a halt when a small, winged faerie with scaly blue skin stepped out from the curb right in front of her. Wren's arm tightened almost imperceptibly around my waist, holding me in place.

"What is going on?" I whispered, clutching at Elera's mane as she shook her large head and snorted her annoyance. She only continued walking once the small faerie had finished crossing the road.

I felt Wren shrug. "I put a glamour over us."

"You *what*? Why?"

He huffed. "Because like I said, bookworm, I don't want any gossip."

My blood heated, and I wriggled forward, trying to put some space between our bodies. "Then what was all of that bullshit about posture?"

"You have a nasty little mouth on you, don't you?"

"Wren!"

"What?"

I sighed deeply. "Nothing."

Every muscle and nerve ending in my body ached for the journey to be over soon.

The scent of fruit-filled pies and fresh bread filled my nose as we passed a bakery, followed by herbs and spices I couldn't name wafting out of a large cauldron at a stall two doors up, filled with a delicious-looking orange soup. A faerie who resembled an Ogre with a large bald head and wrinkly sage-coloured skin was standing behind it, using his enormous, thick-fingered hands to wield a ladle and goblet as he served the line of customers trailing down the street.

The crowd thickened as we veered around the queue, and Wren suddenly leaned down, almost horizontal to the ground, and swiped a sprig of grapes from the top of a straw shopping bag on the arm of a purple, three-horned faerie. He offered one to me, but I shoved him off.

I could feel Wren mocking me in his head, and I almost went to say something—but then I heard the crunch of the grape skin bursting as he popped one into his mouth, and I had to brace myself against my stomach's ravenous complaints.

Baskets of wine bottles and freshly cut flowers lined the road, and a stall towards the far end of the marketplace had a display of hanging crystals that spun in the breeze and cast sharp rainbows on the off-white canopy.

My heart clenched.

Brynn would have loved this place, too.

"Does the glamour bother you that much?" Wren asked, poking me in the ribs.

"No. It's not that." There was no use in pretending that he couldn't detect even the slightest shift in my mood based on body language anymore.

"Then what?"

"Please, don't start acting like you care about me now."

Much to my relief, Wren didn't deign to respond.

He was sullenly quiet for the rest of the ride out of the little township. I matched his hostility—until Elera veered off the cobblestone road onto a dirt lane that was concealed by a thick overgrowth of trees and weeds.

"This is taking forever," I complained. "Why aren't we there yet?"

I felt Wren turn his head from one side to the other by the brush of his nose against the back of my hair. "Do you even know where we're going?"

"No," I admitted tersely. *It's not exactly like you offered up that information.* "Tell me."

"It won't make the trip any shorter if I do," he challenged wryly.

I've encountered humans like this before.

Veritable brick walls.

"Honestly." I sighed. "I don't know how much longer I can stand to be around you."

Wren patted one of my thighs. "Then it's a good thing you're sitting down."

Frustrated, tired, and beginning to feel a little sore, I gave up on conversation with him. I had no response, no snippy remark that could ever match up to his apparently bottomless well of bad attitude and deflection skills.

I might cry again. Truthfully, I was tempted to, simply because I was just so tired. But then I saw the house.

Not a house, but a mansion. A grand building of four levels, carved from blue-grey stone with multiple smoking chimneys and a manicured lawn dotted with routinely pruned and clipped hedge trees. Soft lace curtains billowed out from the open windows on the upper levels like a haunted house, and enormous cobalt statues of knights in shining armour stood to either side of a pebbled driveway leading up to the front doors.

Elera saw it, too, and veered towards it. My heart thumped a little louder with each crunch of her hooves on the white gravel.

"Oh, look at that. We're here." Wren dug his knuckles into my ribs again, harder this time. "Long may I remember your benevolence in tolerating me thus far."

As thankful as I was to finally have arrived at our destination—and immensely grateful for it being large enough to put a lot of space between myself and Wren—it was not a castle by any means. And that meant there was likely no High King or dark and dingy dungeon beneath, and essentially no point to my being there aside from the aforementioned freedom from my obnoxious travel companion.

"I forgot to mention this earlier," Wren went on, as Elera slowed to a stop in the broad front courtyard. "It's best to look sharp when you're meeting the High King. A little late for that now," he lamented, fluffing my hair, "but oh well."

Shaking off his hands, I forced my stiff muscles to move far enough for me to turn back to look at him, eyes wide with dismay. "*This* is where the High King lives?"

A haunted house with a basement rather than a castle with a dungeon?

Wren nimbly slipped down from Elera's back and extended his arms to assist me. I accepted the help only because my muscles were cramping, and I wasn't sure that I could make it down safely on my own. Elera was quite large.

"Sometimes. This is the House, his safe house," Wren amended, gripping me under the arms and lifting me from the enormous creature as if I was nothing but a stack of kindling.

"Why is he staying in a safe house?" I asked, feeling the pressure of solid earth gradually reconnecting with the bones in my legs as I touched the ground. It was a strange but extremely satisfying sensation.

Wren pulled a face. "Bookworm," he crooned, somewhat remorsefully. "Did I forget to mention there's a war going on?"

SEVENTEEN

The Court of Pretty Little Human Things with Sharp and Nasty Tongues

"**Y**ou brought me into a *war zone*?" I hissed, as Wren marched with purpose up the three stone steps towards the mansion's black oak door.

Carved in the middle, the Belgrave—and the Court of Light—insignia was painted in white-gold and sat above a brass door knocker shaped like a cauldron. Wren bypassed it, reaching for the handle instead. I glanced behind us in time to see Elera trotting around the side of the house, deliberately excusing herself from the brewing argument as the door swung back without so much as a creak. It opened into a long, dimly lit hallway lined with a tasselled mahogany floor runner. Candles burned in their sconces upon the walls, and a huge chandelier was hanging at the end of the corridor, right before a grand staircase.

It was not a homely sort of mansion, but nothing like an ominous castle, either.

Definitely a haunted house.

Wren held the sturdy door open and beckoned for me to go inside. His eyes were molten gold again—not quite as bright as they had been in the bookstore but more radiant than they'd been during our travels. I studied his nonchalant expression for a moment longer before I took a step over the threshold.

The door closed, plunging us into a moody gloom and eerie quiet, and Wren leaned against it with his hands in his pockets, wrists fitting between glinting silver weapons on both sides. He suddenly looked very much like a butcher.

"If you dedicate enough of your few remaining human brain cells to trying, you may recall that I told you about the Malum and their diabolical plans."

Eyes flashing, I crossed my arms over my waist and bent my head forward as I whispered, "You didn't tell me that they'd waged a *war*."

Clicking his tongue, he waved a hand at me dismissively as he pushed away from the door and began to stride down the hallway. He took exceptionally long steps. "Details, details," he muttered.

Wren was bad enough on his own, but something about being left alone in the corridor of the haunted house felt worse, so I hurried to keep up with him.

Although there were no signs of life elsewhere, I tucked my hair behind my ears and attempted to straighten my clothes. No longer stained by the blood of my apparent enemies, they were still wrinkled and smelled like horsehair. I desperately needed a brush, some toothpaste, and a shower.

The hallway was lined with polished wooden consoles—some cleared, and others hosting vases and age-stained candelabras—and had about a dozen closed doors dotted on either side. We passed all of them, heading straight for the staircase at the end.

"Honestly," Wren grumbled, shaking his head as he began the ascent. He took the stairs two at a time, forcing me into a near-jog to keep up. "What did you think was going to happen when I said the High King might want to summon all of faeriekind to his behest?"

"Not an all-out war," I snapped breathlessly. "Maybe a threat or something, but—" I huffed, pushing my shoulders back. "I really don't give a damn about faerie politics."

"A threat against the High King is as good as a declaration of war," he countered evenly. "Nobody's slumming it in the trenches yet, but things are all amiss on the Map."

I stopped when we reached the next landing and made to grab for the sleeve of his shirt, but he moved so quickly that my grip snagged on his wrist instead. He grasped my hand as if on instinct, and my fingers slipped through his as I pulled it back, biting down on the inside of my cheeks to keep them from going red.

Wren gave me a strange look.

A stream of sparkling daylight pooled over him from the reinforced window behind me. The top of his blond hair glowed silver like a halo. With Wren's strong features, mesmerising stare, and boyish haircut—not to mention his sheer *height*—one might easily mistake him for an angel.

An angel cast out for never taking anything seriously enough, of course, but an angel, nonetheless.

I felt it again at that moment—the magic, brushing against me with an invisible hand, asking to be let in.

No.

Wren's eyes bored into mine, the colour of absolute bliss, darkening slightly as he searched my face for something. "Yes, bookworm?" he purred.

Space.

The haunted house had plenty of space. I simply needed to get through the initial induction, and then I could move far away from Wren and work the last nagging traces of him out of my system.

"The Map?" I queried in a voice weaker than I would have liked.

He lifted his head, expression smoothing over into cool disinterest. "The Map of Faerie. Ancient, powerful thing. Handed over to each High King at the start of their reign. Very important in the grand scheme of things. Not important right now."

I didn't know why, but I pressed. "What's amiss on the Map?"

He studied me intently for a moment, lips pursed. "Blythe, the High Lady of the Court of Darkness, went missing some seven odd years ago. Hasn't been seen or heard from since, and nobody has dared to go looking for her because her Court seems to have vanished from the Map."

One of my eyebrows rose. "There's a Court of Darkness?"

"There are six Courts." He began listing them off on his fingers. "Fire, Water, Wind, Earth, Light and Darkness. The Court of Darkness was formally called The Court of Pretty Little Human Things with Sharp and Nasty Tongues"—he paused, wiggling four of his outstretched fingers in my face before I swatted his hand away—"but much like their namesake, they didn't understand the very serious concept of war, so they succumbed to the enemy quicksmart." He gave me a self-impressed, crooked smile.

"Oh, is that so?" I folded my arms over my chest, smiling back saccharinely.

His lips pulled back into a grin at that. "Blythe's Court has been blacked out on the Map. It was all shady and shadowy before, but now it's just *gone*. Malum infestation," he added. He made a comical face and shuddered, brushing invisible muck off the sleeves of his shirt. "And now the Court of Earth is acting suspicious, which is an issue because they border against the Court of Darkness, and even more of an issue because Gregor's the second most powerful High Lord and won't need much convincing to cause a scene."

I fell into step beside him as he nodded towards the last flight of stairs and began to move again. "Who's the most powerful?"

"The High King, naturally."

Studying his profile as we climbed, Wren taking the stairs one at a time, I did my best to put the pieces together. "So, the High King—and or Queen—is decided based on power?"

Actual, raw power—more than the perceived power of human leaders. In my world, we often bowed to jokers, fools, and conmen based on smoke and mirrors. I couldn't imagine the danger of a man like that with any measure of material influence. I'd have to tread very carefully indeed.

"Yes," he agreed, and he started to move his hands in animated gestures as he elaborated. "The most powerful High Lord or Lady at any given time is crowned the ruler. It's not even a conscious choice but a demand from the High Mother. Nobody can wear the crown if someone possessing more power is alive at the same time. The land rejects them. We don't get a choice."

That sounded to me like a recipe for disaster, but I wasn't about to get into a debate with him over the morals of faeries and their politics. "And what does this have to do with the Malum?"

"The Malum desire a seat amongst the High King's inner circle and have been denied, so they're resorting to other means."

Wren came to a stop at the next floor, leading me towards a wide corridor lined by a tall row of bay windows overlooking the rear of the property. I drifted towards them, unsure where to let my eyes wander first.

Rich, finely mowed grass covered the land in green with spots of turquoise, and a bubbling water fountain sat in the stone-paved courtyard below. Thickly padded chaises and lounges were positioned next to glass tables beneath plants that looked like gigantic palm fronds, with faeries of all different shapes, sizes, and colours pottering around with broomsticks and silver trays of sparkling lemonade glasses.

Beyond the courtyard, the land was mostly bare, though bone-coloured rocks began to appear a fair way out as the property descended into a dip towards the horizon between two towering ridges. Glimmering in the distance was the sliver of a sapphire-blue lake or ocean.

Remembering Wren's warnings about Merfolk, I immediately turned my back on the glass and redirected my train of thought. "I didn't think Lesser Fae would even consider asking for something like that," I mused.

Wren barked a laugh. "Lesser Fae?"

Shaking my head vaguely, I gave him a questioning look. "Not—Lesser—?"

"It's the twenty-first century. High Mother spare you, Aura." He resisted the smile tugging at the corners of his mouth. "We're civilised and quite progressive, you realise. We don't use that term anymore."

"You don't?"

"Nobody does." His lashes fluttered, barely concealing the caustic roll of his eyes. "We call them by their names, or if it's not personal enough to warrant a name, we use their origin race or simply the word *faerie.* High Fae is a heritage, a race of its own—descendants of the first High Mother-blessed—but Lesser Fae was a derogatory, blanket term coined afterwards and used to discriminate long ago when they were enslaved to us. They aren't now."

I rolled my tongue around in my mouth, embarrassment pooling in my gut. "So, you're telling me—"

"I'm not telling you anything that you don't need to know," he cut in, sliding a hand through his hair. "But you really should do yourself a favour and visit the library. Read some books by faerie authors. Brush up on your myth and legend. Reconsider taking an interest in faerie politics, perhaps."

Out of every comment that Wren had ever made to me, that one might have been the fairest, so I nodded and swallowed my pride.

"If the Malum aren't considered...unworthy," I began, making a visible effort to choose my words with more care, "then why have they been denied? Don't all races of faeries have the right to a seat amongst the High King's inner circle?"

Wren grimaced. "Not quite. It's complicated. The Malum are—or *were*—High Fae."

"What? Like...you?" Shock contorted my features. I'd expected the Malum to *look* like Malum—whatever that was—but certainly not like Wren.

He dragged both hands down his face, the fabric of his wide shirtsleeves straining against the tension in his muscles, and he pulled his lower lids down until I could see the whites of his eyes.

"Let me guess," I murmured, and then I sighed. "I should look this up in the library."

He cracked a smile that didn't reach his eyes. "No. You won't find this in there."

"So...tell me what I need to know."

A long pause stretched out between us, our locked gazes thickening the tension in the atmosphere.

"It was during the Gift War," he began, mimicking me with a sigh. "A particular faction of High Fae decided to use the distraction of pandemonium to slip into the night unnoticed and begin heinous experiments with Witch Covens—an idea they'd brought before the High King, and he'd rightfully shut down. For centuries," he went on, leaning back on his hands against the console behind him, "the Witches have refused to consort with us, preferring to practise what they believe is *pure* magic derived straight from the land, rather than the *gifted* magic the High Fae were blessed with by the High Mother. These idiot deserters believed we would lose the war, so they thought to give themselves an advantage by trying to merge their power with that of a Witch. They convinced themselves that if they could harness the essence of the Witches, then they could not be rendered completely powerless if we were defeated and lost our gifted magic."

"And the Witches cursed them?" I guessed. I was certain that my mother had read me the same story at bedtime before.

Wren's throat bobbed, and he looked away from me, towards the window over my shoulder. "No. A horde of *fucking* Banshees tricked them. The whole of Faerie was a burning, bleeding mess at the time, and magic was in a state of utter panic, leaking across the land like melting snow. A tribe of Banshees went trawling through battlefields, picking at the lingering remnants of fallen High Fae like vultures, and used the collected power to temporarily transform themselves into beautiful creatures. The similarity they bore to true Witches allowed them to get close enough to the rebels, and they gutted the magic right out of them. Banshees are like leeches where magic is concerned.

"But they should have known better," he said, swearing under his breath as his gaze fell upon the floor beneath his feet. I could have sworn that a line of silver tears glimmered in his eyes. "Witches are too smart to be trifled with, and there was so much madness going on. I—" He broke off abruptly, glancing up as if he'd just remembered that I was standing there. "The Banshees have wanted to infiltrate the High King's inner circle for millennium, but they've proven time and time again that they can't be trusted. Each time they're granted a seat, they violate the agreement and kill someone for their magic. They have no natural-born powers of their own, and they can't control themselves around us. They're drainers, and once they start, they can't stop. The rebels should have known better."

Drainers.

The Banshee on the lane didn't want to eat me. It wanted to *drain* me.

I stiffened against a stomach-twisting shudder and wrapped my arms a little tighter around myself. Wren was oblivious, his eyes glazed over as if he were miles and miles away from me as we stood together in the corridor.

It was strange to see him like that; a statue, no different from the carvings of soldiers in the front yard, or an illustration in a book. I had already suspected that Wren was probably hundreds, if not thousands, of years old, but the way he told the story had confirmed it. He was there when it happened a long time ago, and he'd seen things that would probably give me nightmares.

"The Banshee on the road here wasn't beautiful," I murmured. I didn't know what else to say.

It was not quite a question, but Wren nodded his understanding, simmering golden eyes still trapped somewhere in the past. "When the High King found out what they had done, he confiscated their stolen magic and banished them to the Ruins," he explained. "And then tried to return it to the High Fae—even though many members of the inner circle were not convinced they deserved it after their treachery—but couldn't find a way to do it. And so, the race of Malum was born."

"Born?" I repeated, a dull sense of nausea knotting in my stomach. "Or created?"

He grimaced again, opening his mouth as he twisted his head away. "Uh, they were born. Or as close to it as they could get after what they'd done." His eyes darted back to mine apologetically. "The rebels mated with the Banshees—a sacrilegious abuse against our true mating rituals—and whatever was conceived during the process devoured them from the inside out within days, but it left enough of them behind that they...suffered. Conscious the whole time but without their autonomy or magic."

It was my turn to grimace. A stomach-churning, spine-warping shudder came over me at the thought.

"The High Fae can't interbreed," he admitted in a low voice. His eyes flicked back to mine and then quickly darted away. "Not...us. We can, but not with any others."

It took me far longer than it should have to realise that he wasn't talking about him and me, but rather the High Fae and humans. I wanted to ask what made humans different from other faeries—however, I wanted to stop thinking about breeding and mating more.

"Out of shame," he continued, promptly changing the subject, "the Malum went into hiding, and it seems like whatever anti-magic disease the Banshees passed onto them has worsened over time. They've adapted but decayed. No longer do they bear resemblance to their former selves, yet they still remember their homes—though I'm not convinced they remember anything else."

I couldn't put my finger on the feeling that swept between us in the moments of silence that followed his story.

Like a tendril of his magic had stretched out to greet me, I was overcome by a profound and hollow sense of loss, sadness, and...guilt. But for the life of me, I could not understand why Wren would feel so personally responsible for what had happened to the Malum. Even more perplexing than that, I could not understand why I related to what had happened to the Malum so well. Why I felt like...

"What is it?" he whispered, and his voice was hoarse.

My heart began to bob up and down in my chest, undecided between sinking and swimming. "I need to go home."

It was Wren's turn to give me an inquisitive look. "You—why?"

"Because of the Malum." Glancing away from him nervously, I sucked on my lower lip and braced myself for the impact of his outrage that he had just spent two days trekking through the Court of Light at human speed for nothing.

It didn't come.

"You'll be safe here," he told me quietly. "And your family will be safer with you here."

"It's not that."

"Then what?"

The pinprick of welling tears tickled the backs of my eyes. I tried to take a calming breath, but it came out like a sniffle. Tension clutched the cave of my heart. "I don't want...to become the Malum."

"Unless you're planning to mate with a Banshee, bookworm, that's rather unlikely."

"No." I sniffled again, turning my head towards the row of windows. "Symbolically."

There was a long pause, and then, "I'm sorry?"

My eyes were stinging, but the pain was dulled by irritation at having to explain myself—even though he wasn't being rude, for once. I wiped my nose with the back of my hand and whirled around. Wren was studying me intently, like he was annoyed that he couldn't pluck the answer straight out of my mind.

"I've wanted to run away from home since I was eight years old," I confessed, dropping my eyes to his boots because I couldn't bear to meet his questioning gaze. "It was always my plan. As soon as I was old enough, I would leave and go somewhere else. Somewhere *safe*. And so, when my mother told me she was pregnant again, I was furious. I stormed out of the house and went and sat down by the docks for hours, trying to work up the courage to stow away on one of the boats. In the end, I couldn't bring myself to do it."

I took a deep, unsteady breath. "I was so mad at her for bringing another child into that life and for forcing me to remain in it for the sake of a younger sibling. I sulked throughout the entire pregnancy, told myself that I would wait and see the baby safely delivered, and then I would leave. But I saw Brynn that day, and I... I knew I couldn't abandon her. I knew that I couldn't leave her to witness and experience the horrible things that I had, all alone. Even then, though, I was desperate to run away and build a new life for myself somewhere else."

Wren politely averted his gaze as a few stray tears leaked down my cheeks, and I scrubbed them away ferociously, snivelling like a child.

"That feeling never entirely went away," I admitted, clearing my throat as I straightened my spine. I watched charcoal-coloured storm clouds rolling in from the ocean in a thick, angry swirl. "I mean, when you showed up blabbering nonsense about faerie fathers and demon hunters, I didn't think twice before I agreed to go with you. I didn't think about it at all. I just...*left*. I left Brynn like I thought you had left me on that lane, and I keep telling myself that it's to keep her safe like it always has been, and part of it *is*—but part of it isn't about her at all. It's about me."

Wren stared down the corridor, clenching and unclenching his fists around the edge of the table. He gave no indication that he saw the parallels I was drawing between myself and the Malum—that he saw how much my fear might cost me, how I might also be punished for abandoning my post in the middle of the night.

And how I had been selfish and cruel long before I learned that it was my birthright.

I whispered, "I'm sorry for what happened to the Malum back then, and I'm sorry for what you're saying is going to happen now. But I don't want to know who my father is or what kind of magic I may or may not have. I want to go home before it's too late. Before I forget who I really am, before too much time has passed, and while they still might recognise me. I never should have left them in the first place."

Wren gave me a sidelong glance, one eyebrow arched speculatively. "I *could* force you to stay here, you know."

Blood rushed straight to my head. I gaped at him in horror.

Immediately, I wished that I could take it all back, the feeling like desperately trying to put the flood of spilled water back into its jug with nothing but my bare hands. The guilt, the confession, all the broken little pieces of me that I'd offered up to him as payment. My skin tingled with shame, simmering beneath the surface, threatening to engulf me and leave nothing except charred remains behind.

I shouldn't have trusted him with anything else that belonged to me. He already had too much. I should not have admitted to any of that out loud, not even to someone like him. Panic began to set in, seizing the blood in my veins on its mad rush back to my heart.

"It's not your fault," Wren said suddenly, his voice barely a whisper. He cleared his throat. "Faerie has an...*allure* to humans. Even more so when you're part-faerie. I don't think you would have been able to say no to me, regardless. And I don't think you'll feel the same way about it tomorrow, but I'll take you back to the gateway if you do."

I managed to roll my eyes at the arrogance underpinning his tone, and then I nodded vaguely. An act of kindness from the High Fae, however small or self-serving, was a rarity to cherish. I willed the tears to stop trickling over my lower lids.

"And if I'd known that a little history lesson would put you in such a state, I wouldn't have bothered," he quipped, shaking his head at the floor. "You're polluting my air with the tang of salt, so if it'll help you get yourself under control again, you may as well know that your family will not forget you."

My eyes turned dry. "What?"

Wren peered at me, studying the slow evaporation of moisture on my cheeks. He rose from his perch on the table and closed the distance between us, bringing his hands up to cradle the sides of my face. I tensed, but I let him hold me there.

"Your mother believes she received a call from a hospital in the next state, claiming that your father had been admitted for alcohol poisoning," he stated, wiping the tears from my cheeks with his thumbs. "They wanted to discuss his condition with his next of kin and arrange placement in a rehabilitation facility should he make a full recovery. You offered to go so that she can keep Brynn at home, and you'll be staying there in nearby accommodation until further notice. I spelled it so that she'll think you're keeping in touch with her every couple of days, though she won't be able to remember exactly the last time the two of you spoke or what was said."

Gratitude rose to my lips, stronger than any feelings of surprise and confusion, but I stopped myself from forming the words as Wren's thumb swiped across my mouth, gathering the last traces of salt from my face.

He returned to his perch on the table by the wall as if he hadn't noticed the way my eyes had softened. "No faerie fathers or demon hunters, as requested. You're free to return to your old life whenever you wish. However, I strongly advise against it."

The question stumbled up my throat, snagging on numb lips. "And—"

"No, your father will not be going back to them. Not any time soon."

Wren had given me a way home. In my paranoia and desperation, I hadn't asked him to do that. I'd done the total opposite; I'd asked him to erase me, but he'd made a loophole.

I didn't ask why my father figure wouldn't be going back. I didn't care.

They were safe. My mother and Brynn were safe, and I was—

I was *free*.

It took every last ounce of my strength not to show him how I felt. To keep my gratitude and vulnerability to myself. I needed a reality check.

Free, but he could still force me to stay. He still kept a man trapped in a basement or a dungeon and tortured him. He was still High Fae, and I was still a human in Faerie.

Taking a deep breath, I forced my features to smooth over into bored curiosity as I asked, "What do you think prompted the Malum to want to come home now, then?" I turned back towards the window, keeping my gaze low. He was dangling a carrot in front of me, and I would not bite. "You won the war ages ago."

A deep voice, rough with a slight accent, answered in his place. "Actually, we lost the war."

I whirled, and my eyes fell upon the most prepossessing and intimidating man I had ever seen in my life. He commanded the air in the room with his presence—and commanded Wren, too.

My jaunty escort practically leapt from his perch against the wall and crashed to the floor, boots squeaking against the hardwood as he inexpertly fell onto one knee before the speaker.

"Your Majesty," he hummed, looking up from beneath slightly furrowed brows. The absolute commitment he displayed, the dedication he offered to that man with his eyes was unnerving to witness. Even his voice was exaggerated when he spoke. "Auralie, please say hello to the High King of Faerie, Lucais Starfire."

EIGHTEEN

Lucais

It was the face from my dreams, gazing back at me at long last.

Every thought and feeling that once took shelter within my being abandoned me. Too stupefied to react with any trace of recognition or emotion, all I could do was stare blankly at his face. His beautiful, coveted face.

I knew his body from my dreams almost as well as I knew my own. The sensual lines, curves, and ridges of muscle were visible even beneath his simple clothing. He wore a black tunic and pants with only a dagger in his belt, its golden hilt bejewelled with gleaming red stones. He was as tall and strong as I remembered from all of the nights he'd spent withstanding the impact of iron weapons in my mental prison, though I found nothing when my eyes scanned him for signs of harm.

Confusion flickered across my face for a heartbeat before my eyes locked with his again. They were wise eyes of deepest chestnut, and widening by the second. I would have thought him to be far too young to be the High King based on his appearance if it wasn't for the centuries of time weighing down those eyes.

His skin was a lovely shade of brown, with olive-gold undertones that I had only ever viewed eclipsed by silver moonlight and shadows before. Hair as black as a midnight ocean, it was shaved into a sharp crew cut with long, loose curls left to fall across his forehead. Soft, rounded features distinguished his face, and two elongated ears rose up into sharp points on either side of his head. A fraction smaller than Wren's ears, I noticed, as though he was tucking them in like wings.

He absolutely radiated warmth, to the point where the air began to feel a little bit stifled like the sun had burned its very essence into his being, and he carried light with him in every breath.

Lucais.

Lucais was the High King of Faerie.

Unharmed and free—and standing right in front of me.

I caught the exact moment that some form of recognition crossed his chestnut eyes like he'd been dreaming of me screaming for him in that cell, too.

He knew who I was.

Judging by the fleeting look the two High Fae men exchanged, Wren knew something about that as well. My opinion of him had been shifting and switching for days, but every ounce of affection I'd ever felt for him was snuffed out like a candle when I remembered that he'd heard me calling for his High King in my sleep. I had told him that the Banshee wanted me to divulge the High King's location before I was attacked.

And he hadn't said *anything*.

Wren, the scoundrel, rose to his feet with as little grace as he'd displayed whilst bowing. I tried not to ogle, but I found it odd, considering how much time he must spend licking Lucais's boots clean.

What had he told me? Something about the High King being the most handsome and clever man that I would ever meet?

Glancing at Lucais again, I had to admit that he might not be wrong.

The High King returned my gaze with a gentle scrutiny of his own, a curiosity that one might bestow upon a leopard prowling across the beach. I sensed fear, confusion, and wonderment in his eyes, and I considered running for my life before he decided to cage me and send me back to the swamp.

Lucais's lips curved into a tentative smile. "I've been worried for you," he purred, the true panther revealed. His eyes darted to Wren, who cleared his throat uncomfortably, but I was clinging on to the sound of Lucais's voice—smooth as honey and deep as the ocean. It was everything I'd imagined it to be when he wasn't grunting quietly in pain. "You look exhausted, Auralie."

The way he said my *name*...

"I'm sorry," I breathed.

Lucais's brow twitched, but he said nothing. He simply extended his arm to me, a regal and gentlemanly gesture that put Wren and his playful, wandering hands to shame. I accepted, linking my elbow with his, and he began leading me down the corridor.

My head swam with fatigue and racing thoughts, the walls of my mind feeling almost non-existent—as if my consciousness might float away into oblivion if it wasn't for my arm being linked with Lucais's.

"On behalf of your escort, I apologise. He really should have allowed you to rest before bombarding you with a history lesson—and an inaccurate account of it, at that," he added, calling Wren out over his shoulder with a meaningful look.

"I was getting to it," Wren muttered, dragging his feet on the floor runner as he trailed after us.

The exchange slipped over me like throwing sand against a wall. Wren probably could have made the whole thing up, and it would have ceased to matter because I'd forgotten it a few minutes later.

Lucais was the *High King* of Faerie.

I'd found him, the man from my dreams, so quickly and easily and in the exact opposite position to what I was expecting.

I had been dreaming of the High King of Faerie as a prisoner.

"You need to rest," Lucais went on, his voice a melodious purr in my ear. I was vaguely aware of our pace quickening as we turned a corner at the end of the hall. "The House is enchanted to ease the workload of its staff, so it will take care of you. There is some urgent business I must attend to right now, but I will send someone to check on you later tonight and escort you to dinner. I'll advise them not to disturb you if you're sleeping..."

I was not in my own body, not in my own mind.

Lucais as a prisoner.

Lucais as the High King.

The High King as a prisoner.

A prisoner as the High King.

All one and the same, yet such entirely different potential storylines.

My head was positively spinning as we came to a stop in front of a large oak door, which swung open without a single touch to reveal a lavish bedroom within. Both of them were watching me, waiting for me to move, say something, or take a breath.

"Thank you." I reclaimed my arm and forced my legs to take a step, and then another, until I had crossed the threshold of the guest suite. "Thank you," I said again.

I had nothing else to offer. There was nothing but a roaring in my head. A loud vibrational warning, though for whom it was intended, I had absolutely no idea.

Turning around in a slow circle, I instructed my eyes to focus on the room. It was grand enough to rival any penthouse apartment in a human hotel, and certainly more luxurious than any room I'd ever stayed in before.

An enormous four-poster bed sat in the centre of the room, adorned with a canopy that looked as though it could have been crafted with the delicate web of a spider. In one corner, a small desk sat beside a floor-to-ceiling bookcase filled with fiction and fairytales, and a russet velvet armchair sat against the wall on the other side. The similarity it bore to Dante's Bookstore was startling but comforting.

A huge bay window overlooked the gardens, an abundant spread of soft green and lilac pillows and blankets on its seat, with patterned white lace looped over two brass hooks on either side. At the opposite end of the room, a gossamer curtain was the only door to the bathroom, hanging down from the open archway and faintly obscuring what appeared to be a marble bathtub and long sink.

"Auralie, I wouldn't leave you like this if I didn't absolutely have to," the High King murmured from the doorway.

My throat had closed up like I was having an allergic reaction to the air in the room. I felt suddenly dizzy as I nodded my head and made to turn around, pausing only to examine the antique wardrobe standing in the corner of the room and the familiar insignia carved into its doors. I had to tear my eyes away from it, fixing my gaze on Lucais once more.

Later.

I could ponder the shared symbol later, and the revelation about my dreams and what to do with my newfound freedom.

The face I'd longed to see for so long was handsome and kind, but Lucais's eyes were visibly guarded by an emotion too strong for me to properly discern. He bowed his head to me as he pulled the door closed, a gesture that stunned me so completely that I couldn't even think to say goodbye...

And then he locked it from the outside.

A vulgar word rang out in my mind repeatedly.

The unmistakably damning *click* was so faint, but it instantly sobered me up.

Heart spluttering, I lunged for the doorknob. My steps were near-silent on the plush carpet, and I had almost clasped my hand around it when I heard Lucais's voice on the other side. Swearing quietly at a silent Wren, the High King was hurling questions at him about what he was thinking and what he was doing as their voices faded down the corridor.

It had to have been about me—about Wren taking me there. Because I was human. Because I hadn't imagined it. Lucais knew something. About my dreams, or dreams of his own...

The hallway fell silent.

They hadn't realised that I'd heard the lock.

I held in my screams, my shouts, and the urge to try to break down the door. My hand fell back to my side. The doorknob was useless. Mortal limbs were useless.

I was a human in Faerie.

The moment of relief I'd felt earlier—the fleeting brush against freedom—was merely another faerie trick.

I was a *human*. In *Faerie*.

Walking backwards, my mind running a million miles an hour, I halted when I was in line with the bathtub on the other side of the lace curtain. And then I strode through it, wrestling my smelly cardigan over my head without bothering to undo the buttons. The curtain clung to me as I entered, and I swatted it away, wildly throwing my clothes around the room as I undressed.

Fine. Lucais and Wren could lock me in here. One of them had already dragged me across the countryside for two days with minimal regard for my welfare. But my family was safe, and there was no prisoner in the basement.

I was a madwoman, almost completely deranged, slowly losing her grip on the last threads of sanity. What did it matter if I took the opportunity to relax in a hot bath while I had a mental breakdown and resumed plotting my escape?

The bathroom resembled a snow globe. It was a large, circular chamber with an arched roof carved from jade stone, smoothed into tiles across the floor but left rough and exposed along the walls. A wide marble sink sat beside an oval-shaped, full-body mirror to one side, and I was only a little bit surprised to find a normal, flushing toilet on the other.

In the middle of the room, a marble bath took up most of the space, large enough to be a hot tub. It was deep enough to require the addition of stairs, with benches spanning across every other side. Beyond it, French doors had been pulled back, opening out onto a large balcony covered by crawling wisteria vines. They perfumed the air, nearly overwhelming in strength, as a gentle breeze slipped into the room and swept up the curtains—a matching set with the ones across the bay window in the bedroom.

I went to the doors, pulling them partially closed, and turned around to find that the bath—which had been empty moments ago—was filled nearly to the brim. Wisps of steam curled up from its glassy surface, heating the cool stone room.

What had Lucais said?

The House is enchanted. As if it was a person or a pet. Not house, but House. Not haunted, but enchanted.

My eyes bulged out of my head as it hit me. *The Forest had been enchanted, too.* Only this time, I wasn't completely certain I could trust it, so I eyed the ceiling warily before I stripped off my underwear and dipped my toes into the bath water.

It was the perfect temperature.

"Okay, thanks," I uttered quietly, to no part of the House in particular.

I scanned the room again, looking for eyes or ears, but I suddenly felt very much like the House had given me privacy—and perhaps that I had made it blush a little when I'd undressed without warning. I would have thought the House ought to be used to it if Wren lived there, but I still sent a silent apology out of my mind. And then I finally slipped into the beautifully warm water, soaking my tired muscles and weary bones.

Maybe I had found my way to that place I should not have been in, after all, but at least it was better than the dungeon.

NINETEEN

I'm Not a Water Faerie

An hour or two passed, and I was still in the bath.

I'd made use of the tin of soap and jar of bubble bath that had appeared at my side. I had scrubbed my nails, washed my hair, and shaved my legs. My skin was pruning, but I had half a mind to remain in the water until I drowned from prolonged exposure to it. The enchanted House, to its credit, never let the bath go cold.

"Don't you think the smell is gone yet?"

Wren's voice came from the balcony.

I jolted upright, and my arms, which had been resting on the sides of the bathtub, fell into the water with an enormous splash. More water poured over the edges in small rolls as I brought my knees to my chest and checked to make sure the generous supply of bubbles hadn't started to dissipate over anything important.

"What smell?" I hissed, shooting him a vicious look over my shoulder.

He was standing in the gap I had left between the doors—which I'd intended for the breeze, not burglars—with his arms crossed as he surveyed the overflow of bubbles and water leaking from the sides of the bathtub with visible distaste.

"You," he answered simply, bringing his sinless gaze up to my face. "You've been in here for hours. Figured you must be self-conscious about your stink."

I could have sworn the water in the bathtub began to boil alongside my internal rage. "You're the one who made a bargain in order to keep my panties in your pocket," I snapped, reaching for the bathrobe the House had brought for me earlier. It was sopping wet thanks to Wren's intrusion, so I let it fall to the floor with a defeated slap and brought my arm back beneath the water to cover myself. "Obviously, I can't smell *that* bad."

Wren gave me a bewildered look and lifted a hand in the air. In the blink of an eye, he was holding a new bathrobe—this one in black. "Did I say I think you smell bad?" he asked, striding towards me with the robe in hand.

"It was implied." I gave him a withering glare. "What are you doing here, anyway?"

He held the robe up by the shoulders for me, but he tugged it away as I reached for it. "I *did* knock," he offered, "but you didn't answer. I thought you might have drowned."

I highly doubted he would care if I had.

"So, instead of coming in through the door like a normal person, you decided to jump onto the balcony?" I grabbed for the gown again, using the arm not fighting for its life to cover my breasts beneath the water, but he dangled it out of my reach. "Will you *stop* that?"

Wren shrugged. "The door was locked." He brought the gown closer, then stepped back and gave me an exasperated look. "Would you just stand up and let me be a gentleman and help you?"

"You're being a pervert."

He frowned at that, then chose to ignore it. "You want me to put it down?" he questioned, nodding at the puddles of water on the edge of the bathtub and the floor. "You've flooded the bathroom."

"So, magic it away!" I exclaimed.

"I'm not a water faerie."

Against my better judgement, I groaned out of frustration. "You have the *audacity* to come in here without warning—"

"He told you he'd send someone—"

"He also *locked* me in here!"

"What?" Wren dropped the robe right over a wet patch along the edge of the bath. "You think we locked you in here?"

All of a sudden, I didn't care that he was still standing a foot away from the tub or that the fresh robe was now soaking up bath water from the first one. I snatched it up and rose to my feet, putting it on backwards so that Wren didn't see anything I really didn't want him to see.

He didn't look the least bit interested, though.

His eyes were an angry shade of gold as he glared at me. "The door was locked from the inside, you *idiot*."

"What?"

"The House locked the door from the inside," he repeated slowly, as if he were speaking with an illiterate child. "So that no one accidentally wanders in here." He shook his head and turned away as I began to climb out of the bathtub. "None of the High King's inner circle know that you're here, and they've been canoodling all day, and High Fae don't particularly care which room or what bed they go to when they—"

"I get it," I interjected, my cheeks burning with every imaginable form of mortification.

Wren cut me a glance out of the corner of his eye. "I don't think you do." He took a deep breath and then aimed for the archway into the bedroom. "I came to take you to dinner. Clothes are in the wardrobe. I'll be waiting in the hall."

"I can find it myself," I said impulsively. The heat colouring my cheeks flared, but Wren didn't turn back to me.

He stalked out of the room, slamming the bedroom door shut behind him. The force was enough to send tremors through the floor, and I wondered absently if that caused any feelings of hurt to the House. However, a moment later, both the bathtub and the bathroom floor were magically dried.

Shock cleared the colour from my face, and I made an aggravated gesture at the floor. The House had witnessed the whole exchange with Wren and chose not to intervene until it wasn't urgent anymore.

"Oh, thanks a lot," I grumbled, tying the waist of my robe. "I was about to feel sorry for you, too."

The enchanted House did not deign to respond in any form, and so I didn't bother asking why it had locked the bedroom door for me but still allowed Wren passage through the balcony. I didn't care. I didn't even care how long I left him waiting for me out in the hall while I dried myself off and got dressed.

The only reason I was going downstairs at all was because I was starving.

And because maybe—hopefully—I had been wrong about the High King of Faerie in one way and right about him in another.

TWENTY

You're Not Invited to Book Club

The House either didn't know or didn't care what my usual wardrobe contained. After the stunt it pulled with the water in the bathroom, I was inclined to tell it to mind its own business in any case.

Even without knowledge of runes, spells, and enchantments, the magic of the House *felt* the same as the magic in the Forest of Eyes and Ears, except the Forest had very determinedly been on my side, whereas the House seemed to have a similar attitude to Wren and an impassive, neutral allegiance.

I didn't like it.

And I didn't much like the clothes it was offering me, either.

Dresses of varying lengths and styles were hung up behind the two oak doors, alongside sets of silk or velvet shirts and pants that loosely resembled pyjamas. I pushed the hangers aside and searched the drawers, but I found only a selection of different coloured socks and scarves within them. No underwear. No normal clothes.

Choosing a set of midnight blue silk—simply because I wouldn't be caught dead wearing a dress in Faerie—proved to be even more frustrating. The silk shirt was cropped at mid-length, with the lower half of the bodice replaced by scantily detailed lace.

A dress was dangerous, though, so I would have to grin and bear it.

Wishing I could have been offered a bralette for security purposes, I ran a hand through my hair before I turned to the door. The House had provided a toothbrush, mint paste, and a hairbrush—all of which felt like an apology, and one that I'd reluctantly accepted—and I was feeling more human than I had in days.

Human in all of the good ways, that is.

The House opened the bedroom door for me before I touched the handle, and I gave it a disapproving stare before I stepped out into the hall. I was highly suspicious that it might be banking favours with the intention to come back and claim them in the future.

Wren was not waiting outside my room.

Candlelight illuminated the hallway in a murky golden glow from the sconces burning along the sepia-coloured walls, casting flickering shadows across closed doorways and between wooden cabinets and hanging tapestries. I did wonder very briefly why the

High King had chosen to use fire when organic orbs and flares of pure light seemed to be so easily accessible to members of his Court, but I was grateful for any illumination as I began to walk down the corridor alone.

Of course Wren didn't wait for me.

I had told him not to—after accusing him and his sovereign of locking me in the bedroom like a prisoner.

Despite the fact that I'd been warned about the House and its enchantment, I refused to feel bad about any of it after I'd considered that there was still every chance they were torturing prisoners in the basement. If they were, the House knew about it and hadn't done anything to stop it. My conspiracy theory was becoming less likely, but I had to keep my guard up, and that meant assuming the worst of everyone and every*thing.*

Especially Wren.

When I made it back to the corridor of windows at the end of the hall, the candlelight behind me died off, and the flames burned brighter down the staircase. I was tempted to tell the House that I could find my way to dinner without help, thanks very much, but I didn't want to risk losing light altogether, so I descended the staircase with my hand on the rail.

At the first landing, the candles leading to the ground floor had been snuffed out, and a string of firelight led the way down a wide corridor. Still, there were no signs of life, no sound beyond my footsteps padding along the mahogany floor runner as I followed the House's directions.

My muscles tensed as I walked further along the hall, preparing for someone or something to jump out at me. Part of me wished that the High King's inner circle *had* been alerted to my presence, if only to save the awkwardness of an encounter with any of them.

Ancient weapons, suits of armour, and arrays of crystals and gemstones were displayed in glass cases along the walls. When my gaze lingered on any of them for too long, I felt that humming presence circle back to me expectantly. Averting my eyes, I stifled a shudder and quickened my pace down the hallway.

Every so often, a dark corridor would branch off between cabinets or doorways, but the candlelight continued in a straight line ahead until two huge double doors, left slightly ajar, appeared at the very end. The clink of glasses filtered out through the space, accompanied by a low murmur of voices.

Taking a grounding breath, I braced myself and pushed the doors open.

The term *dining room* didn't feel quite right, although a huge buffet table stretched down the centre of the room with a dozen high-backed chairs padded with emerald-green cushioning. Platters, trays, and crystal towers filled to the brim with food were cluttering the spaces between woven gold placemats. No places were set with plates or cutlery for guests, aside from the three seats at the other end of the table.

Bookcases that had certainly seen better days lined the walls on the far corner of the room, where chaise lounges and side tables had been positioned around a circular green rug. Books had been left open, stacked on top of one another or barely hanging on to the edge of each wooden row, and quills and ink were haphazardly abandoned in the empty spaces between them.

The opposite wall was lined by floor-to-ceiling windows overlooking the rear garden. A midnight sky swallowed the horizon, but the courtyard below was illuminated by blue light. That same blue light bobbed between the exposed beams above me like stars had been hung from the ceiling by invisible threads.

"It's faelight," Lucais called from across the room.

As if he had willed it to do so, one of the floating lights drifted down to meet me in the doorway. It was small, no bigger than a raindrop, though it had a hazy glow around it like it was blending into the very air. Although similar to a flame in shape, I could very clearly see that the little orb was, in fact, the branding in the Belgrave insignia.

The insignia shared with the Court of Light.

It was so peculiar, so ethereal, that it was no wonder we had been mistaking it for flame all that time. The faelight orb was not a concept that I could have conjured up myself—to have light appear right in front of me as if it had been scooped out of the sky in near-material form without any source of external power. *As* a source of power.

Once I'd spent a moment examining it, the faelight returned to its space among the rafters, and I walked around to the side of the table closest to the windows in order to avoid Wren.

He was sitting beside the High King, who naturally occupied the head, reclined back on his chair's rear legs with his boots on the table as he flipped through a book.

I considered moving the third and last place setting to a different spot, but I was starving, so I took my intended seat on Lucais's other side. Across from Wren.

"Now I understand where you get that nasty little tongue of yours from," he remarked without looking up from his book. "Do all human women use such crude language when requesting intimate favours from their human mates?"

I frowned, eyes dropping to the cover...

Not Wren's book.

My book. The book I'd been reading in Dante's that night.

"Where did you get that?" I demanded, jumping up from my chair. I made a wild grab for it across the table—decorum be damned—but the space was simply too wide.

Wren defensively lifted the novel over one shoulder with both hands and looked me up and down. "Careful, now, or you're bound to get sauce all over that pretty little blouse."

Blood boiled beneath my cheeks as I glanced down and realised that my breasts were scarcely a moment away from knocking over a sterling sauce boat. Mentally cursing the House for not supplying underwear, I braced my hands flat on the table and straightened my spine, willing myself to look him dead in the eyes. "Give it back."

Wren's full mouth turned down in a pout. "But I'm not finished with it yet."

"Give it *back*."

He glanced towards the High King, and I copied the gesture to find that Lucais was watching us with an unreadable expression on his face. It was as if we were children, and he was an estranged uncle only in town for a funeral. He looked damn near offended that I was leaning so close to the sauceboat. When he caught my eye, he cleared his throat.

Lucais did his best to look like he cared as he faced his companion and nodded his head towards me. "Give it back," he encouraged with a grimace, his voice much quieter than I would have expected.

"Fine." Wren rolled his eyes melodramatically and slammed the book closed, giving me a pointed look. "But you're not invited to book club anymore."

"What?" I blinked at him. *Is he drunk?* "You don't have a book club."

"Sure I do." He threw a glance over his shoulder towards the bookcases in the far corner of the room. "Those are all mine. I meet with other book lovers in the Court as often as I can to discuss what we're all reading. You work in a bookstore. Surely, you're familiar with the concept?"

I stared beyond him, over the top of his head, at the enormous shelves and couches—at the *reading nook*.

Those are all Wren's books?

There had to have been hundreds of them. And the reading pattern... With the way he'd discarded so many of them, he was either in such a hurry to get to the next one or he was in a major DNF slump where nothing he opened quite hit the right spot.

Or he was lying. But...he couldn't lie.

I turned my deadpan gaze back onto his face. "You haven't invited me to any book club."

"True," he agreed thoughtfully. "I might have, but then you got snippy with me, so now I won't. Either way," he went on with a shrug, "I'm not going to judge you for reading smut, bookworm." He passed my spicy hockey romance novel across the spread of food and sauces, and I snatched it off him, quickly hiding it on my lap beneath the table. "You're welcome, too."

I was too overwhelmed to ask what he thought I should be thanking him for, but the effort was rendered unnecessary as Wren reached down and lifted my handbag into the air. It levitated to me over the table, and I caught it right before it fell into that infernal sauceboat. I couldn't remember where I'd left it in the human world, and I had no idea why he'd thought to retrieve it for me or why he hadn't bothered to say anything about it until then.

Wren stared at me expectantly, and I stared right back.

"If you are finished flirting with each other," Lucais said at last, clearing his throat again. "I would like to begin the meal sometime soon."

"Why would I flirt with her when I have your handsome face to make those—what are they called again, Aura?—those *fuck-me* eyes at?" Wren waggled both eyebrows at his High King, who exhaled a long-suffering sigh in reply. "That's what you think, isn't it?" he continued, swinging his attention back to me.

I bit my tongue. Truthfully, I couldn't care less if Wren was Lucais's lover, but I couldn't come up with a better explanation for his initial description of the High King. Especially when it turned out to be so accurate.

Ignoring his probing gaze, I turned towards Lucais. "Your companion informed me very early on that the High King of Faerie was the most handsome and creative man I would ever meet," I informed him pleasantly. "I can assure you that he and I have not been flirting."

The High King rested an elbow on the table, his mouth forming a hard line. He looked at me as if he didn't believe me. "That's what he told you?" he asked. He didn't wait for me to respond before he turned his head towards Wren and said with depthless disbelief, "High Mother spare you, my friend."

"Oh, enough." Wren waved a hand at us and began piling food onto his plate. "You're not in the least bit creative. I used the word *clever*, but I must've been thinking of some other handsome man."

Lucais huffed a laugh as he waited for Wren to finish plating up his food.

Until a moment before, I hadn't actually thought about either of their sexualities or preferences. I hadn't given a thought as to what their relationship might be at all. But watching the High King of Faerie patiently waiting for Wren, who had to be some kind of courtier at best, to select the largest cuts of meat and the nicest vegetables for himself had me absolutely stumped.

Kings and Queens were at the top of the food chain. Amongst any human aristocracy, behaviour like that would be considered disrespectful. Was it really so different in Faerie?

Lucais, noticing my observation of them, coughed loudly. Wren paused with his fork, loaded with roasted bean shoots, halfway to his open mouth. Slowly, he lowered his cutlery back to his plate and stared down at the pile of steaming food like he could become invisible at will.

"It is only the three of us tonight," Lucais explained, reaching for the platter of roasted meats. "I would not be so cruel as to throw you into one of our typical dinner parties on your very first night here."

Out of the corner of my eye, I surveyed the spread of food that spanned all the way to the other end of the table. There was enough food for an entire army laid out for us, and every chair had a gold place mat in front of it, so the decision to exclude everyone else must have been made very last minute.

"We're old friends," he went on, pouring some kind of black sauce all over the meat on his plate.

"Close friends," Wren added suggestively, though his tone was lacking its usual humour, and the implication didn't quite make its mark. I glanced over at him to find that he was still staring down at his untouched food.

"Not that close," Lucais muttered. He offered me a small, forced smile—one that didn't reach his eyes, which were guarded by that same hard, chestnut wall I'd seen on him upstairs. My stomach turned anxiously at the sight of it. "He's my right-hand man. Please, eat."

I had suddenly lost my appetite.

Lucais waited for a few moments before deciding to start his own meal, and Wren followed his lead a few moments after that. I remained motionless in my seat, my fingers curling around the edges of the book on my lap as I stared down at my empty plate.

Meticulously and repeatedly, I went through all of my knowledge of the two men and their world in my head. The Malum and their vicious pets, stalking me into the human world. The small group of High Fae I had witnessed lounging in the courtyard, who had simply vanished into thin air. The Court of Darkness disappearing on the Map ahead of a brewing war. And the table full of food intended for many more people than had actually been invited or shown up.

When I lifted my head again, I found Wren watching me. I registered the fear in his eyes before he blinked it away.

Swallowing the saliva pooling in my mouth, I turned back to the High King. "You knew I was coming here." He'd said he was worried about me, and he'd recognised me almost immediately upstairs—like we'd been introduced before. "Why doesn't your Court?"

Lucais took longer than he should have to chew his food. He tilted his head to the side, towards Wren, as he swallowed, and his black curls shifted across his forehead until they touched his eyebrows. He glanced at his fair-haired companion, whose face was angled towards his plate again, and my heart began to race in a disjointed rhythm.

"Why are you looking at him?" My voice echoed in the otherwise deathly quiet room.

The two men shared a look, the picture of that moment worth a thousand words over a thousand years. An entire conversation passed between their eyes, so knowing and intense that no emotions were spared, and I found my hands, curled into fists, were beginning to shake beneath the table.

"They know," Lucais blurted before I could explode into a thousand pieces. Wren glared at him, but he turned away from his friend, the wall of solid wood in his eyes beginning to split. "The Court knows that you're here."

My legs began to shake, too. My whole *body*. "You lied to me." I shot daggers at Wren with my eyes, trembling harder with each moment that he refused to meet them with his own. "But you told me that you couldn't lie."

Eventually, Wren's sharp, unrelenting gaze switched from the High King's face to mine. His expression was hard and unapologetic. "That was a lie."

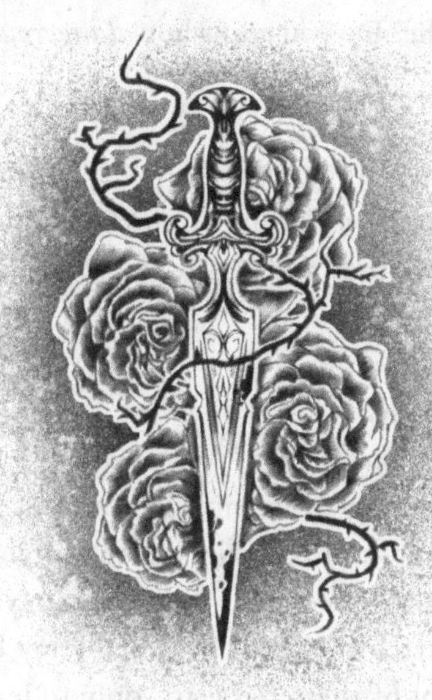

TWENTY-ONE

Wicked Gold Eyes

I felt my soul, my consciousness, beginning to detach from the rest of my body, but I forced myself to maintain Wren's unforgiving stare with one of my own. "You sick son of a—"

"I told you that you aren't asking the right questions," he snarled, leaning on the table as if he was ready to flip it over. His hair was silver beneath the faelight, but his eyes were burning like the flames of the candles in the hall. "Do you know how *easy* it has been for me to lie to you, Auralie? Do you know how *dangerous* that makes me?"

No.

No.

NO.

Everything—everything from the moment he erased the memories of my mother and sister, to the promise of taking me home...

He lied.

He lied to me.

He lied. To *me.*

My heart began to crumble like ancient stone beneath the hammer of the gods, and the pain was too intense for me to even consider why it felt so personal. Why his betrayal felt like he had stripped me of my clothes, grabbed me by my hair, and dragged me through a pool of shattered glass, only to leave me naked and bleeding on the stairs.

Wren watched those emotions crossing my face, his own an impenetrable mask of cruelty.

"Alright," Lucais interjected, his voice more like that of a mediator than a King. "We need some context here." His tone changed in an instant, rumbling with command. "Wren. By the Oracle, you need to calm down. *Now.*"

The villain across from me did not move, speak, or breathe.

I sank down in my chair, pinned in place by his wicked gold eyes.

"Auralie, I know this sounds crazy," Lucais continued, voice softening, "but it's important for you to understand this. Faeries cannot lie, but we *can* deceive you—and we're very good at it."

I must have looked as though I didn't hear him properly because the High King sighed.

"We cannot tell you, with conviction, that the sky is a colour that it's not," he went on. "We *can* make a sarcastic remark that the sky is blue when it's not. Auralie, are you listening to me?"

My face turned in his direction, tears flowing freely down my ice-cold cheeks. I could only shake my head, even though I had been listening.

He narrowed his eyes at me. "It's—" Lucais broke off with a sharp exhale, and I felt heat bloom on my cheeks. Wren had lied to me, and Lucais was tired of me. "It's easier for us to offer mistruths when we aren't responding to a direct question, when we're making subjective remarks or offering opinions. If you ask a faerie a direct question, you must pay careful attention to your wording and theirs."

I just stared at him, at the crease between his eyebrows and the dark curls falling across his forehead, with blurry eyes. I couldn't even look at Wren, couldn't feel his gaze on me anymore as my entire body went numb from head to toe.

Lucais shoved his plate aside with a clatter and lay his hands down flat on the table, fingers splayed out over the surface. "Aura, ask me who the High King of Faerie is."

There was a bang on the table, causing the glasses and cutlery to clink, and I started. Wren had either punched or kicked the wood.

He was still seething. I ignored him.

"Who is the High King of Faerie?" I asked, lifting my shaky hands to wipe the tears from my face.

"Lucais Starfire." The High King looked at me with wide, open eyes. "That was the truth. Now, ask me if I know who the High King of Faerie is."

I took a deep breath, shifting in my seat now that Wren was no longer looking at me like he was going to strangle me to death. I asked, "Do you know who the High King of Faerie is?"

Lucais's throat bobbed as he swallowed. "Yes." A brief pause. "Gregor Woodburn from the Court of Earth." He coughed with his mouth closed, shaking his head as if to clear it. "That was almost a lie, see? Yes, I do know who the High King is, but I added the second part to mislead you. Questions and answers can vary depending on the context, and we can refuse to respond if we don't wish to tell the truth, but we cannot outright lie to your face if you ask us the right questions."

My head felt heavy, my blood thick and sluggish in my veins, but I nodded to convey understanding—though it was the most basic kind and utterly useless.

"One more." Lucais's voice was acting like an antidote to Wren's poison. With each exhausted blink, my eyes began to clear. "Ask me if I can show you where the paperdove eggs are."

Weakly, I arched an eyebrow at the name, but I took a deep breath and said, "Can you show me where the paper dove eggs are?"

The High King nodded and replied with, "Yes."

I watched as he reached over a goblet of red wine and pointed to a dish of what looked like purple grapes, which were about five platters away from the only bowl of boiled eggs I could see on the table.

"Matching your actions to words is the foundation of honesty for humans," Lucais explained. "The High Fae have long considered this to be our greatest weakness, so we've found ways to work around it. Technically speaking, I answered your question truthfully, even though I showed you the wrong thing. You'll get used to it, and learn to adapt, too."

Bringing my elbows up onto the table, I buried my face in my hands and took measured, deep breaths until my face felt warm again. Even if I *could* trust either of them to tell me the truth, I didn't want to ask how Wren had deceived me earlier. I wanted to figure it out for myself.

I wracked my brain, trying to recall the specific words.

"I said the Court doesn't know you're here." Wren's voice was like a distant echo of thunder. "I was referring to the specific room you were in, but I let you believe whatever you wanted. That's the art of deception. That's what I've been *trying* to tell you—"

"I don't care!" My fists came down on the table with a bang. I looked straight at Wren, at his beautifully deceitful face, and swore at him—a filthy word that he might have recognised from the book he stole from me. "Stop talking to me."

A muscle in his jaw flickered, but he kept his mouth shut.

I turned back to Lucais, and immediately, part of my guard dissipated. He was sunlight where Wren was frostbite, and I could've melted into the expression on his face, the way he sat in the chair with the backs of his hands flat on the table as if he was ready to catch me if I fell. He didn't look tired of me anymore. He looked almost impressed.

"Take your time," he murmured encouragingly, noting my concentration as I tried to phrase the right sort of question.

I had absolutely no confidence in myself—not anymore—because it was so easy to become lost in language, and communicating with faeries was like the practice of reading and understanding all of the fine print.

But I could learn. I could adapt, like Lucais said.

"What caused you...to worry about me?"

His attentive frown slackened, chestnut eyes softening as they roamed my face. "I worried because I knew when the two of you crossed the border, and it took you days to arrive here when it should have taken minutes."

"Why should it have taken minutes?"

He cocked his head to the side at the same time as Wren let out a discouraging groan. "It only takes minutes to evanesce from the House to the border," he stated plainly.

My eyes shuttered. "But I'm human. You knew I was human. I can't—"

"Oh, here we fucking go." Wren tossed his head back, covering his face with his hands.

Lucais smacked his lips together, nodding at the table. "You let her think you couldn't evanesce with her."

Another falsehood. Or half-truth. Or lie by omission.

I looked at Wren, my fingers twitching against the smooth wood on either side of my placemat. He had dragged me across the countryside without sufficient food or water, let a Banshee attack me, and forced me to walk until my heels had bled while he sat his lazy ass on his unicorn.

He pulled his head back, eyes drowsy and half-lidded, and gave me an emotionless, crooked smile. I only had one question.

"*Why?*"

His smile became whole. "To teach you something so that we could've avoided all of this—"

"Have you lied to me about anything else?" I cut in. "Have you left out important details from anything else you've said to me or in answers you've given to questions that I've asked?" Hands braced on the table, I pushed myself out of my chair, my voice rising with me. My book fell to the floor with a thump. "Have you misled me or failed to correct me or *deceived* me about anything *else*?"

Wren didn't answer.

Because he *couldn't*.

I laughed breathlessly once. My chest felt like it was about to cave in. But my arms were strong, strong enough to hold myself up. "Tell me what it is," I demanded.

Still, there was no reply.

He stared at me as if the tables had turned, the power had shifted, and it was *my* unapologetic stare pinning *him* to his seat. It was only his sheer stubbornness preventing me from getting an answer. His throat worked, and I could see the restraint on his face and in his burning eyes as my conviction dragged the words up, only to become trapped behind his clenched jaw.

"Tell me what it is," I repeated. And then a thought occurred to me. A new strategy. I lifted my chin, emphasising my position in our power struggle. "What are you thinking right now?"

His pupils enlarged, like black holes ready to swallow the gold in his eyes, and his knuckles turned white around two handfuls of the place mat before him.

"Hmm." Lucais's voice was a quietly conflicted moan. "Good girl, but that's enough."

I whirled on him. "Why?"

He made a similar noise in the back of his throat and pressed his mouth into a tight line.

Laughter trickled out of my mouth. A soft giggle at first, and then a full-blown cackle. "That's it?" I gasped for breath. "That's all it takes?"

"No." Lucais rose from his seat, reaching for me with a hand. "I *want* to tell you—"

"So tell me what *you're* thinking—"

"Stop it!"

In the blink of an eye, three things happened.

First, Wren's roar shattered the two rows of empty champagne glasses lined up along the table. It was nothing but sound. The piercing explosions were contained, raining glass down on the spread of food without shooting over the edges of the table where Lucais and I were standing.

Second, he ripped the napery right off the table, taking countless trays and bowls of food with it. Sauce slathered the backs of chairs, grapes spilled out of their overturned bowls and rolled onto the floor, where they landed atop the mess of food and drink and linen.

And third, he leapt over the table, barely giving me enough time to stagger backwards before he rose to his full height before me. Close enough that his chest brushed against my chin as it expanded with each heavy breath.

He backed me all the way up against the window, breathing raggedly, and bent down far enough to place the tip of his nose against mine.

"You have a lot to learn," he growled, and the menacing edge to his voice raised the hairs on my arms. In contrast, his breath caressed my lips, hot and heady. "The first is that our thoughts are considered the most private part of our beings, and it is an offence against our people to attempt to pry into them. You may take a nice long look at my cock, if you like, but you will stay *the fuck* out of my head."

I gulped but showed no other sign of fear—or anything else.

"The second is that most faeries would sooner kill you than sit through a performance like that," he went on, his pupils dilating. "Listen to me very carefully, bookworm. If you have power, you do not wield it blindly. You do not *wield* it at all. You *are* your power. If someone is stronger than you, you will be faster. If someone is faster than you, you will be smarter. And if someone is smarter than you, you will be more determined. You. Rely on nothing else. *You* are all that is required here. You. Are. *Everything*."

Footsteps, as light as a cat, came towards us, but my eyes were locked with Wren's, transfixed by the smouldering colour. I realised that I had stopped breathing at some point and took a sudden breath. His cologne, that intoxicating scent, had almost knocked me out, and I managed to break the stare only so I could turn my face away to find some other type of air that did not belong to him.

"What are you?" he asked, his voice low but strong enough to command an army.

"Human," I whispered. Wren's eyes narrowed, so I corrected myself. "Part-faerie."

"No. *Listen* to me." His enunciation of each word was so perfect that I caught a glimpse of his razor-sharp canines. "*What* are you?"

A phantom hand brushed against mine. Wren hadn't moved. Lucais was still standing a few feet away as if preparing to intercept.

I felt it again, asking for acceptance, looking for a tear in my flesh armour, and I ignored it. Shoved it away. But Wren's face...

"Everything," I whispered.

"And?"

"Power." The word was a dose of poison on my mouth, but I let it out, and then I bit down on my lower lip to stop anything else from escaping its cage under his instruction.

Wren's gaze tracked the movement straight to my mouth. "That's more like it." He closed his eyes and took a deep, calming breath before stepping away from me.

I remained against the glass if only to feel the sobering chill seeping into my back through the silk and lace of my shirt.

Lucais stepped forward, an embodiment of concern, as Wren turned on his heels and prowled back to the table. I allowed the High King to take my hand, allowed his warmth to flow into me through his touch, and felt the thunderous echo of my heart as it started to beat again.

"You weren't supposed to find out like this," Lucais murmured. "But I assume you know that the caenim were hunting you?"

I nodded, eyes darting towards Wren, who was holding up two pieces of a chair he'd broken to examine them.

"She knows about the Malum and Blythe's Court, too," Wren called over his shoulder, as he tried to fit the leg of the chair back into one of its splintered corners.

The High King nodded, taking a deep breath. He was less perturbed about the damage to his property than I would have expected. "The missing piece is the Oracle then," he told me. "Would you like me to be honest with you, Auralie?"

"Don't lie to me," I answered, loud enough for both of them to hear. "No matter what."

Lucais inclined his head to me. "The Oracle offers a prediction on the success of each ruler's reign, and the whole of Faerie stands to bear witness to it. Unfortunately, the last one wasn't very clear, and it caused some unrest across the realm, which seems to be escalating now. For as long as we've been a civilisation," he went on, oblivious to Wren's continued efforts to repair the broken chair by force, "Faerie has been ruled by a High King or Queen—or both, or two of one or the other—hailing from one Court. That Court tends to receive the most benefit from the reign, as the crown feeds into the land, so the High King's power is strongest wherever he is.

"Mates—as in soulmates—rarely occur between two different Courts and have *never* occurred between different Courts for the High Kings or Queens. But this time, the Oracle claimed it would be different. At first, it seemed like a union between the Court of Light and the Court of Darkness was going to happen, but then the Oracle showed us that the new High King would take a mate from the human realm." He shook his head, laughing without humour. "That's never happened before."

I did not particularly like where this was going, but I let him continue.

"The Court of Darkness has since vanished, so it seems we misunderstood at least part of the Oracle's message. Soon after, there was a dramatic increase in the number of human bodies found in various Courts." Lucais stared down at our hands, at my limp fingers he held in his grip. He looked like he wanted to drop them. "Most of them are discovered near the gateways. Caenim attacks, usually. We think they leave the bodies there to send a message because they're all young women who..."

What? Who what?

"...look and smell like you."

Like me. My genetic makeup.

Like my mother.

My hand fell out of Lucais's hand.

"The Malum wish to create a peace pact by forcing an arranged marriage," he added. "We can only assume that they're aware of the prophecy and they consider a human mate—or any mate—to stand in the way of their plans. There is no world in which a union between the High King of Faerie and a Malum bride would ever take place, but you can't reason with them." Lucais reached for my hand again, but I pulled away.

"So, you're telling me that I look like this girl," I whispered. "They're killing... It's not half-breeds, it's—"

The High King tilted his head down, looking up at me through thick black lashes with apologetic eyes. "It's you, Auralie." Lucais's tone was gentle, but I detected a faint trace of brewing hysteria underneath. "The Oracle claimed that you would be the High King of Faerie's mate."

Heart beating up my throat, I braced a hand along the window behind me to steady myself as I began to sidestep away from him. Lucais looked like he was trying to find something else to say, but he knew as well as I did that there was nothing to follow.

Mates.

Soulmates.

The concept was familiar enough. Faeries only ever married for love, but the allocation of soulmates was less about emotional connections and more about physical compatibility. The mating bond came first, and union of love second—if at all. They believed in fate, but love was as fickle in Faerie as it was in my own world.

I can say no.

In the books I had read before, sometimes, they said no. Sometimes, the love was unrequited, and the union never happened. Even if they tried to force me, I would *never* let them—

My hand curled around what felt like a doorknob. I realised that the windows were actually glass doors leading onto a narrow balcony concealed mostly by darkness, so I maintained eye contact with the High King as I checked to make sure it wasn't locked—and prayed to the House, my only witness, that it would stay that way.

It was unlocked, so I pushed down on the handle and held the High King's stormy and highly suspicious gaze.

If he would accept the word *no* from a High Fae mate, he could accept it from me, too.

"I reject the bond," I declared loudly, and it was only the expression on his face that told me I had used the right words.

Faster than he could react, I shoved the door open and fled into the darkness before the guilt could set in. Lucais's eyes had widened in fear, anticipating the words...

But it was Wren who roared, the sound full of violent rage as I ran after the tiny orb of faelight that had followed me through the balcony doors. It was Wren's furious dismay that shook me to my core while Lucais remained silent, exactly where I'd left him, as if I'd taken his heart out of his chest and carried it with me.

I had always felt that if emotions had a soundtrack, then disappointment was loud and ferocious and all-consuming. Heartbreak, for me, had always been quiet. The final traces of the music as it faded into silence right as the playlist came to its end.

Sadly, I realised that Lucais must have felt the same.

TWENTY-TWO

Wren

Winter arrived in Faerie that night.

It was early spring in the human world, and from what I had gleaned from the Court of Light so far, the seasons seemed to work the same, but snow had dusted my windowpane when I woke at dawn the next morning to shooting pains of hunger, squeezing and releasing my stomach with an iron fist.

I didn't remember falling asleep the previous night, nor did I recall tucking myself in underneath the blankets when the temperature had plummeted.

The faelight orb had guided me around a shallow balcony walled by a swirling gold railing until I found another glass door, at which point the House took over and led me back to my bedroom by manipulating the candlelight. I'd locked the door from the inside myself and leapt onto the bed, muffling my cries with the feather-down pillows.

I had half expected Wren to storm into my room at some point during the night and throw me out of the House, but nobody had come to my door. There wasn't a single sound above the howling wind as the snowstorm seized control and drove icicles into the heart of the land.

Breath clouding in front of me, I pushed myself into a sitting position and tried to peer through the fern frost on my window.

Instead of light and colour, the sky was a cool shade of dark grey, and the clouds were heavy and thick, throwing snowflakes between them rather than crystals. Pulling the blankets up to my chin, I swallowed down a wave of nausea as my stomach growled again. I hadn't touched any of the food the night before, and I couldn't bring myself to get out of bed and go downstairs in search of breakfast—not after what I had said to the High King.

Lucais's deafening silence had remained in my head like part of my brain had gone quiet and shut down. Wren's roaring, too, like he had vocalised the agony that had caused his High King to be lost for words.

Did I hurt him?

Would it hurt to have the mating bond rejected in such a sudden and careless way?

There was no love between us. Perhaps a shared nightmare or two, and maybe even the most basic and carnal form of attraction.

Lucais was handsome and had behaved decently enough, so it wasn't because I found him repulsive, but...

It was ridiculous; the entire story was absurd.

And yet, I had offended both of them with my questions about their thoughts. Faerie customs were so peculiar to my human brain, and some of the things Wren had said and done were deeply offensive to humans, but I supposed that High Fae were a race of people with their own culture and customs, and they should be treated as such.

Magic and madness aside, they were a people, and I was a guest in their home. A tourist in their homeland. And my behaviour...

My behaviour had been appalling. So appalling that even in some human countries, it might have gotten me thrown into a dungeon.

I couldn't face either of them after that. Even if it meant that I would die from starvation as my stomach twisted again.

As if the House was privy to my thoughts, a breakfast tray appeared in front of me a moment later, filled with plates of pancakes and fried eggs and chopped fruits. It was only the rich, greasy smell that stopped me from accidentally knocking it over in surprise. My hands were reaching for a slice of buttered toast before the rest of my body could react.

"Thank you," I told the House, hoping it could understand me through a mouthful of pancakes drenched in syrup.

A pot of black coffee, pitcher of milk, and dish of sugar cubes appeared in reply.

I devoured everything on the tray, though there was enough food to feed three adults, and put all the milk and sugar cubes into the coffee pot, stirring it with one hand as I used my other to finish the last of the raspberry crumpets.

After drinking as much of the sweet caffeine as I could stomach, I pushed the tray to the end of the bed and curled up on my side.

Belly filled, fingers and toes warming beneath the blankets, I closed my eyes against the blinding white snowstorm whipping against my window and fell back to sleep to the melancholy lullaby of the howling wind.

I had no idea how much time had passed when I woke again, yanked from my sleep by an ear-splitting crack of thunder.

The snowstorm was over.

It was like it had never happened at all. The sky had turned a dark and malicious seaweed green colour as black clouds rolled across the horizon at double their natural speed. Ultraviolet streaks of jagged lightning split the clouds in two, and rain began to fall, pounding against the House with so much force that I began to worry that hail would smash through the window.

In wild weather back home, I would have curled up with Brynn in my mother's bed and waited for the storm to pass. But I was alone, and a little elemental temper tantrum would not spook me.

The House had cleared away my breakfast dishes, so I threw back the coverlet and hurried into the bathroom, where it had drawn me another hot bubble bath. I saw to all of my other needs before climbing into the tub and sinking below the surface of the water to drown out the sounds of the storm.

It was still raging when I resurfaced a moment later, and a fluffy white robe appeared folded up on the edge of the marble tub. I closed my eyes and leaned back, soaking up the heat.

Something brushed against my arm.

Opening one eye, I found the robe had been moved closer to me.

The House was bossing me around. Mothering me.

I was inclined to ignore it, but the storm was intensifying outside. It had grown so dark that I could no longer tell if it was night or day, and each stroke of lightning illuminated the room in a harsh, violet light.

After quickly washing and drying myself, I found that a new set of clothes in black velvet had been plucked from the wardrobe and placed on the edge of the tub. It wasn't until I dressed and strode back into the bedroom that I understood why the House had been in such a hurry to get me out of the bath and presentable.

Wren was standing by the bed, studying the titles of books on the shelves in the corner.

Orbs of faelight danced around him, the same molten gold colour of his eyes. He turned towards me, and they flared bright enough to light up the whole room in a soft, warm glow.

Strikingly handsome in a neatly pressed black shirt and pants, Wren was without his weapon belt and his usual revolting smirk. His blond hair was combed up, fringe hanging over his forehead in thick strands as if it had been gelled, and he was unshaven, the stubble along his chiselled jawline glittering beneath the faelight.

"I'm sorry about the storm," he said quietly, as the glowing orbs settled up against the ceiling like light globes. "The High King is in a bad mood. It'll pass soon."

I frowned. "What does that—oh." Lucais had inferred that the High King's original Court stood to gain the most from his reign, and that the crown fed into the land. Perhaps his Court also stood to lose the most, then. "He meant that literally."

Wren nodded once in confirmation. His eyes were weighed down by something that almost looked like apprehension. He was quieter than normal, too, and standing back instead of getting right in my face.

"It's that...intense?" I queried, risking a step forward. "Having a High King in Faerie? He—his moods?"

I could not imagine the death and destruction that would occur if human leaders had such an intricate and primal connection to their lands, but then again, we had shunned the High Mother long ago, while the High Fae still lived in worship.

"Not always," Wren murmured, tugging at the collar of his shirt like it was scratching him. "The bond between the High King and the land is tenuous, both linked as equals to the High Mother. You can judge his strength based on the prosperity brought to the land during his reign, and occasionally acquire an inkling as to his overall mood or health. He can't control it, and most of the time, it's a very mild flow-on effect. But, sometimes, like right now," he continued, making a sheepish gesture towards the storm-lashed window, "it's just downright embarrassing."

Glancing at the lightning whipping the sky outside, I swallowed a fat ball of acid guilt.

The blizzard-slashed winter morning. The electrical summer storm. Both occurred on the same day.

The day after I had said those words to him.

"I must have upset him very much, then," I lamented, standing on the tips of my toes as I crossed my ankles and stared at the floor.

My hair spilled over my shoulders, already dried after the bath, and I balanced on one foot as I straightened up and gazed back at the High King's right-hand man with as much resolution as I could muster.

I did not regret my words, but perhaps I did regret the way I'd delivered them.

Wren shrugged, a fluid motion across his broad shoulders. "It's not as personal as you might think." Slowly, he dragged a finger across a shelf in the bookcase like he was absentmindedly checking for dust. "I could tell you that Lucais Starfire has been waiting to meet his mate for his entire life, that he's a sappy old romantic for how much he's looked forward to it. But he didn't know it was you until the moment he laid eyes on you for the first time, and you were looking right back at him."

Blinking, I recalled the look of realisation I had seen crossing Lucais's face when I'd arrived.

"The Oracle doesn't show faces," Wren explained, sensing my confusion. "You might catch a whiff of their scent, maybe a blurry memory from a former life with vague details like flame-red hair, but it wasn't about having you. Or loving you. Or even wanting you. It was the *idea* of you. And you would not be the first person who rejected the idea of falling in love with your soulmate because you were told to do so by some external force. This is exactly why I kept it from you."

Clouds filled my mind, dripping with knowledge and feelings. Hazy and profuse, like searching for signposts on a fog-consumed road.

Lucais hadn't been dreaming of me.

He knew who I was because of the mating bond, because some Oracle had shown him—

"When?" I stumbled forward, steadying myself against the closest bedpost. "When did this Oracle—"

"Three months ago." Wren bowed his head to me. "I'd wager it was around the same time your dreams started."

Soulmate.

Were my dreams a memory, like the Oracle had shown Lucais? Did he suffer like that, or is it yet to happen? How many beatings has he endured—or will he endure? And, above all, did the idea of me help him survive that, like I tried to do when I screamed for him every night? Or is that why I'm here now?

Without answers, without anything but the feeling that lingered on my skin like perfume, I was emptied and completed at once.

Blank and bursting with colour.

"Look," Wren said tightly, halting my motionless downwards fall. "Forget him. The mating bond has been primarily used to produce strong, healthy faelings, but it's not uncommon for the crown to switch Courts between reigns, so having an heir doesn't really matter. It's the modern age now, anyway, and nobody is going to tell you what to do. Not even the High King of Faerie."

Eyeing him warily, I wrapped an arm around the bedpost and sagged against it. "You sound like you know an awful lot about this."

A wistful look gleamed in his eyes. "He's my best friend. My brother. We've been through everything together. All of this, and all the years beforehand." Shaking off the memories, he gave me an appraising look. "He's disappointed, but he'll get over it. And besides, his foul mood is not just about you." He waved a hand towards the window again. "There's an awful lot happening at the moment, and by no means should you feel guilty for any of it. You have every right to say no." His hand fell back to his side, and he heaved a deep breath. "To go home."

I jerked my head towards him, my throat tightening. "Is that why you're here?"

He ran his tongue along his lower lip, then his teeth, and he broke our stare for a second before offering me a small, sad smile. "Would you like me to take you home, bookworm?"

For a moment, I couldn't speak. All I could do was stare at him as that one potential, budding truth began to bloom between us until all of his lies were buried beneath it.

But they were buried in a shallow grave.

Still, I couldn't form an answer.

Is it smarter to go home now? Can I ask him to make me *forget?*

There was still hope for that life in a quiet town far away from the gateways into Faerie, where my mother and sister could live in safety, and I could...

I could be safe, too. Safe in stories I could close and walk away from without elemental repercussions or feelings so strong that they demanded a sacrifice. Like I'd always desired. Like I'd always told myself that I desired.

"Do you want me to go home?" The words came out before I could stop them, the question posed before I could make sense of it.

Wren's reply was immediate and final. "No."

Reassurance flooded through me, opening up my lungs and steadying my hands. I'd braced myself for a different answer, although I didn't know why. Of course he wouldn't want to take me back. He didn't want to carry me while he evanesced, and he hated the long walk.

And of course I couldn't go home. Not yet, not after what I'd said the night before. I couldn't leave when I still hadn't discovered how or when Lucais had or would become a prisoner, or if his best friend had anything to do with it.

"Then we're agreed." I tried, and failed, to make my voice sound light.

He smiled again, soft and affectionate, and I started saying his name in my head over and over again so I wouldn't forget who he was. The man who likely tortured people, the butcher in the hallway; not this, whatever it was, presenting itself to me draped in sheepskin and romantic faelight by the bookcase.

"What is it you want?" I asked suddenly. His warning look, though not harsh, immediately cured me of longing for an answer. "Never mind. Sorry."

Wren's sensual chuckle filled the room as he turned away and plucked a book from the shelf. "This has always helped me get through the storms," he mused, extending it to me as he closed the space between us in a few long steps.

I reached for the book, entitled *The Sins of Stars,* and his thumb brushed mine as he released it and pulled back his hand.

The only part of my brain still functioning in spite of my confusion awakened to the sense of that *thing* circling back to me again, filled with magic or memories that I rejected with a tall wall of mental adamant.

"We have quite a few meetings coming up," he informed me softly. "If you need one of us, we'll come as soon as we can. But, in the meantime, we'll send a maid up to check on you. Her name is Delia. I think you'll get on well."

I watched as Wren put one hand in his pocket, leaving the enormous hardcover book in my grasp, and hesitated before pulling his other hand away.

Before I could react, his fingers threaded into my hair, palm cupped around the side of my head as he brushed it behind my ear.

"For what it's worth," he whispered, stroking my temple with his thumb, "I wish it was different, bookworm. I really do."

Wish what was different?

Then he was gone. His touch was missing like someone had ripped the blankets off me right as I was beginning to fall asleep, and he disappeared through the open doorway.

The magic swirling around me reached for him, stretching between us as far as it could go before it just...*snapped*. Like thread against a blade. Dissipating into thin air as the faelights dimmed and eventually disappeared with Wren and everything else he had taken with him.

Suddenly exposed to the dark and cold again, I hugged the book close to my chest, ignoring the way its hard corners dug into my skin, and swung around the post until I collapsed onto the mattress.

Wren, Wren, Wren, Wren.

There was a final, almighty groan of thunder outside like the creaky slam of a door flying off its hinges.

And then, as if it had been sucked out of the sky by a holy vacuum, the storm stopped.

TWENTY-THREE

Obsidian

The next morning, I awoke to the sound of knuckles rapping against my bedroom door. Bleary-eyed, I stumbled out from under the tangle of blankets and went to unlock it.

After Wren's visit, the House had made itself unavailable to me as if I had committed some offence against it, refusing to even provide fresh towelling when I went to wash my face before tucking myself into bed for the night.

The old linen would have sufficed, but it had taken that away.

I didn't *need* the House, though.

Barely even wanted it.

Flicking back the lock, I turned the doorknob and yanked back the wooden door. I was half expecting to find Lucais in the hallway because I knew that Wren wouldn't have bothered to knock, but the person standing there was a young High Fae woman, and she handed me a note before I could scream.

Bookworm—this is Delia. Be nice to her, will you? She's lovely, and here to help you with whatever you need while we are otherwise engaged. Poor communication skills, though. Pity about that.

Wren's words were scrawled across a torn-off piece of parchment paper with blotches of ink and other liquid stains I didn't care to study too closely.

I glanced back at Delia, trying to conceal my expression with a hand over my mouth, but I was well aware that it was a futile attempt and that I was being incredibly rude.

She was beautiful with peach skin and long white hair draped over her shoulder in a braid. Her irises were dark silver, and they glittered like starlight as she stared back at me with a level of patience honed down into an art form after years—or centuries—of practice.

Because her mouth, as white as bone, had been sewn shut with thick metallic-grey thread.

Poor communication skills? The bastard brothers have sent me a maid who can't speak!

A maid who could not be forced to tell me the truth if I was clever enough to ask the right questions.

"I am so sorry," I whispered, taking a quick step backwards to allow her into the room. "Have you read this note?"

Delia gave me a knowing look as she strode past me and set down a breakfast tray at the end of my bed. It told me all I needed to know—that she had indeed read the note, she was well acquainted with Wren, and that we would, in fact, get along very well.

When her hands were free, she gestured to the stitching across her mouth and shrugged as if to say that she was used to it. I decided not to do her the dishonour of apologising again, and instead focussed my attention on the food.

Thanking her for bringing the tray up for me, I settled in the middle of the bed with my legs crossed and began to dig in. I'd eaten about three meals worth of food at breakfast the previous morning, which was fortunate, considering the House was shunning me, but the early sense of hunger was already stirring in my belly again.

Delia left the room, but she didn't close the door. A moment later, she returned carrying fresh linen and clothes, which she placed beyond the sheer curtain in the bathroom, and then kicked the bedroom door shut behind her when she came back once more with a large wooden bucket.

I froze with a porcelain cup of coffee halfway to my mouth.

The wooden bucket was familiar—a dark, stained walnut plated with iron rims. Delia's hands were placed strategically against the wood, and I'd seen the burn marks on Lucais's throat when they'd shoved his head into it...

She paused before the curtain, looking at me over her shoulder like my growing fear had taken physical form and struck her over the back of her head.

She gave me a pointed look and nodded, and then glanced down at herself with the same expression and shook her head gently.

I put my cup down before I dropped it and asked, "It won't hurt me because I'm human?"

A reassuring nod.

"But why do you even have it?"

Delia filled her cheeks with air to emphasise the stitches sealing her mouth, and I winced at the way they tugged at her skin. When she continued her walk into the bathroom, I could have sworn her shoulders were moving with silent laughter.

I could not imagine being able to laugh at all after someone did that to my mouth. I could not imagine why Lucais hadn't done anything about it, or why Delia had remained in his service if he was refusing to help her—or worse, if *he* had done it.

And I couldn't ask her, either.

But I had no time to consider these things any further, because as soon as Delia began her work in the bathroom, I realised that the House truly was trying to oust me.

She'd brought the bucket in for the purpose of filling the bath with hot water because the marble tub had no taps or drain, and the House was being obstinate.

Delia began hauling the bucket back and forth from the sink, and I discarded my breakfast to offer her some help. I tried to tell her not to bother because the idea of manually emptying it out afterwards seemed exhausting, but she wouldn't hear it. Waving me off, she continued moving with graceful ease between the marble tub and sink until the enormous bath was nearly half-filled with steaming water.

She motioned for me to undress and climb in while she retrieved a comb from the counter. I obeyed if only to avoid causing her any more grief than she was already receiving on a regular basis from Wren.

As Delia began to pull the comb through my hair, twisting and twirling it until my curls were more pronounced than ever before, I quietly mused on Wren's behaviour from the previous night. Not only the things he'd told me, but the way he'd spoken to me, the way he'd looked...

The way he'd looked at me.

I wish things were different.

After he'd left, I had spent the rest of the day perched on the window seat, reading the book he'd given me. It was a story about star-crossed lovers that felt far too soft for his tastes, detailing a time in Faerie's history when *Lesser Fae* was still a commonplace term.

The main character was a young High Fae man called Micael who came from a noble house, and he was falling in love with a Swapling—which I realised was the word being used to describe a Shapeshifter—called Livia, who had been enslaved to his family.

Despite the author's insinuations that their relationship bordered on the unnatural and blasphemous, it hit all the right spots for a romantic tragedy and had me completely entranced. I'd read until my eyes started to sting, and then I'd carried it back to the bed with me and left it at my side while I curled up beneath the covers and thought about the enormous, brutish High Fae who'd given it to me reading it himself through every storm.

The thought was somehow warm, if thoughts could be considered by temperature, and I had drifted off to sleep feeling less lonely than I had in years.

I didn't like Wren. He didn't like me, either. But we didn't have to like each other in order to understand.

Except before I had a chance to finish processing our newfound understanding, he'd proceeded to send me a snarky message the very next morning, accompanied by a poorly written note.

His mood swings were like the strikes of a whip. Sharp, grating pain between brief moments of solace. And honestly, I preferred to just take the lashings until he'd seen so much of my flesh and blood that he got sick of it.

But no, he continued to offer those little pieces of himself to me—tiny, insufficient splinters of humanity that I grappled for like a life rope—because he wanted to manipulate the tides so he could pick when and where I washed ashore.

Anger started to take shape in my mind, like a cobra ready to strike.

He had used Delia to send me a message. A warning. Delia—who was a person, who deserved more respect, and who probably didn't agree to being used like a pawn in his wicked games.

And the games! The games made me *furious*.

Wren was as hot as a summer with no shelter, and then he was as cold as the blizzard that tore through Faerie the morning before. He was dark as night and bright as day, a protector and a predator. He couldn't seem to make up his mind because he wanted it all. He wanted it all, and he—

I wish things were different.

Everything went dark.

Like a thick curtain of midnight velvet had fallen across the room, blocking out all of the light. Panic seized my throat, my heart slamming into my chest, and it was only Delia's hands on my head, halting in the middle of gathering hair for another braid, that allowed me to remember where I was.

Who I was.

What I was.

Because something inside of me had caught on fire. My hands burned, palms pressed against my stomach, and there was something leaking out of me like blood. I couldn't hear it dripping down into the bath water around my hips, but I could *feel* it...

"Something is wrong," I whispered to Delia frantically. "Stand back—get help—"

She moved just in time.

Her lightning-fast faerie speed might very well have saved her life.

Because the wound inside of me, the burning hole of which my lifeblood was pouring out, exploded.

It was silent, but I screamed.

The sound tore out of me like someone was ripping out my fingernails as a whoosh of wind and midnight and ribbons of ebony rippled across the room. Glass doors rattled, the steam on the stone walls hissed, and the tins lined up on the counter clinked to the ground and echoed as they rolled.

Delia was silent, but I felt it.

The sudden emptiness. The finality of darkness enveloping me and everything surrounding me, maybe even the whole House.

Breathing heavily, I waited with my head tucked between my knees for the water in the tub to stop swishing from one side to the other. Until the vibrations of that silent impact stopped. And then I lifted my head. Slowly.

And gasped.

Colour had been drained from the bathroom. Its jade green stone had been washed out by greyscale shadows, like the ink on a black-and-white photograph. The marble tub and countertop were now obsidian, depthless in their appearance. And on the ground in the corner of the room, a small figure with dark hair was curled up in a ball.

She lifted her head and—

"Delia?" My voice was hoarse.

The young woman was familiar with silver eyes and metallic thread sewn across her mouth, but her hair was as black as night.

It was supposed to be white. It *had* been white.

"What have I done?"

Delia's eyes softened, moisture making the silver glisten, and inclined her head to me in clear confirmation of my very worst fears.

Perhaps you found your magic.

"No, no. I'm so sorry." My hands slipped against the marble as I pulled myself out of the bathtub and went straight to the clothes that were on the floor.

A set of silk pants and matching shirt that had been red when she brought them in were now as black as her hair. I donned them regardless, letting them soak up the water droplets on my body and stick to my freezing skin.

"Please, please don't tell anyone," I begged, completely ignoring my inconsiderate phrasing. She couldn't vocalise it to anyone, but she could nod, and she could probably write things down. "I swear it won't ever—" I broke off, glancing over my shoulder and finding Delia rising to her feet. She reached one hand out to stop me as I raced for the archway into the bedroom, towards the door to the hall. "I'm so sorry," I told her again.

And then I ran for my mortal life.

There was no one in the hallways to stop me.

The House was perpetually empty, and with its enchantment effectively giving me the cold shoulder, I was left to stumble down dark and twisted stairways and corridors, searching for a door to the outside. Glass cabinets filled with ancient relics and suits of armour turned my own fear-stricken reflection on me as I sprinted past them, avoiding eye contact and any recognition of that whispering hum as it followed me down the hall, throwing questions at me like spears in my back.

Will you let me in, let me in, let me in now?

Every door in the House was closed, and I did not dare try to open them for fear of what might be hidden on the other side. Torture chambers filled with iron-rimmed buckets, women with their mouths sewn shut, or weapons like the blades Wren carried on his belt. Or something worse.

I knew there was something worse because Wren was planning it. He told me he wished things were different, and then he sent me a message—to keep my mouth closed, to stop asking questions.

Why else would he have brought me back to Faerie with him?

It wasn't for the High King, who had shown very little interest in me after his initial shock and the reluctant revelation about a prophecy. No—I was a decoy of some sort, an excuse to have Malum track us through an unnecessarily long trip back from the border, or something else sinister.

I had to be. I was a blight, not a bride. And Wren was in the dungeon with Lucais in my dreams, but he was not a prisoner.

I burst out through the first exit I could find—a glass door into the garden—and its frame rattled as it swung closed behind me.

Strong perfume filled my nose, the delicate scent of wisteria mixed with roses and thyme, as I cut through the lines of flowerbeds spanning a mile away from the House. The soil was damp, the ground muddy beneath my bare feet, and some of the large, vibrant petals looked weatherbeaten and ice blue with frost as they drank in the warmth from the light sky and recovered from the blizzard.

I almost told them not to bother, almost warned them that the real storm was still to come, but the plants could fend for themselves. Even if they did have faces outlined by seeds in their cores, and I could've sworn they turned to blink after me sleepily as I fled.

Flowers with faces and monsters with teeth for eyes and a girl with her mouth sewn shut, whose hair had gone from white to black in the blink of an eye.

The injury I'd felt earlier was gone, like the blast of night had been a bullet fired from a gun, and I was left to steady myself against the reverberations and pray to the gods that I was not reloaded.

Racing for the distant line of trees, obscuring the dirt road towards the little town called Sthiara, I went over my knowledge in my head.

Magic was temperamental. I'd read about half-faeries and changelings before, and it was a common conception that emotions fuelled their powers. If the High King's emotions could summon a storm, then it must be true—and it had happened to me when I'd let myself feel my own. It started to rise up again, provoked by the memory of how I'd felt in the bath. The idea that Wren was a traitor to everyone and everything that ever mattered—

No.

I shoved it down. Beat it back. Boxed it up.

Never again.

I would not accept it, would not consent to it, would not acknowledge it.

Wren was wrong.

I was not power. I had no choice, I had no control, and I was mortal.

The line of trees parted as if to embrace me, and I dove into the shadows they cast on the ground, almost falling to my knees as I skidded to a stop and pressed myself against a rough trunk to catch my breath.

Magic halted with me.

Is it time, is it time, is it time yet?

"Never," I breathed, sweat dripping from my brow. My chest burned; my throat was on fire. I swore at the presence that had stalked me into the woodland and kicked at the stones and fallen leaves on its floor. "You're about ten fucking years too late."

It recoiled, letting fresh and clean air reclaim space around me, but then it growled. A deep, wet sound that came from a copse of trees a few feet ahead.

That was odd.

The magic had never made a sound before, not outside of my own head.

Not me, not me, not me, it sang.

I willed it to go away and leave me alone, but the warning gave me a moment's notice. Time enough to throw myself out of the way as the wind changed direction and the smell of rotting death filled my nose, barrelling straight towards me as the caenim lunged from the shadows.

TWENTY-FOUR

Caenim

The caenim were as slow as I'd imagined when I had seen the overlarge figure sauntering down the main road through Belgrave.

Perhaps it set a careful pace due to its blindness, in order to avoid tripping over obstacles it couldn't see and making itself vulnerable to its prey. Either way, I was not about to hang around and wait for that to happen.

Running for the road, I jumped over unearthed roots as small as steps and darted around trees, leaving a long and winding trail of my scent for the caenim to take its sweet time following. It was the best I could do, considering I didn't even have a baseball bat at my disposal, and I could not return to the House.

But I couldn't go home, either.

That had been my intention—to return through the gateway to the human world, where the absence of magic had dulled the kernel of poison inside of me. And maybe where any last traces of me would mysteriously vanish between one place and the next.

I didn't know what I would do with the caenim tracking me all the way to the High King's safe house, though. Soulmate or not, I didn't think there was enough perfume or dung in the world to cover my scent there.

Planning my future took a backseat to my present as soon as I broke through the last of the trees and skidded onto the dirt road.

Caenim—dozens of them—were trudging through the forest on the other side of the road. Forked tongues flicking out of their eyes, they caught my scent alongside the death reek of their comrade as the wind came from behind me, tousling my loose auburn curls, and their black and empty mouths pulled back into wide grins.

I swore violently and didn't care that nobody heard me.

The Malum had sent a small army into Sthiara.

Returning to the House was not an option. Not if Wren was working with the Malum to overthrow the High King.

Lucais's vision through the Oracle had contained memories, as if the concept of soulmates defied all logic of time and space, but I was almost certain that mine had been a premonition. A warning.

And I had about five seconds to make a choice that would change that future.

I turned towards the township of Sthiara, knowing full well that there was every chance the caenim had already raided it.

My eyes watched the thicket on either side of the road as I ran, an action that was strangely familiar, like checking for kangaroos while speeding down an outback highway in a sedan. In either situation, I stood to sustain the most damage without a weapon or a bull bar.

Thankfully, none of them jumped out at me, so I decided to risk a glance over my shoulder and immediately regretted it.

Two small armies were joining from both sides of the woodland in the middle of the road, plodding after me at a disconcertingly confident pace.

I realised that I probably should have asked questions about them before I left. How many would have to be killed in order for me to be safe again? Could the Malum create more? Was that why Wren was working with them, because he had access to magic that they didn't, and they made perfect, blind scapegoats?

The wind changed again, blowing towards me from Sthiara, and my heart withered against the smell of death the breeze carried from the little town.

Caenim attack, Malum infestation, or something else that was very wrong.

I couldn't go into town when there was every chance that a dozen more of the caenim were waiting there, so I cast a backwards glance to ascertain how much distance I'd gained before I ran back into the forest.

My calves were burning, muscles threatening to seize up, and it made me clumsy.

Sharp branches sliced at my skin, leaves caught and broke off in my hair, and the skin of my toes started to bleed as I tripped and stumbled over roots and rocks.

A hungry, feral growl sounded from behind me as the coppery tang of my blood tainted the air. They were much closer than they had been before.

I was relieved when light pierced the forest, opening up a clearing ahead, though it was short-lived as shadows moved across the golden grass and began to form a line of starving death.

They were everywhere.

There was nowhere to hide.

A sob caught in my throat, rocking my chest, and I wished that I could peel my skin off—could climb out of my body and fly away, leaving my scent in a pile of flesh and bones for them to devour on the ground.

But I couldn't.

The Malum had enlisted an apex predator for a long hunt. Speed didn't matter when you couldn't hide. Sight and sound were irrelevant when the description of the target was a smell that couldn't be discarded.

I am going to die here.

I made it to the clearing, and I stopped running.

The pungent reek grew more and more unbearable as they closed in around me, skin as grey as the bathroom walls had been when I left the House. Their hoods were up, tattered cloaks billowing out behind them, but their tongues were as red as blood as they extended out of their eye sockets and tasted the air swirling around me.

I closed my ears against the sound of their rumbling hunger until the world went quiet, and not even the rustling grasses pierced my mind.

Heartbreak was silent. Death was silent. I didn't want to hear a single thing as they killed me; I wanted the world to shut down the same way it had ten years ago, so the circle of my life could be completed at last. The debt would be repaid.

"Do you hear me?" I whispered shakily. "The debt will be repaid."

None of them smiled this time.

They were close enough for me to strike, but my hands hung limp at my sides.

Maybe they'll beat me to death.

I hoped they would. That would be fitting.

Sinking to my knees in the grass, I closed my eyes. The line of caenim already treading across the field would get to me soon.

A scream rang out in my head—sharp, soul-wrenching, and final. My mother's scream as I sat on the floor like a discarded tissue and remained quiet.

A memory.

The memory that had haunted me throughout my life, which would hopefully be laid to rest at last in my death. We deserved that peace.

I thought about Brynn in the brief moments before I died. The happy moments—picking strawberries at the farm two towns away from our home, flooding the kitchen stove with more popcorn than we had room for in our bowls because she had accidentally tipped the entire bag of corn kernels into the pot, reading stories about unicorns, fairies, and mermaids before she fell asleep in my arms—because those were the memories I wanted to take with me.

Those were the memories I needed to hold onto when I inevitably found myself in some hell loop on the other side, reliving the worst day of my life until my soul had been ground down into nothing.

Brynn smiled at me in my mind, twirling a curl of her blonde hair around her finger like I once did to soothe her to sleep, and used her other hand to point behind me.

The caenim was reflected in her eyes, a clawed hand hovering over my head, aiming to swing down and—

"No!"

I screamed and ducked to the side.

She can't see this. She isn't supposed to see this.

My eyes flew open, desperate to show her something else, but there was nothing but dark, lumpy figures closing in around me on all sides.

The one she had seen, with its arm hanging over me like a guillotine, took another step to close the extra distance and—

Its head fell into my lap, green blood squirting into my face as its mangled body became limp and flopped to the ground.

The scream that followed was my own.

I braced my hands on the dirt behind me and twisted my hips, urging the head to roll off me, and then I very nearly covered the corpse with a spew of bile that choked the scream catapulting out of my throat.

Wren didn't even look at me as he whirled, sword dripping with filth, and swung it around at the two caenim approaching him from behind. The third one was a little shorter, so instead of a clean decapitation, his sword cut into its head and became stuck, lodged halfway through its skull.

He grunted with annoyance and kicked its stomach, reaching for his weapons belt and drawing another blade. He took that blade—the poniard he'd used to peel his apple at the cottage we'd stopped at on our journey through the Court of Light—and threw it at me.

Not *at* me—behind me, straight into the heart of the caenim that was extending two clawed hands right towards my spine.

Pulling his sword from the other caenim's skull, Wren acquired another small dagger and tossed it on the ground in front of my knees. I stared at it, then at him.

What is he doing?

"Not to pierce the illusion of chivalry," he said, throwing me a brief look over his shoulder as he speared his sword through the chest of another beast, "but you're welcome to participate."

I had no opportunity to reply as he charged forward, his steps like a dance, skewering caenim and slicing off limbs and heads as he pirouetted through the long golden grass.

His movements left an opening for one to stalk forward, taking his place in front of me, and it was instinct for my hands to grab the weapon he'd left, though I had never used one before in my life. I felt human and helpless as I cried out, eyes darting across the caenim's body, searching for an opening between its arms as it lunged.

Shrieking again, I drove the blade into its chest, and its iron-tipped nails, closing around my arms, barely scratched my skin as it sagged and tumbled to the ground like a pile of bricks. My heart was beating so loud, I thought it was going to burst from my chest and take flight to the skies.

Wren jogged back and nodded in approval. "Very good, bookworm," he remarked with a healthy amount of condescension. He leaned over me, dripping caenim blood into my lap, and yanked the blade out of my kill. Giving me a wicked smile, his green-splattered face only an inch away from mine, his eyes glowed like wildfire as he placed the hilt of the dagger back in my hand. "Now do that again, pretty girl."

Caenim bodies were littering the field, and Wren resumed his dance, felling monsters that came too close or tried too hard. He ducked and weaved through skinny arms and outstretched claws as he brandished his sword, the high-pitched whip of it slicing through everything in its path the only sound I could hear. Green, festering blood coloured the land, squirting across the sky like paint being squeezed from its tube. My hands were covered in it, its texture thick and oily.

Most of the caenim lost their heads or suffered a blade through the chest, but others he took apart slowly—an arm, and then a hand, and finally a slash across the belly that sent grey mucus pouring out of their bodies as they withered to the ground like dying flowers.

It was over before I could get to my feet.

Wren twirled the sword in his hand, a flash of silver against the dark forest as he faced down the final caenim.

This one was tall and gangly, wearing an ill-fitting robe that revealed its canine-like hind legs, impossibly long and misshapen. I couldn't be sure, but I had a feeling that it knew it was over, too. Still, the monster made one last, valiant effort to kill its attacker, lunging at Wren with a wide mouth open—

He ducked and rolled, leaping to his feet behind it, and brought the blade upwards between its legs with unimaginable strength, nearly slicing the creature in half. Making a disgusted face, he spared a glance in my direction as the caenim's body hit the ground, his sword still wedged inside it.

The horror-struck look lasted for a split-second before Wren vanished, abandoning his sword in the body of his last kill, evanescing through the air in a blur of black and gold.

He reappeared at my side, almost stepping on me as the toes of his boots touched the dirt and he tackled a straggler to the ground behind me.

I'd been so enthralled with his violence, I hadn't even realised...

The caenim was bigger than him, almost as big as the last one, and he didn't have the advantage of a sharp sword to spread between them. In a swift move, the caenim twisted, pinning Wren to the ground. It was all the High Fae warrior could do to bring his knee up at the last second, creating a barrier to keep the monster's enormous mouth at bay.

The caenim lifted an arm in the air, iron-tipped nails glinting in the light, poised to slice open his throat.

Wren snatched its raised arm first, and then its other, holding the caenim's hands down by its wrists. The beast's neck was so short that it was prevented from leaning down and chewing off Wren's head, and he kept his knee firmly between their bodies while it struggled to free its arms.

I waited, eyes wide with shock, for him to make the killing blow.

He didn't have access to his weapons, but he didn't need them. He *was* a weapon. Wren had magic in his veins strong enough to light up an entire city with an arrogant wink, but instead of frying the creature from the inside out with the scalding light on his palms, he looked at me.

"Kill it," he ordered, his tone as light as it would be if he was asking me to close a window. Golden eyes bore into mine, simmering with impatient expectation.

I didn't move, didn't give him even a hint of salvation in my own gaze. I had no weapons, and I couldn't remember where I'd dropped his dagger.

The caenim snarled, mouth dripping with saliva, and Wren craned his neck away from it, giving me a demanding look. "Aura, my love," he said with lethal sweetness, voice tightening, "will you please pick up the dagger at your feet and *kill* it?"

I glanced down at the blade in the grass, edges dulled with crusted green gunk, and then back at Wren.

He was beginning to squirm.

The caenim struggled against him, teeth-filled eyes hissing and snapping, and I saw the killing blow—my killing blow, if I picked up the blade and drove its point right into the base of its neck.

And I hesitated.

Wren saw it. His face folded in disbelief—a handsome face, a truly handsome face that some part of me might have eventually missed being able to appreciate from afar.

But maybe Lucais could commission a statue created in his likeness using marble, which was probably the only type of rock that would do justice to Wren's strong features and sharp jawline. Although, I wondered what they would do for his eyes, which were incomparable and fast glazing over with hurt as he watched me and understood.

I had stopped hesitating.

I was refusing.

And I thought that, for some reason, my refusal hurt him the most—more than anyone else—because there was not even a spark of magic left at his fingertips.

The whole world saw my choice to let Wren die.

I hoped the damn Oracle saw it, too, and gave me some sort of sign in my next dream that I had made the right choice for the High King of Faerie. For Lucais, who would probably never understand.

Not the way Wren did as he glowered at me.

And let go.

Twenty-Five

Touching Her is Suicide, and Speaking About Her is Treason

The Oracle did not see me allowing Wren to die...but the High King's Guard certainly did.

In the blink of an eye, they appeared on horseback, charging through the clearing with their swords raised in the air. It was as if their horses, without horns like Elera, had simply evanesced through the woodland. I only knew that they were the High King's Guard because of their uniforms, which were a regal set of white pants and gold coats. They looked rather ridiculous, I thought, as they galloped towards us to save the traitor to their High King.

Alleged traitor, I supposed.

There was no real proof yet.

It was a feeling I had, an explanation for the peculiarities that nobody else could or would give me, but I did still find myself exhaling in relief when a dagger came spinning through the air, landing in the caenim's back before it could spill Wren's throat.

He hadn't moved to stop it himself, hadn't blasted a hole of light through its torso or vanished into thin air beneath it. He hadn't done anything but let the caenim go while he held onto me with his burning eyes.

Aside from that shuddering breath of repose, I felt numb from head to toe, from the inside and out.

The collective shouting of the Guard was a distant murmur, even as they came to a stop around us, and the one who had thrown the dagger jumped down from his midnight stallion. He was taller than Lucais but shorter than Wren, and he had a mean face, nose pinched, and mouth turned down as he stalked towards me and raised a large, plump hand in the air. His palm connected with the side of my face with a crisp slap, but it did nothing to wake me up.

I let the blow throw me to the ground, bracing myself with my hands as I landed on my backside in a pool of sticky caenim blood.

Even then, I didn't move.

I sat there in the muck, tunnelling down into myself, trying to make sense of the choice I'd made. Trying to remember what had felt right about it in the moment when I suddenly felt so empty and broken at the very thought of Wren dying.

The sentry was yelling at me, shouting filthy and horrific slurs as he grabbed my arms and hauled me to my feet.

I barely even heard him. I looked at Wren to make sure he was still okay, just in time to see him shoving the caenim's lifeless body off himself and leaping to his feet without the assistance of his hands. His beautiful face was the picture of absolute fury, and I braced myself as he stormed over to me, ready for another strike, knowing that I probably deserved it.

But Wren didn't hit me, though the action he took still woke me up and brought full light and proper sound back to my awareness.

He ripped the sentry away from me, light flaring on his palms, and punched him in the face. A muffled cry made its way up my throat as the sentry staggered backwards, guilt and incredulity rolling over his features as a trickle of red blood leaked from a cut on his cheekbone.

Wren struck him again, sending him to the ground. Blood gushed out of his nose this time. He became wedged between two dark corpses, but his eyes were glued to Wren's face. He looked like he was about to cry. Wren looked like he wanted to hit him again.

"You lay a hand on her, and I will have your head severed from the rest of your body," Wren snarled.

"But—Your—"

"I am in the perfect mood," he began, with slow and spine-chilling emphasis, "to shatter your jaw..." he continued, cocking his head to the side, "...with my boot." He narrowed his eyes at the sentry on the ground, a vicious challenge glinting in the gold, and then lifted his chin. He appeared to address the entire clearing, his volume increasing to a boom. "Are we *clear*? Do you all understand that touching her is suicide, and speaking about her is treason?"

The sentry didn't speak again. In fact, none of them did. All of them, even their horses, quickly found more interesting things to look at before Wren turned around and stalked towards me, still in an absolute, palpable rage.

Despite the fact that I knew he was talking about me, I felt his warning in the very marrow of my bones and would have cowered if I had the strength. It was as though there was another girl here and I had threatened her.

Maybe he will hit me now.

I tensed, bracing myself for his hands to close around my throat. He would likely be able to snap my neck one-handed.

The blow I was expecting never came. Instead, I was overcome by a completely different but equally shocking sensation as he pulled me into an embrace. Wren held me tightly against his chest, and then there was nothing but wind so intense that I had to close my eyes until...

"Sit down."

I opened my eyes straight into Wren's pectorals. It was the same view I'd had when I first met him, only this time, his shirt was stuck to his skin with blood. He let go of me, and an icy shiver skittered across my skin. Swaying, I lost my balance, and he pushed me back into a cushioned armchair.

We were in a room at the House, identifiable by the similarity it bore to my own bedroom with a four-poster bed and the archway blocked by a gossamer curtain leading into a bathroom. It had to be Wren's bedroom, judging by the mess. Apparently, he treated all of his possessions with disregard, not only the books he kept in the reading nook downstairs.

His bed was unmade, clothes and weapons strewn around the room in no obvious pattern, and his wardrobe doors had been left open.

"Please accept my apologies on behalf of Hanson," he said, peeling off his shirt. It was ripped and torn, which wasn't really surprising considering he had single-handedly cut down almost an entire army of iron-taloned monsters. "I'm working off the assumption that you would be physically unwell if I were to have him killed, but if the apology is insufficient, please say so."

As if.

Wren turned and strode towards the bathroom, tossing the shirt behind the curtain, and I really tried not to stare, but I couldn't help it. He had the most beautiful body I had ever seen. It was almost—but not quite—identical to the one in my dreams.

Broad, strong shoulders and arms corded with thick muscle, the tendons and veins in his hands stretched up his forearm like vines. His abdomen was carved with more precision than a statue, a maze of grooves and ridges sharp enough to break a tooth, and dipped down on an angle over his hips, beneath the waistband of his pants.

He walked back to me, and I thanked the High Mother that he was keeping those on.

Wren was a soldier, a warrior. His perfectly smooth, light-kissed skin was flecked with golden scars, whereas Lucais had sleeves of tattoos down his arms, likely markings relating to his royalty. If it wasn't for the absence of those tattoos on Wren, I could have almost mistaken them. But the High Fae were naturally beautiful and violent, so I imagined they all looked much the same—sculpted to impossible standards. Wren was the most beautiful simply because he was the only one I'd seen so much of in person.

"Are you staring at me because you're concussed or because you're wondering if I'll send you a nude self-portrait if you ask nicely enough?"

"Thank you," I blurted, my gaze snapping to his face. *For reminding me that I don't like you.*

He smirked at me, lowering himself to his knees between my legs. *You're welcome.*

I tried to close the space he was sliding into, but it was too late. I should have sat down with my legs crossed.

"You're going to be the death of me, bookworm," he muttered absently, reaching up to cup my chin. He tilted my head to the side so he could examine my cheek, which was aching but didn't feel significantly damaged. "But that's the hope, isn't it?"

I clenched my jaw and stared at the far wall.

I couldn't believe that I'd been willing to let him die, alleged traitor or not, and I had already promised myself I'd never do something like that again. There was no point in admitting any of it to him, though.

"I'm not working with the Malum," he told me. "But you did well today to refuse me aid."

"What?" I jerked my head back, out of his grip.

"You thought I was the enemy, so you were prepared to let me die," he said, angling his face towards mine. "Your enemies in Faerie will take on many different forms and try many different tactics to force you to yield, so that was good." He reached for my cheek again, but I swatted his hand away, and he growled softly. "Fine. It doesn't look fractured, anyway."

"How do you know that?" I snapped. "About the Malum."

He gave me a wry smile. "I can scent the suspicion on you every time we're in the same room. It started the night you woke up in the cottage, screaming like a newborn faeling."

Rolling my eyes to conceal my horror at being discovered so easily, I leaned back in my seat to create some semblance of distance between us because he was still kneeling between my legs. Somehow, it only made it much worse. "I don't know what you're talking about," I huffed, trying to distract myself.

"Oh, so you just wanted to watch me squirm?" Wren arched a golden eyebrow, his hair windswept across his face. "In that case, tell me, is there anything else you'd like to watch me do?" Without breaking eye contact, he braced his forearms on my thighs and let his hands dangle suggestively between my legs.

Something wicked and made of fire woke up inside of me.

It wasn't magic this time; it was worse. The budding sparks of electricity caressed my nerves, linking to his hands, their proximity, and his every tiny movement, and I frantically reached for the main switch to shut them all down.

If he did touch me in that particular moment, I had no idea what I would do. *How would I react? Would I like it?*

I crossed my arms over my chest because I did not dare move my legs. I was trapped. My scent—my stupid, stupid scent—was going to be my doom in Faerie. The one thing I couldn't control, and he was so close...

Wren's eyes travelled to my folded arms, and then lower.

"You disgust me."

"Your sharp little tongue can lie," he murmured, sliding his arms off my thighs with borderline unwillingness, and the knowing glint in his eyes completed the rest of the sentence. *But the rest of your body cannot.*

I squirmed, lifting one leg, and kicked him in the chest. It was gentle enough to push him away from me, to avert his face from where it was inclined towards a part of my body I was still trying to bring back under my control.

Wren laughed and leaned back on his hands. "Oh, relax. It's not the first time. It happened when I was teaching you to ride my..." He trailed off, a sinful smile taking shape across his full mouth as I forced myself to keep my eyes on his face. "*Horse*," he finished.

And, just like that, I wished that I'd let him become afternoon tea for the caenim.

"Where's Lucais?" I enquired politely, and the scowl that followed the death of Wren's smirk told me he understood why I'd asked.

I was still his High King's mate, bonded or not.

"Everyone went to the field. They're on their way back now."

"How come you found me first?"

"You forget," he started to say, as he climbed to his feet and brushed the dust from his pants. "I spent two days with the salt from your sweat and tears stuffed up my nose. I've become accustomed to you. It didn't take long. Especially not with the trace of your magic lining a path from the disaster in your bathroom to the disaster in that field. Are you seeing a pattern here, Aura?"

Bringing my legs up onto my seat, I curled into a ball and resisted the urge to start rocking back and forth. "I do not want to talk about that."

Yes, I had a pattern. I had a pattern that I was doing everything I could to break.

"You didn't hurt anyone," Wren offered, his tone toeing the edge of gentleness.

I scoffed. "Not this time, at least."

But I had come close to it again if I'd had anything to do with Delia's hair.

Something had escaped from me—like magic, but worse—and it would never, ever happen again. I would not acknowledge it. I would not accept anyone else's acknowledgement of it, either.

Wren's inquisitive stare coaxed my eyes up to meet his, but before I could fabricate a response that wouldn't condemn me, Lucais appeared in the middle of the room in a blur of red and gold.

The High King's wide eyes fell on Wren first, and he said, a little breathlessly, "I really wish you hadn't struck Hanson."

My heart stopped.

I was in trouble.

Of course I'm in trouble; I almost let the High King of Faerie's best friend and right-hand man die. On purpose. Whether or not he was also willing to let it happen is an entirely different matter. There is no apology in the world—

Lucais's eyes settled on my face, and his eyes went wide, as if he didn't realise that I was in there. A soft sigh escaped him, and his shoulders slumped forward. "I would have liked to do it myself," he finished quietly.

For a moment, I stared at him—the High King of Faerie, the man from my dreams.

His clothes were ruffled—a silver-trimmed tunic and black pants—and he carried no weapons. He didn't need them. Lucais radiated warmth, power, and light, and his features held onto absolutely no traces of heartbreak, disappointment, or resentment for what I had said to him and what I had done.

The High King of Faerie had already forgiven me—perhaps never thought I'd needed it to begin with—and, in that moment, something charged between us. Hot, intense, and familiar.

The *bond*.

I could almost feel a tangible connection threading through the air between us.

I know you. I have known you always. I will know you forever. You and I are the same. We are one.

Lucais was not my prisoner.

He was not my High King.

He was my soulmate.

He was a safe place for me to land, to immerse myself in all of my wildest and most frantic dreams. He had a face that would never lay blame for his darkest emotions over me, hands that would never act them out on me, and a voice that would never be used against me. And even if fate had orchestrated it, did that make it any less real? Were we any less worthy if we listened to the stars? If I gave it—the stars, the High King, and even the damned Oracle—a chance?

My heart stuttered, beating to the sound of a thousand lives falling into each other across time and space, and something cracked open in my chest and bled light into the room between us.

Lucais saw the change. Wren probably saw it, too, but I wasn't looking at him. I wasn't looking at anything or anyone other than the dark-haired man in front of me who was offering me everything I had ever wanted in the depthless world of his eyes.

Something like sparks glittered in my peripheral, possibly coming from my fingertips. I flinched, barely—too consumed with the ache to remember the lives our souls had met in before. Lucais saw it happen, though, and he reacted more appropriately.

"Oh, fuck, Aura," he muttered, practically leaping to step towards me. He clasped both of my hands in one of his and lifted the other to brush the hair back from my face.

I was consumed. I'd never had someone look at me the way Lucais looked at me—like I was his sole purpose in life, and the world simply ceased to exist from every other angle.

There was a beat of hesitation, and then he wrapped me in his strong embrace, covering me in the scent of smoke, heat, and sunlight. It was an unusual scent—unfamiliar but fulfilling, as though he truly was the piece of me that I had been missing all my life.

And so maybe that meant I could try.

At best, perhaps I would learn to love my soulmate. At the very least, I could do my best to keep him alive.

I didn't owe him anything. He didn't expect anything. But I had dreamed of him for months, and that had left me with something to offer him. After all, Lucais had waited for me his entire life, and I had done enough damage to enough people already.

"I'm sorry. I'm so sorry," I whispered against his chest.

His hand came up to stroke my hair, fingers threading through it, tightening against my scalp in a possessive way. "Don't you dare apologise. You never apologise."

"I didn't mean it. I take it back. I'll...try."

I heard his heart physically skip a beat, loud and alarming, and he squeezed me a little tighter. "Don't run, Aura. You don't have to run. Say the word, and we'll take you wherever it is you need to go, no questions asked. You don't have to hide from us. We would never—"

Maybe it was a delayed reaction to a near-death experience or a culmination of everything bad that had ever happened to me, but I suddenly felt as close to being in love as I ever had in my life.

And so, I pulled back, looked up at him, and kissed him.

Lucais started, as if my lips had electrified him, and his fingers flexed against my spine. He made a small, tortured sound, and pulled away, the colour in his eyes dancing, sparks flicking off a bonfire. "Aura, you don't have to do that," he whispered.

My heart was absolutely racing, sending my blood tearing through my veins like wildfire. "Let me try."

Lucais nodded slowly and cupped my chin with his hand. Conflict was caught in his eyes, but it vanished in a blink. He tilted my head back towards his with excruciating slowness and parted his feather-soft lips as his mouth met mine again. Heat and light consumed me, fireworks streaking out of my nerves and burning me up from the inside out.

As my mouth opened for him, I couldn't believe what I was doing. I couldn't believe who I was doing it with or the things I quickly began wanting to do next. Lucais's tongue brushed against mine, tasting sweet and smoky, and I sagged against him, his arm fastening around my waist to hold me up. He felt as hard as granite, every last inch of him. Arousal filled the air, flowing out of me in waves, so strong that for once I could actually understand what Wren was talking about...

Wren.

I jumped back, cheeks aflame, and Lucais copied my movements.

But when I scanned the room, heart pounding furiously, I found that we were alone.

Wren was gone.

TWENTY-SIX

One Week

He was gone for seven days.

Twenty-Seven

Two Weeks

Fourteen.

Twenty-Eight

Three Weeks

Twenty-one.

Twenty-Nine

Until My Lungs Were Starving

I was used to being alone in the bookstore back home, but Wren's disappearance rattled me. After he vanished from his own bedroom that day, I didn't see or hear from him again for three weeks. They felt much longer than they should have, and that was partly due to the fact that Lucais also became absent most of the time.

The High King remained at the House in physical form, at least. He was sometimes distant but never unkind.

We dined together in the evening most days, and it quickly stopped feeling so awkward. He made me laugh and then pretended that he wasn't trying to be funny, which made me laugh even more.

We sat in the library together a few times a week, which was a massive room on the third floor that was far grander than the shabby reading nook downstairs. He would flip through something, and I would read another book, and it felt like we had known each other forever. He'd pull my legs onto his lap, and I'd watch his eyes widen while I read the steamy passages from my books out loud to him.

He would stop and talk to me if he was ever passing through a part of the House that I was in, and one time, he sought me out on one of my twice-daily walks around the perimeter of the gardens.

He even took me down to the inlet one afternoon when the sun finally came out again. We lay on the sand between the long grasses, bathing in its warmth together, while he asked me about all the books I'd read and loved, and then he kissed me until my lungs were starving and my lips were swollen, and we both got sand *everywhere*.

He never came to my bedroom, though, and we never specifically mentioned what had transpired between us in Wren's.

He didn't mention Wren at all, actually. No one did, and I didn't ask.

Delia came and went, some days more often than others, and some days not at all. She couldn't tell me what she was doing or where she was the rest of the time, and I could never find her when I went looking. Still, I was grateful for her presence, even if it was inconsistent. It was keeping me sane, reminding me of when Amelia would drop by Dante's Bookstore and disturb the monotony of a long day without customers or deliveries.

I stayed mostly within the boundaries of the House since the slaughter in the clearing, per Lucais's request. He explained that the

House was protected by runes and enchantments, shielding us from outside threats, and told me I would be safe if I remained within the boundary lines while he was unavailable.

He hadn't informed me of any new caenim sightings, but I was confident that the Malum knew my location. I'd stepped out of bounds, beyond the fence line, for a split second once or twice a day every day for the last three weeks—simply in case they needed a reminder of where my scent would lead to and where it would not. I had to do something to ensure that my decision to travel there and remain in the strange House was worth it for my mother and sister, especially when I had no idea what Wren or even Lucais were really doing since the attack.

Delia gave me a healing tonic that cleaned up the mess Lucais's sentry had made of one side of my face, and nobody had spoken of it again. I didn't think the man was allowed anywhere near the House now.

In those three weeks, when I wasn't with Lucais, I spent most of my time searching for clues. Anything to suggest that there might be a dungeon hidden somewhere underground or that Wren might have been involved in other nefarious activities.

I found *nothing*.

The House was back to speaking with me when it felt like it, but it did not help me with my searches. In fact, I had cause to believe that it was deliberately getting in my way. Every door I came upon was suspiciously locked, and every abandoned corridor was left in the dark. It refused to let me move the ladder in the library to different sections so that I could reach the higher shelves that contained most of the non-fiction and historical artefacts, and it often kept me waiting for things like meal trays and hot water in the mornings, which felt like a delay tactic.

In the end, I gave in. The House was an enigma. There was probably no dungeon. Wren was likely out on a bender somewhere, blowing off steam. And Lucais was...

Well, I wasn't sure.

Sometimes, I caught him looking at me in such a way that could very nearly set me on fire. But then he would glance away. I would receive the affectionate brush of a thumb across my cheekbone or a foot massage in the library. Maybe even a kiss like that day on the sand, but it never went any further, even when I showed interest. In fact, he had abruptly left me panting and hot on more than one occasion with no explanation.

I actually felt like he was avoiding me some days, so I didn't tell him about my dreams and my search for the dungeon. Not even the books I was trying to reach in the library on the days he didn't join me there. I didn't say very much at all about it, and to be perfectly honest, neither did he.

Until sometime after my third week in the House, when he knocked on my bedroom door.

THIRTY

A Very Clear Case of Dark Magic

"It all feels so...*forced*. I wish I didn't have to put you through any of this."

Threading my fingers through Lucais's as he guided me through the maze of hallways in the House, I sighed. "The caenim that attacked my mother set us up, really."

His long fingers tensed around mine, sending a shiver of pleasure skittering up my arm. The High King didn't make gestures often, and they were normally casual and cool. This one echoed with a subtle and raw form of possession, though.

I had to admit that I didn't *not* like it.

"The whole point of this was only ever to keep you alive," he replied. "With so many human girls showing up dead, it stopped being about the mating bond and instead became about preventing them from killing humans in pursuit of you. We didn't know who you were, and when we realised, we wanted to protect you. From all of it." The High King paused, mulling over his words. "His methods," he went on, cautiously referring to Wren for the first time in weeks, "would not be my first choice. He's done the best he can, given the situation."

I let go of his hand as we descended the staircase. Lucais was a smidge closer to my height, but he was still so huge that I had to bend my elbow to keep my hand in his. The gesture was odd—it felt comfortable, but I couldn't remember who had taken whose hand first or why.

Wren *had* saved my life.

If anything, that acknowledgment served to turn my intense dislike for him into indifference. He was obviously an important member of the High King's inner circle, and I still didn't have any proof that he was a traitor. Or that he *would* be a traitor. He had disappeared from his own bedroom at some point during my embrace with his High King, which hinted at something, but I couldn't quite put my finger on what.

Lucais was accompanying me to a meeting downstairs. Apparently, if it involved the caenim, it had to involve me, too. When Lucais mentioned to me that Wren was waiting there, I scoffed without thinking it through first.

"Are there sections of the library that are closed off?" I asked to change the subject as he gestured for me to walk ahead through a doorway.

I entered yet another new hall illuminated with candlelight. They kept appearing, though I'd been combing through the place from top to bottom. It was as if the House was moving its halls and doors, like the Forest had changed the position of its trees.

Lucais gave me a strange look. "No," he answered. "Of course not. You're welcome to anything of mine in this House. The library should present no exception. Is there anything in particular you're searching for in there?"

"The Malum," I admitted. I had tried to overcome it myself for long enough. "And the Oracle's prophecy. Anything to help me understand more about the connection between the two, and how that involves me. Wren said—" I broke off, scrunching my nose at the way his name felt on my tongue. "He told me that there were books I could read to brush up on my history, but I can't get to them."

"I'll have some sent to your room," Lucais offered immediately. "There's really not much in terms of the Malum or the Oracle, though. The Malum wish to create a union that will give them equal rights to sit at the High King's table, and the Oracle appears once or twice during every High King or High Queen's reign to spit arbitrary gossip out of a crystal ball."

"Are you saying they want to *marry* into the inner circle?" I clarified, as we strode past some familiar yet entirely out of place glass cases and cabinets. The House was definitely reorganising its doors and hallways.

Bastard thing.

"They have a bride ready and everything," he muttered, shaking his head at the floor. "They were all—I mean, we knew them once. Lived among them, fought beside them. Some were considered close friends. Their bride was a member of my Court before she joined the rebellion and…" He trailed off into an uneasy silence.

"You know her?" I frowned, coming to a stop in the middle of the hall.

"Knew her, yes." Lucais's gaze fell back to the floor. "It's not really her anymore, and even if it was, she's not the intended High Queen. Or even a desired substitute. Not that the real one is under any obligation." He gave me a meaningful look, accompanied by the most breathtakingly handsome smile of which I had ever been the recipient.

Intended High Queen.

Brynn would have a field day.

"They seized the Court of Darkness after the initial proposal was rejected," Lucais continued. "It seems they would prefer to orchestrate a marriage and rule Faerie as equal parts Malum and High Fae, because they still don't fully understand how far removed from us that they've become. However, we would be foolish to assume that they're not well-prepared to try and take it by force."

I raised my eyebrows at my own reflection, visible in the glass cabinet over his shoulder. "Why do they still want me dead when you've already rejected the proposal, and we aren't even… I mean, it's not like…" I took a sharp breath and spat it out. "We're not married."

Lucais gave me a crooked smile and chuckled, running a hand through his dark hair. "Aura, we wouldn't marry. High Fae *don't* marry. We mate." His woodfire eyes were sparkling with faint amusement. "The Malum are offering marriage because there is no mating bond between our kinds, and therefore no other way for their bride to be recognised as High Queen. There can't be a Malum Queen. It goes against the High Mother. So, while they may believe it's their best option to join us again, it's practically an impossibility. It wouldn't make a difference if you accepted the bond, but they don't care."

"I don't understand. Wren said the rebels mated with the Banshees, and that the High Fae in your Court were...canoodling that first night. So, they're all mated?"

Lucais's eyes darkened. "No." He averted his gaze from mine and sighed deeply. "By the Oracle, I'm going to kill him." A pause. "Aura, we can bed whomever we like for pleasure, and we very frequently do. It is reproducing that requires a mated pair because they have been blessed with a bond by the High Mother, signalling genetic compatibility for the creation of strong, healthy faelings."

I felt my cheeks burning, and we shared a heated look before I asked, "How did the rebels manage to mate with the Banshees, then?"

Lucais cleared his throat. "We didn't think it possible until it happened. The rebels were unknowingly harvesting their essence under the misapprehension that it belonged to the Witches, and Banshees are magic drainers. When the process became so intimate, something went terribly wrong. Like a merger between the two. It never should have happened, and what was born of their sins is the furthest thing from a faeling. Some of us believe that it was an intervention of the High Mother to punish them for their faithlessness."

"Okay. So, when Wren said *mate*, he meant—"

"They were fucking each other, Auralie," he said soberly, the warmth in his eyes flaring as he took a step towards me. I stumbled backwards, brushing up against the wall. "And it produced something, almost in the way that it's supposed to when a bonded couple do it with the intention to conceive a faeling."

Mortification swam circles in my head, and I could only nod.

Wren had more or less confirmed their extremely prolonged lifespans with his firsthand recollections of a long-ago war, so it made sense that the fertility myth was true, too—but to restrict procreation to mates when love was a choice, and the bond wasn't?

I wanted to know what Lucais thought about these things, but the conversation felt far too intimate for the middle of a draughty hallway, so he backed up from me, and we continued to walk. His fingers brushed against mine, and I wasn't sure whether it was on purpose or not.

Mercifully, we arrived at our destination only a few moments later.

The double doors to the dining room were closed, and Lucais motioned for me to wait in the hallway as he cracked one door open and slipped inside. He didn't click the door shut behind him, so when a sharp, lilting voice spoke, it filtered out through the gap.

"It's a very clear case of dark magic," she was saying.

"Except it was light magic that killed the Banshee on the road here," Wren countered. His deep voice had adopted a casual tone that was annoyingly burned into my memory. The hairs on my arms rose at the sound of it, the budding start of a shudder knitting around the top of my spine.

"Hmph. *Your* magic."

"Was not."

"Can we—" Lucais interjected, but he was immediately interrupted.

"You expect me to believe that she was being attacked and you were physically able to do *nothing*?" the stranger demanded, scorn ripe in her tone. "Is she even who we think she is?"

Wren's voice turned as cold as death. "She most certainly is, and you will treat her accordingly."

A tinkering laugh. "I heard she rejected it."

"She didn't know what she was saying."

"Seriously—" Lucais tried again.

"She gets nothing until she becomes something," the stranger persisted, a cutting edge to her voice.

"Oh, please." Wren groaned. "You're just jealous."

"And you're completely blinded by loyalty—"

Shoving against the door with my shoulder, I very nearly fell into the room.

Lucais's hands shot out to steady me, and I gave him a grateful smile before turning to face the stranger, who had pissed me off with the tone she was using while talking about me. I didn't care that she was criticising Wren's blind obedience to the High King or that he was defending me because of that obedience. But to say that I was *nothing*...

Astonishment washed over her face and silenced the room.

As I surveyed the beautiful woman standing at the far end of the table, I began to lose my nerve.

If Lucais and Wren were beautiful, the High Fae woman was glorious.

She had long chestnut-brown hair pulled up into a high ponytail, accentuating the sharp definition of her cheekbones. Everything about her was narrow and angular, from her tall figure to her pointed ears and nose, and to the long red nails on her bony fingers, clutching a leather-bound notebook. Wearing a shimmering teal gown of silk chiffon with a neckline that plunged almost down to her navel, she held her head high as if she knew as well as I did at a glance that she could have been the High Queen.

"Auralie," Lucais murmured, taking my hand to bring me around to the other side of the long table. "I'd like you to meet Morgoya."

The ethereal beauty gave me a lazy once over, something wicked and ravenous glinting in her eyes. "I see," she murmured. "I'm sure the pleasure will be mine, Aura. May I call you that?"

Words simply evaded me.

That was the first time any of the High Fae had asked permission to use my nickname. Both Wren and Lucais had simply assumed, and none of them had told me how they knew so much about me. I gathered it was because of the Oracle, but had everyone in Faerie witnessed that premonition?

"Dear little thing," she purred, drinking in my disorientation with her feline, emerald green eyes. "I hope you won't take offence to the things you overheard. I just hadn't laid eyes on you yet."

My gaze darted towards Wren, who was sitting in Lucais's chair at the head of the table, watching me with disdain, before finally settling back on her face. "Does that make a difference?" I asked.

She cocked her head to the side and sniffed the air. "Let's just say it leaves no doubt." A delicate, one-shouldered shrug. "You are his mate."

There was no emphasis, no underlying inference in her tone. She said it like a statement, like it just made perfect sense, and it was that easy for her to accept it.

The echo lingered in the room, clinging to the air around me.

Soulmate soulmate soulmate—

Wren pushed his chair back, obnoxiously scraping it against the floorboards, and sketched a bow for the High King. "I was defending the chair," he explained, giving Morgoya an exaggeratedly suspicious look out of the corner of his eyes.

She sniffed again, decidedly ignoring the fiend. "Indeed," she murmured to no one in particular. But her eyes were locked on me.

Nearly blushing beneath her gaze, I was only partially aware of Lucais taking his seat at the head of the table and Morgoya slipping into hers. It left me hovering beside Wren awkwardly, both of us aware that there was only one seat left directly beside the High King.

Lucais's right-hand man looked inclined to shove me out of the way in order to claim it, but he cleared his throat and announced, "I'll stand."

Faeries and their politics and pride. They behaved as if there were not two dozen other empty seats at the table, which was bare save for a few unlit candelabras and the notebook Morgoya had placed in front of her.

Before I could move or object, the beautiful woman gave me a pointed look, waving a perfectly manicured hand towards the High King. "Why don't you sit on his lap?" she suggested lightly.

My heart skipped a beat—because she was serious.

"Go on," she urged, directing me towards him with her eyes. "It's perfectly acceptable behaviour in our circle, and we're all friends." Her sparkling gaze drifted up, over my shoulder, until it landed on Wren. "Aren't we?"

"I hardly think that's necessary," he replied in a tone that made me wonder if they *were* friends. "Aura's a half-breed. She doesn't know the first thing about the Court or what behaviour to expect or display. It's confusing, and she tends to spook easily."

Wren spoke about me like I was a wild horse needing to be broken, and I bristled, balling my fists at my sides. Lucais gave me a wary look, but he leaned back as if to offer me the choice.

Without so much as a glance in Wren's direction, I brushed past him and settled into the High King's lap.

It didn't feel as uncomfortable as I had thought it would. Everything about the High King's Court was informal, from the lack of respect Wren had shown by sitting in the High King's chair initially, down to their behaviour when they dined in private.

The intimate gesture was no different.

The seat was wide and high-backed with two sturdy wooden arms carved into small waves at their ends, and Lucais filled the space almost completely. My legs dangled over one of his knees, crossed at the ankles, and I folded my hands in my lap, one shoulder pressed into the soft spot between his arm and his chest.

Balancing on an angle, I deliberately faced Morgoya, and Lucais's arm instinctively came up to create a barrier between my spine and the hard edge of the chair. His right arm rested on the other side, hand dangling loosely over the end, and I found myself studying the veins and tendons on his hand and wrist, disappearing beneath his long-sleeved tunic. I matched my breaths to his deep, even breathing, remembering the feeling of his mouth against mine.

"My, my," Morgoya purred, studying us intently. Her nostrils flared delicately. "It is *delicious*. Even when it's all so unofficial."

The High King shifted in his seat, drawing me a little closer as he tightened his arm around me. "Tell me what's happened," he instructed calmly.

Morgoya straightened her spine, all traces of delight leaving her eyes like stormwater rushing down a drain. "There was another attack last week. They're all coming from the Court of Earth, through the eastern passes beneath the Metal Mountains," she began, interlocking her fingers as she placed her hands on the table. "We estimate about one hundred caenim per horde, the most we've ever seen at once. There's been no word from Gregor or his sentries at the Watch, so they're either all dead and he's too busy to respond, or...they're *letting* them through."

"The gateways are intact, running at full power," Wren added redundantly.

I felt, more than heard, Lucais inhale a lengthy breath. "Where?"

"Sthiara was raided again," Morgoya reported quietly. "Minimal structural damage, but that makes seven dead and two still missing. We can't find where they're hiding out. Our scouts picked up traces of the caenim along the road out of town, all the way back to the edge of the Forest along the coast. We're scouting the Ruins now, but there's no indication that they attempted to enter or skirt the Forest." Her eyes flicked to mine and quickly dropped to her hands. "It's pretty clear what they wanted and that they'll keep trying."

I stiffened, and Lucais's thumb brushed against my arm in silent comfort.

"As far as we can tell," she went on, "none of the caenim have gone near the portals, so it's unclear if they'll send any through to Belgrave—"

"But my concern is Caeludor," Wren cut in, bracing his elbows on the table and leaning forward. "If we stay here much longer, they might make a move on the city to provoke us, to draw us out."

Morgoya sat back in her chair, nails clicking on the wood. "It's far more likely they'll come back here if they know Aura is with us and suspect their first army got even half as close as they really did. So, that begs the question, what are you willing to risk?" She maintained eye contact with Wren, though the question was clearly posed at Lucais.

The High King turned his head towards mine, so close that his breath tickled my nose. Even seated on his lap, our faces were barely at equal height. My gaze dropped to his mouth as he murmured, "Caeludor is the City of Light. It's our home."

Blinking through the fog his proximity unleashed in my mind, I looked up into his eyes. "So, obviously, you can't stay here if there's a risk to your home."

"No." Wren's voice was a gentle growl in reply to a question no one had asked him. "We're not going to risk losing two things at once."

"Two things?" I repeated, throwing my head back to peer at him quizzically. His displeasure was even more pronounced upside-down. "What's the second?"

He stared me down, and I challenged him to say it out loud. *You.*

Using his free hand, Lucais tilted my face back to his. "He's right." His eyes roamed over my features indulgently as he tucked my hair behind my ear. "I wouldn't dare. You didn't ask for any of this."

"Neither did you." I spoke without meaning to, without thinking about it.

The High King smiled at me. "Oh, I know." He dropped his hand from my face, but instead of returning to the arm of the chair, his forearm fell across my lap as he turned to Morgoya.

Every muscle in my body tightened and then forcibly relaxed.

"We'll stay here and monitor the situation closely," Lucais decided. "If we return home now, it might prompt an attack on our capital that may not have otherwise happened. Keep at Gregor until you get an answer, and ask Enyd for a meeting as soon as possible. Start making the arrangements. Her Court might be their next target if they're going as far south as the Metal Mountains. We'll warn Caeludor, too, but keep it quiet. We don't need unwanted attention on the city right now."

Morgoya nodded, glancing at Wren. He remained quiet, ever the devoted servant to the High King of Faerie.

His loyalty to Lucais might be preserving my life, but I wasn't foolish enough to trick myself into believing that he was happy about it.

Wren's sullen disposition quite literally tainted the air as their discussions continued—going over the details of hosting company from the Court of Wind and selecting which of the Guard to use for increased patrols on the streets of Caeludor—and I could feel his eyes burning holes as hot as the sun into my back every so often.

I wish things were different.

Different how?

Wishing the Malum weren't trying to stage a hostile takeover of the High King was one thing. That was arguably an obvious thought for everyone in the room.

It felt like more than that—still, three weeks later, it felt like more than that.

As the three members of the inner circle conversed, I mulled over his words.

I'd assumed Wren meant treason, a desire to overthrow the High King and claim the crown for himself, but the land wouldn't allow it. Lucais had confirmed as much when he told me the Malum could never rule, and Wren certainly wasn't the first or even the second most powerful of the High Fae. Maybe the third, at best, after Lucais and Gregor.

How many would he have to kill to claim that title for himself?

What else could he have meant?

Their discussion deepened, and I felt Lucais fall into a familiar state of relaxation. He was at ease in his role, accustomed to discussing the fate of Faerie, and perfectly content with me sitting quietly in his lap while he did so.

His body language created a ripple effect on me. And so, when he leaned forward to tilt his head around me, deep in conversation with Wren about ward security, I found my arm moving from where I had rigidly wedged it between our chests. I snaked it around the back of his neck to allow him more room, casually draping one hand over his shoulder. The motion was so natural that the High King didn't miss a beat, and his thumb began to stroke my thigh.

My focus became fixated on that touch—the absentminded simplicity that spoke in volumes, echoing within my body, and the warmth we shared that I suddenly felt as if I would die without—and I struggled to pretend otherwise, to ignore it.

The woman in front of me didn't even try to ignore it, though. Her gaze locked onto us, and she attempted to conceal a small, satisfied smile—and failed.

"What are we going to do about *her*?" Wren demanded. I hadn't even heard the topic of conversation changing, and again felt those holes of blistering heat scorching my back. "She can't stay with us."

"Is it not safer that way?" the High King countered evenly, his thumb still brushing over my leg. "They'll track Aura by scent. They don't care where *we* are while she's alive."

"No," Morgoya agreed, her gaze following the High King's hand as it slowly travelled further up my thigh until it was nearly against my hip. "But all of this magnifies her scent. If it continues and we leave," she murmured, studying the strong arms around my body before glancing at Wren, "it won't be long before the Malum catch a whiff—not to mention the rest of Faerie. And then we'll have questions I'm not sure we can answer yet."

"I'm sorry," I interrupted a little breathlessly. I wriggled in Lucais's lap, feeling like an insect beneath a microscope, and his palm slid down to my knee. A line of fire burned in its wake, threatening to warm my cheeks, and I hoped they couldn't hear the slight acceleration of my heart. "Scent? Questions?"

Morgoya looked between the men as if asking for permission before she spoke. "High Fae have a heightened sense of smell, and the bond between mates is very potent," she explained. "Think of it like a wedding ring on humans, something to tell others that an individual is spoken for. And with the way things are right now, it's going to be a little stronger than normal until everything settles down."

She had used the word *delicious* to refer to my scent. *Our* scent, entwined as we sat together, emphasised by the *thing* charging between us as Lucais's fingers traced the seam of my pants, down to my calves, back to my knees, and up to my hip.

Lucais didn't know what he was doing. He couldn't have because they were talking about it right in front of us, and his hands were making it worse. His brown eyes were clear as he looked at me, murmuring something about the High King's connection to the land and how intense it can be during certain life events.

But I didn't care if the mating bond stretched over the whole of Faerie and made all of its residents aware of my presence. At that moment, I was more worried about what Wren and Morgoya were about to become aware of as his hand trailed up my leg, silk slipping between our skin as if it was about to fall off, and my body reacted in the only way it knew how.

Lucais noticed it first, saw the panicked tears pricking my eyes as every other part of my body began to melt like ice cream in full sun as a thrumming and lightheaded tension began to build in my core, and his hand froze on my leg.

"Leave the room," he commanded quietly, and Morgoya immediately rose to her feet. Lucais didn't take his eyes from my face, but I could only assume he spoke directly to Wren as he added, his voice a quiet snarl, "Now. We'll discuss this later."

THIRTY-ONE

Yes... Please

If Wren protested, I didn't hear it. If he left the room, I didn't see it.

There was a whisper of movement, the swish of Morgoya's gown and clink of heels against the floor, and the echo of the doors as they closed.

Then my heart, pounding in my chest like a war drum, as I watched Lucais's eyes slide down my neck, over the buttons of my shirt, to where the ends of my hair were sitting in tangled curls over my chest. The silence was tense, like the strain of a match scraping against the side of the box, only moments away from catching ablaze. I could feel the hairs on my arms beginning to raise, rough against my silk sleeves, and the heat growing between my hips, resistant to my thighs pressing together to squash it.

I cursed the House, cursed the absence of underwear, cursed the whole of Faerie, and yet I remained in Lucais's lap. I was too scared to stay but far too curious to leave.

With deliberate, steady leisure, he brushed my hair over my shoulder with the backs of his hands. The curls dragged over my breasts with featherlight pressure—only enough to send a small wave of dull, aching pleasure rolling out across my body—but it was his eyes, his focus on the shape of my nipples poking through the white silk as hard as stone, and the dark satisfaction in his gaze that undid me.

I bit back a small whimper, half desire and half desperation, as his throat bobbed, and he looked up at me again.

Lucais dragged a hand down his face and held it up between us, studying it as if it belonged to someone else. "If my hands ever go anywhere you don't want them to," he said, voice low and thick, "then you have my absolute permission to slap me."

Pressing my lips together, I shook my head and writhed in his lap, trying to avoid the inevitable as I felt the wetness pooling between my thighs. The mating bond was stretched between us, taut and ready to snap, but it was also as thick as a cloud of heady smoke, drawing me towards him like I was suffocating, and he was the only source of air.

"What do you need, Aura?" he pressed, keeping his hands still. "Would you like to leave?"

I shook my head again because I didn't know. Every part of my body was suddenly aching with borderline ecstatic tension, electrified by Lucais's proximity, and his hands hadn't been nearly as close or rough or greedy as some unruly and absolutely shameful part of me wanted them to be.

"Why will it be stronger?" I breathed, inhaling the scent of a bonfire so realistic that I could have been choked by it. His throat worked, and I could see the blood pounding through his veins, the barely restrained tightness in his neck as he bent to rest his forehead against mine. My eyes shuttered, trying to contain the explosion of lust-induced fog in my head. "What has to...settle?"

I knew very well that *I* had to settle down, for starters, but I didn't seem able to do that, so I was hoping for another option. An off switch. Or maybe a really strong and off-putting cologne. Absentmindedly, I wondered if Faerie had anything equivalent to a skunk, and if Lucais would agree to being drenched in its scent for a while—just until I got my thoughts under control again.

"Maybe some space would be best for us," he whispered, even as his hand slid up to cradle the side of my face, and he traced the length of my cheekbone with his nose.

"Haven't you had enough space?" I asked boldly. I couldn't stop myself.

He made a strangled noise, half-sigh and half-moan. "I haven't been thinking. I'm not thinking clearly. You really don't have to feel obligated to—to respond."

High Mother spare me. I was going to spontaneously combust.

I touched the tip of my nose to his, the softest caress, and inhaled another unwieldy dose of him. His lips were so close to mine that I could almost taste them again, and I knew I wanted to—hadn't I already decided that I wanted to?—but I was caught in a whirlpool, flailing halfway between fate and reality.

Don't do it don't do it don't do it—

I brushed my mouth against his, a magnetic force tugging us together, and felt the warmth of his lips spilling out across my entire body like a dam bursting in the summer. The ache between my hips throbbed, a contraction of building pressure desperately begging to be released as his lips parted to let me inside, and his tongue stroked mine with slow, deliberate hesitation.

Each part of the kiss was prolonged, giving us both time to change our minds or commit the taste to memory. Lucais's tongue lazily caressed the edge of my teeth, the roof of my mouth, twirling around mine in the steps of a perfectly rehearsed dance. Every stroke had me weakening, heating up, and dripping.

Tentatively, I explored the sharp point of his elongated canines with my tongue, and a shudder came over me as he angled his head to allow me deeper into his mouth.

Hands fisting in my hair, he pulled me in tighter until I was straddling his lap, and the arm he wrapped around my waist brushed against my bare skin as the silk slipped and slid over my body. My breasts felt heavy and full, and when he bit my lower lip and dragged his teeth across it with a soft and breathless moan, a stab of impatient pleasure tightened my nipples.

I braced my hands against the flat surface of the wooden chair so I wouldn't totally collapse onto him and rocked my hips against his lap, against the part of his body that had hardened like stone and began pulsing underneath me.

Lucais pulled back, panting, and gazed at me with heavy, half-lidded eyes. "Aura," he crooned, the slightest hint of warning in his voice. For both of us.

This is not supposed to happen.

The High King had commanded the others to leave the room in order to give me space to clear my head, not for whatever I was on the brink of doing now that we were alone.

Nerves throbbing, my mind one thought away from madness, I rested my hands on his shoulders as I arched my back and tilted my face up towards the ceiling, taking a gasp of fresh air from above. I just needed to *breathe*...

Lucais groaned as if he was in pain, and I looked down to find his eyes locked on my breasts again, the peaks of my nipples at eye level. "You're going to have to slap me in a minute," he said roughly, without moving his gaze.

"I'm not going to slap you," I whispered, because it was true.

His eyes darkened until they were nearly black as he tested my word, holding my gaze a prisoner of his own as his hands trailed up my thighs and over my hips. The silk between us felt like sandpaper as his fingers moved over my stomach, every touch a little more than the last until they were curved beneath my breasts.

He finally glanced down, his admiration like a physical caress, and I gasped quietly as Lucais brushed his thumbs over my nipples, watching my reaction with intense interest. A small moan reverberated in the back of my throat as my hips moved again, grinding the overstimulated bundle of nerves at my centre against his erection. The sensation spread like wildfire throughout my body, and the low ache between my legs demanded *more*.

Lucais released a breath that sounded like a growl and plucked the first button on my shirt open with a single hand, and then the next, until my upper body was completely exposed to him, the shirt hanging loosely at my sides. Eyes glazing over with heated desire, he rubbed his jaw and swore under his breath, and then threw his head back, hard, into the high-backed chair.

God, I was sweating. I couldn't feel it, couldn't smell it, but I was so sure that I was sweating. It was so hot; I was burning up from the inside out.

The High King watched me, taking the view of my body in like an ocean sunset from a famed tourist vantage point, his eyes devouring me, his pulse quickening. I was so exposed, so vulnerable, but I felt so, so...

Safe.

Looking up at me from beneath dark lashes, his eyes sought my permission, which he was unequivocally granted.

Gently, he took one of my exposed nipples between his thumb and forefinger and pinched it, causing me to drive my hips against him in response. His fingers tightened, pulling and twisting harder each time, and then he bent his head forward, capturing my other side between his teeth, his breath scalding against my breast.

I gripped the back of his head with one hand, holding his face to my chest as he indulgently nipped and licked at me, threading my fingers through his dark curls. His tongue was so hot that it nearly burned as he stroked me with it, until his hand and mouth fell into a greedy rhythm that dragged shallow, sharp moans from the depths of my lungs.

Heat bloomed in my core, a tense and expectant desire tightening my lower belly, and I began to move against him in earnest, trying to ease the build up of pressure between my legs.

Lucais dropped his hand from my breast and wrapped it around my waist, rising from the chair in one fluid motion and pinning me down on the long table, his other hand laid flat against the wood beside my head. His mouth released me with one final, sharp tug of his teeth, accompanied by what could only be described as a hollow growl. He pulled back far enough to gauge my expression as his hand explored my body, travelling lower and lower until I could feel the heat of his palm right over my throbbing centre.

I trembled beneath him, breathing unsteadily as he cocked his head to the side and asked, "How would you feel if I touched you down here, Aura? Do you want me to?"

I couldn't speak. I could only nod.

Lucais didn't wait a second longer before he slid his hand beneath the waistband of my pants. His fingertips immediately slipped against my skin, hot and wet, and found their way to my clit, which he began to explore with demanding circular movements that sent pulses of pure bliss out across my body.

He bent his forehead to mine and groaned, the sound deep and raspy. "*Fuck.* You're this wet for me?" He sounded like he couldn't believe it.

"You would have realised sooner—" I gasped, writhing against the table as his fingers dipped further down into the arousal pooling at my entrance. "If you'd stayed a little longer after kissing me these last few weeks."

"Hmm," he murmured, trailing his lips and tongue down the column of my throat and back. "Let me make it up to you." He kissed me deeply while his hand gradually moved lower. "Do you want me inside of you, Aura?" he asked against the corner of my mouth. "Be a good girl and say *please* for me."

I could feel his fingertips barely there, almost within reach, and a flare of pleasure shot out to meet them. "Yes," I breathed, bucking my hips against his hand. "*Please.*"

Lucais slipped two fingers inside of me, an expectant and ecstatic smile on his face, and I gasped in shock at the sudden fullness, rising from the table until I was halfway to sitting. His mouth found mine, and I held onto him with my arms around the back of his neck as he moved his fingers in and out, finding the perfect spot to touch, repeatedly, so deep inside me that his palm massaged my swollen ball of nerves. Each stroke of his hand and brush of his tongue felt like he was adding kindling to a fire that would eventually cause an explosion within me.

He moved his lips to my ear. "I want to taste you," he said. "I love the way you smell right now, all hot and bothered and soaking with need, and I am fucking *dying* to know how you taste. Will you let me?"

Let him? I was practically begging for it. "Anything," I answered, the word catching on a moan as he curled his fingers.

Carefully, he lowered me back onto the table until I was lying flat. I watched as he removed my pants, caught the nearly feral glimmer in his eyes as he appraised my body, stripped bare before him.

He bent to kiss me. My mouth first, where our tongues tangled and our teeth clashed, and then he made his way down my body, licking and suckling, his hands sliding along my sides as he lowered himself to one knee. His lips brushed my hip bone, his tongue caressed my inner thigh, and then Lucais grinned up at me wickedly as he spread my legs with his hands...

And buried his face between them.

We both moaned at the contact, and the vibrations of his sent an almost intolerable wave of pleasure skating through me. It was so intense that it bordered on pain.

His mouth was a welcome warmth as his tongue lapped up my arousal, sliding inside of me in long, languid motions and then circling my clit. After a few moments, he placed his hands on my hips, threw my legs over his shoulders, and tugged me further down the table as if he couldn't get enough, couldn't get close enough.

All I could see was the top of his head, black curls against dark skin against my body, and his large, strong hands gripping my thighs as his arms wrapped around from underneath and held me up to his face. The chair towered over us behind him—the same dark wood as the table beneath me—and I averted my eyes, idly blinking up at the rafters on the ceiling high above us as a destructive wave of pleasure built and built, threatening to utterly destroy me.

He heard my whimper and groaned in reply, a delicious sound that pushed me to the crest, and he rose to his feet, taking me with him, his face crushed against me. I shuddered, trying to hold back a scream as I came against his mouth so hard that I saw stars in my mind.

When I opened my eyes, I found him watching me, an atrociously self-satisfied smile in his own. And that look alone sent me over the edge again—or for longer, I wasn't sure.

Lucais waited until I had stopped writhing and twitching before he softly lowered me back to the table, where the cold wood bit at my bare skin. My legs were shaking violently, and he smoothed his hands over them, tracing circles with his thumbs.

"You are the most perfect, exquisite thing," he told me, and then a dazed look passed over his eyes. "Fuck. I'm never going to be able to sit here and want to eat anything else again." He frowned as if he had only just realised that he had pinned me down on the dining table. I must have paled or ceased shaking, because his expression softened. "Aura?"

We *were* on the dining table, and neither of us cared.

It wasn't supposed to be that easy—to want him in such a way, a man I barely knew. I could've sworn the stars were laughing in my face.

"If we do this," I whispered, glancing at the very obvious and borderline intimidating size of his erection, "will it help? The bond, the scent—"

"Oh, for the High Mother's sake, Aura. No." Lucais's eyes lightened, drilling into mine with sudden clarity. "You're not doing this for *that*—" He broke off and muttered a filthy curse, shaking his head as he took his hands off me and ran them through his hair. "There is nothing you can do about this. I'm sorry if we made you believe otherwise."

The heat fizzled out across my skin, and I gaped at him, momentarily lost for words. I reached for my shirt, pulling it closed around me, but the buttons were magically done up before my shaking fingers could find them. And then my pants were back on.

"I'm not—I'm not *whoring* myself out to the High King to try to save Faerie from another war," I stammered, and I was amazed at how hard my voice was when the rest of my body felt like jelly.

His eyes narrowed. "No, that's not what I meant. The timing is just..." He trailed off with a sigh.

"Time and place, right?" I snapped, scrambling to climb down from the table, fumbling for the sense of control that had been teased, taken, and thrown back at me. "You couldn't have thought about that sooner?"

I recognised the look on his face.

Not quite embarrassment or regret, but—guilt. As if paying our debt to the stars went against some kind of moral instinct. As if we shouldn't have acknowledged the debt in the first place.

I certainly shouldn't have. God, I didn't have to sleep with him to try to save his life.

I still hadn't decided if it was worth saving, for crying out loud.

The High King could lie, and he might still turn a blind eye to the brutal torture of prisoners. For all I knew, that's why the Oracle predicted it would happen to him in the future. Revenge! Did he have enemies? I didn't know. I didn't even know if he had any friends. I had questions—lots and lots of good, reasonable questions—that I hadn't bothered to ask before I jumped into his lap and started purring beneath his touch like a cat. A sudden and intense wave of heat engulfed me from my head down to my toes, and I felt sick.

Mere moments before, I had been completely naked in front of him and had allowed him to possess my body so completely that it qualified as a religious experience, but he hadn't removed a single item of his own clothing. Hadn't shown me even a strip of his own skin.

I'd let my guard down, and the High King's inner circle had started taking me apart piece by piece.

"Auralie," Lucais called as I turned on my heels and stormed towards the doors. Tears burned behind my eyes. "Auralie, wait."

Lucais was not my High King, so I ignored him and slammed the door behind me as I left the room and started my indignant march down the corridor.

I made it all of five steps.

"I see you finally decided to listen to me," a dark voice purred from behind me.

Wren.

THIRTY-TWO

Fooled Me Twice

There is truly nothing sacred left in Faerie, I realised as I came to an abrupt halt and slowly pivoted to face the golden-eyed fiend.

Arms crossed over his chest, he was leaning against the wall beside the double doors of the dining room, an arrogant smile on his face.

He's been here the whole time. Of course he's been here the whole time.

I swallowed hard. "I don't know what you mean."

He cocked an eyebrow and let his arms fall to his sides, hands sliding into his pockets. "Power," he said, pushing off the wall. "What good is magic when you can use your body to get what you want instead, yes?"

Bile rose up my throat in defiance at the vulgar insinuation, but I held it back and willed the flames licking my cheeks to die down. "I hardly think I can be blamed for the sins of the stars," I replied, lifting my chin slightly.

Wren gave me an appraising look. "How much of the book have you actually read?"

"Enough."

Nineteen chapters, to be exact.

But he didn't need to know that.

Micael's older brother had just discovered him with Livia in the barn, and he spent the next few pages trying to persuade him to leave her instead of telling their parents. The angle he chose to take was the question of what would happen when Micael eventually met his mate.

"The bond is predetermined by fate, and it's pretty clear that the author relates that to the stars," I went on, willing my voice to remain casual and businesslike. Wren was no ordinary customer in Dante's Bookstore, though. "And the stars are wrong for denying them, but that's what happens, isn't it? They are forced apart—not by his family, but by his true mate."

Wren's expression gave nothing away. "Keep reading," was all he said.

"You can't blame me for this," I answered sharply. "I saw the way you looked at me in there. I can see the way you're looking at me now."

Amusement cooled the fire in his eyes, and he took a step towards me. I refused to back down. Wren was a puzzle I was on the brink of solving, and that step forward—that possessive, territorial look in his eyes—might very well be the last piece.

The post-orgasm clarity from his High King might have been a factor, too.

"I thought it was the Malum at first," I admitted, sending signal after signal to the muscles in my body to hold steady as he took another slow, predatory step forward. "There was guilt written all over your face when you told me what happened to them. I'm familiar enough with it to know. I figure that since you knew them, maybe one or two of them were even your lovers, and perhaps that made you loyal to them. But it's not the Malum. It's me."

Wren paused a foot away from me, golden eyes flaring with interest.

"You knew who I was as soon as you saw me, didn't you?" I questioned softly, biting down on the fear in my voice. "That's why you told John that you didn't want to take me with you. That's why you made it clear to me that I am a half-breed, and stupid, and slow, and all of the other cruel things you've said and thought about me."

He rolled his shoulders back, cracking his neck, but kept his cards close to his chest as I picked them out one by one until I found the ace of spades.

"Your loyalty *is* with the crown, and you *can't stand* it," I whispered, "that a half-breed human is your intended High Queen." Something like bravery flowed through my limbs, and I used it to take a calculated step towards him until we were as close as we'd ever been. "How *different* do you wish it was, Wren? You said you don't want to take me home, though you keep offering in the hopes that I'll agree. That was a faerie lie, wasn't it? You don't actually want to be around me for that long, but you wish that I was gone. You kept a loophole open for me so I could change my mind. But you know I won't. So, you tell me. Would you rather that I was dead, or would it be easier for you if I had never been born in the first place?"

Eyes of firelight stared down at me, and he parted his lips, exposing his flesh-shredding canines as he ran his tongue along the edge of his teeth. A soft growl rumbled in his chest, and he said, "It would be easier for me if you were never born."

Truth.

Every word echoed with truth. He didn't even try to work his words around it.

The final piece clicked into place, and I felt my courage abandoning me as it did. A cold, empty feeling of loneliness took up its position.

I had finally figured it out.

He was going to let himself die in that clearing—not out of guilt, but because he knew the repercussions of my actions would have been much worse than the slap I received from the sentry. *That* was why he saved me each time. He also knew the consequences that I would face for his death would be no less than what he would receive for letting me, the High King's mate, die.

Wren defended me only in the presence of the High King and played nice when there were eyes on us, but he glamoured me in Sthiara so the townsfolk wouldn't know I was there. Because he didn't intend for me to stay. He tried to bully me into leaving, and then he attempted to convince me by pretending that he understood. Finally, after the army of caenim lay dead in that field, he even tried his luck at trying to seduce me away.

"Now, you tell me," Wren growled softly, eyes of molten gold roaming over my face. "Do you want to go home yet, Auralie? You haven't gotten what you followed me here for, but does it really matter *which* High Fae man finally gives it to you? I can still smell your arousal mixed with the come all over the slit between your legs. If I fill it for you, will you be happy? You're mad at him. So, if I fuck you until you forget and send you home dripping with me for the next *six months*, will you be satisfied? What will it *take* for me to be *rid* of you?"

Fury like nothing I had ever felt before filled me to the point of overflowing, but I sensed the darkness before it erupted, and this time, I held it at bay. Even for Wren, I wouldn't let it consume me again. Not even after that.

Taking a step back, I flexed my fingers, letting the motion send a bolt of self-awareness charge through my veins. I would not let it consume me—would not let it *become* me.

"The next time you throw me a blade," I said with lethal calm, my voice steady against a growing wave of devastation, "you'd do well to think twice."

He laughed bitterly. "The next time I throw a blade at you, bookworm, I don't intend to miss."

There was no one else around to hear the threat. Even the House had gone quiet again, the lights lowering to a dim flicker.

Lucais had probably evanesced from the dining room as soon as I slammed the door, and the only other people I had seen around were Delia and Morgoya. The former was forcibly silenced, and the latter was probably as displeased about the Oracle's predictions for her High Queen as the man standing in front of me, who was visibly shaking with each violent breath.

We stared at each other for a few moments longer until the rage simmered down into a mild shade of hatred, reflected in the soft golden tones taking over the wildfire in his gaze.

There was no way for us to be freed from each other. That was the unspoken truth that hovered between us, bouncing back and forth between our locked eyes.

He was the High King's best friend, and I was the intended High Queen.

And we hated each other. We really, truly hated each other.

He fooled me twice, and I would never forgive him.

Wren turned away before I did, prowling down the hall to the east wing, rattling the glass cabinet doors with each heavy step. I didn't breathe until he had disappeared from my sight, until the burn marks from his eyes had healed over on my skin.

And then I walked back to my bedroom, far too proud to fall apart in the halls, and asked the House to lock my door and leave me alone as I climbed into bed and let the tears soak into the pillowcase beneath my head.

THIRTY-THREE

Morgoya

Morgoya joined me for breakfast the following day, wearing a lime green dress that was far too bright and sparkly for first thing in the morning.

I fretted that she would wrinkle it when she sat down on the end of my bed, but she waved me away and adjusted her skirts as I scrubbed the sleep from my eyes. She hadn't said anything about what had transpired between myself and either of the men in the House, but she had a knowing and sympathetic look in her eyes as she extended a tall glass mug of coffee topped with whipped cream, strawberries, and chocolate sauce to me.

It was a peace offering, as though she had been a fly on the wall during my disastrous encounters with the men in the House last night—or perhaps the arrogant High Fae bastards had also likened her to a whore at one point or another, so the look in my red-rimmed eyes was familiar.

Delia wheeled in a small silver cart about ten minutes later with two breakfast trays instead of one. She was in on the apology tour, too, though why either of the women should feel obliged to take responsibility for the behaviour of the men was beyond my comprehension. Her hair was still black, which unnerved me, but I tried not to think about it because it seemed that no one else—not even Delia herself—was concerned.

"Is it rude for me to ask what happened to her?" I asked at last, after Delia had bowed her head to us in goodbye and disappeared through the door into the hallway.

Morgoya's mouth quirked to the side. "Happened to her? You mean the stitches?"

I nodded, taking a bite of generously buttered toast.

"They didn't tell you," she realised, rolling her eyes towards the ceiling. "Delia is a Secret-Keeper, one of the more curious of our kind. She traded her voice to the High Mother in exchange for answers to all of life's greatest questions."

Frowning, I took another bite of toast and chewed thoughtfully. "You mean she consented to the stitches?"

Morgoya looked a little insulted, but she smiled at me and replied, "Of course. Wren and Lucais might behave like beasts around you, but we're not barbarians."

So she did know.

I decided that I wouldn't ask how and instead steered the conversation back to Delia. "What's the Secret-Keepers, exactly?"

My companion took a deep, considerate breath. "Well, the High Fae date back to the dawn of time, when the High Mother granted the original-blessed the gift of magic. Everyone from that era is worm food nowadays, but our history claims that the Temple of All is the last remaining relic." Her emerald green eyes drifted towards the window wistfully. "Legend says that if you go there, pure of heart and sound of mind, and ask the High Mother to share her knowledge with you, she will. But, in return, you must leave your voice in the Temple and sew your mouth closed with iron-thread to ensure that you keep the secrets of creation to yourself."

I couldn't prevent the grimace that warped the features on my face at the very thought. Iron was toxic to faeries. Painful.

"We can't have the knowledge of the universe landing in the wrong hands," Morgoya explained, noticing my expression. "The iron-thread ensures that, even if magic is used to somehow give the Secret-Keeper a voice again, they won't be able to use it."

"So why offer the secrets at all, if it's so risky?" I asked, reaching for a moon-shaped slice of juicy orange fruit.

Morgoya shrugged delicately. "Faith, I suppose. The world simply cannot sustain every being knowing every detail because that would starve it of passion. Still, people like Delia are a symbol. They prove that there *are* answers to our questions, even if we aren't supposed to know what they are. The Secret-Keepers are, in a sense, the wick allowing the candle to burn."

"Couldn't she just write it all down?"

She arched a perfectly curved eyebrow at me. "Haven't you noticed her hands?"

I shook my head.

"They break their fingers and seal the damage with an enchantment," she murmured, tilting her face towards her breakfast tray. "I'm not doing a great job of convincing you that we aren't barbaric, am I?"

Delia's hands.

If I was honest, I hadn't actually paid attention to her fingers. When she had carried the bucket into my room the morning that she had manually filled the marble tub, she kept one palm flat against the bottom and one obscured from my view on the other side. Ever since then, I'd been too preoccupied to notice any of those details.

Shuddering, I tried to offer Morgoya a placid smile, but something wet and cold was curling up in the bottom of my stomach. "Do you think it's worth it?"

"To me?" Morgoya's catlike eyes widened, long lashes fluttering. "No. To others? Every Secret-Keeper I've ever met has gone back to their normal lives, and they don't seem disappointed."

"Would she know about the Malum? Is that the sort of thing you can ask?"

Morgoya shook her head. "Delia hasn't gone back to the Temple since her initial visit long ago. Some do return. So, theoretically, there could be someone out there who knows the ultimate fate of the Malum. I doubt it, though."

For a fleeting moment, I actually entertained the thought. I considered what it would be like to give my voice up in order to receive answers, and if it might even be worth it, simply to avoid having to deal with Wren while I searched for them the old-fashioned way.

I had not seen or heard from him or the High King of Faerie since our humiliating confrontations. The lingering traces of anger still itched in my veins, but it was a small comfort to discover that they were not responsible for the stitches on Delia's mouth.

"Well." I sighed. "At least she did it to herself. On purpose."

Morgoya chuckled, the sound deep and throaty. "You really thought it was one of us?"

"Wren, actually," I confessed. "He used her as part of some sick joke when he chose her to send up here to be my maid."

Her laughter quieted. "Delia's the only maid in the House."

"Yeah," I scoffed. "Because he scared all the other maids away."

This time, her laugh was loud and genuine. "Oh, darling. That man is all bark and no bite."

Somehow, I doubted that, although I appreciated the comparison to a dog. And not just any dog, either. In my mind, he was a flea-ridden mongrel with a penchant for snapping at people who tried to feed him.

I hope he starves to death.

"You better wipe that look off your face before he sees you again," she warned playfully. "You might hurt his feelings."

Wren didn't have feelings, but that wasn't what gave me pause as I threw my legs over the side of the bed and made to stand up. "How do Secret-Keepers eat and drink?" I asked her.

Morgoya gave me a contemplative look. "We don't really need to eat or drink, darling. Not if our magic is intact and thriving. We do so for pleasure. Most of the things the High Fae do, we do for pleasure."

So, Wren is a masochist.

"Figures," I muttered, striding over to the wardrobe.

All of the clothes provided by the House looked to me like pyjamas, so I wore them to bed every night and changed into a new set each morning. Dresses still dangled inside the wardrobe, pushed to the very end of the rack, and I quickly flicked through the varying shades of silk and velvet shirts.

"Wear a dress," Morgoya suggested. "He likes the colour gold."

I whirled on her, taken aback by the absurdity of the suggestion. "Wren?"

"No." She smiled down at her tray, picking through a bowl of berries. "Lucais."

I'd never seen him wear anything gold except for a jewel encrusted on the hilt of his dagger the first day we met, but Wren had golden eyes. Perhaps that was why Lucais continued to tolerate him—for his pretty eyes.

"I'm afraid that a dress might hinder my ability to run for my life," I murmured derisively, eyeing off a sheer black gown at the end of the rack. "Or, High Mother forbid, give someone the wrong impression."

"I'll try not to be offended," Morgoya said with a laugh. "You would do well to follow my lead. They mean no harm."

Crossing my arms over my waist, I turned around again. "Why are you defending them?" I snapped. "You obviously know what happened. They were probably bragging about it to each other last night. Comparing notes on my—on my *scent*."

"Aura." Her beautiful and slim face widened as her cheeks rolled up around a sympathetic smile. "I can promise you that is not what happened."

I glanced at the floor, shrugging half-heartedly as I considered how easily the High Fae could deceive me. "So, tell me what happened."

Morgoya shifted, folding her manicured hands in her lap, and relaxed her expression into something of calculated calm. "Essentially, they stormed off into their respective quarters and were both brooding when I showed up to ask why neither of them were at dinner. It quickly became clear as to why *you* weren't. If you can't already tell," she went on, glancing over her shoulder, "the High King in particular regrets his words dreadfully."

Indeed, I followed her gaze to find that the light sky had been swallowed up by a melancholy grey. It was faint, as if the rays of colour had been washed out, and reminded me of an overcast morning in the human world, though there were no clouds at all this time.

"The High King's Hand regrets his words, too," she added softly.

I stared at the light grey sky until my eyes began to water. "Hand?"

Morgoya let out a disgruntled sigh. "Honestly, I'm not surprised you're upset with them. They overlooked formal introductions completely. The proper title for the High King's right-hand man is the Hand—of the King, to the King; it varies between Courts—and I am the High Lady of the Court of Light."

"You are?" My nose screwed up. "But Lucais is the High King—"

"Of Faerie," she cut in with a wry smile. "Someone has to tend to local politics while he manages the weather."

I almost laughed, but there was still an awful pit in my stomach, writhing and stretching and seething. "Do you have an issue with my title, too?" I asked her instead, though the assumption that I even had a title made the sickness in my stomach rise up.

"It's not at all what you think," she told me, smoothing down her skirts as she rose to her feet. "But it's a story for another time. We have a meeting to continue downstairs, and this time, *I'll* sit in his lap."

That dragged a laugh out of my mouth; it was a small, feeble sound, but it tickled my throat and loosened the debris left behind after the words I'd exchanged with Wren had triggered such an emotional explosion.

It wasn't long at all before a strange bitterness took its place, provoked by the thought of anyone else sitting in Lucais's lap. I refused the drop of jealousy—very nearly spat it out onto the floor of the wardrobe—and resumed picking through the velvet clothes. There was no way I'd risk wearing silk again.

"Wear a dress," Morgoya repeated, sliding a hand through my hair as she sauntered towards the doors. Her voice had a little more command in it this time. "I'll be in the hallway."

THIRTY-FOUR

A Lesson in Self-Defence, Not Torture

There were two gold dresses in the wardrobe.

It was the only colour available in more than one style, and I chose the paler one. A lightweight rayon with a mid-length, flowing skirt, billowing sleeves, and a respectfully plunging neckline with small buttons down to its empire waist. The colour of my hair brought out the white undertones of the faintly floral pattern, making it an easy yellow rather than pure gold.

I didn't care what Wren thought. I didn't even care what Morgoya thought as she gave me an evaluating stare when I walked out of the bedroom and commented that I looked lovely as we made our way back into that infernal dining room downstairs.

The House was quiet again, in the sense of both the enchantment and the quite literally vacant halls. Candlelight flickered against the walls as we walked, compensating for the gloomy natural light filtering in through the largely spaced windows.

I always felt as if I was being watched, but the persistent emptiness that had fallen over the House since my arrival was really starting to bother me.

"Where is everyone?"

"They've been instructed to make themselves scarce while you settle in," Morgoya replied. "The High King didn't want to spook you, and both Wren and I agreed. You'll meet them tomorrow night."

Spooked—again, like I was a wild horse or a feral cat. I decided against offering commentary on that particular description of my unstable opinion on Faerie.

The bastard brothers were waiting for us, but the seats at the long dining table were empty, and the wood was as bare as it had been the previous day. I straightened my spine against a shudder as the memories touched me like a lover's caress—with the tip of a knife in hand.

Instead, the High King and his Hand were sitting in the reading nook, the former occupying the two-seater couch and the latter sprawled out across a small chaise lounge on the other side of the coffee table. Wren's hands were tucked behind his head, and a book was lying open across his face.

"Straight to business today, please," Morgoya said as she settled into one of the armchairs between them.

Refusing to meet Lucais's guilt-stricken gaze, I took the other armchair and completed the square. The High King didn't look at all affected by my choice of clothing in one way or another. There was only a pleading softness in his eyes as they searched my face for signs of forgiveness.

"We will be hosting the Court of Wind tomorrow night," Morgoya declared. "Arrangements are already underway, and my spies have confirmed that the High Lord of the Court of Earth is indeed alive and well. The Watch is operational, but there are no signs of the caenim near the inland borders."

The book slid off Wren's face and landed on the ground with a thump.

Very slowly, he raised himself to sit, blinking sleepily as if the commencement of the meeting had woken him up from a nap. His neutral gaze fell on me as he made to shuffle around to face the High Lady. Before the turn was complete, his head snapped back towards me, an expression of utter surprise on his face.

I have stopped listening to you, and I do not care, I thought.

Wren gave Morgoya a withering glare and said to the High King, "We consider Gregor a lost cause, then."

"It's a shame," Lucais murmured, leaning back in his seat. "We should keep trying to make contact, but the situation is precarious. The Guard will remain at the border, exercising an increased amount of vigilance, but no one should cross over into his Court. Not until we know for sure what might await us."

"All going well tomorrow night, we may be able to remain here to conduct our business until the Malum send their next message—whether that be another proposal or another army." Morgoya clicked her tongue. "It's not safe to bring Aura into Caeludor yet."

"It's not safe to leave her here either," Wren muttered.

"We've been over this." Lucais's voice was weary. "Nobody is *leaving* Auralie anywhere."

"Fine." Wren exhaled in a long-suffering sigh and ran a hand through his blond, sleep-tousled hair.

"I do agree, though," the High King continued quietly. "It's not safe anywhere, and we can't pull any more of the Guard from the city without leaving it vulnerable."

"What do you suggest?" Morgoya questioned.

The High King looked at me, deep-rooted sorrow in his eyes, and the ghostly presence of magic lunged for me in response. For the first time in *weeks*, damn him.

"No." I folded my hands in my lap obstinately. "Absolutely not."

Lucais sighed. "You took out a Banshee by yourself but nearly died at the hands of the caenim. If you were willing—"

"I am not."

"—then one of us could show you how to get past that mental barrier," he finished with a small, amused smile.

Blinking at him innocently, I pretended I hadn't heard the last part of the sentence. He glanced at Morgoya, and then to Wren, and finally threw his hands up in the air and shrugged.

"Fine. Weapons, then." The High King fixed Wren with a hard look. "Show her the armoury. Teach her to use at least something effectively in case the caenim return here and grab her during one of her tight-rope walks along the perimeter." His stern eyes darted to mine for a split second, causing my cheeks to redden instantly. I hadn't realised he knew what I'd been doing out there each day.

Wren's mouth slackened. "What?"

"She could have died during the last attack," the High King stated. "And I'd like to be sure that won't happen again."

"The wards are secure. I'll push them out past Sthiara. If she hadn't tried to run away the first time, the caenim never would have gotten within a mile of her—"

"Would you like to take that chance again?"

There was a long, tense pause.

I shifted uncomfortably in my seat, trying to find the words to convince them I knew how to use weapons perfectly well without them sensing that it was a lie. The only things I'd ever raised in self-defence before, aside from the blade I'd used on the caenim in the field, were my hands.

And that hadn't really worked out.

"No," Wren grumbled at last, and I wondered how he was able to lie so well.

The matter apparently settled in spite of my input, the discussion continued between the High King of Faerie and the High Lady of the Court of Light, with their obnoxious companion chiming in to argue every so often. I was only half listening, picking up on small tidbits of information about security while the Court of Wind was visiting and the benefits of remote patrols across the land as I mulled over the phrasing of Lucais's question and the ease of Wren's deceitful reply.

Of course he was willing to take that chance.

Faeries couldn't lie, but I was out of my depth against a culture so well-versed in the loopholes of language that its people could evade the truth without blinking an eye.

I wondered if there was a time limit on their honesty or if their thoughts played a part in their ability to deceive.

And then, when Morgoya asked the High King and his Hand what their preferred strategy was for explaining the situation to Enyd without giving too much away, I wondered how often they lied to each other.

"Do they not know?" I blurted, interrupting Lucais mid-sentence.

Three pairs of eyes fell on me, glazed over with surprise, and I realised that I was treading in unfriendly territory again.

None of them opened their mouths to answer.

I gaped at them. "The other Courts don't know about the Malum?"

The three of them swapped apprehensive looks, but it was the High King who spoke.

"No," he said gravely. "No, they don't know about the Malum. We kept the deaths of the human girls as quiet as we could, and the rumour mill decided on its own that it was a rabid pack of Lycanthropes."

"Werewolves?" I braced my hands on the edge of my seat to stop myself from falling over.

"They prefer the term Wolf-Folk," Wren corrected, studying a button on his pale blue shirt. "They're really quite civilised people."

"I don't care." The words tumbled out of my mouth, rebounding off numb lips. I turned back to Lucais. "How can you keep this from the whole of Faerie? Don't they deserve to know they're in danger?"

"They're not in danger ye—" Wren started to say, but Morgoya shushed him.

"They have a lot of questions we don't know how to answer yet," she told me. "Part of the reason we loathe our curse of truth is that when we tell it, we tend to give all of it over at once. It can be overwhelming, making those decisions, shouldering the burdens."

"Just spit it out." Wren scraped the toe of his boot over the plush green rug. "She'll make up something stupid in her own head otherwise."

Morgoya gave him a long look—which he ignored—before speaking again. "If we disclosed the threat the Malum pose, we would have to tell them what—and who—the Malum are."

Shaking my head in disbelief, I sat back in my chair and crossed my arms. "You mean that when this all happened, during the—the whatever war—"

"The Gift War," Wren murmured.

"You didn't tell anyone about it?" I ignored him and tilted my head to the side, eyebrows bunching together. "You said they lived among you, that they were friends. What did you say when people asked? Surely *someone* asked when they didn't come home?"

"It was contained to our inner circle. The rebellion began in this Court." Lucais's voice was strained. "There was so much destruction and pain during the Gift War that when someone didn't come home, they were automatically presumed dead by their loved ones. We simply never corrected them—because they *are* dead, in a manner of speaking. It was too painful—"

"It was guilt," I interrupted, levelling my cool stare on him. "You were the High King then, weren't you?"

Lucais blinked at me.

"You tried to give them their magic back and banished them to the Ruins when you couldn't because you felt guilty for what happened." I felt my voice rising to near hysteria and did nothing to quell it. "That's why you didn't have them executed and why you *still* aren't doing anything about them. You're putting the whole of Faerie at risk and blaming it on *me*—"

"I don't have time for this." Wren jumped to his feet, startling me into silence, and began smoothing out non-existent creases from his clothes. His eyes were on fire when he looked at me. "You want a history lesson? Fine. Go to the library. Read up on the Gift War, and *then* come back to fling accusations at us if you still can't put two and two together."

Heat bloomed over my cheeks, and my hands curled into fists. "I wasn't—"

"Tomorrow morning," he went on, staring at the bookshelf behind Lucais as he straightened the collar of his shirt, "I'll be in the training room. If you want to learn how to get yourself killed, stay here and pass judgement. If you don't, I'll expect to see you there at dawn. Don't be late."

My furious stare burned into his broad shoulders as he turned and stalked for the doors, leaving Lucais with his head in his hands and Morgoya rolling her eyes towards the ceiling.

Wren paused halfway across the room. "Oh," he said, only half twisting around. "And wear something else. It's a lesson in self-defence, not torture. I don't need to see so *much* of you."

His words hit my shield, clinking to the floor like bullets.

The tears that might have sprung to my eyes didn't even bother this time.

My well was empty, and anything that was left would not be going to him. Nor would I be touching any books that he directed me towards—*The Sins of Stars* included. I'd find a fireplace for that or toss it out the window.

I simply turned to Morgoya when he was gone and asked, my voice heavy and head held high, "Will *you* tell me about the Gift War?"

THIRTY-FIVE

Land-Dragons

The High Lady of the Court of Light obliged.

The High King said nothing as we rose to our feet, straightened our skirts, linked our elbows, and fell into step with each other as we strode towards the dining room doors.

I let Morgoya lead the way, hoping she wouldn't escort me to the library. Wren's leash on his temper had slipped this time, even in the presence of his High King, and I was in no mood to see how well he would cope if he found himself alone with me again.

The magic was a humming presence at my side, following me like a lost puppy as I tugged my attention away from it. I didn't want to see how far I could slip, either. Since the swarm of darkness in the bathroom, something had changed. It wasn't asking to be let in anymore. It was asking to be let *out*.

My willpower strengthened considerably after the caenim attack in the clearing when I'd proved to myself for what might have been the very first time that I didn't need magic to do terrible things.

The magic was separate; I was a problem in my own right. Oddly enough, coming to terms with that helped me to keep its poison smoke locked away in a far corner of my mind ever since.

See no evil and hear no evil—and stay the bloody hell away from Wren, so I would speak no evil.

For now.

Morgoya led me down to the ground floor, through a doorway behind the staircase to where a large and luxurious rectangular sitting room opened out onto the courtyard. I didn't have a word for it, other than to call it a *canoodling room*.

Long, wide lounges and cushioned armchairs were positioned around the edge of the room, and small tables adorned with coloured glass smoking pipes and jewel-encrusted cases filled the empty spaces in between. The lingering smell of sweet smoke filled my nose, infused with sweat and potent liquids and the remnants of the inner circle finding pleasure with each other, so I held my breath and tried to avert my eyes from the slightly elevated dais sitting in the centre of the room, fixing a large gold dancing pole against the ceiling.

Morgoya released my arm, elegantly weaving between tables and couches as she sauntered over to the French doors. "Would you like to talk about it?" she offered, holding the door open for me.

I took a quick gasp of fresh air as soon as I stumbled out into the courtyard. "Talk about what?"

"Whatever is on your mind."

It had been magic, but then it was the things that happened in that room.

"No."

She shrugged. "Okay."

The courtyard was empty, sun lounges and side tables bare and gloomy in the grey light, and we crossed it quickly. I'd donned a pair of ballet slippers before leaving my room, which had been the only available option aside from ridiculously high and narrow stilettos. Every choice I'd made since arriving in Faerie, all the way down to what I wore, was based on maximising my chances of survival.

Except the dress.

As the wind stirred, lifting my skirts, I realised that I didn't know why I'd chosen to wear the dress. Especially when the House was still denying me underwear.

Clenching my fists around the billowing fabric, I held the skirt down against my sides as Morgoya began to walk across the flat expanse of green and turquoise grass in the direction of the ocean. We were both silent, listening to the soft song of the wind as it danced over the land like it was trying to bleed colour back into the light sky.

The closer we got to the ocean, the more nervous I became. Water as dark as molten iron glimmered and swished between two towering hills, rising up around it like a cage as the land jutted out towards the approaching horizon on both sides. Bone-coloured rocks grew into the sky, larger than life despite their ageing discolouration and clear signs of wear from the weather.

Not rocks, I realised with a jolt as we began to walk beyond a few of the smaller ones.

Bones.

An enormous skull lay discarded on the earth, weeds curling around it and flowers poking out from its eye sockets. It was bigger than anything I had ever seen before, most certainly not belonging to any creature that existed in the human world.

"Dinosauria," Morgoya said, gesturing to the skeletal remains strewn across the land with a flippant wave of her slim-fingered hand.

From a distance, I had assumed the rock formations had been small and plentiful, and I was horribly wrong. There were actually very few bones, but each of them were impossibly huge. One in particular caught my attention—an enormous spine, half sunken into the soil, with a wide tailbone and broken ribs.

"Dinosaurs?" I repeated incredulously.

"Whatever you want to call them. We called them land-dragons."

My breath thinned in my lungs. "So they were...*real*? And they're extinct here, too?"

"Everything is real, Aura." She gave me a sharp look. "People don't just make things up. The sky-dragons hunted them into extinction."

Land-dragons.

Sky-dragons.

Dinosaurs.

It would have sent me into a panic if I hadn't already seen stranger things.

Morgoya continued down to the sand, making her way precariously close to the water as I paused at the edge of the grass, studying the remains of a skeleton almost as large as a car. It had horns and an enormous plate of bone fanning out around its skull, and I was mesmerised by—

"Do you want to hear about the Gift War, or do you have an interest in palaeontology that takes precedence over current affairs?" the High Lady sang out to me, her voice as sweet as the wind.

Rolling my eyes, I gave the dinosaur bones another moment of awe before I turned and trudged down the slope towards the small beach.

The sand was as soft as silk, giving out beneath my weight, working its way into my shoes and between my toes before I'd even caught up to Morgoya. She removed her heels and sat down with her hands buried in the sand behind her.

"Aren't you worried about the Merfolk?"

She squinted up at me, though the sky was still a melancholy grey. It made the beach look as white as death, and the ocean almost as deadly as a black hole. The air was warm, however. As warm as the High King of Faerie, and carrying his wild scent of burning pyres and grass fires.

"They don't come into the lochs," she assured me, pulling a hand back to pat the space beside her. "We have iron nets to keep them out."

Lowering myself to sit, I made sure to tuck the skirt of my dress in tightly and keep my legs straight and flat against the sand. "That's a little barbaric, isn't it?"

The High Lady snickered. "We learned from the Dragon War not to engage in futile territory battles with others of our kind. The Queen of the Underworld granted us permission to put up iron nets in two inlets—one north and one south—to give us free and safe use of them, in exchange for allowing her people an unrivalled claim to the ocean. That means that any creature who goes out there, beyond the nets, is fair game. And our people can come here, or travel north, if they wish to reacquaint themselves with the sea."

I picked up a handful of sand and let it fall through my fingers. "Underworld?"

"Under our world," she clarified simply.

My eyes travelled upwards to the gloomy skies. "Is there an Aboveworld?"

Morgoya followed my gaze. "There was." Her tone became sad. "We don't think that it survived the Dragon War."

Stiffening against a shudder, I looked back towards the loch. The mountainsides were bathed in shadows and fog, with deep purple and green smeared over the ridges like an oil painting. If I squinted into the distance, I could just make out two low-lying ledges on either side of the bend, where it was likely that the nets had been lowered into the ocean.

"You wanted to know about the Gift War," Morgoya reminded me. "You won't remember it this way, but it was the birth of your world."

My world is the human world, I thought, and gave her a snide look.

"It happened about three hundred years ago," she went on heedlessly. "Faerie had been living in an era of peace and prosperity after the end of the Dragon War, which we'd stayed out of by order of the last High King, and the High King we know now had only recently been crowned. The death of land-dragons weighed heavily on him, and he made an overnight decision within the first year of his reign to outlaw slavery.

"It wasn't the wrong decision," she added quickly, "but he went about it the wrong way. He gave no warning and he wasn't delicate about it either, so many of our kind were quick to anger. They were forced to obey by his power, and the faeries were freed. The term we used—the one starting with the letter L—was then abolished. He hexed it, so even trying to say it scalds our tongues. It left many people disgruntled with him, so when strange things started happening, it didn't take much for the hysteria to build and blame to be laid."

"What do you mean by *strange things*?" I asked quietly. The whole of Faerie seemed strange to me, so it was hard to imagine what might have happened to unnerve the High Fae.

"Coloured lights dancing in the night sky," Morgoya replied, gesturing upwards. "Huge balls of fire flying through the atmosphere. We believe it now to be the Aboveworld ending in the wake of the Dragon War because the sky-dragons were their only source of transport and they had brutally hunted their only source of food to extinction. But the conspiracists believed it was the High Mother handing down her wrath after the slaves were freed.

"They thought the world was ending. They considered the High King's actions and beliefs to be an insult because our history claims that the original-blessed was High Fae, and all of Faerie was built and created from their gifted power. They believed that we were made in the High Mother's image, put in this world to rule and conquer, and he had used the power she granted him to enforce equality with beings they truly felt were supposed to be enslaved. Not everyone shares their opinions, but it doesn't tend to take much, you know."

I nodded. *I know that very well indeed.*

"So," she concluded, "they committed an offence against the High Mother of their own, absolutely convinced that it was what she wanted them to do. They gave their magic back to her. And they became human."

All colour quickly drained from my face.

Morgoya paused, letting it sink in, and then sighed.

"I'm sorry." I shook my head, digging my fingers into the sand until I could feel it jammed underneath my nails. "What?"

"Humans came from High Fae." Morgoya's voice was gentle, barely a whisper of the wind. "You may choose not to believe this, but we once lived in the town you call Belgrave. It was built by the High Lord of the Court of Light, my predecessor."

"So all humans are part-faerie?" I frowned. *This is surely an important piece of information that I should have been given already.*

She made a face. "Not really. They became something else when they gave up their gifts, lost their immortality, and reproduced a world full of mortal children. It's not quite like the Malum," she mused quietly. "They didn't breed into another race of faeries. They simply became a version of us without our gifts."

"But you said this happened three hundred years ago, so it can't be true. My world dates back for much longer—"

"History sometimes rewrites itself in order to offer the easiest explanation to those who seek answers with fear in their hearts," she told me softly. "When magic vanished from their veins, it eventually vanished from their memories, too. The High King was able to fill in the blanks when the war ended. Your world is much younger than you think it is, and many of the horrors you experience now are a consequence of the losses your people sustained."

My throat felt tight. I worked it, wrestling down a gulp of saliva, before I spoke again. "Horrors...such as?"

"You're trapped in one body. Some are forced to undergo expensive and lengthy and invasive procedures in order to feel like themselves." The High Lady frowned as if she couldn't quite imagine it. "Or you're in love, but you can't have a child together. You die if you become too old or too sick. Lose weight and muscle mass if you don't eat—"

"I don't understand," I cut in. "You're saying these things don't exist here?"

Morgoya pursed her lips. "No," she answered, sounding as if she was somewhere far away from where we sat together on the sand. "They don't, not really. We're fluid beings, submerged in power. If we do not feel suited to our current body, or our current body does not suit our long-term desires, we simply change it or summon what it requires. We don't get sick, don't require food—"

"Wait." I held my hand up, fingers splayed in the air. "If a faerie is assigned male at birth, but they're a girl, you just—*what?* Change your entire body with magic?"

The High Lady blinked at me. "Yes. We *are* magic, you know. We can do as we please. The price we pay for balance is an allergy to iron, but we implemented strategies to conquer that a very long time ago."

Chewing on my lower lip, I asked, "Is there any way for you to give that to someone—a human?"

Morgoya arched one perfect brow. "Why? Is there something you need?"

"No." I shook my head. "But Amelia has a younger sister. It would—it would mean the world to her. She's Brynn's best friend at school. Her only friend, actually."

"Hmmm." She scraped her nail along her lip, considering. "We'll ask Lucais. I don't tend to meddle in human affairs, and I doubt it's been done before, but if there's a way, he'll find it for you."

The way she said *for you* sent a ripple of excitement skittering across my skin, but I shook it off. I had to focus and retain all of that information if there was even the slightest chance it was true.

I stuck my bottom lip out and sighed through my nose. "Okay, you're all fancy magical beings with insane power and privilege. Got it, maybe. But you still haven't explained why there was a war. A bunch of High Fae gave up magic, and humans were made. Where did the conflict arise?"

"Well, they continued to live among us at first, but strange things kept happening, so then they tried to force *everyone* to give back their magic." The High Lady's sweet, lilting voice turned dark and lethally quiet. "We didn't want to. But we didn't want to slaughter them, either. The battles were brutal and long. Mortal weapons against our gifts, which were kept on a tight leash to prevent bloodshed and were only intended to be used as a defence until they gave up. It sent some of the soldiers mad."

"But they did give up?"

"No." She shook her head, staring out at the horizon. "Eventually, the High King decided to divide the land. We lured them out to the borders we know now and fought the last battles—a final, desperate attempt to convince them to stop, to come back to us—and lost. The High King glamoured what was left of Faerie and created the gateways in case anyone wanted to change their minds.

"We lost so much that the survival of our race alone isn't considered a victory by most. Every so often, we go back there to the land that used to be ours and the descendants of the people we used to know. They've forgotten us, and the land is barren, but call it a morbid curiosity. Some of us have obviously gotten involved," she added, gesturing to me, "and produced what you refer to as part-faerie. More like half-faerie, I suppose. Though, we don't know how it happens because usually one parent is absent before the birth, so it's unclear if there is still a lingering trace of us in humans or if it's something else." She paused. "Well, actually, I suppose you prove that there is—with the mating bond."

My mouth fell open. "Because I'm human—"

And faelings are usually conceived by mates. Half-faerie children, too. For my mate to be one of the High Fae, even though I was born into a hopelessly human family, that suggests there are mating bonds between the parents of people like me.

My father—my real father—was my mother's mate.

"So, if they find their human mates, why do they leave them?" I exclaimed, much louder than I had intended.

Morgoya gave me a puzzled look. "Your mother would have been given a choice, Aura. To stay with us or return to the human world. Most of the time, it is the human's choice. They carry with them either the fascination or the fear of magic, handed down through the dilution of their bloodlines, but they almost always want to go home in the end."

My mother.

In Faerie.

I didn't want to believe it and didn't want to talk about it anymore.

The life she could have given me instead...

"So, it was a war over your gifted magic," I stated, to distract myself from everything else. From the anger I couldn't justify, and therefore couldn't acknowledge. "That's why the rebels wanted to harvest the essence of the Witch Covens and ended up turning into Malum. But can you explain to me then why nobody told the rest of Faerie what had actually happened?"

Morgoya sat forward, drawing a pattern of lines and swirls in the sand. "We were in mourning," she murmured. "The High King—*he* was in mourning. His father was the leader of the rebellion, the architect of the spell intended to harvest the essence of the Witches. The spell that bred them into Malum instead."

"Oh, no." My heart...*cracked*. Moisture blurred my eyes, and my hands were too weak to wipe it away. "And I said all those awful things to him."

The High Lady sighed morosely, looking at me over her shoulder. "It gets worse. The intended Malum bride is—or *was*—Wren's sister."

THIRTY-SIX

Lochgrub

As I sat alone on the beach, watching Morgoya's tall, thin figure getting smaller and smaller as she walked along the water's edge, I thought about it.

About the nights that I had spent lying awake in my single bed, tucked up beneath layers of blankets pulled all the way over my head with only my face free, and thought about killing my father.

My father figure.

My mortal louse.

Dark, disturbed thoughts—too wicked to be entertained by such a small child, but entertained and enjoyed, nonetheless.

I had wanted to end him, end his reign of tyranny over my mother. I had desperately wanted to make things right and safe and okay in a way that would be permanent.

But I could never bring myself to take it further than a single thought. It never became an idea or a fully thought-out plan. It didn't matter how badly he beat her, or how much of our money he stole and gambled away, or how many pieces of furniture he broke in our home, or even what irreplaceable things he so violently ripped away from us.

I could never do it.

Would never do it.

And so I understood why Lucais couldn't do it, either, even if it was the right thing to do. Even if, maybe, the execution of the Malum would be a kindness.

There had been humans who wanted to hurt my father, too.

I had a boyfriend when I was sixteen, whom I had met at a regional school sporting event, and even he wanted to hurt him. He had seen the bruises on my mother, the large fingerprints marking my own skin, and he had promised that he wouldn't let it happen again. He talked me through the violent things he would like to do to that man...and I had broken up with him the next day.

Some of my father figure's friends had acted on similar thoughts. Better matched by age and strength, and fuelled by too many beers, I could recall more than one night where more than one friend had stood up to him for us. Swearing, bleeding, and throwing punches out into the street until the police were called.

But they never came back after that. Even if he didn't.

A part of me had liked their violence. Related to it.

The other part of me was scared to death—not of them or what they might have done if they were ten years older or a few drinks more sober, but of the silence that would have followed once my father's playlist came to an end.

The piece of my heart still hanging on by a thread and bruised to the point of blackness—the part of me who never grew up and out of those rose-coloured glasses and would be the same age as Brynn was forever—would have broken irreparably to lose a parent. Even one whom I hated.

Even one whom, as it turned out, was never really my parent at all.

Lucais had let the Malum live in exile after committing a heinous crime while attempting to commit another.

A crime against the High Fae's mating rituals, and an attempted assault on the Witch Covens.

Why had his father been able to disobey him when the whole of Faerie had been forced to bend to his will in freeing the slaves?

Had he reigned in his power and used only his words to give the order not to do it? Had he refused to play the crown's card because it was his own flesh and blood?

Maybe it *was* his fault, his error in judgement. A new High King, a new era in Faerie, and a war that ended in the creation of the human race happening all at once must have been overwhelming for even the most powerful of the High Fae.

Lucais's guilt was raw and genuine. He couldn't be blamed for wanting to prevent the hunt that would have begun for his family members—and for Wren's, too.

Fuck.

Wren had a sister. Wren had *lost* a sister. And he'd gone straight upstairs the night the caenim attacked us at my home in Belgrave to check on mine.

I'd accused him of being loyal to a lover.

It was his *sister*.

The soft whirring of the wind alerted me to his arrival as he evanesced, and then his voice followed, quiet and low as the purr of a cat.

"Auralie?"

As I climbed to my feet and brushed sand from the back of my legs, I caught sight of Morgoya in the distance, waving a hand in the air to signal goodbye before she vanished in a flash of green and gold.

"The High Lady filled me in," I mumbled a little sheepishly, as I smoothed down the already smooth fabric of my skirts and stared at his polished boots, "and it turns out that we aren't so different after all. Maybe some part of me still wants to blame you, but I can't. For any of it. Because I understand."

I understood what pain could do to people—what it had done to me. How it could speak for you, and sometimes act for you, too. What it could take away, what it could offer up in replacement, and how some nights you couldn't even tell the difference anymore.

The relief of passing it onto someone else was familiar to me, as was the self-hatred that followed. And then the denial. The blame. The explanations and the excuses.

Anything to keep on hurting. At least then, I was capable of feeling something.

At least then, the High King and what was left of his inner circle after the war were capable of feeling something.

"She's gone, Auralie. My sister is gone, and I've had about three hundred years to make peace with that."

Slowly, as if in a daze, I lifted my gaze to meet the chestnut brown eyes that were caressing me as softly as his lips had. "Morgoya said it was Wren's sister."

The High King's shoulders jerked upwards in a casual dismissal. "Margot was like a sister to both of us."

"Oh." I nodded, feeling a sudden wave of vertigo rolling over me. Shivering, I brushed it off. Clamped my mental fist around the magic that stalked me before it could move or speak. "Well, I'm sorry for what I said..."

Lucais smiled at me forlornly. "As am I."

"Call it even, then?" I asked, squinting up at him and trying for a smile.

He nodded, taking a step forward, and his midnight curls fell over the creases on his brow. "We made some grave errors during the war and the months after it ended. Consequently, it will be much harder to put the Malum down now. But we will. Aura, I promise you that we will."

Letting him take both of my hands in his, I breathed in the scent of smoke and sunlight emanating from the High King of Faerie and waited for the grey skies to fade back into the rainbows of dancing light.

The magic hissed.

I silenced it again.

We had made up, so his mood should be improving...

A piping shriek rang out, and I whirled, backing up against the hard planes of Lucais's chest, searching for the source. It was a soprano, ringing out through the air like a song, so it couldn't be the caenim. It echoed with fear and panic and—

"Calm down," the High King said with a laugh, wrapping one arm around my waist and placing his other hand across my thundering heart. His long fingers splayed out, spanning nearly the entire length of my collarbone. He bent his head to mine, nudging my face towards the water with the bridge of his nose against my cheekbone.

The sea had risen up like a fountain, like an enormous orb of water was being sucked from the surface, and inside of it was a—

"*Mer—*"

"No." The High King placed his lips against my temple so I felt his smile. "We have iron nets to keep us safe here. That's a lochgrub. They're usually harmless."

A lochgrub—that's what Wren had called me when I'd refused to step through the gateway.

Eyes wide and heart stuttering, I blinked at the blob of seawater hovering above the surface, trying to peer through the ripples and glare of grey light to glimpse the creature inside.

"The Merfolk clip their wings so they'll be easier to hunt," the High King explained, his breath tickling my ear. "Some of them risked fleeing into these inlets when we lowered the iron nets before that could happen, but they remain trapped in the water, too scared to take flight in case they land on the wrong side of the nets. That's what it's doing now—trying to fly—but it just can't bring itself to break through."

I stared and stared and stared at the creature in the moments that passed as the fountain of water slowly began to fall back into the sea.

It was small, but it looked almost human. With two short arms and legs, webbed feet, and long fingers, it had skin instead of scales that shimmered like a pearl. The wings were translucent, the gold-tipped outlines barely visible as they shuddered, and its body-length hair was the colour of seaweed and starlight.

Right before it sank beneath the surface again, the creature turned to face us.

An angelic face, huge eyes wide and glistening with regret, stared back at us as we stood together on the sand. It lasted for a heartbeat before it disappeared, sending small, dark waves crashing upon the shoreline.

"That's a lochgrub?" I whispered.

"That's a lochgrub," the High King confirmed, pressing a warm and affectionate kiss to the top of my head.

I took his hand and let him lead me away from the inlet, back towards the House, but I wasn't aware of anything as we walked.

If he spoke, I couldn't hear him. If the dinosaur remains were still there, I couldn't see them. If the courtyard or the room beyond it were empty or filled with faeries again, I couldn't notice. And if the light sky had indeed begun to clear, I hadn't looked at it.

After Lucais walked me back to my room and I frantically searched for the copy of *The Sins of Stars* I had kicked under the bed, all I could think about for the rest of the afternoon was the ethereal vision I had seen along the beach.

The lochgrub.

The creature Wren had likened me to before he brought me into the Court of Light.

He could have called me anything—any number of creatures who froze on the spot and refused to move or were painfully slow and indecisive.

But he'd called me a lochgrub.

And now that I had seen one for myself, seen that it was so different from what I had imagined, the magic in my veins had started to squirm again. Trying to speak, trying to be noticed. Wren had called me a lochgrub, and everything—*everything*—stopped making sense.

Because lochgrubs were strange, but they were absolutely and incomparably *beautiful*.

THIRTY-SEVEN

The Armoury

The next morning, I had well and truly convinced myself that I was overthinking everything.

I was halfway through *The Sins of Stars* before I fell asleep, and nothing I read did anything to convince me that my original thoughts were wrong.

Micael and Livia were doomed.

His brother eventually told their parents, and Livia was sold into service at another noble household. Fate was getting in the way of a perfectly good love story, and I wondered why Wren gave me the book to read when it was so obvious that he detested the idea of Lucais being my mate.

Maybe he thought it would convince me that the mating bond was wrong. That if I went back to the human world, I would find true love like the High Fae and the Swapling had.

I didn't care.

I shoved the book back under my bed when I awoke before dawn and plodded into the bathing room to brush my teeth and wash my face.

The bath could wait until later. I'd need it to wash off the stench of Wren's arrogance after he showed me the weapons collection hidden somewhere in the House.

Morgoya was walking down the hallway when I emerged. She gave me a nod of approval as she surveyed the dress I'd chosen—a sleeveless, floor-length gown in indigo that had a tall neckline and billowing chiffon skirts with a thigh-high split.

If Wren didn't want to see so *much* of me, then he could look away.

"I admire you," the High Lady purred as we glided through the halls. As usual, she was draped in a brilliant shimmering gown—this one a startling shade of crimson, matching the colour of her lips.

I gave her a sidelong glance. "How so?"

"Most people do what he says without question."

"You don't," I mused, recalling the argument between them in the dining room the day I first met the High Lady.

"I find it an attractive quality in others, too," she replied through a smile. "But rare indeed."

Squinting down the hall, I took a steadying breath and muttered, "You mustn't know many faeries, then."

Morgoya laughed, the sound musical. "I know plenty, especially the women." She gestured ahead to where a single door was left slightly ajar and ran her fingers through my hair with that soft, sensual touch again. "Good luck."

Giving her a grim smile, I made an effort to keep my posture straight as I continued on alone.

The doorway led into a stone stairwell, which twisted around itself tightly as it spiralled upwards. It must lead to the roof—unless there was another floor of the House that I had missed entirely in my searches—because Morgoya escorted me to the highest level, and I was climbing even higher.

At the top of the stairwell, an identical doorway opened into a new room in the House. It was not quite an attic or rooftop, but not quite a whole new floor either.

Bland concrete, as cool as melting ice, spanned out across the enormous space. Thin rectangles ran vertically along the walls, which were the same blue stone as the exterior of the House, like tiny open windows.

In contrast, the entire ceiling was made of glass. Light filtered down from the sky as it slowly regained its colour, and the reinforcements criss-crossing over the fragile window panes cast lines of thick shadows onto the floor.

Wren was standing in one such shadow, leaning against a wooden bench on the far side of the room with his arms folded over his chest. He was shirtless, wearing only a loose pair of black lounge pants. A wall behind him displayed weapons; some hanging, others laid flat on the bench, and some in glass cabinets illuminated by tiny balls of faelight.

As I had expected, he didn't look the least bit happy to see me.

"Unless you're planning to distract your enemies to death—which won't work on the caenim, by the way, seeing as though they're *blind*—then get changed." He jerked his chin towards a plain wooden cupboard to my right.

Gazing around the room, I found that the wall at my back mirrored the one across from me. Swords, shields, and maces were strung up, and small tables were cluttered with daggers and other dangerous-looking items I couldn't name.

A warning chill made its way down my spine, pricking me with its claws.

I had willingly walked into a room of near-certain death with my closest enemy.

Wren watched me, his eyes half-lidded, and extended a large, heavily muscled arm out towards the far wall. He looked like he could tear down the House with his bare hands.

Swallowing the lump in my throat, I lifted my chin and took a step forward. I was barefoot, the concrete stinging my skin, and a sharp breeze was ripping through the slits in the walls, gently rustling the skirts of my dress.

"I'm quite content the way I am, but thank you," I told him, trying not to flinch at the way his eyes darkened with ire at the words.

"I'm not showing you anything when you look like that," he replied, his voice close to a growl.

Willing my bones not to melt at the very sight of his muscles as they flexed, I shook my head and tried to make it look effortless. "I don't think different clothes will fix it. My hair will still be red, the meat still on my bones, the mark still above my eye."

His gaze drifted to that mark—the birthmark above my left eyebrow, like a smudge of dark pink paint that wouldn't wash off. Wren had never picked on it before, though I was certain he'd ridiculed me for it internally and likely banked his best insult for a future argument. His throat bobbed as if the degrading comment was making its way to his lips, but he simply said, "Fine."

I swallowed again. Hard. "Fine."

The silence that stretched between us could have lasted forever as we glowered at each other from opposing sides.

"This is the armoury," he declared at last, waving a careless hand in the air as he pushed away from the bench. At his full height, even from a distance, he absolutely towered over me. "It's glamoured for reasons that I won't explain, even if they're not obvious to you."

I took a step forward instead of rolling my eyes. "Because you keep weapons here."

He arched a brow, lips curving upwards in mock surprise. "You're a genius."

Giving him a sweet smile, I inclined my head to him. "Why, thank you."

"Unlike humans," he went on, ignoring my grin, "High Fae don't beat each other with large wooden sticks. I noticed you had one in your home. Is there anything else you know how to use?"

I froze, momentarily stunned, as I remembered the baseball bat I brought home one day to protect my mother and little sister and wondered if they would remember it.

Wren told me he didn't erase their memories of me, but what if he did?

"Didn't think so," he said with a sigh, half turning towards the table. He picked up a thin silver blade with edges so sharp that they almost blurred into the gloomy stonework and flipped it in his hand. "How's your aim?" he enquired, throwing me a wicked smile over his shoulder.

Returning it with one of my own, I took another step towards him.

"I don't know," I crooned, tilting my head as I examined the blade again. My gaze drifted to Wren's body a moment later, searching the hard and unyielding planes of his chest for any soft spots, any weaknesses. His eyes, burning like the edge of the sun, tracked their every movement. "Would you like to be the one to find out?"

THIRTY-EIGHT

What Happened to You?

Knife-throwing was easy.

Wren astutely decided not to volunteer himself for target practice. Instead, he wheeled out a thickly padded dummy strung up against a pole a bit like a scarecrow, covered in fabric that might have once looked white. Red and black ink had been applied to outline critical areas of the human—or rather, the faerie—body.

I missed a few times, but in the first ten minutes, I hit the red sections thrice and the black sections five times, with minimal instruction. The weight of the knives had thrown me off a little, being so much heavier than the darts at The Water Dragon.

"Beginner's luck," Wren muttered.

"The Water Dragon's Annual Dart Champion, five years and counting," I corrected with a wink. "I also played netball for seven years. Made it all the way to nationals in goal attack."

He frowned, casually looping his arm around the dummy's shoulders like they were old friends. "You played with a *what* ball?"

"Netball." I picked up the last throwing knife and weighed it in my hand. My balance was okay as long as I kept my focus away from the razor-sharp edges and pointed tip. It was a simple silver carving, polished to defy the ages, with a much flatter and longer handle than the darts I'd wielded before. "It's a sport."

Wren's beautiful face screwed up into a look of utter confusion. "You—you hit people with balls made out of nets?"

"No." I rolled my eyes. "It's a non-contact sport."

"I don't like it," he declared, shaking his head as he straightened up and removed his arm from the dummy. "I enjoy many things that involve a great deal of contact indeed."

When he turned around, I made an exaggerated gagging face at the ground, and then I threw the last of the knives towards the red circle outlining the dummy's heart.

My aim was perfect, and the blade plunged into the target all the way down to the slight outwards curve before the handle.

Apparently, faeries did have hearts—and they were in the same place as mine. Wren told me that if my aim was true and my arm was strong, I could kill one of them with a knife to the heart.

Not him, he added with a smirk, but perhaps another faerie.

Immortality was a concept I still didn't fully understand. To live forever—but only if you were lucky enough not to be killed by any of the monsters lurking within this realm.

"Your ability to throw things at people is passable," he commented reluctantly, striding to the thick wooden bench along the wall. Weapons and objects that didn't look at all familiar to me were lined up on strips of old cloth and leather. "Your perception of things is severely lacking, though."

"What's that supposed to mean?"

He picked up a small blade with a finely crafted golden hilt, twirled it in his hand, and put it back. "You didn't notice the caenim until it had almost clawed out your spine."

Instinctively, I opened my mouth to argue, but he was right.

"It's unlikely that you'll find yourself in a situation like that again," he went on, sidestepping along the table with his back still turned to me, "unless you pull another half-brained stunt like that. But if magic is still so repulsive to you, then—"

A blade came slicing through the air as Wren whirled on me.

I barely had time to move out of the way before it whooshed past me, not even a hair's breadth away from where I was standing.

Adrenaline seized my heart, stabbing through it like it was the knife Wren had thrown at me.

Swearing viciously, I checked to make sure he wasn't about to pelt another sharp object in my direction before I started screaming at him.

"What is *wrong* with you?" My voice broke at its highest pitch. "What in the *hell* was that for?"

He shrugged, leaning back on his hands, and angled his face towards the light pouring in through the glass ceiling. Pure light returned to the sky, as if Lucais's mood had improved for some unbeknownst reason at last, and illuminated Wren like a demon bathing in holy fire.

"Are you determined to have us both executed for trying to kill each other?" I demanded, tucking a loose strand of hair behind my ear. My cheek was stinging with a phantom pain right where the blade almost cut me.

"Your reflexes suck," he stated, meeting my furious stare with a look of cool contemplation. "Knife-throwing is no good if you can't get out of the way when people inevitably start throwing them back at you." He rubbed his chin, the stubble glimmering in the light. "Your magic is completely dormant, too. I just can't figure out why."

I glared at him, rage simmering beneath my skin. "You don't need to know why."

"Ah." His golden eyes lit up like the core of the sun in a dawn sky. "There *is* a reason. You didn't kill that Banshee on purpose."

"I didn't kill that Banshee at all," I spat.

Wren had saved my life, ulterior motive or not, on more than one occasion. I still wasn't convinced that I truly defended myself on the road into Sthiara—especially not with light magic when it was incompatible with the thing that escaped from me in the bathroom that day with Delia.

"We can stand here all day if you like." He shrugged and folded his arms across his chest. "More than half of the weapons in this room are designed to be wielded by those with magic, and you'll pose a greater risk to yourself than to anyone else if you touch the other half of them while you're dancing around in the gaps in between."

Staring through the window-crack in the wall, I dug my teeth into my lower lip to stop myself from pouting. If the room was designed to be accessed by people with magic, then I had absolutely no right to be in it.

"Those weapons," Wren went on, pointing to the row of glass cabinets illuminated by blue faelight, "are magical relics. On their own, they're useless—but partnered with the power of the High Fae, they can be used as well as any blade. Better, even."

Watching him out of the corner of my eye, I took a few careful steps towards the cabinet. I was not supposed to be in the armoury. Not when I had no magic, when I refused the offer as it lingered at my side, curling around my wrists like a hand—but curiosity was humming in my blood. Wren remained against the table, crossing his arm back over his chest.

"I'm not High Fae," I murmured, though he surely didn't need to be reminded.

"Maybe you could be."

The words were so simple. *But no.*

Ignoring his strange remark, I surveyed the cabinets. Fixed my attention on the contents.

The top shelf was filled with rocks. All different shapes and sizes and colours of plain old rocks.

"Witch-Lapis," he told me. "It doesn't reveal its true form to humans, but carried by High Fae in battle it can duplicate a killing blow up to five times without taking a drop of energy or power from its wielder. Below that is the Blood Lock," he continued, and I dropped my gaze to the lower shelf. "Coat that in the blood of the willing, and the wearer will be able to channel their combined strength."

The Blood Lock was a necklace crafted from solid gold, displayed in its open case. The chain was thin, the amulet small, a circle filled with what looked to be the remnants of dried, crusted blood. A shudder rippled down my spine as I examined it, forcing me to look away.

"You can throw things at people, or we can cut down a tree branch for you, but you will remain your greatest enemy so long as you refuse to accept what you truly carry with you in every breath."

He meant magic. I knew he meant magic, and he was wrong.

I did carry something with me in every breath, but it wasn't magic. It wasn't a gift.

"You can feel it, can't you?" Wren whispered. "Right here in this room, filling the air, growing with each beat of your heart." Hands sliding into his pockets, he took a step towards me. And then another. My blood thumped through my veins. "How did you feel when you killed that Banshee, Aura? Do you remember?"

Shaking my head, I watched his reflection in the glass cabinet as he approached, each step slow and predatory. "No."

"You don't remember the high?" he purred. "The way it felt to have that *release*? The build up of magic as it refilled in your veins, pooling in your body ready to spill out all over again?"

I gritted my teeth together. "No."

Shock. I remembered being shocked—and angry at him for having left me in the first place, only to come sauntering back on his magical horse at the very last possible moment. I remembered being tired, sore, and hungry after trekking through the Court of Light, and after the unleashing of power that had been thrumming beneath my skin...

"*No*."

"No?" Wren came to a stop behind me, lifting a hand to brush my hair over my shoulder, the same way he had when we were riding Elera together. His knuckles grazed my cheek, and I stiffened, reinforcing my walls as the smell of paper and ink swirled around me like perfume.

Home.

Why does Wren smell like home? Like Belgrave, like Dante's Bookstore?

It had to be a trick.

"I remember," he breathed. And—High Mother spare me—the caress of his breath against my skin sent a crack splintering through my foundations. "You were so riled up. It wasn't merely my hands around your waist," he murmured, sliding the palms of his hands against my hips. *Lower.* He nipped my ear, and his voice was a sinfully sensual purr. "It was the comedown from that *release*—"

"Stop it!" I slapped his hands away and stumbled forward, stopping only when I almost knocked into the cabinet of magical relics. A flood of dark and bitter magic leapt for me as if it was coming straight out of the Blood Lock. I sidestepped away from it.

"We can do this the hard way," he threatened, blazing golden eyes tracking the movements of my hands as they curled into fists at my side. "I can send you out of here with a sheath of throwing knives and wish you luck, but we'll end up in that field again. I'll save your life, and you'll forget to thank me."

My upper lip curled. "I *did* thank you."

Wren winked, one corner of his mouth pulling up into a dangerous half-smile. "Not properly."

"You wish I was dead, anyway," I hissed. "So, what's the point of all this?" I gestured to the room, to the space between us.

Wren held my stare unflinchingly. "I'm bound to the High King."

"So am I."

"I know." He sighed sharply and shook his head. "It would be easier for everyone if you weren't human. He won't admit it to you, but *I will*—"

"Then we're going to do this the hard way," I snapped.

And then I turned on my heels and marched towards the doorway.

Fuck Wren.

Fuck the whole thing, and fuck the whole place.

I didn't go up there to be humiliated—

"You can shield yourself," he called after me as one of my feet hovered over the threshold. "Others, too. I can teach you how."

I hesitated but didn't turn around.

"There are wards in place around the House. Around Sthiara now, too." Wren's voice was soft, a salesman trying to make his daily commission. "Some are large enough to protect entire cities, like Caeludor. They're hard to break. Even harder when people don't know they're being used. You could put one around yourself. Around anyone you like."

A shield. A shield.

I felt the words of damnation coming out of my mouth like a steam train with failing brakes instead of the questions that some dark and twisted part of me wanted to ask instead. "It's too late for that. Besides, I'm only half a faerie, and until last week, I didn't even know that I was a faerie at all. It's *too late*."

Wren fell silent as I left the room and began to descend the stone steps. I didn't think he was going to say anything, but then he spoke, sounding closer than he should have. As though he followed me to the doorway.

"Bookworm," he called down the passage, the rumble of his voice echoing off the stone walls. "What happened to you?"

I stopped.

Placed my palm flat against the wall to balance myself.

And then I ignored him and continued to walk down the stairs.

Nothing. Nothing happened to me.

It hadn't happened to *me*.

THIRTY-NINE

You Didn't Ask for This

Instead of returning to my bedroom or finding somewhere else to hide, I walked through the House in search of Lucais. He was my antidote to the poison Wren spat on me at every opportunity.

We hadn't talked about what happened in the dining room, but we made up on the beach—and it felt like that was for everything, sealed by the kiss he placed on the top of my head before he left me in my bedroom. Though, I was so preoccupied trying to figure out the mystery of Wren that I hadn't even paused for a moment to consider why Lucais remained so distant. To figure out why he had kissed my hair instead of my mouth.

It felt forced, yes, but at the same time, the pull between us was pure nature. Instinct. Like he and I were made from the same cut of cloth, the same threads tidying our edges, the same stitching joining us at the seams. I wanted to explore that with him, to learn more about him and discover what made him tick, if only he was willing—

"Aura?"

Halfway down another seemingly endless and stock standard hallway, I started and spun around. Lucais was poking his head out from one of the many doorways, his dark hair a tangled snare draping over his brow. I blushed, feeling suddenly coy. He knew I was meant to be in the training room with Wren.

"Are you—" As he stepped over the threshold, his breath hitched. I don't know if it was the look on my face or the feelings spilling into my scent that tipped him off. "Aura," he murmured, the sound so rich and deep that I experienced it almost like a physical caress. There was a hint of hesitation, though, and I bristled at it.

"I don't understand," I told him, using my annoyance as fuel for my brazen confidence. I wasn't completely sure if the heat in my blood was stoked by Wren or Lucais, but I was determined to use it on the latter. I stepped towards him, and his feline gaze swept along my body, from the top of my head right down to my toes, as if he wanted to commit my figure to memory before he pounced.

"Go on, then," he urged, eyes darkening.

"You learn about me but send your right-hand man into my world to retrieve me. Okay, fine, you're the High King and maybe you *can't* leave. But then you shove me into one of these gazillion bedrooms and disappear for hours as soon as I arrive. You send *him* back up, later that night, to bring me down to dinner. If it was anyone else, I would understand—but for your intended High Queen? You can be informal with Wren in the dining room and allow him to stuff his face before you pick up so much as a piece of bread, but you wouldn't come back to check on *me* yourself?"

Lucais's throat worked. "I regret the way I handled that."

Nodding my head in support of that sentiment, I went on, "Enough to change your behaviour from that point on? I don't understand the way you look at me. Half the time, I feel like I've offended you somehow. The other half, I feel like you're so turned on by my presence that you're sitting there and picturing me naked."

His full lips twitched, and he ran his tongue over them, shifting his position so that he was leaning against the doorframe with his arms folded over his chest. "Would it upset you if I was?"

My lower belly clenched, heat blooming between my legs. I took a measured, equal breath in an attempt to steady my cantankerous heart. "It upsets me that you can't seem to decide on one," I answered quietly. "We kissed, and it was pure warmth...and then you went cold. You left me to my own devices for almost a month, forgetting about me—"

"I never forgot about you," he cut in, glaring at me. "Yes, I had some rather pressing matters to attend to that arose with little notice, but I was never far from you. I watched you in the garden twice a day to make sure that you always returned to the House safely when you were finished scattering your scent along the boundary line. I made sure that Delia was here on the days when the power feeding into the House's enchantment had to be temporarily redeployed. And I waited, every night, to make sure that you were sleeping soundly before I left to attend to other matters, in case you needed me—"

"I do need you," I insisted, practically falling a step forward. Another. "I need more than small talk over dinner and a kiss on the top of my head, Lucais. I don't know why you keep taking back everything that you give me—"

His irises flared with sudden rage. "Because you *didn't ask for this*," he snarled, and the sound sent chills racing across my skin.

I shook them off and closed the distance between us. I had to tilt my head almost all the way back to glare up at him. "Neither did *you*."

Lucais huffed a humourless laugh. "Whether or not that's true, it is irrelevant. I have no interest in taking anything from you that I'm not entitled to take, Aura. And right now, that's nothing. I am entitled to *nothing*. If you wish the situation between the two of us to be different, you're not asking the right person."

"You want my permission?" My brow creased. He already had it. "You want me to ask for it?"

His entire body went still. "Ask for what, exactly?" he murmured, eyes narrowing with heated suspicion.

"You," I whispered.

Lucais groaned, throwing his head back as he moved to press my body against the wall, boxing me in between his arms. He bent down to press his forehead against mine, his breath warm and deliciously smoky as it fanned my face. "Be more specific," he said, his voice tinged with desperation.

I pushed up on the tips of my toes until I could brush my lips against his ear. "I want to finish what we started in the dining room," I whispered. He made a small noise in the back of his throat and wrapped one arm around my waist. "I want you to touch me like that again." The other hand came down and gripped the back of my neck. "I want to know what you feel like—"

He closed the distance between our bodies, and we fell through the wall.

Gasping for breath as Lucais wrapped one hand beneath my leg and hitched it around his hips, I opened my eyes to see that we were in a bedroom. My heart was absolutely thrashing in my chest, like a fish out of water. He had evanesced with me through the wall.

The room doesn't look occupied or even like it has been slept in—

My thoughts about the room tumbled away as he applied pressure between my legs, using his impressive erection. He was thick and hard, and I moved against him, searching for friction.

Lucais swore, the sound low and throaty. He twisted, and then we were in between one place and the next for a split second before we landed on the bed together, a tangle of limbs and tongues as he pulled me in for a kiss. He opened his mouth, drawing me in deeper, his tongue skating along the edge of my teeth and reaching back to caress the roof of my mouth. I moaned as he pushed one of his knees between my legs, sending a pulse of energy rolling through me. He had one hand beneath me, curled around my waist, and the other fisted in my hair, holding me against him like he was afraid I might vanish from his sight if he let go.

He broke away, bending his head to my neck. He took the fabric of my dress between his teeth and pulled until it tore straight down the middle. I shifted until it slid off my chest completely, gasping as cold air rushed to greet my skin. My nipples pebbled, then warmed as he took them into his mouth, one by one. They tightened to the point of pain when the air met them, wet from his tongue, as his mouth sought out mine once more.

"You want to finish what we started in the dining room," he repeated against my lips, "but I still have the taste of you coming against my mouth all over my tongue."

His words—his *voice*—made me throb against him, and he gently but firmly ground his knee into my centre in reply. I moaned against his mouth, and he swept his tongue across my bottom lip before grazing it with his teeth.

"You want me to touch you like that again," he continued, pausing to kiss me, sliding his tongue against mine as my nails dug into his shoulders, silently begging for more. "But I've already imagined a thousand ways to take you, Auralie, and I don't have the patience to wait much longer before I start." He relaxed the hand gripping my hair and trailed it down the side of my face, over my chin, across my breasts. "So, I'm going to make you come on my hand this time, baby. But you have to tell me that's what you want, that I'm understanding you correctly when you say that you want to know how I feel."

Writhing against him, I struggled to form the words as he kissed the side of my neck, twisting one of my nipples between two of his fingers as he sucked and pulled at my skin with his mouth. He groaned as I reached for him, and the sensation ricocheted through me, shaking me to my very core. I felt a spill of warmth flood the space between my legs, and he moved his hand towards it in response.

"That's what I want," I managed to get out, gasping as he hiked the skirt of my dress up and slid his hand between my legs. His fingers slipped against the evidence of my arousal, soaking it up with long, lazy strokes.

"You want to do what?" he asked, teasing my entrance with two of his fingers. "Against what?"

I shot him a glare, and he laughed. The sound was full of pure ecstasy.

"Fuck, you're the most beautiful woman in the world," he remarked quietly, shaking his head as his gazed down at me. His fingers continued their indulgent movements over my clit, adding to the building tension in my core. "When you're angry, and sad, and confused, and determined—you're always the most beautiful, Aura. Always the place that my eyes most want to land. You think that I was expecting you, but you're so wrong. No one could have expected the way you make me feel."

I sighed, a warmth spreading from my chest that had nothing to do with his hands, and lifted my head to meet his mouth.

"And when you're ecstatic," he purred, scraping his teeth against the corner of my lips, "you're beyond beautiful. When you fall apart for me, all over me, because of me, I think that's the greatest thing that's ever happened to me. I want you to do it again. And again."

"*Please*," I begged.

"What are you going to do?" he prompted.

My eyes rolled back in my head as he dipped two fingers inside me, pulling them straight back out. "I'm going to come," I said, my voice sounding like it belonged to somebody else—someone up high, strung out, beyond reason.

Lucais pushed his fingers inside of me again, and I groaned, bucking my hips against his hand. He curled his fingers until they hit that perfect spot, but then he pulled back a fraction, using his other hand to hold me still. "Where?" he demanded, voice rough.

"On your hand," I bit out, sighing.

"Good girl," he crooned, beginning to move his fingers inside of me again.

Each time he hit that spot, I couldn't help the noise I made. It almost didn't sound human. Lucais was an expert, working at the perfect pace, finding exactly the right rhythm, and commanding my body with his knee and other arm to remain in the correct position for the ideal angle. He watched me, his eyes burning with deep-rooted desire, and responded as if he could read my mind.

If I moved to bring him in deeper, he held me in place and found a way to go deeper. When I gasped, wishing he would move faster, he swallowed the sound I made with his mouth as he started to work his hand faster. And when I gripped his wrist, gently rocking up and down with every movement as I held on to him, he began to fuck me with his fingers harder until the breast that was not pressed into his chest bounced with so much force that it nearly touched my chin, and my climax built and built to completion within seconds. He looked down at my body and moaned a string of filthy and flattering curse words, the sound of his voice almost a growl, and I was undone.

An orgasm like nothing I had ever felt before crashed into me, and if Lucais's arms hadn't been so firmly secured around my body, I could have sworn that the force of it would have sent me flying across the room.

The sound that left my throat, deep and raw, was almost a scream. Tears sprang to my eyes as my body pulsated around Lucais's fingers, the sounds of contact wet and fulfilling as he gradually began to slow down until my body allowed him to leave it and reclaim his hand. He rested it against me, palm sealing in the heat as I relaxed, and leaned his head against mine, both of us panting into the silent chasm the sounds of my orgasm seemed to have opened.

Finally, he removed his hand and covered our bodies with a blanket, pulling me tightly against him and tucking my head beneath his chin. "I haven't forgotten that you were supposed to be training in the armoury right now," he muttered into my hair.

My eyes flew open and I tensed. "I didn't—I wasn't coming here to get out of it. That's not why I was looking for you—"

"Shhh, baby," he crooned, his chest trembling with quiet laughter against me. "Right now, I am so lovesick and selfish that I couldn't care less about anything you're meant to be doing that doesn't involve me and the sounds you make for me when I touch you."

I shivered and felt his cock twitch in reply, but when I went to turn around to face him, he tightened his hold on me with his arms.

"The Court of Wind will start to arrive soon," he reminded me. "And I have no intention of rushing it when I do make you come with my cock—or the begging you'll be doing before we get to that part," he added, his voice taking on a rougher edge. He cleared his throat, then sighed. "So, would you like a drink or something to eat? I can have a bath running if you'd prefer to rest in there—"

"No." I shook my head and pressed myself closer to him. "I just want you to stay with me like this."

He went to press a kiss to the top of my head, but then he moved his hand under my chin and tilted my face back to his. Lucais pressed his lips over mine, warm and soft, and whispered, "As you wish, my Queen."

FORTY

Unicorn Hair

Later that evening, I was in my bedroom alone again, preparing for the Court of Wind's arrival.

Lucais and I lay together, wrapped in an unyielding embrace, until the very last possible second. He evanesced us back to my bedroom before kissing me, hard and long, and explaining that he was required to attend to matters involving our visitors and the wards. As he left, he flicked my chin affectionately and told me he would see me later in the night.

I was still thinking about what we did in the other room when Delia came to my bedroom to deliver a note from the High Lady. It was accompanied by a small parcel wrapped in huge, brown, leathery leaves tied up with twine.

A few things to remind you of who you are while you figure out who you wish to be. – M

My good mood took a nosedive. Morgoya had spoken with Wren. That much was obvious from the note alone, but I tore into the package as soon as Delia had closed the door and disappeared behind the bathroom curtain.

Makeup?

The High Lady of the Court of Light had gifted me make-up—and a gold necklace with a thin, circular charm emblazoned with Belgrave's insignia.

Because it *was* Belgrave's insignia to me, even if my small town had once been part of Faerie—and even if the orb of light originally belonged to Lucais's Court, the symbol would always mean home to me. I wondered what it meant to her to give it to me.

Nearly giddy with happiness, I sifted through the contents of the package. It was selfish and vain, but I'd lived without the add-ons from my human life since the day I'd crossed through the gateway. To have access to them again, to have a means of levelling the playing field when I dined with the Court of Wind...

Nobody mentioned the birthmark. Nobody even suggested that my inferiority stemmed from my looks—except for Wren—but I wanted to make sure it stayed that way as my circle of tricksters and thieves inevitably grew.

Powders and creams were contained in small clamshells and jars. The few brushes included in the parcel were nothing like the ones

I had back home, seemingly crafted from polished twigs and hair so fine and shimmery that it could have belonged to a unicorn.

Pausing, I squinted at a brush and held it up to the fading daylight.

It probably *was* unicorn hair.

Stifling a sound of abhorrence at the thought, I packed everything back into the small woven basket. When I reached for the wrapping and twine, I found that the House had already disposed of it for me.

Delia emerged from the curtain, smiling at me through the iron-thread stitches on her mouth. She gestured towards the room and bowed her head, making her way towards the door.

"Wait," I called, scrambling to rise from my perch in the middle of the bed.

She turned, an eyebrow arching over one silver eye.

I swallowed the lump in my throat and said, "I'm so sorry about your hair."

Her eyes widened, the smile spreading across her face. She lifted a hand and ran it through her midnight-black locks, twirled the ends around her fingers, and shook her head at me as if to say she liked the new colour.

As she played with the last few strands, I noticed her broken fingers for the very first time. If I hadn't known to look for damage, I might not have realised they bent the wrong way or that her knuckles were gnarled and swollen. There was no discolouration on her pale pink skin, but I could see very clearly that at least three of her fingers on each hand wouldn't curl well enough to hold a pen.

Delia placed her hands over her heart and inclined her head to me before leaving the room, her eyes sparkling with a knowing sort of delight that made absolutely no sense to me.

"Wait!" I raced after her, catching the bedroom door right before it closed, and swung my head out into the hallway. "Did you know?"

The Secret-Keeper continued down the hall as if she hadn't heard me, but I saw the way her elongated ears pricked.

She couldn't answer. She was not allowed to divulge any information that she had gleaned from the Temple of All. It was wrong of me to have even asked, and embarrassment stained my cheeks. Even so, I couldn't shake the feeling that I was right—that Delia had seen the future and knew I would go there, and that would happen.

The thought was a cold, slimy pit in the bottom of my stomach as I trudged into the bathroom to get dressed for dinner. *What else does she know?*

I didn't know very much about the High Mother—or the Oracle, for that matter—but the idea that I was being featured in so many visions and fortune-tellings regarding the fate of Faerie stirred the nausea I buried underneath whatever other feelings I could snare to smother it.

And the thought of visiting the Temple of All appealed to me again, even as the House filled the bathtub for me, and I sank beneath the surface and held my breath.

FORTY-ONE

You Look Ridiculous

Faerie makeup was something else entirely.

I covered my birthmark with one of the creams Morgoya sent me, and when I was done, there was no trace left to be seen.

In the human world, I needed to use three different products before I got close to full coverage; but one cream from the High Fae and it was like I'd enchanted myself with brand new, unblemished skin.

My reflection stared back at me in reverence.

Silver glittered around my eyelids like starlight was bleeding down my cheeks. I had brushed my eyebrows upwards to mimic the straight, upturned style of the High Fae, and used one of the darker powders to give the effect of sharper and more lifted cheekbones. The last thing I did was dab some red-tinted gloss over my lips.

After a moment of marvelling at my own reflection, I turned away from the mirror.

I was beautiful, yes, but I looked more like them than ever before. That was my intention until I saw the finished product. Until I realised how much it frightened me.

My ears were still human and rounded, and I wore the necklace that reminded me of Belgrave. I found myself touching the insignia every few minutes, just to ground myself. To remember which place was home.

Delia had laid out a beautiful golden gown for me; it was the second dress from the wardrobe in that colour and had spaghetti straps with a plunging cowl neckline. It shone like the fabric held the light of the sun, even in the shadowed bathroom, and I left it behind when I walked back into the main bedroom.

I knew that it represented Lucais and his power, but all it reminded me of was the colour of Wren's eyes.

A set of white velvet would have to do instead.

Leaving my hair down, I made sure to scrunch my curls with one of the jasmine-scented oils provided by the House until they were light and fluffy. Then I slid into a pair of velveteen slippers and took a deep breath before opening the door.

"Where do you think you're going?"

Three steps.

I made it all of *three steps* down the hallway before Wren's voice stopped me in my tracks. On instinct, I turned towards the sound and found him standing at the other end of the hall as if he'd just stepped out of the open doorway behind him.

That couldn't be his bedroom, because I'd been in his bedroom once before and it wasn't...

It wasn't right up the hall from mine, was it?

"To dinner," I replied, keeping my voice steady against the strain building in my chest.

"No, you are not." He strode towards me, eyes narrowing. "What is that on your face?"

My stomach churned. "Nothing."

When he was close enough to touch me, he reached out and roughly swiped a finger across my forehead. Morgoya hadn't included a setting spray in her little gift basket, and apparently faerie makeup didn't set quite like I thought it would because Wren's fingertips came away coated in the shade of cream I'd used to cover my birthmark.

He scowled down at his hand, positively livid. "Wash it off."

I let out a disgruntled sigh and made to wipe his finger clean with the sleeve of my shirt. He jerked his hand back, brows pulling together.

"No," he snapped, throwing his arm out behind him. He pointed to my bedroom door. "Wash it off your face. You look ridiculous."

My mouth fell open as blood flooded to my cheeks. "I—"

"Aura." My name came out of his mouth like a curse. "You are not presenting yourself to our guests from the Court of Wind looking like someone you are not. Wash it off before you come downstairs, or I'll put a glamour over you."

Face flushing a shade of absolute rage, I balled my fists at my sides.

We were both bound to the High King of Faerie, and earlier the very same day, our exchange had been tense but amicable. I was prepared to deal with him as part of the bargain with Lucais, but the brute behaviour would have to stop.

Or I am going to strangle Wren in his sleep.

"Do those human ears of yours still work?" he jeered.

I might've strangled him right there in the hallway.

Tears welled up behind my eyes, and even though my mind was a dizzying cyclone of insults and hateful threats all directed at Wren, my voice had disappeared. I couldn't even feel my way down my throat to find it and drag the words up as a chilling, empty numbness began to spread across my body.

Before the first drop of moisture trickled over my lower lid, I rushed past him and slammed my bedroom door closed between us.

I hate him.

I hate him so much.

He had *no right* to treat me so poorly. There was *no reason*.

Leaning against the door for support, I sank to the floor and wrapped my arms around my legs as I brought my knees to my chest.

By the time my brain was able to send out the command to hold steady against the wave of emotions wrecking my body, it was too late. The tears streamed down my face freely, and I would have to wipe the rest of the makeup off when I was done crying.

Wren ruined everything.

He ruined *everything*.

From the moment I went to close the stair gate in Dante's Bookstore that fateful night until the moment I picked myself up off the floor and wiped all traces of joy and sadness from my face, Wren flaunted his continued existence in my mind. A dark, looming presence tainting every single memory he touched.

I hated him.

I hated him even more than I hated myself.

The hateful brute was standing outside of my bedroom door when I opened it again, red-eyed but fresh-faced.

I shot him a disdainful glare, my stomach twisting in protest at the very sight of his beautiful, cruel eyes. "What do you want?"

He glanced up at me without tilting his head away from the floor, strands of his blond hair tangling with his thick eyebrows. "I'm sorry."

The door slammed closed behind me, but it was his words that startled me. I blinked at him, the knot in my belly tightening. "You're...*what*?"

He lifted his head and rolled his eyes skyward. "You did look ridiculous," he began, holding up a hand to stop me as I opened my mouth to curse him. "But I should not have spoken to you like that."

Closing my eyes, I blew out a sharp breath through my nose, and then fixed him with a hard look. "I don't care."

His eyes roved over my face, no doubt marking the tear-stained redness that couldn't be washed off, and he nodded—slowly, like he didn't believe me, and was recalculating his next move. "The birthmark above your eye," he said, lifting his chin towards me. "You shouldn't be ashamed of it."

I shook my head at him. "I don't understand you. Since when do you apologise for anything?"

Wren's eyes dropped to the floor. "It doesn't happen often. But I know when I've crossed a line, and for that I'm sorry."

That he thinks this *was crossing a line, after everything else that has happened—*

"Okay."

He raised an eyebrow at me, folding his arms over his chest. "Okay?"

"Okay," I repeated blandly.

That was the best he would get from me. I had no interest in setting his clearly conflicted feelings at ease by accepting his apology. I'd appreciate it much more if he would simply disappear.

Wren nodded again, thoughtfully. "Okay." He started to turn but halted. There was something raw and bitter gleaming in his gaze. He took a sharp breath and waved a large hand in the air between us. "I know you don't like me, and I don't expect you to. I never expected that from you, Aura. But I need you to know that this has nothing to do with you."

My throat tightened, heat rising up to melt my brain. "You can dismiss me all you like—"

"Not *you*," Wren snarled, though his voice was mild. He gave me a beseeching look, free of its usual condescending edge.

I squinted at him, exhaustion beginning to creep over me. It was such a common feeling around him. "What are you trying to tell me, Wren? That if I was born High Fae, and I was not the fated mate of your High King, then you might actually *like* me?"

The corners of his mouth turned down, and he shrugged. Something like relief loosened his shoulders. "Perhaps."

If he was trying to make me sick with these hot and cold flushes, I wouldn't let it work. One day he was behaving like an ass, belittling me and wishing I was dead, and the next he was offering me twisted compliments and wishing things were different.

I gave him the sweetest smile I could muster as I began to walk down the hallway in the direction of the staircase. "Like I said, I don't care."

His eyes shuttered, barely concealing another eye roll. "Good. I suppose this means you can escort yourself to dinner then?"

"*Please.*" I didn't turn back to him as I replied or even glance over my shoulder to watch him evanesce.

I didn't need to.

One moment, I felt him standing there behind me. The next, the feeling vanished. Because *he* had.

The days we spent travelling into Faerie together seemed to have attuned me to Wren every bit as much as it had done for him, and I didn't like it. I couldn't shake it off, though. Even as I walked through the House alone to meet Lucais downstairs, I couldn't shake the imprint Wren's fingers had left on my forehead.

I stomped, more than stepped, down the stairs and cursed him repeatedly as I approached the dining room doors.

My furious fixation on Wren was short-lived. As soon as I stepped up to the doorway, two members of the High King's Guard appeared out of thin air on either side. I vaguely recalled the slight ripple of their silhouettes as being the effects of a glamour and wondered why the High King had thought it necessary to hide two sentries at the entrance to the room for this occasion.

My stomach flipped as I considered the possibility that they had been there all along—even on days when he had made everyone else leave the room—but I refused to let it show on my face as I regarded them both with the best impersonation of an impatient, entitled glare as I could manage.

They inclined their heads to me respectfully and moved in perfect synchrony to push the double doors open.

Concealing my surprise that the look I acquired worked, I gave them each a brisk nod as I lifted my chin and stepped into the dining room.

Except it wasn't the dining room anymore. Not really.

My confident steps faltered as I cleared the threshold and felt the faint whoosh of air hit the nape of my neck when the doors closed behind me.

That wasn't the dining room. It wasn't even the pleasure room from downstairs. It was like I had stepped inside a faerie nightclub, the two rooms combined to make one entirely new world of High Fae society.

Plum-coloured velvet curtains were lowered across the wide windows lining one wall. The banquet table that normally occupied the centre of the room had been moved against it, filled with platters and bowls and towers of food much like it had been the first night I dined at the House.

Cushioned armchairs and chaise lounges had been set up, filling the empty spaces in a similar design to that of the strong-smelling room I'd hurried through downstairs. As I blinked ahead, trying to force my eyes to adjust to the phenomenon before me, I noticed that the side tables holding pipes and bejewelled boxes had been relocated to the dining room, too.

With blue faelight orbs hovering throughout the room, some against the ceiling and others down at eye level or lower, I felt as if I was walking through the stars as I took my first step.

Everything was painted in a dim, ultraviolet glow and had a delayed effect—like time had been told to slow down, and my eyes witnessed movement before it actually occurred.

I searched the room for Lucais, but I hadn't seen a crowd of faeries like that since I'd rode through Sthiara on Elera with Wren. Faeries of all different shapes and sizes and colours flooded the room; some with wings tucked in between their shoulder blades or tails curled around one of their ankles, others with horns that rose high above their heads and bumped into faelight orbs as they moved.

Every last one of them was dressed elegantly, but scantily. I looked down at myself and felt the urge to cover up, keenly aware of my lack of underwear beneath my long-sleeved clothing, as bare shoulders and backs and midriffs and legs breezed past me with an eclectic buzz.

There was no glamour.

This is Faerie. This is the High King's inner circle, and his guests from the Court of Wind.

I couldn't tell them apart. Light magic was easy to spot in Wren's eyes, and I could feel it pouring off Lucais by the warmth that encircled him like a second skin, but how did wind magic present itself?

A flash of dark hair caught my attention on the other side of the room, and I took a careful step towards the crowd of faeries standing in the open space in the centre, swaying and rocking their hips as a low, sensual beat began to vibrate beneath my feet.

I cursed under my breath.

Is this how their dinners were always hosted? Is this why Lucais asked his inner circle to steer clear of me while I adjusted?

No amount of time would have prepared me for this. Certainly not when both the High King and his Hand—and his High Lady, for that matter—neglected to mention that the High Fae paid more attention to each other than they did to their food during meal times.

I needed to find Lucais.

I was sure that I had seen a glimpse of his head on the other side of the room, but there was a sea of bodies between us and the thought of getting any closer to them as the music began to follow the rhythm of their movements made me uneasy.

It was tame. The way that they touched each other... It was tame, but I wasn't naïve enough to think that it would stay that way. If I was going to cross the room and curl up into a ball beside Lucais, I had to do it quickly.

Taking a deep breath to steel myself, I began to wade into the crowd.

A few faces glanced towards me, eyes half-lidded and mouths turned up at the corners, and their dazed expressions quickly flattened. Nostrils flared softly and murmurs began to ripple across the room, prompting other faces to turn in my direction.

I was glad that my blush was concealed beneath the soft cosmic lighting because the burn spread down to my collarbone as a few heads bobbed around me. Nodding—or bowing—as they scented the mating bond to their High King that branded me. It must have been extremely potent, given what we'd done that afternoon.

Some groups took a step back to clear a path for me, but others remained glued to the floor where they stood, watching me with rounded eyes.

High Fae were easy to spot due to their resemblance to humans, but the other races of faeries present in the room were harder for me to discern. There were no monsters like the caenim or the Banshees, but I had to be mindful of webbed feet and antlers as I made my way through the assembly.

Every last one of them was beautiful. Strange, but attractive in the sort of way that unrealistic things always were. I tried not to ogle at them, but I met as many stares as I could and offered them a shy, appreciative smile.

My appreciation was as much to do with their unique beauty as it was to do with the fact that none of them tried to eat me when I walked past them.

As the crowd thinned, I spotted a dais against the far wall. The long couch from the reading nook—which had either been physically removed from the room or glamoured—was placed atop it, and both the High King and his Hand were sitting there.

I stumbled over my own feet at the sight of them.

There was no throne, and Lucais didn't wear a crown. The two of them lounged back in their seats like equals, like brothers who ruled the land together and bowed to no one. Not even each other.

And certainly not to the girl on her knees between them, her head tilted towards Wren.

I swore again—out loud—as the sea of dancers closed in behind me.

The black hair I'd glimpsed did not belong to Lucais, though he was sitting upon the slightly elevated dais beside her. His entire body was angled away from the girl, his head inclined towards the short faerie standing beside him with thin feathered wings and a crown of horns. He hadn't noticed me entering the room or sliding through the spread of his guests, but Wren had.

Wren—who had unbuttoned his white shirt entirely and reclined in his seat with his elbows resting on the back of the couch. His blond hair was ruffled, tinted with lilac, and his loose-fitting pants hung low around his hips. His physique was on display for the entire room to admire, and the antsy behaviour of the guests swarming the dance floor suddenly made perfect sense.

Skin glimmering beneath the lights like he had painted it with oil, his abdominal muscles rippled as a thin, stark white hand stretched up his core from between his legs. He threw his head back slightly, lips parting, as the dark-haired girl on her knees switched her full attention to him.

I didn't look at Lucais to see if he had noticed me yet, to learn if he had banished her at the sight of me or if he would have asked her to step back either way. I didn't care as the deathly white hand and its slender, splayed fingers climbed up Wren's perfectly chiselled chest, and his hips rocked gently, urging her to squeeze in between his open legs.

Her face was hidden, midnight tresses falling almost to the floor as his arms slid down from the back of the couch, and he brushed her hair over her shoulders with more affection than I'd ever seen him implement. He gathered her hair in his hands, threading his fingers through it, and I wanted to be sick.

I wanted to turn around and run away, but I was paralysed by the scene unfolding before me, and he could tell.

Wren met my gaze, disgust and greed warring in my eyes, and his hands fisted in the girl's hair as he urged her to climb onto his lap. The pit in my stomach clenched, a brutal and shattering warmth spreading down between my legs until my thighs began to tremble as she obeyed.

When she was straddling him, his hands began to roam across her body. Our stare was locked the entire time and thick, red-hot bile shot up the back of my throat.

Lucais.

I forced the image of the High King into my mind, forced my eyes to tear away from Wren's and seek out my mate.

He was still oblivious to my presence, deeply engaged in conversation with the winged faerie at his side.

The beast in my lower belly roared, twisting and flinching as hazy thoughts began to intrude upon my mind.

I was less than five feet away from him, and he hadn't noticed me. Hadn't scented me. Hadn't felt me the way I could feel him.

High Mother spare me, I even felt Wren's presence. But the High King was ignorant to my own—his mate?

Wren was still watching me as the girl climbed him like he was a tree.

A tree she put her mouth on and *sucked.*

I looked down, studying the way my feet were positioned on the ground. Putting all of my energy and focus on the left one, I willed it to move. I had to leave, had to get out of there.

He moaned.

The sound intertwined itself with every cell in my being, shaking me to my very core.

My head shot up, eyes racing to find his face again.

The girl had buried her head against Wren's neck, nibbling on the erogenous zone beneath his ear where his jugular vein protruded. His head was tilted back, eyes hooded and mouth open as another soul-destroying moan of pleasure rumbled out of him and punched me in the stomach.

Heat flooded me. In my core, down through my chest, across my face. Even my bones felt hot.

The sound was everything. The dawn of time, the end of the world, and every moment in between.

It was rough and deep and guttural. I could have sworn my ears pricked the way the High Fae's did, aching to hear him again.

His hands fell limply to his sides, palms facing the roof, and though his eyes became unclear and unsteady as the molten gold flashed like fireworks, he tried his best to hold my stare as the girl began to grind against his lap, moving up and down on a part of his body I couldn't see, her mouth still fixed around his neck as she sucked, and—

Blood.

There was blood on his chest.

FORTY-TWO

Vampyr

The sight of Wren's blood spilling down his chest slapped me back to reality, and my muscles loosened up enough to pry my thighs apart from where they were pressed together. I almost fell over, but a hand caught my wrist.

"*Vampyr*," Morgoya whispered in my ear.

Blood-sucking creatures that could only be killed by a wooden stake, depending on the version of mythology being read. I was familiar enough with the different records to understand that Wren was not in danger; he was enjoying the experience of being fed from—and most likely fucked at the same time—and the simmering heat started to blaze through my veins again.

The High Lady began to guide me across the room, back the way I'd come.

I fumbled for my voice, furiously tearing through memories to bring up the name of my mate. "Lucais—"

"He'll be preoccupied tonight," she murmured, linking her elbow with mine for support as my steps became clumsy and leaden over the slick floor. "They both will. This is probably not the best event to have you sitting in his lap."

With Morgoya leading the way, we slipped through the crowd twice as fast as I did by myself, and she steered me towards a couch opposite the dais on the other side of the room. I sank into it, feeling my muscles tense against the soft pillows as if they'd been longing for something else.

"Preoccupied with what?" I dared to ask.

The High Lady adjusted the transparent lace skirts of her black gown before she sat down in a nearby armchair, and I could've sworn her eyes darkened with chagrin as she glanced towards the High King. "Business, I suppose," she muttered. "For the record," she went on, turning her steely gaze on me, "I told them that this was a terrible idea."

"Didn't you arrange it?" I questioned, but as soon as the words were out, I realised that I'd misunderstood her meaning. "Oh. The...girls."

There were, in fact, multiple of them. I assumed they were all Vampyrs, based on their colourless skin and shadowy hair, and the way they pawed at Wren's body like seductive predators while two drank from either side of his neck, and the third licked his chest and stomach clean from the spill.

His head was tilted all the way back, giving them complete access, and his arms were loosely draped around their shoulders. I knew the third was licking the spilled blood from his chest, but the way her head was bobbing up and down as she knelt between his legs...

The High Lady slapped her hands down on her thighs, abruptly drawing my attention back to her. "Well, never mind all that. We show Enyd and her Court a good time, and we'll be better off for it. Can I get you something to drink?"

My mouth was dry and papery. I nodded on instinct, but my hand came out to grab hers as she rose from her seat and turned towards the refreshments table. "Uh, faerie wine?"

Half of my focus was snared on Wren, like a second sight that always found its way to him. My head felt cloudy, but I had a distinct memory of humans losing more than their wits after consuming faerie wine.

I didn't feel like I had much left to lose, so it seemed important to hold on to whatever was left.

Her mouth pulled up on one side. "I'm assuming you'd like to avoid it?"

"Please."

The High Lady's tinkering laughter lingered behind her as she made her way towards the curtained windows, and I resisted the urge to fold my legs beneath myself as I shrank into the couch and fought the desire to look back at Wren with every ounce of strength left in my body.

"It's quite a crowd," someone remarked, the piercing voice causing me to jump in my seat.

I looked up to find a tall, wide, large faerie standing in front of me with a warm smile curving the corners of her mouth. The action provoked a set of dimples, and though I knew the High Fae woman had to be decades older than me, I was struck by how adorable and sweet her facial features were.

The rest of her body was the complete opposite. Her figure was bold and proud, with rolls and curves emphasised beneath the silky green garment she wore, exposing freckled skin that appeared to be turquoise beneath the strange lighting.

"My name is Batre," she said kindly, lowering herself to sit beside me. "I've heard a lot about you."

I didn't want to tell Batre that I hadn't heard a single thing about her, so I offered her an uneasy smile and bowed my head. "It's nice to meet you."

She draped her long twin braids over one shoulder and inclined her head towards mine. "Full disclosure. I'm incredibly nosy. Have you felt it yet?"

Rolling my lips between my teeth, I followed her gaze across the room to where Lucais and Wren were lounging upon the dais. The three Vampyrs had disappeared, but the trace of their saliva and Wren's blood still lingered on his bare chest and open white shirt in uneven lines of smudged darkness. His pants were still around his hips, but I couldn't tell if his zipper was undone or not. I clenched my jaw, then relaxed it and clenched my fists instead.

"The pull?" Batre prompted. "That creeping, crawling feeling under your skin. Like an extra layer of flesh you can't shake off."

"Wren?"

She choked on a gasp of breath. "No, *Lucais*." There was a quiet and disbelieving laugh before she whispered, "The mating bond?"

"Oh." A breath whooshed out of me. My head swam with mortification. *Of course she wasn't talking about Wren.* "Is that what it feels like?"

"For most people, I think so."

I felt her looking at me, so I kept my gaze locked on the man sitting across the room. Sensing my attention, his golden eyes flared as he gazed back.

"No." I shook my head too hard, too fast, and had to throw a hand out to brace myself against the arm of the couch. "I mean yes. I don't know."

Heart beating wildly, I willed the blood in my veins to cool. Wren's eyes felt like knives pricking against my skin, slicing me to ribbons without drawing a single drop of blood. I glanced towards Lucais, his conversation with the winged faerie concluded, and found that he was studying his glass of wine intently.

He didn't return my gaze.

Why won't he return my gaze?

"Batre!" Morgoya exclaimed, picking up her pace as she crossed the room. "Oh, my love. I told you to leave the poor thing alone tonight."

The stunning woman at my side blushed, visible only because her freckles momentarily vanished, and gave me an apologetic sideways glance. "I'm sorry. I couldn't help myself."

Morgoya grimaced, affection clear in her eyes, but there was something else, too. Almost like guilt. She handed me a glass of clear liquid.

"Water?" I checked, sniffing it.

The High Lady gave me a withering look. "Of course."

As I sipped the cool, plain liquid and willed it to calm the fire still smouldering in my core, the High Lady settled into Batre's lap.

"This was not how I envisioned this introduction, but I'd like you to meet my girlfriend," she told me, nudging Batre's softly rounded nose with her own.

Batre's cheeks flushed again, and she nuzzled her head against Morgoya's chest before turning towards me. "Apologies, I skipped an important part of the getting-to-know-you process."

"What *were* you hassling her about?" the High Lady enquired. Her tone was soft, but there was a strain to it that didn't quite make sense to me.

Batre eyed the dais across the room suggestively, and Morgoya's throat tightened in response. When she fixed her gaze on me again, there was a question in her eyes.

I didn't have an answer. I couldn't decipher it.

"Was it like that for you?" I asked instead, shifting in my seat so that my body was facing the couple. "The feeling under your skin?"

To be honest, I didn't know why I posed the question to them or what I hoped the answer would be. Thin wisps of smoke were beginning to cloud the ceiling, giving the effect of a starry night above us as they danced around the faelight orbs, and I was beginning to worry about the potential effects of secondhand exposure to faerie drugs.

"She gets under my skin," Batre murmured, linking her fingers with the High Lady. "But...no. We aren't mates."

Hurt flashed across Morgoya's eyes, and I wished that I could take it back. *She said they didn't experience the horrors of humankind. I assumed...*

"I'm so sorry—"

Morgoya raised her free hand to stop me. "It's fine. We've made our peace with it. We're in love, and that's all that matters."

Wren made a comment that Morgoya was jealous. He hadn't meant jealousy of the throne or even of me, but rather that the High King had met his fated mate and Morgoya's love interest hadn't triggered the bond.

Absentmindedly, I wondered if Wren had ever met his mate. Or thought about it. For her sake, I hoped he never did.

"Dance with me?" Batre murmured, her sultry voice barely loud enough for me to hear.

Morgoya shot me a glance.

"I'll be fine," I assured her. I gestured to the dance floor. "Please."

Her mouth twisted as if she was considering staying, but she heaved a sigh and climbed off her girlfriend's lap, leading her by hand towards an empty space left by the portion of the crowd who had gone off to utilise the pipes presently filling the room with smoke.

It was stupid of me to ask her about the mating bond. I knew it was a sensitive subject for High Fae, and though this encounter only prompted more questions, I made a mental note never to pry like that again.

Curled up with my hand cushioning my head as I rested it on the side of the couch, I watched the two beautiful women dancing together until the moment became too private for me to witness.

Looking away from them only made me search for Lucais again, and the slimy pit of melting ice in my stomach hardened when I found that he still hadn't noticed me.

The creeping, crawling feeling.

Like a second layer of flesh you can't shake.

Evidently, it was not like that for Lucais. If I was truthful, I didn't feel that way about him, either. But I didn't want to be truthful because that opened up far too many questions, and each one of them left the gaping wound in my chest a little bigger.

When he and I were together, I felt like I was home, but when we were apart, I felt...perfectly fine.

Morgoya and Batre had a natural, easy sort of affection for one another. It was obvious to anyone who saw them together. Somehow, the absence of the mating bond only made it seem all the more raw and genuine. Like Micael and Livia.

My eyes, High Mother take them from me, drifted back towards Wren.

He was still sitting on the dais with Lucais, and a dark-haired High Fae woman was perched between them. There was nothing suggestive about the position of his arm resting on the couch behind her, or the way she inclined her head towards him to allow him to speak into her ear over the noise.

Still, I felt the flutter of rage building up. Hot enough to melt the ice, and wild enough to make me wonder where the hell it had come from.

Wren was under my skin.

He was the feeling I couldn't shake. The smell of home, the sense of familiarity that ran so deep that I couldn't even begin to explain where it had started.

"No." I said the word out loud to force myself to acknowledge it.

Wren was nothing. He was *nothing*.

He was arrogant and rude, and above all else, he was cruel. His apologies were worthless, and he undid every kindness he ever displayed by following it with something unforgivable. He hated me and wished that I had never been born and he...

And he was looking right at me again.

I cursed myself under my breath and glanced away. In the heat of the moment, and under the influence of whatever was coming from those pipes, I had no idea what feelings my face betrayed. But he saw something, and now it was too late.

Hastily ending his conversation with the dark-haired woman and the High King, Wren rose to his feet and descended the few steps of the dais. My heart thudded in my chest, forcing the blood to rush through my veins three times faster than normal, and I began to feel a little lightheaded as the crowd of dancers parted for him like they found his presence repugnant.

There was no repulsion on their faces as they bowed their heads to him, though.

There was only respect—and maybe a twinge of admiration, too.

For their High King's closest friend and most trusted advisor.

For the High Fae brute who had come into my life like a wrecking ball, and who was prowling towards me with a dangerous look in his golden eyes.

I sat up straight, steadying myself with my hands flat against the couch.

Wren was a figure of nightmares and dreams bleeding into one another as he approached me, his broad shoulders blocking out most of the room as he came to a stop with the toes of his shoes touching mine. A smirk twisted his mouth, his eyes foggy from indulging in the pleasure of Vampyrs, and no doubt a few glasses of faerie wine.

"Are you bored, my love?" he drawled.

Words. Words escaped me.

I had nothing to offer back as he bent down until his face was directly in front of mine. No sound came out of my mouth. Not even a squeak when his breath caressed my face, a heady sweetness that reeked of magic and madness.

Words.

Aura, say something.

I couldn't.

So, I stood up instead. It was one form of language that I could master, at least. Moving my body. Taking back some of the personal space that his enormous figure and devastatingly handsome face was crowding.

Wren moved with me, keeping the same painstaking distance between us as I straightened my spine and looked directly up at him and into those eyes of wildfire and pure gold.

Say something.

"I am so *sick* of seeing your face," I whispered.

The fire in his eyes flashed without a trace of anger. He spoke to me through his perfect, razor-sharp teeth. "So why don't you ever stop *looking* at it?"

Saliva pooled in my mouth, thickening in the back of my throat, but I refused to swallow it down in one gulp. I held his gaze as I lifted a hand and stroked my fingertips along his jaw, ignoring the shudder that prickled along my spine at the sensation of his bare skin, and pressed my thumb and forefinger down on either side of his mouth.

And then I pointedly turned his face away from mine.

There was little resistance. His head twisted to the side, his gaze bouncing between the ceiling and the floor as he swiped his tongue along his bottom lip and a breathless chuckle rumbled through him.

Wren tilted his head, giving me a sidelong look, and shook his head. "Spiteful little beast."

My pulse jumped. "*Bite* me."

He pulled his lips back, flashing his flesh-shredding canines at me before he bent his head to my ear. I stiffened at his proximity, heart racing a hundred miles a minute, and had to clamp my teeth down on my lower lip to keep in the sound that threatened to escape as one of those canines grazed the edge of my ear.

"Don't tempt me," he purred, the faint whisper of his breath threatening to knock me over. "I can hear your heartbeat like it's legato, and I'd love to make it staccato."

Oh, fuck. High Mother, spare me.

He was drunk, and I was...

I didn't know what I was, except for being grateful that my long sleeves concealed the way my skin prickled and the light dimmed the fire warming the skin from my hairline to my chest.

Wren leaned away with perfect balance and made a point of averting his eyes from my face. With a theatrical bow, he turned on his heels and strode back through the path of faeries who were watching the exchange with enlarged eyes and open mouths.

The dread sank in, like a leaden weight crashing to the bottom of my stomach, as some of those eyes remained glued to my face as Wren made his way back to the dais.

My vision went slightly blurry.

They were staring at me.

They had been staring at us.

The whole time.

An entire room filled with faeries had witnessed the exchange, and it would have appeared far too intimate for the High King's Hand and his mate. The way I stood up and aligned my body with his, and the way he bent his head to mine and nipped at my ear...

Morgoya's green, catlike eyes were filled with fear when I found her standing to the side of the dance floor. Batre had a hand over her mouth.

Wren was oblivious. He didn't care.

He fell back into his seat and made a gesture for the room to continue as it had been, prompting most of the faeries to start moving again. I stood there and took their glances like arrows to the chest for a moment longer before I looked up at the High King.

Lucais was staring into his empty glass, his knuckles as white as death as he gripped it.

It was the dark-haired woman between them who caught my attention, though. Her head was angled to the side, a strip of grey fabric tied around her forehead, and her dark eyes were deep and full of contemplation as she examined me.

Enyd. High Lady of the Court of Wind. It's a pleasure to meet you.

The words came into my head like a thought, but in a voice that was not my own.

Don't panic, Aura. There's no time to explain, but as you seem to be the only person from your Court with whom I can communicate like this, I need you to share this message with your mate.

I blinked at the woman across the room, then flicked my gaze to Lucais. He was studiously ignoring me, and it made me want to scream at him.

Your mate, Enyd repeated in my mind.

Glancing at Wren, I pressed the back of my knees into the couch to steady myself and swallowed the hard lump in my throat before my eyes fell back on the High Lady of the Court of Wind. He was watching me out of the corner of his eyes, fist curled around the edge of his seat, and it brought me the strangest sense of comfort to know that at least I wasn't being totally ignored by both of them at the same time.

Two of my sentries are dead. They were stationed on the outskirts of Lucais's ward as a precaution—

The voice in my head became choked, then abruptly broke off. My eyes widened, my body swaying back towards the couch as I tried to capture Enyd's gaze once more. Pain flared in her eyes, visible even at a distance.

Three are dead, she corrected with a wince. *Two are on their way to the House right now.*

The next thought was my own. *Caenim.*

A small army, she agreed. *Led by a Malum General.*

The breath disappeared from my lungs. I didn't exhale; it just vanished. Looking towards Lucais again, I tried to let the fear curling in my gut show in my eyes. I couldn't communicate via thoughts, even if I wanted to. I was very good at reading body language, but that was useless when he refused to look at me.

By the time I gave up and returned Wren's piercing stare instead, it was too late.

The warning rang out in my head, in the voice that Enyd had used to infiltrate my mind somehow—

Get down!

I ducked against the couch as the double doors behind me burst open, and shards of wood splintered across the room.

Light flared around me, white-gold and glowing ferociously, enveloping me in a bubble like a shield.

Lucais.

The shards of wood and pieces of metal missed me entirely, but one of them speared straight into the heart of the first Vampyr girl, and it was Wren's blood that poured out of her as she collapsed on the ground.

Forty-Three

Nothing Between Us

Faerie screams were terrifying.

It was like listening to the cries of children locked in a burning building. Those beings were ancient and sometimes scary, but the sound of their pain was raw and brand new.

The two Vampyr girls crouched over their fallen sister, whimpering and sobbing, as members of the High King and Enyd's Courts scrambled to move out of the way.

Despite my better judgement and instincts of self-preservation, I lifted my head to peek over the back of the couch as a figure stumbled into the room. The shield of light remained around me for a moment longer before Lucais, sensing no immediate danger, let it drop.

Because it was not caenim.

The man was dressed in dark grey uniform, the same colour as the strip of fabric across Enyd's forehead, but his fair skin was streaked with black veins. Each one grew, protruding from his flesh, as he stumbled into the room with a hand braced against the side of his head.

Members of the High King's Guard followed him, expressions of disgust and shock plastered onto their bone-white faces, boots sliding on the blood the man was leaking onto the floor.

Enyd's sentry locked eyes with his High Lady and fell to his knees. The impact knocked his hand from where it was resting against the side of his neck, and his head fell to the side, his throat almost completely severed. Green-black blood poured out of him, running across the floor like an oil spill in the ocean as the weight of his decapitated head hanging on by the skin pulled the rest of his body down.

There was no smell of rotting death, though the colour and texture of the blood were similar to the caenim massacre in the bookstore and field.

Enyd cried out, the sound audible to the entire room as the gathered faeries fell into a stunned silence—save for the Vampyr girls weeping over the corpse of their friend.

The sentry hadn't meant to kill anyone. He couldn't use his hands, so he blasted the doors open with his wind magic. I glanced around the room to make sure that no one else had been hurt before I searched for Wren's face.

He was already up and stalking across the room.

His steps prompted one of the Vampyrs to look up and I gasped at the blood-red tears streaming down her face. She opened her mouth in a snarl, exposing teeth sharper than any other race of faerie I had encountered thus far, and crouched down on her legs, ready to spring towards the High King's Hand as he strode past her.

With a flick of his fingers and not so much as a glance in their direction, both of the Vampyr girls were bound in iron chains. The manacles hissed against their skin, curls of steam rising from where their hands and feet were bound, and both of the girls shouted in pain.

Wren paused beside them, his mouth pressed into a tight line. "These will remain until you calm down. Your nest will be generously compensated for the loss of your friend. Please accept my deepest apologies."

They hissed and snarled at him, but neither one of them moved to break free from their chains.

Distractedly, my hand went to the place on my forearm with the scar left by the gold manacle from Wren's trickery in the Forest of Eyes and Ears. The mark was so small that I'd almost completely forgotten it was there, but I traced its slightly raised edge beneath the sleeve of my shirt.

I wondered if he had one, too. I hadn't even thought to look for it when he was shirtless in the armoury.

Wren continued walking until he was standing in front of the dead sentry. "Your man, I take it?" he asked Enyd.

The Court of Wind's High Lady was standing on the dais, a hand clutching her stomach. "You know me," she replied, making a visible effort to keep her voice light. It was the same voice that had spoken into my mind. "Can never be too careful."

"In star formation around my wards?"

"Yes. Four dead."

He raised an eyebrow at her. "So, where's the other one?"

Enyd closed her eyes, falling into an almost trancelike state, and sighed. When she opened her eyes again, relief had swept away the clouds of pain. "Your bastard soldiers are holding him hostage downstairs."

Wren gave her a heartbreakingly beautiful smile and winked. "Can never be too careful." He turned to me, eyes narrowing. "You, go to your room. The door will lock from the inside." He didn't give me a chance to argue before he put his back to me, facing the rest of the assembled guests. "I apologise for the commotion. Unfortunately, it seems the House has a little pest problem. Please return to your rooms while we deal with it. *Within* the wards around the House, you'll be safe."

Enyd scoffed at the pointed look he gave her and gestured for members of her Court to disperse.

Batre made a beeline for me, dodging the body of the staked Vampyr, and took my hand in hers. "I'll take you upstairs," she whispered.

I caught sight of Morgoya watching her partner with a furrowed brow, but she turned away before I could grab her attention. Lucais was speaking quietly with a small assembly of his Guard in the far corner of the room as the guests shuffled towards the doorway, and for the first time all night, he felt my eyes on him.

He turned away from his conversation, lips parted around an unfinished word, and shook his head at me gently. I didn't know what that meant.

While Batre escorted me from the room, our pace lagging as we filed out behind half of the other guests, I mulled over the predicament.

Lucais must have witnessed the tense moment I'd shared with Wren, but he had still shielded me with his light magic, so maybe he could forgive me.

Even though there was nothing to forgive except for the mortifying impression it had left upon his guests. Wren had sobered up quickly when the dead man burst into the room, but he'd been intoxicated when his mouth touched me, and I had simply reminded him that I couldn't stand to look at him.

The encounter meant nothing.

There is nothing between us.

Even the hatred I felt towards him had dissipated, cooling down into mild indifference again. If Lucais had actually bothered to look at me before the very sudden end of the party, he would have seen that.

He would have seen it.

But he didn't. Instead, both the High King and his Court had seen something else. Something that was misunderstood and reflected with horror in their eyes. And after everything we said and did this afternoon, when I'd asked him to stay consistent with me, and he swore he'd see me later...

"It will be okay," Batre murmured, rubbing her free hand along my arm as she steered me towards the staircase. "He does this all the time. Some things might change, but other things will take some adjustments."

"What do you mean?" I asked, my voice hoarse.

"Oh, you know... The sex and the violence." She patted my forearm. "Morgoya tried to warn him, but he's stubborn."

The pit in my stomach became permanent. My door opened for me as we neared my room, and Batre gave me a reassuring smile, but I was too far gone to attempt one myself.

Sex.

Lucais didn't meet my eager gaze all night, though he knew that I was there. He must have known that I was there.

The Vampyr had been kneeling between them when I arrived. *What happened before I crossed the room?*

Batre's words echoed in my head as she mumbled something about calling her if I needed her right before the House promptly shut and locked the door between us.

Sex.

The dais was a display for the dancers touching and kissing and moving with one another in the centre of the room. *What did they see before I crossed it?*

It wasn't hard to take a guess. He had been left hard as a rock after our activities earlier in the day, though that was his own choice. *Tame* was the display I'd witnessed of the Vampyr girls quite literally sucking the life out of Wren. Something else must have happened with the High King first.

Why else would Lucais have dodged me all night?

Violence, though...

It hit me too late.

I realised far too late that Lucais was planning to go beyond the wards and hunt down the caenim himself. Wren would likely join him, and I hadn't told either of them that the army was being led by a Malum General.

I ran back to the door, almost smashing my nose into it as I fumbled for the lock on the handle and pulled.

It didn't budge.

I yanked it again, twisting and turning it until my hands were so clammy they slipped right off.

"You let me out right now," I demanded of the House, voice shaking.

The inside lock clicking back into place was my only answer.

It was locked from both sides.

Pain throbbed through my toes, shooting all the way to my ankle as I kicked at the door. It was useless. The blasted House had locked me in from both sides, keeping me prisoner for the very first time.

Enyd will tell them about the Malum General. She wanted me to do that, and she'll find out soon enough that I hadn't been able to, and then she'll fill them in...

I staggered back from the door, breathing raggedly, and pinned my hateful stare on the ceiling. "If he dies, it's on you," I told the House.

The question that popped into my head was in my own voice, but I had an unnerving feeling that the House had put it there—even though that was impossible.

Which one?

FORTY-FOUR

Poisoned

The sound of galloping horses stirred me from a light, restless sleep.

I opened my eyes to find the glass window only an inch from my face, the sky outside barely beginning to lighten from onyx into a steely blue.

Dawn was still a fair way off. I'd paced the length of my bedroom long into the night, occasionally trying to reason with the House or make a bargain for my release from the bedroom, but I must have fallen asleep when I eventually conceded and took up watch by the window.

There had been nothing to see. My window provided a view across the back gardens and the loch, and the shadows remained undisturbed all night.

Scrubbing the sleep from my eyes, I pushed away from the window and shuffled around on the seat to face my door. Absolute silence enveloped the House as if all of the occupants were fast asleep, and I wondered if Wren and Lucais had come back yet.

I checked the doorknob. Locked.

Right as I was about to recommence cussing out the House, there was a crash in the hallway. Another blanket of eerie silence followed, and I pulled my leg back, ready to kick at the door until the House let me out.

The *flick* as the locks switched stopped me.

When I pulled it open, I found the hallway empty. The walls flickered with shadows cast by the faint candlelight from the sconces, and the air was chilly. I swept my gaze down both ends of the hall before I stepped outside.

Something wet and sticky touched my bare feet, and I looked down to find the carpet smothered with blood. The trail ended a few feet away, just before a corner of the hallway. I followed the river of blood towards the doorway that Wren had been standing in front of the previous night.

Glass was shattered on the floor, a cabinet of magical relics was pushed on its side, and a blood-soaked body was lying slumped over in the middle of the mess.

The blond hair was more familiar to me than my own reflection.

Wren.

Stifling a scream, I dropped to my knees and scooted across the shards of glass, covering my hands with my sleeves and being careful to keep my bare feet elevated behind me. When I was close enough to touch his outstretched hand, I grabbed it and began to shake his arm.

"Wren," I said, my voice trembling. "Wren, wake up."

He was clad in black leather, slick with moisture, but there were no visible injuries. I found myself praying to the human gods that we were not lying in his blood.

"Wren," I repeated, louder. "Wren, *wake up!*"

He cracked open a bloodshot eye and swore at me. "Let me sleep, heathen."

His eyes closed before he could see the disbelieving look I gave him, so I dug my knuckles into his rib cage and shouted his name. The groan that rumbled out of his chest turned my blood into ice.

It was filled with pain. He was injured, but I couldn't tell *where.*

Moving closer to him, I pressed the palm of my hand against his cheek and brushed the hair back from his face. "Wren, you're hurt. You need to move. You're lying in broken glass."

Both eyes flew open, his gaze going straight to the overturned glass cabinet. Before I could say anything else, he shot to his feet, swaying like he'd spent the night consuming more of that faerie wine instead of hunting down caenim beyond the wards.

He leaned against the wall and examined the mess on the ground with dazed, half-lidded eyes. "What have you done to me?" he demanded. "Why have you made such a mess?"

I didn't have it in me to react to the absurd accusation because my eyes were trained on the fleshy spike protruding from his side.

It was not a weapon, nothing like a sword or a knife. The spike looked like it was meant to be part of another creature, like a giant faerie-sized splinter, and was leaking a watery purple fluid from both the end shoved into his stomach and the raw side where it had broken off from its original owner.

"What happened?" I breathed.

"I think I should be asking you that question," he drawled, struggling to keep his eyes open. He pointed a shaking hand towards the broken cabinet. "Clearly, you attacked me."

"*What?*"

He swayed, eyes shuttering, and I didn't have time to protect my hands and feet from the broken glass. I rushed over to him, wincing at the slices against my heels, and caught him before he fell back to the ground.

By the High Mother, he is heavy.

With my elbows underneath his armpits, I threw all of my strength into holding him upright as I dragged him backwards. My feet were screaming at the additional weight, pushing them deeper into the pieces of glass that had stuck to my skin, so I closed my eyes and put all of that pain into yelling out for Batre.

"Batre! Batre! Somebody! *Help!*"

Wren stirred in my arms, struggling to get to his feet again. I kept my hands on his biceps as he straightened, bracing a hand against the wall for support. He was floating in and out of awareness, so I screamed out for help again as I tugged his arm and started to walk towards the nearest door.

Balancing on one foot at a time, I brushed as much of the glass from my feet as I could, trying not to react to the sensation of blood trickling down from where it had broken through my skin.

Wren followed me obediently, his eyes beginning to glaze over.

The closest doorway wouldn't open, though I shoved against it with all my might, so I urged him around the corner and down towards my bedroom instead. Halfway there, he gained back his awareness and shook off my hands.

Confident that he could stand by the time we made it to my room, I left him leaning against the doorframe and sprinted into the bathroom to wet some washcloths.

When I came back, he was staring at my bed suspiciously.

"You're very pretty," he said without looking at me. "So please don't take this the wrong way."

Frowning, I ignored his nonsense and started wiping the blood from his face with a warm washcloth.

He swatted my hand away. "Please," he said, his voice clear and strong. "I have a mate."

My chest ached with a sudden pang as I realised what he was thinking, despite the fact that he was still out of his mind. "So do I," I muttered, turning my attention to the spike in his side. *If I move it, he could bleed out, couldn't he? How am I supposed to deal with High Fae injuries?*

"You do?" Wren swayed against the doorframe. "He's a very lucky man."

"Come and lay on the bed, please." I placed a hand on the small of his back and gestured towards it.

"I told you—"

"Wren!" I shouted, startling him. "Please. You're injured, and I need to get help."

He gave me a confused sideways glance. "Who?"

"You," I groaned.

"No, you said Wren. Wren is injured. What happened to him?"

"Oh, for High Mother's sake—"

"Wren!" He was shouting. "Wren-*lock*! Where are you? Wren-*lock*!"

I almost smothered him with my hand, but I figured his insanity was loud enough to draw attention, and we needed help. "*Please* go to the bed."

He rolled his eyes but sauntered towards the bed and lay down. Somehow, he remained completely oblivious to the spike sticking out of his stomach. I didn't want to leave him, but I had to go for help, so I placed one of the washcloths across his forehead and turned towards the door.

Batre was standing there, wide-eyed, and I sagged against the nearest bedpost in relief.

"By the Elements," she whispered. "He's been stung by a locust. We need to take out the spike."

"A locust?" I repeated with uncertainty. "Like a grasshopper?"

She gave me a stern look as she rushed over to the bed. "Not in Faerie, they're not. That spike is poisoned, and every second it stays in his body, the poisoning is getting worse."

I swore at the High Mother, at the Elements, at myself.

Batre wasted no time in pulling the spike from Wren's stomach, immediately applying pressure to the wound with two of the damp cloths I handed to her. His scream almost sent me to my knees—a tortured sound, like the echo of pain I'd heard in my dreams every night for three months—

"We need more," she told me.

I didn't move.

His scream.

I'd heard it before.

Where have I heard it before?

"Aura! Towels!"

Batre's voice startled me back to reality, and I nodded, mumbling an apology as I raced back into the bathroom to wet the remaining washcloths.

When I returned, she was unbuttoning his leather clothing, and he was glaring at her.

"Keep your hands to yourself," he huffed, lifting a hand to stop her. "I am a person, not some piece of meat for you women to have your way with whensoever you like."

"Hush," she hissed, placing his hand back on the bed at his side. "You've been poisoned. I need to close the wound before we give you the antidote, or it will bleed straight out of you."

"I've not been poisoned, wench," he argued.

"Quiet," I scolded him. "You're not yourself. You're unwell."

His eyes fell upon my face, the golden light slowly leaking out of them. "You. This is *your* fault."

Hurt stabbed through me, but I pushed it away. He was not himself. He was poisoned.

Wren turned his attention back to Batre, who had managed to rip open the buttons of his shirt and peel back the leather to expose his chest and the gaping wound on his side. She covered it with fresh cloths, slowing the bleeding.

"I've not been poisoned," he repeated. He raised a hand, forefinger extended in my general direction. "If I *am* unwell, then it is *her* fault."

I almost growled at him like some kind of feral animal. Even on the brink of death, he was still such an asshole.

He blinked a few times as he swung his gaze back to me. "I knew this would happen," he murmured, beginning to slur as his eyes fought to slam shut again. "I'm so in love with you, it's made me sick."

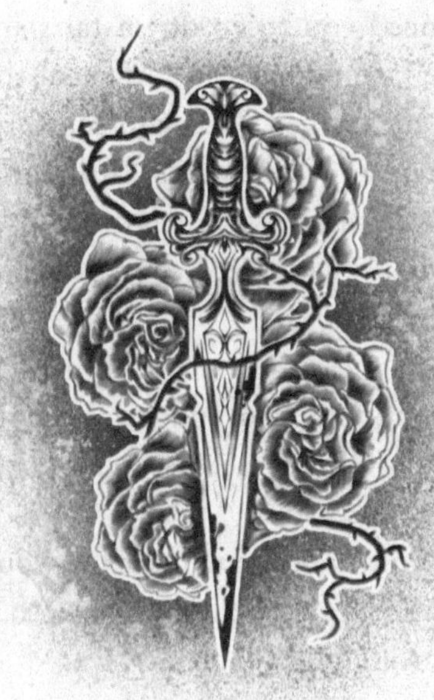

FORTY-FIVE

His Majesty

Batre moved in my peripheral vision and uttered something like an apology on Wren's behalf as his eyes finally closed again.

She might have told me that it wasn't my fault and reminded me that he wasn't himself, but I couldn't be sure.

I'm so in love with you, it's made me sick.

I'm so in love with you.

In love with you.

"Aura, I need you to go downstairs and find a healer." Batre's voice came from above the surface of the water in which my head had been submerged. A distant echo growing louder and clearer with each repeat of her words. "Aura, he needs a healer to close the wound. We don't have much time."

"Downstairs," I whispered, my gaze locked on Wren's face.

I'm so in love with you.

"Yes. Now."

I was not in control of my body as I fled from my bedroom, almost falling down the staircase in search of help.

A healer.

I needed to find a healer to close the wound. I should have asked about the antidote, about what he'd need to counteract the poison coursing through his blood—

I'm so in love with you, it's made me sick.

The hallways were empty, so I made my way to the dining hall, nearly tripping over my feet as I raced around corners and dodged the slightly raised edges of carpet rugs.

The dining room doors were open, but there was no one inside.

Swearing filthily, I turned on my heels and ran back to the stairs. Halfway down, I heard a low murmur of voices.

I couldn't make out what they were saying.

I'm so in love with you.

Faeries were scattered on the ground floor, talking in small groups along the edges of the hallway and between the open doors.

"I need a healer!" I shouted.

All of them turned to look at me.

"Please, I need a healer. Wren is injured. Batre is with him upstairs—"

"Wren isn't back yet," a short High Fae woman with dirty blonde hair called out.

Panic shot up my throat like hot coals. "Yes, he is!" I screamed. "He's upstairs with Batre, in my bedroom—"

"In your bedroom?" another faerie scoffed. He was wearing Enyd's grey uniform, altered to accommodate a long furry tail. "Nobody tell Lucais that."

A gurgle of laughter rippled across the group.

"He's been stung by a locust." A desperate sob broke free from my chest. "Please."

The laughter stopped. Somebody swore under their breath.

"He must have gone to join Lucais's group in the forest," another whispered.

And then, finally, one of them stepped forward and said, "I can help."

If I had access to my magic, I might have sent a blast of power out to knock the rest of them onto their asses. But I didn't have time to wrestle my magic free from the chains I had locked around it, so I extended my hand towards the woman and nodded my head.

I didn't even have time to question if the High Fae who had volunteered was really qualified to help, considering she looked no older than ten years of age. The girl took my hand, and we vanished, sucked up into a gust of calming wind, and evanesced into my bedroom doorway.

"Move," she commanded, and Batre obeyed.

I remained in the doorway, gripping its worn wooden edges for dear life as Batre retreated to the corner of the room and the girl began to work.

She healed Wren the same way that he had healed my mother, by holding her hands above his wound and letting tendrils of light magic flow between them. I didn't need to move any closer to know that she was stitching his skin back together with nothing more than a concentrated thought.

Batre had specifically told me to ask for a healer, and part of me wondered if it was a particular skill set unique to certain faeries—and if so, how Wren had managed to lay claim to such a wide variety of power.

He was unconscious, his head resting on my pillow and his arms lying limp at his sides, and I stared at the half of his face visible to me as the healer put her magic to work.

I almost screamed when flames burst out across his clothes, but Batre shot me a warning look, so I dug my teeth into my bottom lip and pressed my cheek into the grooves in the doorframe.

The fire wasn't hurting him; it was removing obstacles, like the bloody washcloths and his torn shirt. It blazed without smoke, controlled and calm, and didn't singe the linen on my bed as it wrapped itself around his limbs and magically cleared away the part of his shirt trapped against the coverlet beneath his back.

Wren's features softened as the healer worked, the one sign that his pain was lessening.

Mine only increased.

It is her fault.

I'm so in love with you, it's made me sick.

"The antidote, please," the healer said, one hand hovering above his stomach as she extended the other behind her.

Batre looked at me, her mouth stretched into a tight and apprehensive grimace. "It's your blood, Aura."

But I was already moving towards the bed, craning my head around the healer's body, following the line of ink that had appeared on Wren's skin as the last of his sleeve burned away and the fire went out.

The fire went out.

Like the light in my eyes as they traced the swirls of tattoos up and down his arms.

The scar from the golden manacle, twin to my own, may have escaped my notice previously. I had a distinct memory of studying his arms, though. I'd traced the corded muscle with my eyes along clear, unmarked skin.

It wasn't clear anymore.

And I no longer cared that the scar from the manacle was, in fact, still on his wrist, like a matching friendship bracelet carved in flesh.

Or that, on the silver chain around his neck, the round Belgrave insignia that rested atop the middle of his chest was identical to the one on mine.

I no longer cared about anything as I saw Wren's naked arms for the very first time.

He had two sleeves of tattoos, and if I had never seen them before, there was a chance that I might have been convinced it was part of the healing ritual, but I *had* seen them before.

In my dreams every single night for three long months.

When the healer explained why my blood was needed to counteract the poison in his system, it was too late.

It had already clicked.

"I can make a tonic if you have a blood phobia," she grumbled, "but his mate's lifeblood is the quickest and easiest way to cure him."

And as every other thought, feeling, and drop of knowledge abandoned me, I considered refusing.

I considered refusing to save the life of the man who had haunted my dreams through the winter, and who had lied to me for weeks and tormented me with his touches, smiles, and double-edged words, and who was ultimately a stranger.

I didn't even know his name.

"She hasn't accepted the bond yet." Morgoya's voice came from behind me.

I stiffened but didn't turn towards her. If we were to continue our friendship at some point in the future, the High Lady could not see the hateful emotions crippling my features as I stared down at the man on my bed.

"No matter," the healer declared with a shrug. "It will work either way, though His Majesty's recovery may take a few extra days."

His Majesty.

His Majesty.

Morgoya's voice softened. "Aura—"

"You shut the fuck up."

There was a stifled gasp from Batre, but I shut the rest of the room out as I extended my hand towards the girl who had healed *His Majesty.*

"He has to drink it?" I asked, my voice suddenly unfamiliar to my own ears.

"Yes," she answered carefully. She placed a small blade in my open palm. "Make sure he takes an entire mouthful."

Oh, he'll get a full fucking mouthful.

Taking the blade from the healer, I passed it into my other hand and then sliced it across my right palm.

Cupping my hand to let the blood pool there, I dropped the blade to the ground and lowered myself to sit on the edge of my bed. Then I propped his head up and brought my bleeding hand to his mouth.

His lips parted, though his eyes remained closed.

His breathing pattern became uneven as he drank from me.

I pressed my lips against his forehead, aware of the healer quietly retreating. To her and Batre—to anyone outside of the High King's corrupted, traitorous inner circle—I was no more than his mate, murmuring loving reassurances as I healed him with my blood.

But only he could hear me.

"Take as much as you need," I whispered, brushing my lips across his skin as I moved my mouth to his ear. "Because when you wake up, I am going to fucking kill you."

FORTY-SIX

His Mate

Before she left, the healer offered to fix the cut on my hand so that it wouldn't scar. I let her seal it to prevent infection but requested that she let the scar form naturally.

I wanted to keep it as proof.

She gave me a list of instructions while the man in my bed healed, and I gave her a list of my own.

Nobody was to be allowed into my bedroom except for her when she returned for twice daily checks on her patient.

With a puzzled look, she agreed to my conditions and left the room to attend to the commotion downstairs as everyone returned from the conflict with the caenim to the sanctuary within the wards.

Nobody had mentioned what had actually happened yet, and I didn't care to ask while I had so many other pressing issues on my mind.

I assumed there was no longer any immediate danger, so I sat on the window seat while the man in my bed dozed, his even breathing indicating a deep and restful sleep.

As I watched him, I went over everything in my head. Again and again and again.

It took me all morning to recall the exact wording of our very first encounter, and my frustration only magnified when I finally did.

"Who are you?" I had asked him.

A rookie error.

"You can call me Wren."

And I did.

I had called him Wren ever since, and not once had I realised that nobody else ever did.

Lucais Starfire was the High King of Faerie. They made sure that truth sank in during the brief lesson they'd given me on how to word my questions, but I'd never thought to confirm their names and identities.

The references to Lucais and Wren had been blurry. It was always the High King and his Hand, or vague uses of their pronouns, or some other form of faerie trickery. Intertwined and overlapping, a scheme designed to keep me in the dark.

I just couldn't figure out why.

And as I sat on the window seat while the gloomy day passed us by outside, my anger only increased. At him, at all of them, and at myself.

Lucais Starfire was the High King of Faerie, and he was recovering from locust poisoning in my bed.

His eyes were the colour of light. His hair was the colour of light. Even his skin was drenched in it.

The only time he ever spoke nicely about another person had been in the kitchen of my house in Belgrave, when he had told me that the High King of Faerie was handsome and clever.

He was talking about himself. *Of course he was talking about himself!*

When he bowed to his dark-haired friend that first day in the House before he'd given him a chance to speak, the gesture had thrown him off-balance. Then he had slipped up twice in front of me. Possibly even more often than that, and I was just too blind to see it.

When he was the first to serve up his plate at dinner, something felt off. Had they told me about the mating bond to distract me from prying into their true hierarchy?

I was too distracted with my own problems with magic to question anything else when I walked into the dining room and found him lounging at the head of the table like he owned it the day I met Morgoya.

And Morgoya—

My hands balled into fists.

She had accused him of saving me from the Banshee, claiming that he couldn't possibly stand by and do nothing while I was attacked.

Because I am his mate.

And she *knew* that I was his mate.

She had said as much right in front of me. *"Let's just say, it leaves no doubt. You are his mate."*

She was toying with us when she told me to sit in Lucais's lap—fake Lucais, my fake mate, while the real one simmered with rage beside me. The looks she had given us. The dress she had me wear. The *gold dress* matching the colour of his eyes. His favourite colour.

By the Elements, even the way he'd looked at me when I was wearing it should have told me that something was wrong, that I was being lied to.

He displayed immense power, unlike anyone else. Even the dark-haired man who let me believe that he was the High King, with nothing substantial to back it up outside of a fabricated story and feelings provoked by lies.

It had taken a fraction of the amount of time it took everyone else for him to find me in that field full of caenim.

A member of his Guard had slapped me for wanting to let him die that day. Because I wasn't trying to kill the Hand; I was watching on as the caenim snapped and drooled all over the fucking High King of Faerie himself.

He'd threatened the man, punched him twice for putting his hands on me, and kept his inner circle away from me for that exact reason.

Even the glamour when we rode through Sthiara made more sense.

Because they all knew the truth. Even the Banshee on the road into town had known it, had scented him on me. I was the only person in Faerie who didn't know that he was the High King, and I was his mate.

I am his mate.

*And that makes him...*mine.

A scream coiled in my chest, ready to tear free from my body, and I forced the magic in my veins to be quiet for a little while longer.

For every memory I dredged up and every piece of the puzzle I put into place, it was wriggling free from its constraints.

Is it time, is it time yet?
And I was letting it.
Almost.
"Let me explain before you explode and take the whole of Sthiara down with you," the High King said.

FORTY-SEVEN

Fate

My gaze snapped towards the true High King of Faerie.

He was awake and alert.

"You son of a bitch," I breathed.

He rolled his eyes, grunting as he pushed himself up into a sitting position on my bed. "Considering she's Malum now, you're not wrong."

I took a mental shovel out on the relief that rushed through me at the sight of him sitting up, clear-eyed and skin healed, and tried to bury it beneath my rage.

His blond hair was matted with crusted blood, as was the diamond hoop in his earlobe, but the fire had cleansed the rest of his face, chest and the chain tying the insignia to him. He was still wearing his leather pants, splattered with mud and blood, and I hadn't bothered to pull the covers over him.

"What is your name?" My voice threatened to shake, threatened to break into a million little pieces.

He held my gaze, some of the fire returning to his eyes. "Try again."

The healer had propped him up with three of my pillows, but there was one on the bed next to him. If I was fast, I probably could have grabbed it and held it down over his head until he stopped breathing.

I lifted myself off my perch on the window and began to walk towards it, moving slowly as the blood trickled back down into my stiff legs. It had grown dark outside, barely a streak of light left in the sky.

"What is your full, real name?" I asked, leaning down with my hands on the bed so we were eye-to-eye. "What is the name that your parents gave you, the name that the other faeries know you as?"

He didn't blink. Even as molten gold swirled in his irises. "Lucais Starfire."

The impact his answer had on me was unprecedented. I felt like I was going to die, but I ploughed onwards.

"Are you, Lucais Starfire, the High King of Faerie?"

"Yes."

Breathe, I told myself.

I closed my eyes and took a deep breath. "Am I your mate?"

"No."

My eyes flew open. He was smirking at me, but there was a hint of regret in his eyes.

"You are *supposed* to be my mate," he clarified, and I sagged forward, kneeling on the edge of the mattress. "Technically, you aren't my mate until you accept the bond. Keep working on your phrasing. You're getting better."

"I hate you."

His eyes followed a lazy line over my body on their way back to mine. "And I think the feeling is mutual, bookworm," he murmured, but his mouth twisted to one side.

"No," I said, adjusting to sit down on the bed. "I really hate you."

Wren's—*Lucais's*—face was the portrait of innocent alarm. "I know. You threatened to kill me while I was drinking your blood." He arched his golden eyebrows. "Thank you, by the way. I've spent weeks wondering how you taste, and this part of you, at least, did not disappoint."

I made a gagging face. "You make me sick."

He smiled softly. "I recall saying something similar to you not long ago."

Intent on sprinting towards the point instead of jumping over the hurdles in his games, I leaned towards him and propped myself up with my elbows on the mattress. He mirrored me, coming as close as he could with a hand braced on the bed.

"Why?" I demanded. "No lies, no trickery, no bullshit. Tell me why."

Some of the light in his eyes dimmed. "You want the truth?"

"Always." I narrowed my eyes at him and added, "Even if it kills you. Especially then."

He gave me a withering look. "Fine. I didn't want you to know that you were designed to be my mate because I don't want you here. I meant what I said—that it would be easier for me if you were never born, because the things that they will do to you if they find out..."

I flinched, and he grasped one of my hands. The touch was warm, affectionate. I pulled away.

"Aura," he murmured, flexing his fingers as he stared at my hand. "They will pull you apart in ways that prevent me from ever putting you back together. If you accepted the bond, then I'm signing your death warrant, and I can't even fathom how I would survive that. How Faerie would survive that—"

A bitter laugh bubbled out of my mouth, and I shook my head at him. "All because some Oracle showed you a vision?"

Wren's—*Lucais's*—eyes softened in a way I had never witnessed before. The rest of his face followed, smoothing down into an expression of handsome desire. "The vision made me curious. I wanted to meet you until the Malum sent their first message, and I realised how dangerous it would be if we ever did. I had no idea who you were when I returned to Belgrave, but the moment I appeared in that bookstore, and it was covered in your scent..." He closed his eyes and took a deep breath. "If you hadn't come back that night, I would have slaughtered the caenim and destroyed the portal and thrown a ward up around your town. And come home."

"So, why didn't you?"

"Because you came back," he answered simply, opening his eyes. "Even after catching a glimpse of the monsters following you. Didn't you ever wonder why?"

Because I'd left my keys behind.

No.

Because he was there.

"I knew the moment I laid eyes on you for the first time that you were my mate, and that I couldn't leave you," he went on. "I couldn't even *pretend* to leave you without putting the whole of Faerie in jeopardy from the storms it could create, but you couldn't know the truth. It was better for you to hate me if it meant keeping you and my world safe."

My gaze dropped to his mouth, my heart beating out of rhythm. The question was on my lips, but I was too afraid to press further.

"In the cottage," he said, answering it anyway. "I knew that the bond was real and true in the cottage that night when you woke up from a bad dream, screaming for me. Hearing my name on your lips like that for the first time broke my heart. I felt it first in the Forest of Eyes and Ears when you had the whole damn thing attack me, but that night cemented it."

Part of me wanted to touch him. Lucais. Not the Lucais I had been introduced to, but *him*. The one in front of me. The man from my dreams.

His hand was resting on the bed, so close to mine, and I wanted to hold onto it because I was reminded of the way he screamed as the spike was pulled from his torso. The scream that had tormented me for months, from the man I had wanted so desperately to save. The man I had wanted to *love*.

He was staring right at me with a warmth in his eyes that I had missed before now, a warmth that I had felt mirrored in my own eyes so many times.

But he's been staring at me for weeks.

Lying to me.

He doesn't love me.

I frowned at the empty space between our hands. "You realise that you fat-shamed me to your horse?"

He lifted his hand, cupping my chin, and tilted my face up towards his. Lucais dropped his voice to a near-growl and said, "You realise that I'm a liar?"

A shiver ran down my spine, and I almost leaned into his touch.

The magic in my veins leapt with joy, ecstatic that the rest of me was finally catching on to what it had been trying to tell me all this time.

Every question I had was being answered. The confusion was clearing like a wind pulling the clouds from the sky.

I'd had no idea who he was, but I had felt all along that it wasn't who he let me believe he was.

"Those wicked things I said to you were mostly part of the ruse, Aura. But I really don't want you to like me. You felt it the moment we met. I saw it on your face, and so I spent the next few weeks trying to override those feelings, to convince you they were wrong." His thumb brushed my cheek. "I tried to convince myself that they were wrong initially, too. But I realised early on that it was futile."

I shook my head, making no effort to reduce the impact of my words as I whispered, "But I was attracted to Lucais—I mean Wren."

Lucais's grip tightened almost imperceptibly on my chin, but he said with intense calm, "You can be attracted to whoever you like, bookworm. The mating bond doesn't mean anything."

I slapped his hand away from me. He let it drop but gave me an exasperated look.

"Why?" I hissed. "Why would you let him use me like that?"

He arched a brow, a hard look in his eyes. "Use you? He tried to *stop* you—"

Groaning, I threw myself face down on the bed and covered the back of my head with my hands. The things that I had done with Lucais—fake Lucais, real Wren—in the dining room, and in the room off the hallway, and even in *my mate's bedroom.*

Fake Wren, real Lucais had watched. He'd waited outside and listened and said horrible things to me in the hallway afterwards. I had a better understanding of his anger now, but it didn't explain why he had let it happen in the first place.

When it became hard to breathe against the mattress, I rolled over and sat up. I was closer to the true High King than I had been before, and by the way his shoulders tensed, I knew he was aware of it too.

"You enjoy his company," he said too quietly. "Does part of me want to snap his wrists? Yes. Are those feelings warranted? No. They belong to the bond, which answers to the stars, not the High King."

I sighed. "None of it was warranted."

"Wrenlock didn't actually agree to the plan," he confessed. "It was a foolish, split-second decision I made alone in Belgrave when I gave you his name instead of mine, and then I didn't provide him with a chance to argue when we arrived back at the House. I figured if there was something real budding between the two of you—"

"*Is* something," I corrected.

"Then maybe," he ground out, fists balling around the covers, "I could convince people that we weren't mates, that the Oracle was mistaken somehow. And maybe being with him instead of me could save your life if you chose to stay with us." He gave me a sidelong glance. "It's not only the Malum, Aura. There are enemies among my own people, carrying around a centuries-old hatchet and waiting for the right time to use it."

Because he freed the slaves.

Lucais, my fated soulmate, had started a war by granting freedom to faeries far and wide. It was the action of a High King, an action that had stirred affection deep within my heart, even though it put a bounty on our heads.

But what else did I not know about him? About his reign as High King, about his past, about his personality?

I sighed and turned towards him, the weight of all the truth becoming too much for me to bear. "You tricked me," I stated.

Lucais's golden eyes narrowed—not out of anger, but in preparation for the blows to come.

"Instead of letting me prepare myself to face the real enemies I may have, you had me believe that *you* were one," I said, keeping my voice even. I felt hollow like my heart had been carved out of my chest.

Lucais had haunted my dreams, and when I met him as Wren, I'd known that he was in that dungeon with me. I had been so sure of it, and the only explanation I could find was that he had been one of the men who had tortured my prisoner.

But he was the prisoner I'd screamed for all along.

How different would things have been if he had simply told me the truth from the start?

"You let me fall for your best friend based on a lie," I went on, banishing the fantasy in my head. "I would have done anything for you—pretended to love Wren, even—if I'd known who you were. But instead, you *bullied* me, made me feel *worthless,* and pushed me further and further into his waiting arms like I'm nothing more than a sheep being herded into a corral. And then you *slut-shamed* me for it! I don't know much about your mating bond, but I do know that if I was truly your mate and I was truly the intended High Queen, then I deserved better."

"You do deserve better," he told me, his eyes going to some faraway place as they studied my face intently. Like he was imagining the same fantasy of our storyline following the truth instead. "I realise that you don't want to know me, bookworm, and I realise that it's because I am destined to disappoint you by order of the Oracle."

I felt my magic flickering in delight at his acknowledgement of fate, even as the pit in my stomach flipped and shrieked.

"And you *are* the intended High Queen of Faerie. It doesn't make a difference whether you like me or not."

I took a deep breath. "Yes, it does."

FORTY-EIGHT

Where Your Loyalty Lies

Later, I found the real Wren pacing up and down the candlelit hallway outside my room.

He froze when he heard my footsteps, the colour of his cheeks deepening, and as soon as he opened his mouth, I knew that I was about to hear another useless apology.

"Don't bother," I called, striding towards him. "He already told me that it wasn't your idea, and it doesn't make a difference."

"Aura, please." The impersonator ran a hand through his dark hair. "I am bound to serve him. I couldn't tell you, no matter how much I wanted to."

I came to a stop in front of him and crossed my arms. "And the—the *other stuff*? He made you do that, too?"

Real Wren blushed. "No. By the Elements, Aura, I tried to stay away from you. I wanted to wait until you could know who I really was, but it was impossible. *You* are impossible. I am completely and utterly under your spell. I never lied to you, I swear it."

My eyes narrowed. "You never told me the truth, either."

The High King's true Hand cursed at the ceiling. "So much of it was true. Everything I said upstairs, in the bedroom, was real. In the dining hall—"

"Please." I exhaled sharply. "Don't."

Shaking his head, Lucais—no, *Wren*—reached a hand out towards me but thought better of it and let it fall to his side. "We had to try to keep you in the dark. If you knew and chose to stay in Belgrave, it was only a matter of time before we would have had your head delivered to us in a box."

Dread snaked down my spine, and I swallowed back a dose of watered-down bile. Saving my life was one thing, but forcing me into a lie was another.

"Why was it so easy for me to believe it?"

Real Wren's throat worked. His expression was tortured. "Because it's not the bond, baby," he whispered. "It's us. It's real. You decided to love me all on your own."

I shook my head. "Did I?"

I couldn't explain why I fell head-over-heels for Fake Lucais that day in the dining hall, purring in his lap like a cat on catnip after Real Lucais had riled me up in his bedroom. I'd blamed it on the mating bond when the whole time I was falling for a scheme. It wasn't my fault. It wasn't real.

Knowing that didn't make me feel any less sick, though.

"You didn't think to stop it, to make him tell me the truth, or find a way to tell me without saying it out loud, even once?"

Wren's face fell. "I tried. The first time we kissed, he nearly killed me. Morgoya broke it up and calmed him down, and I told him how I felt about you. We were going to call it off, but..."

"But what?"

He sighed again and threw his hands up. "But fucking *politics*. Your magic is unhinged, and we couldn't risk it when we needed to investigate Gregor's Court and meet with Enyd and her Court."

I scoffed. "Gee, thanks. That's nice to know." I stalked towards the windows; it was the same row of glass overlooking the backyard that I had stood beside the day I met him. "How long were you planning to avoid it?" I asked. "Your mouth, then your hand—"

"Aura, be careful asking these questions," he warned. "You might not want to know the answer."

Incensed, I whirled on him. "Just *tell* me!"

Wren stepped up beside me and looked me dead in the eye. "If you had asked me a third time, we agreed that he'd have to tell you the truth. To test it, he let his glamour drop the day Morgoya told you about the Gift War."

The day I'd walked down to the water and saw the lochgrub.

My magic had roiled, trying to tell me that something was wrong. I'd confused them when Wren had arrived in Lucais's place—

"I don't know how differently it would have gone if the asshole hadn't gotten himself stung by a locust and blown his stupid plan to pieces," he confessed. "I hoped it would be much better. You deserve so much better than this." He sighed. "But please believe me when I tell you that I would not have taken it any further without your informed consent. As badly as I want to give you what you wanted from me—to do anything you ask of me—I actually think he would have killed me for it, and I wouldn't have let Morgoya stop him this time."

I glowered at him. "I'm so glad I know where your loyalty lies." The hurt that flashed in his eyes made me feel sick, but I refused to feel sorry for it. "Kiss me," I said, taking a step towards him. "I want to see the difference now that I know."

Lucais's—no, it was Wren's dark, chestnut brown eyes that were wary as he closed the distance between us. "Are you sure?"

"Yes. If you have no objections, then I'd like to do this to clear my head."

"No objections," he breathed. His hand shook slightly as he lifted it to cup my cheek, bending his head to mine.

Real Wren's mouth slanted over mine, soft, warm, and as intoxicating as it had been yesterday afternoon. I felt my heart flutter, chest expanding with desire. My blood heated, my stomach clenched, and my toes curled as I reached up to wrap my arms around the back of his neck. I hated what he had done, all the lies and tricks, but I loved what he was doing with his hands on my waist and my hips, travelling over my backside as he walked me back against the wall. And I loved what he was doing with his *tongue*—

A door creaked open.

I broke away from Wren's mouth with a small whimper of annoyance and whipped my head towards the sound.

The High King of Faerie stood in the hallway, an unreadable expression on his face.

My *mate*.

He looked between my wide eyes and the strong arms that were around me, and then he vanished back into my bedroom. The door slammed closed.

Wren sighed, resting his forehead against my temple. He inhaled deeply like his lungs could consume me and form a permanent attachment stronger than any star-told bond. "Aura?"

My heart clenched. *His voice. The way he said my name...*

The real Lucais, the golden fiend who brought me into Faerie, said that hearing me call his name from the cottage that night broke his heart. Because we were fated mates.

So how was it possible that another man's voice would break mine?

"I've fallen in love with the wrong man," I whispered, staring down the empty hall. Slowly, I turned to face him and found the most gut-wrenching smile on his face. The contents of my stomach turned to ice, and I pushed him away, turning my head so that I didn't have to watch that smile breaking when I said, "But it doesn't change what you did... Wren, I don't want this."

FORTY-NINE

The Body Downstairs

Lucais Starfire spent his three days of recovery in my bedroom.

I didn't ask him to go back to his own room, and he didn't suggest it.

At night, I placed a two-pillow barrier between us, and we stuck to our respective sides of the bed. During the day, he dozed on and off while I read *The Sins of Stars* by the window.

The House brought meals to us, and I excused myself for an hour or two each day while Delia came in to help him bathe.

He promised not to look if I wanted to use the bath myself, but I simply rolled my eyes at him and used the empty guest room down the hall when I needed to.

On the third day, I finished the book.

I slammed it shut loud enough to wake him, and when he didn't stir, I threw it at him instead. The hardcover landed on his outstretched hand, which was resting on my half of the mattress as he lay on his side.

"What was that for?" Lucais asked with forced politeness, cracking open a golden eye.

"Why do you keep pretending to be asleep when you're not?"

He opened his other eye. "I like listening to you read."

I frowned. "I'm not reading it out loud."

"No," he agreed, propping himself up on an elbow. "But your breathing pattern and your heartbeat tell me where you're at with it. And you pelting it at me tells me that you're done. What do you think?"

"I think you're an idiot."

He rolled his eyes skyward. "Of the *book*."

"I think you're an idiot," I repeated, walking towards the bed. "This whole idiotic mess you made came from this one *stupid* book." I snatched it up and threw it down on the mattress again for emphasis.

Micael and Livia were mates.

The mating bond was exclusive to members of the High Fae, which made it easy to believe that there wasn't one between the two main characters because Livia was constantly referred to as a

Swapling—a completely different race of faerie. At the time, she was considered one of the Lesser Fae.

But Livia wasn't a Swapling.

She was a fucking Princess of Faerie who had fallen from the Aboveworld at the start of the Dragon War to escape an arranged marriage with one of the Dragon Masters. She had cut part of her own ears off to make her unrecognisable, and simply never corrected anyone who accused her of being a Swapling.

Slavery was her hiding place.

When the Dragon Master sent spies down from the clouds to search for her, none of them bothered to look twice at a Cinderella-esque serving girl with small, rounded ears.

Livia was Micael's mate.

He'd known it all along—because of some weird, territorial nonsense that affected faerie men more than women—so when the war ended and she returned to the Aboveworld to claim her rightful place on the throne, he followed her.

The Dragon Master's surviving heir accused Micael of kidnapping the Princess, and she was chained to her throne while they tried and executed her soulmate.

"I always thought it was a true story," Lucais murmured, reaching a hand out to stroke the book's worn spine. "That one of the Secret-Keepers had managed to find a way around their bargain with the High Mother and tell the story of how the Aboveworld truly ended, by presenting it to us as fiction."

I sat down on the bed with my legs crossed while he flipped the cover open and ran a long finger over the front page. He glanced up at me, tracing a circle on the empty space around the title.

"There's no author," I realised.

Lucais nodded. "I asked my parents when I found the book in our library, and neither of them knew where it had come from. I think I was meant to find it as a warning."

Tilting my head to the side, I studied his face. His hair was clean and fluffed from sleep, the blond as delicate as starlight in the dawn glow, and he looked fragile. Breakable.

I'd never seen him like that before.

His golden eyes were haunted.

"Because history has a habit of repeating itself," I finished for him. "You know, in the human world, we have a name for this. It's called superstition."

He flipped the lid of the book closed and shrugged, leaning back with his hands behind his head. The fragility had vanished, replaced by an arrogant smirk. "The Malum will do worse things to you than execution. What sort of a mate would I be if I let that happen?"

"You're not my mate," I reminded him, crossing my arms over my chest.

He snorted. "Yet."

Before I could think of what to say next, my bedroom door flew open, and Morgoya appeared. She was dressed in a set of green velvet, and her hair was pulled back into a high ponytail. Her cheeks were flushed.

"Get up," was all she said to the High King.

"That's no way to speak to a man recovering from a life-threatening injury," he replied indignantly.

She rolled her eyes as she stalked across the room. "Oh, please." She yanked the covers back. "You were fully healed two days ago."

My eyes widened at him. "You were?"

Lucais gave me a sly smile and winked. "I've been enjoying our quality time together. You moan in your sleep, you know. It's adorable."

"You bastard," I gasped, whacking him over the head with the nearest pillow. "I was trying to be nice to you!"

"There's still time for you to practise, bookworm."

"Oh, enough." Morgoya dragged a hand down her face. "We have a situation downstairs. The honeymoon is over."

Lucais groaned, nudging her out of the way with one of his feet as he swung his legs over the side of the bed. It was the first time I'd seen him stand since the attack, aside from that brief moment in the hall, and I felt my muscles tense as if they were preparing to catch him.

He rose to his feet with perfect ease, however, and took a step towards the door.

And then he shouted in pain, bending over with his hands clutching his stomach.

I lurched forward. "What's wrong?" I asked, panic ripe in my voice.

"Poison," he rasped. "You didn't...give me enough...blood. Need—*more*."

Frantically, I scanned the room for a knife. When I couldn't find one, I was half tempted to tear my wrist open with my own teeth, but Morgoya slapped him across the back of the head before I could move.

"Cut it out," she chided.

A split-second later, Lucais straightened up and started laughing. The sound was like soft music that grated against all of my nerves in all of the best ways.

"Worth a shot," he chuckled, a roguish smile on his face. "I haven't had a vacation in over three hundred years, and I meant what I said about the way you taste."

The High Lady made a choking sound.

With a wave of his hand, Wren—*Lucais,* for fuck's sake—was fully dressed in a smart black jacket with golden trim and polished boots. He straightened his lapels and brushed invisible dust from his knees before turning to face me as he combed his hands through his sleep-tousled hair.

"Are you staying with us?" he enquired, turning to find a mirror. He let out a rough breath when he couldn't find one and gave Morgoya a questioning look, gesturing to himself.

She rolled her eyes. "You look beautiful. Even better if you'd pick up the pace."

Lucais's answering smile was nothing short of charming.

"Staying," I blurted when they both turned to look at me.

I hadn't even thought about leaving. I hadn't fully processed my feelings yet, either. But the idea of going home, of leaving Faerie, made everything seem so much worse.

Wren had ruined our chance of happiness together by lying to me. I knew that much already. And Lucais had let it go too far for any reparations to be made to what was left of the mating bond. But I had to admit that I understood why.

While he had feared for my life because of *The Sins of Stars*, I had spent three months fearing for his life because of my dreams.

I didn't love him, not like I had loved the man in my dreams before I met him in real life. But the thought of him being tortured still made me queasy, and I had questions about the premonition.

"I'm not... I'm not ready to go home yet."

A flicker of pain crossed Lucais's eyes, but he smiled broadly and nodded. "Very good. I have a cramped schedule to tackle, so this will save me time. There's a body downstairs I need to examine, and then we need to go and find your father."

My stomach dropped. "What?"

Morgoya echoed me, and then asked, "Why?"

The High King shrugged and brushed his hands together before stuffing them into his pockets. "To ask him for Aura's hand in marriage, naturally."

I rolled my eyes. "No, seriously. Why?"

He sighed brusquely. "Where's the trust?"

"You dropped it in Dante's Bookstore," I snapped.

"Okay, fair. We need to find your father because I have a theory I'd like to test."

Morgoya frowned at him. "That's not any clearer."

"The truth, remember?" I prompted, climbing off the bed.

Lucais's eyes were apologetic, but he put his hand on my shoulder and shoved me back down onto the bed. "Sit," he said. "I think I know what happened to Blythe."

The High Lady of the Court of Darkness.

"What?" Morgoya demanded.

He looked down at me and traced his fingertips over the side of my face. "She was finally ousted by her heir."

"You can't be serious."

Lucais ignored her and crouched down in front of me. He took both of my hands in one of his and used his other to draw soothing lines across my palms. "I tasted something else in your blood," he murmured, slowly lifting his eyes to mine. "Aura... I don't think your father was from the Court of Light, my love. I don't think your magic is dormant, either. I think your power is very much alive, and it has chained itself up to protect you from it."

My body was deprived of oxygen.

"I think you were born to the Court of Darkness," he went on, "and I think you are Blythe's heir."

"That's impossible," Morgoya breathed. "Not just a human mate, but one descended from a different Court. It's *unheard* of."

We both ignored her.

Lucais noted the fear in my eyes and let go of my hands, baring his palms to me. His gaze was stern, irises a solid and brilliant shade of gold. I was paralysed by his train of thought.

"Fuck the Oracle," he said. "You have my permission to take whatever you need from me, and leave the rest."

I reached for one of his hands.

I had a theory of my own to test.

Holding Lucais's gaze, I offered up a thought to the tether between us. The link I had felt since the moment I'd walked into him, growing stronger and more surreal with every passing day.

I'm scared.

His gaze softened, and I heard his voice in my mind like an echo down a phone line. I'd heard it before, I realised—but now it was clear, a sound I could identify and follow to safety through a blinding storm. *No, you're powerful. Don't confuse the two.*

You realise fear is a feeling, right?

Fear is a state of being, and so is power.

I looked away, breaking our stare, but kept my hand in his.

This doesn't mean that I forgive you.

Good. I like it better when you hate me. It makes you bold.

I kicked his ankle as he rose to his feet, his fingers still linked with mine.

"The body downstairs," he began, turning his head towards Morgoya. "One of Enyd's?"

The High Lady nodded, all the colour drained from her cheeks.

"Let's go and play coroner then." Lucais glanced at me over his shoulder. "Coming?"

Blythe's heir.

Court of Darkness.

Faerie father with questionable allegiances.

"Sure," I agreed, dropping his hand as I rose to my feet. He slipped it back into his pocket. "Does anyone want to tell me how you ended up in the fight with a locust?"

He made a face. "Not really."

"Ask Wren," Morgoya muttered, trailing behind us as we left my bedroom.

Lucais glanced back at her with mock horror. "Whose side are you on?"

"Aura's. Thanks to you, I have a lot of grovelling to do."

"Mmm," he mused as we marched towards the staircase. "Well, to aid the process, I should probably tell you that my High Lady was violently opposed to my scheme. But I pulled rank on her. She still found a way to interfere, though." He glanced up at her as we descended the stairs. "The gold dress? Brilliant. Evil, but brilliant."

"I wasn't trying to make it worse for you, Aura," she said. "Not for you. I was trying to make a point to the High King."

"Point taken. Cross my heart and hope to die," Lucais sang, acting out the words with his hand, "I'll never do it again."

"I'll get over it," I told the High Lady.

I *would* get over it, but her interference *had* made it worse for me. Much worse. Morgoya had been my one true friend.

The three of us left the House, joining a small group of High Fae in the courtyard outside. Gravel crunched beneath our steps, and the babble of voices quietened into hushed whispers as we approached.

Standing in a circle, I spied Wren and Enyd among the crowd.

Wren flinched when he saw me and averted his eyes. Mine prickled with sharp, bubbling tears, but my anger quickly dissolved them.

Enyd was too preoccupied talking to one of her sentries to look up as we came to a stop at the edge of the circle.

I saw the reason a moment later.

Lying on the ground in the middle of the circle, there was a mangled body writhing against the stones.

"I thought you told me he was dead," Lucais said, scrunching his nose.

Enyd's head snapped up. "He *is* dead. There's no pulse, but he won't stop twitching. Do you want to tell me what in the Elements is going on?"

Lucais hummed and took a step closer to the body.

The grey uniform of the Court of Wind was in tatters, concealing only the man's most private parts. His skin was a sickly green colour, covered with protruding black veins like his decapitated comrade. But this time, the veins were pulsing, like the blackness came from a fluid oozing through his body.

His eye sockets were swollen, his face sallow and bruised, and his hair was black as night. The tips of his fingers were black, too. Like his extremities were slowly dying.

The High King crouched beside the body and began poking and prodding it.

"We have a problem," he announced after a few moments of scrutiny.

"No shit," Enyd hissed. "What has happened to my men, Lucais?"

"Malum," he answered gravely. "He's in transition." He cleared his throat and cast his gaze around the group. "Anyone have a sword handy?"

A member of his Guard stepped forward and extended one to him.

"What are you doing?" Enyd exclaimed as Lucais raised the sword in the air over the man's throat.

He looked at her, face screwed up with confusion. "I'm sorry. Did you want to keep him as a pet or something?"

The High Lady of the Court of Wind blanched.

"Morgoya, darling," he called over his shoulder, eyes on the squirming body at his feet. "Can you do your job for once, please?"

She stepped forward, hands across her stomach, and began explaining the Malum to Enyd and her Court. When she was done, the sentry standing beside Enyd turned around and vomited onto the stones.

His High Lady stared at the body on the ground for a long moment before finally declaring, "Do what you must."

Lucais raised the sword again and brought it down upon the body with perfect form, slicing it clean through the neck. The body stopped moving as a cloud of thin grey smoke hissed out of the wound.

"They're making more," the High King announced, holding the hilt of the sword out to its original owner as he turned and stepped back to my side. "They left this one as a message."

"How do you know?" Wren enquired.

"They took faeries during the raid on Sthiara, and the High Mother knows what they've done with Blythe's Court," Lucais answered tightly. "Gregor is probably offering his help in the hopes that he can avoid the same fate for his own, but it's just a matter of time."

"Why has it taken you this long to tell me?" said Enyd.

Lucais regarded her with a frown. "Need-to-know basis. If you weren't so paranoid, stationing your men beyond my wards, then I wouldn't have had to tell you at all."

Enyd glared at him and threw out her hand, sending a torrent of wind towards him. It wasn't strong enough to knock him over, but it did make his hair stick up like he'd been electrocuted.

He rolled his eyes and began to smooth it down. "That was rude."

"So was keeping this information from me," she seethed. "Who else knows?"

"Only my favourite High Ladies," he answered with a grin, glancing pointedly between Enyd and Morgoya.

"Your favourite," Enyd sneered. "And yet you asked me here to see if I was conspiring with them, I presume?"

"Oh." Lucais pulled a face. "Yes. About that. You didn't bring the Malum General with you and sacrifice your own men because it would make you look innocent, did you?"

"No," she growled through her teeth.

He held his hands up in submission. "Just checking."

"I need to return to my Court," Enyd told him. "I would ask for a week to mourn my dead, and then I am at your disposal." Despite the scene before her, she bowed low. "If it's war they want, then we will give them hell."

Lucais nodded. "I rather think they're already in hell, considering most of them look like *that*," he replied, gesturing to the corpse, "but I appreciate the enthusiasm. Take your week. That gives us enough time."

"For what?" Morgoya asked him.

But it was to me he turned with the answer, his eyes sparkling with pure light. "To go home," Lucais replied. "I'm taking bookworm here to Caeludor."

Oh, no, you're not.

I smiled at the High King, and then I unclipped the leash. Somehow, Wren already knew what I was doing, but his shout of warning came too late.

I turned the lights off in Faerie and disappeared into the dark.

The End

Thank You For Reading!

Whether this was the best or worst thing you've ever read—or a nice spot in between—I would appreciate it so immensely if you would consider leaving a review somewhere. Anywhere. Social media, Amazon, Goodreads, local bus stops—okay, perhaps not there, but you get the picture. Reviews are everything to authors because they let other readers know that the book is safe to pick up and open. Sorry, one moment—

What do you mean other people aren't worried about hexes?

Well, it's too late now. I already wrote it.

FINE.

Reviews are everything for authors because, as well as declaring them free from hexes, they let other people know that the book was worth picking up in the first place. Unless, of course, you feel that it wasn't, in which case I'd suggest you include this in your review—

GIVE ME MY PEN BACK.

Join Book Club

Love Letters by Loren
Newsletter

Wren's Book Club
The Online Reader's Group

Stalk Me on Socials
Instagram, Threads, TikTok & Facebook

Books & Biography
Goodreads, Amazon, BookBub

Obligatory Author Website Plug

www.lorenlittle.com

Acknowledgements

B. For bullying me into publishing when I thought I'd reconciled myself to the idea of this story being a trophy on my private bookshelf for eternity. For your patience, as I swore up and down the house, followed shortly thereafter by blushing and giggling on the couch, then repeat. And for doing all that washing.

My betas: Lexie, Jo, Caitlin, Tori, Shannon, and Caitlin. I am so thankful we found each other. You handled my fragile heart and unpolished manuscript with such grace and care. Your insights and cheerleading for both me and this book are invaluable.

My editor, Brittany Bitossi, from BLD Editing. You made the process so much fun! Over-steeping tea, screaming into the void, and all those capital letters. With your help, I remembered why I fell in love with writing in the first place, and I was able to experience how special this story is all over again. Thank you.

The bookstagrammers, booktokers, admins and members of book clubs on Facebook—you made me realise this was possible. *You made this possible.* Since day one, you have shown up for me. Every day since, I've watched you showing up for each other—readers and storytellers alike—all over the world, and I am filled with so much delight and pride to be part of this with you. Keep doing what you do, and know that you are seen, valued, and appreciated beyond your wildest imaginings. You are the main characters.

My echo and my shadow, who are the centre of everything, my anchor in time and space, and the reason I ever came back from Faerie to write about it in the first place. I love you harder than humans do.

Last, but not least... *Wren*. Thank you for all of those conversations. Here's to many more.

***

Oh, actually. You know what? Me. I want to acknowledge me, too. For seven-year-old me, who just wanted to read, write, and rhyme. For ten-year-old me, who used books as a shield. For thirteen-year-old me, who sat and wrote through entire weekends. For fifteen-year-old me, who believed she would be a published author. For eighteen-year-old me, who gave up on her dreams. For twenty-one-year-old me, who started again. For twenty-four-year-old me, who wasn't sure—but she wrote this anyway. And for twenty-seven-year-old me, who finally fucking did it. Loren...*you're a published author!*

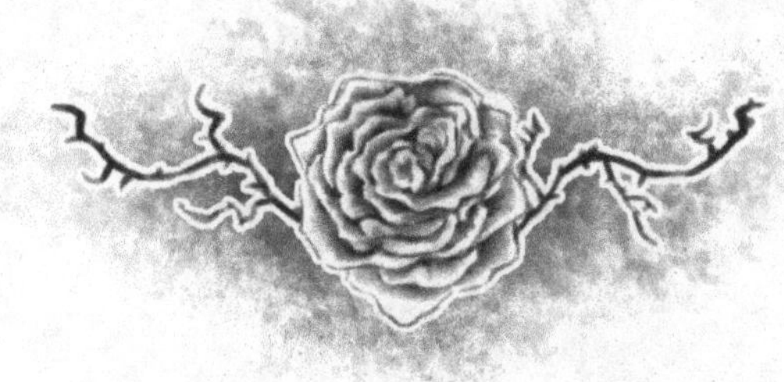

About the Author

Loren Little is an Australian indie author who writes tales of romance in fantasy, dystopian, and contemporary settings based on her imaginary friends. Her stories are filled with banter, steamy scenes, and a lot of wishful thinking. She likes to flirt with the line between light and fluffy and dark and depraved, and she is in an ongoing love affair with morally grey characters and plot twists.

Glossary

Proper Nouns

High Fae
- A race of faeries descended from the High Mother.

High Mother
- The deity worshipped in Faerie and creator of magic.

High King
- The ruler of all rulers.

High Lord
- The ruler of a specific Element or Court.

High Lady
- The ruler of a specific Element or Court.

Secret-Keepers
- Faeries who give up their voice in exchange for answers to all of life's greatest questions.

Dragon Master
- The riders and owners of sky-dragons in the Aboveworld.

Hand
- The trusted advisor of the High King or High Queen of Faerie.

Prince
- The title used to describe an heir of royalty.

Princess
- The title used to describe an heir of royalty.

Faerie
- Ruled by the High King Lucais Starfire.

Caeludor
- The City of Light and Faerie's capital.

Court of Light
- Ruled by the High Lady Morgoya Maudgold.

Court of Wind
- Ruled by the High Lady Enyd Windfall.

Court of Darkness
- Ruled by the High Lady Blythe Darkcloud.

Court of Fire
- Ruled by the High Lord Owain Everspark.

Court of Earth
- Ruled by the High Lord Gregor Woodburn.

Court of Water
- Ruled by the High Lady Ulyssa Pondrop.

Belgrave

- Auralie's small hometown in the human world.

Dante's Bookstore

- Auralie's place of employment in the human world.

The Water Dragon

- A public house in Belgrave.

Sthiara

- A small town in Faerie.

Forest of Eyes and Ears

- The sentient forest that will protect those who enter at all costs.

House

- The High King's safe house, enchanted to care for guests in the ways their lives have lacked.

Opiate Desert

- A bone-dry, barren expanse of land.

Metal Mountains

- The mountain range that splits Faerie down the middle, bordering the capital city.

Temple of All

- The High Mother's place of worship.

Ruins

- The outskirts of Faerie to where creatures like the Malum and the Banshees are exiled.

Aboveworld

- The world that belongs to faeries who live in the sky.

Underworld
- The world that belongs to faeries who live under the sea.

The Watch
- A wall and watchtower in the Court of Earth that oversees the mountain range.

Malum
- The creatures born of Banshee and High Fae.

Banshee
- A non-magical race of faeries exiled for draining magic from others.

Hobgoblin
- A race of faeries known to be grumpy and anti-social.

Ogre
- A race of faeries who are larger than life and talented cooks.

Witches
- A race of faeries who believe in using pure magic derived from the earth.

Vampyrs
- A race of fanged faeries who drink blood for pleasure and sustenance.

Sprites
- A race of small, winged faeries who are kind to the people they like.

The Little Folk
- A race of miniscule faeries who bring gifts to human children that still believe.

Swapling
- A race of faeries who can shapeshift.

Merfolk
- A race of faeries who live in the Underworld.

Goblin
- A race of faeries who value privacy and do not like to be observed by strangers.

Wolf-Folk
- A race of faeries who can transition at will from humanoid form into wolves.

Elements
- Variations of magic gifted to faeries.

Coven
- The name for a group of Witches.

Witch-Lapis
- A weapon that can duplicate a killing blow up to five times without taking energy from the carrier.

Blood Lock
- An amplifier that will give the wearer the combined strength of all parties who willingly bleed onto it.

Guard
- The High King's personal regiment of sentries, soldiers, and spies.

Oracle
- The prophetic magical entity that appears at random to offer glimpses into the future.

The Sins of Stars

• A book without a known author, detailing a story of how the Aboveworld might have ended during the Dragon War.

Gift War

• The fight between High Fae, which resulted in the creation of human beings and split the world into one magical and one non-magical realm.

Dragon War

• The fight between land-dragons and sky-dragons that occurred when the risk of land-dragons becoming extinct was first identified.

Map

• The Map of Faerie.

Nouns

Caenim

• A type of creature that can be kept like pets or trained like soldiers.

Land-dragons

• A type of creature who lived in Faerie like dinosaurs, but are now extinct.

Sky-dragons

• A type of creature who lived in the Aboveworld like dinosaurs, but their status is unknown.

Lochgrub

• A type of winged creature with unparalleled beauty that lives in the ocean and is hunted by Merfolk for sport.

Paperdove
- A type of creature, like a bird, that lays eggs to be consumed purely as food.

Locust
- A highly venomous type of creature that loses a stinger to its victims, but regrows them.

Faelight
- A magical form of light wielded by the High King.

Fae-lily
- A faerie drug designed to render humans who inhale the substance unconscious.

Faerie
- The species of magical beings when referred to as a group of people.

Unicorn
- A magical type of horse.

A PALACE OF SMOKE & MIRRORS

B lood stained the white fabric between my fingers.

I scrubbed and scrubbed at it with a bar of soap, rinsing and repeating, but the marks wouldn't fade. The water ran red first, and then pink, and still the bloodstains on the sheet remained.

Fingers numb and bones aching from the icy water, I dropped the linen with a flat, wet slap. Let it gather at the bottom of the sink, suffocating the drain as I pushed myself up on the tips of my toes and stretched over the steel basin to turn off the faucet.

It shrieked, metal against metal, and I sighed to break the heavy silence that followed. The dead quiet of the house weighed on me like a ball and chain around my ankles, like my bones had been replaced by iron bars. The leaden weight inside me was the only thing keeping me tethered to the earth, the pressure on my lungs the only thing preventing me from screaming until flesh shredded and bone shattered.

His flesh.

His bones.

I found him in the kitchen.

Standing beside the stove with a beer in hand, staring at the array of empty bottles littered across our small wooden table. Glaring at the brand-new highchair next to it, a pattern of blue bears and silver balloons on its padded seat and an unnaturally, immaculately clean feeding tray attached to it.

He didn't look up at me as I approached, though I trudged into the room with my invisible ball and chain in tow, dragging my heels along the floor.

"We need new sheets," I said. My voice was sweet, youthful, and monotone—like a flatline on the hospital monitors in the throat of an eleven-year-old girl.

A grunt was the only response offered to me by the hollow-eyed man near the stove.

Then he took a swig of beer.

The ugly smell stuffed itself up my nose like mouldy fruit left in the fridge for too long.

"We need new sheets," I repeated.

Bloodshot eyes slid to mine. "I heard you."

"You haven't moved."

His eyebrows slowly crumpled into a frown. "You want me to go right now?" he asked, pointing towards the door with the neck of his beer bottle.

"There are no fresh sheets," I stated. *Careful. I have to be so careful.* "She's going to need them changed again by morning."

"It's late. Put some in the dryer."

A rush of cold seized my chest, but I put a hand on the back of the nearest chair to steady myself. Calmly—like I wasn't repeating myself all over again—I told him, "They're stained."

He made a dismissive gesture at the ceiling and began to stride for the doorway. "At least they'll be dry," he muttered. "I'm going to crash on the couch."

Something alive and tangible inside of my chest lunged for him with razor-sharp teeth and talon-like claws—but, instead of sinking into its prey, the hateful beast stumbled headfirst into my heart with a ferocious, painful *thump*.

"No."

He paused in the doorway. "What?"

"*No*," I said again with emphasis. My chest rumbled faintly as if the beast was feeling its way around the obstacle of my blood organ, still determinedly set in its pursuit.

There was no way I would replace her bedding with bloodstained sheets. Again. She deserved clean, untainted linen. Even if it didn't stay that way for long. She was in there sobbing and bleeding and in unimaginable pain. She was hurt in ways that could never be healed, losing parts of herself that could never be replaced because of him—

Because of him.

"You don't want to push me tonight, Auralie," he warned in a voice laced with violence and suffering and the only promises he ever kept.

The dark things hiding beneath that voice were my constant companions, so my knees did not buckle beneath the weight of his threat. Instinct cautioned me against it, but I opened my mouth once more inside of an unpleasant smile.

"Three days," I observed quietly. "Is that a new record for you?"

He turned slowly. His eyes were foggy, glazed by the liquor, and he strained to pull his focus onto me. "What?"

"It's been three days since you last threatened me," I clarified, my cheeks swelling with a vitriolic grin. "If you don't count when I was a baby—which I don't, because I can't remember any of it—or the months you spend on the run, I'm sure this is some kind of record."

The air between us trembled and pulled taut.

He clenched his fists, eyeballs swimming in his head, spending a moment searching for something...

Alas, all he could come up with was more anger and irritation. Shoulders twitching, he shook the beer bottle in his hand and screwed his nose up at me.

"Shut up," he spat, droplets of saliva spraying from his mouth.

Silently, I lifted my middle finger up in the air between us.

The atmosphere cracked.

"Shut up!" he roared again. The bottle went flying and exploded against the wall behind me in a spray of beer and glass that tickled the back of my neck. "Shut up! Shut the *fuck* up!"

The words assaulted me like a punch in the nose, but I latched onto the abuse like a starving beast and greedily devoured the ugly expression on his face. My own heated to near the point of delirium as blood flooded to my cheeks and filled my head—a warmth, a sensation I hadn't felt in weeks.

Something. *I'm feeling something—*

"Hit me!" I screamed back at him. My voice box felt like it had caught on fire, positively quivering in the wake of the falsetto, but it was too late for me to stop. "Go ahead and *do* it!" I shrieked. "Just get it over with! Because if I have to spend *one more moment* in this house, I am going to fucking *kill* you, you asshole!"

He took a thunderous step towards me. "Aura—"

I didn't wait for him to finish. I couldn't take it any longer. I could not be in that house with him, sleeping with one eye open every night, chewing nervous holes through my blankets every time I heard a creak from one of the floorboards down the hall. I couldn't do it. I *wouldn't*.

Heaving an enormous breath that stretched my lungs to bursting point, I released the most blood-curdling scream I could muster and closed my eyelids against the darkness that splintered across the room in flashes of nightmares and artificial lights. There was the sound of my terror and loathing as I spent every last scrap of my voice at once in that single scream, followed by a symphony of what sounded like bullets raining down on me—and then there was nothing.

Complete and utter silence.

Part of me prayed that someone had heard me and intervened, but I couldn't sense the presence of anyone else in the room. It was only me and the monsters...

Or perhaps it was only monsters.

Before I opened my eyes, I tried to gather enough saliva to force down my swollen throat, but my vocal cords were paralysed and my stomach was in knots. I felt the chilling heat of my scream settling in my chest, curled up between my collarbones like a dragon. When I tried to take a breath of air in through my nose, I was hit with the stench of exposed flesh and burning wood. I doubled over and nearly choked as a mouthful of my own blood came hurtling out at an alarming speed, and my eyelids were ripped back on instinct.

All the lights were out.

The whole room would have been in complete darkness had there not been some kind of fire glowing in the cabinet underneath the kitchen sink and a second blaze sparking against the doorframe behind my father's body.

Limply, he lay on the linoleum with his arms and legs spread out, bent in unshapely forms. Everything around him was in jagged pieces—cutlery, crockery, wooden furniture, and chunks of plaster. I was seeing all of it in black and white. Even the dark blood pooling beneath his head, turned away from mine.

My stomach churned around a knot of unease once more, and I dropped to my knees as I retched and spat another mouthful of metallic-tasting fluid onto the ground. Seconds later, my head followed and turned the whole world off with a skull-splitting slam.

I slept for a long time.

I almost thought I'd never wake up.

I almost hoped I wouldn't.

When the white-haired woman appeared in the doorway, I must have been dreaming.

And when I eventually woke up, it was daylight, and the world was colourful again. I was in my bedroom, tucked under the covers. The fires were all out. The light globes were working. The parts of our kitchen that had appeared to be shattered and broken were whole. My mother had fresh, clean sheets.

And my father was gone.

S omething brushed against my upper lip, tickling my nose. I shrugged it off because I was trying to get the sleep I so desperately needed. The world was finally dark again, and I was so, *so* tired—

Sniff.

There it was again. Scrunching my nose up, I turned my head away, making sure to keep my eyes tightly closed against any rebellious flares of light, because I—

Sniff.

It came back with a vengeance, with the persistence only a sentient being could demonstrate.

Alright, I thought. *That's it.*

My head thrashed from side to side as I tried to rouse myself from the depths of my dream-snared reprieve. Heavy as an iron ball, my eyelids felt tender and swollen when I tried to pry them open with sheer will alone. With my arms feeling like jelly, I couldn't seem to call upon my own hands for help.

Loud roaring echoed in my ears like cars speeding down a newly paved highway, irritating me further. *I have to find the window and close it so I can get some rest.*

A bright particle of light sliced through my vision as my lids slowly pulled apart.

It *hurt.*

My eyes watered, lashes fluttering with the intensity of broken butterfly wings while I fought to unravel the circling lines of shooting stars. With some difficulty, I managed to force my sight to wade through the blurry whirlpool of shapes and emerge on the other side of the obnoxious luminescence beyond them.

A white thing with feathered edges bleeding into the murky background swiped across my vision, making my nose tingle, and I shouted at it—even though I knew it was likely some sort of insect and would not care to hear my protests. I bent my neck from left to right, rubbing the far corners of my eyes against my shoulders, and searched for my sense of balance in spite of my struggles to sit upright.

And then, when I found it, I shouted again—an incoherent gurgle of annoyance at discovering my new surroundings.

I was sitting in some kind of carriage, slumped against the wall, and the roaring in my ears was the sound of the wind and earth falling away through the open window as we travelled through the countryside at an alarming speed. A red velvet curtain was pulled halfway across it, guiding a beam of light with firm, rigid boundaries to pour into the space in front of me and land...

...all over Wren.